PENGUIN  CLASSICS

SAGAS OF WARRIOR-POETS

DIANA WHALEY is Reader in Medieval Studies at the University of Newcastle upon Tyne, where she has taught since 1978. Born in York in 1951, she holds degrees in medieval English and Icelandic from the Universities of Durham and Iceland, and a D.Phil. from the University of Oxford. She has published books and articles on a wide range of medieval subjects, including *Heimskringla: An Introduction* (1991) and *The Poetry of Arnórr jarlaskáld* (1998). She was President of the Viking Society for Northern Research in 1996–8. Her current research includes work on a collaborative re-edition of the corpus of skaldic poetry, and on a dictionary of Lake District place-names.

WORLD OF THE SAGAS

Editor Örnólfur Thorsson
Assistant Editor Bernard Scudder

Advisory Editorial Board

Translators

Katrina Attwood
Alison Finlay
Marianne Kalinke
Rory McTurk
Diana Whaley

SAGAS OF
WARRIOR-POETS

Kormak's Saga

The Saga of Hallfred Troublesome-poet

The Saga of Gunnlaug Serpent-tongue

*The Saga of Bjorn, Champion of
the Hitardal People*

Viglund's Saga

With an Introduction and Notes by
DIANA WHALEY

PENGUIN BOOKS

PENGUIN BOOKS

Published by the Penguin Group
Penguin Books Ltd, 80 Strand, London WC2R ORL, England
Penguin Putnam Inc., 375 Hudson Street, New York, New York 10014, USA
Penguin Books Australia Ltd, 250 Camberwell Road, Camberwell, Victoria 3124, Australia
Penguin Books Canada Ltd, 10 Alcorn Avenue, Toronto, Ontario, Canada M4V 3B2
Penguin Books India (P) Ltd, 11 Community Centre, Panchsheel Park, New Delhi – 110 017, India
Penguin Books (NZ) Ltd, Cnr Rosedale and Airborne Roads, Albany, Auckland, New Zealand
Penguin Books (South Africa) (Pty) Ltd, 24 Sturdee Avenue, Rosebank 2196, South Africa

Penguin Books Ltd, Registered Offices: 80 Strand, London WC2R ORL, England

www.Penguin.com

Translations first published in *The Complete Sagas of Icelanders (Including 49 Tales)*, I and II,
edited by Viðar Hreinsson (General Editor), Robert Cook, Terry Gunnell, Keneva Kunz
and Bernard Scudder. Leifur Eiríksson Publishing Ltd, Iceland 1997
First published by Penguin Classics 2002

021

Translation copyright © Leifur Eiríksson, 1997
Editorial matter copyright © Diana Whaley, 2002

Leifur Eiríksson Publishing Ltd gratefully acknowledges the support of the
Nordic Cultural Fund, Ariane Programme of the European Union, UNESCO,
Icelandair and others.

Set in 10.25/12.5 pt PostScript Monotype Janson
Typeset by Rowland Phototypesetting Ltd, Bury St Edmunds, Suffolk
Printed and bound in Great Britain by Clays Ltd, Elcograf S.p.A.

www.greenpenguin.co.uk

Contents

CONTENTS

Acknowledgements

This volume is the result of cooperation between many people. The work of the five translators was fundamental, as was the editorial work of Viðar Hreinsson for *The Complete Sagas of Icelanders*, in which the translations were originally published. Diana Whaley wrote the Introduction and produced the Further Reading, Note on the Translations, Notes, Plot Summaries (with Bernard Scudder), and the notes on Rulers, Early Icelandic Literature and Techniques of Skaldic Poetry within the Reference Section; she also collaborated in putting together the remainder of the volume, including revision of translations. The remainder of the Reference Section is the work of the staff at Leifur Eiríksson Publishing, Reykjavík: Viðar Hreinsson, Örnólfur Thorsson, and Bernard Scudder, who assisted in the editing of the entire volume. The maps were produced by Jean-Pierre Biard. Jón Torfason compiled the Index of Characters.

Three-cornered dealings are not always easy, as the protagonists of the sagas of poets knew only too well, but I would like to thank all concerned for goodwill and shared enthusiasm for these remarkable sagas, especially Bernard Scudder of Leifur Eiríksson Publishing and Lindeth Vasey and Hilary Laurie of Penguin Books. Early drafts of the Introduction were also read by Vésteinn Ólason and Marlene Robertson, representing the 'specialist' and 'interested non-specialist' readership, and I am greatly indebted to them. Finally, all who work on Icelandic sagas learn a great deal from previous editors, commentators, lexicographers and others, and while it is not always possible to acknowledge specific debts, the listing of works in the

Further Reading and the Note on the Translations mark our gratitude to them.

Diana Whaley
University of Newcastle upon Tyne

Introduction*

An Icelandic champion famed for dragon-slaying abroad is ambushed by twenty-four men in a rock-strewn meadow. He offers a desperate defence using the shears with which he was about to trim his horses' manes ... A famous poet and fighter spends an illicit night at the summer pastures with a woman he failed to marry long before. Her husband has no choice but to seek redress ...

Composed in the thirteenth and fourteenth centuries, and set over two hundred years earlier, the Icelandic sagas in this volume enact the meeting of the old Viking ethos of honour and heroic adventure with the newer ethos of romantic infatuation. The sagas about Kormak, Hallfred, Gunnlaug and Bjorn are distinguished by their combination of three important features, all of which appear in other sagas but rarely so prominently. First, at least one central character (usually the titular hero) is a skald, or poet, and hence the prose saga is exceptionally rich in poetic utterances; second, there is a 'love triangle' plot involving disappointed love and concomitant rivalry between the hero and the man who marries his beloved; and third, the hero's travels abroad, especially in the service of Scandinavian rulers, form a major strand in the narrative. It is on the basis of these features, together with certain literary links between them, that the

* For brief surveys of the historical context of the sagas, and of the main literary works referred to in the Introduction and Notes, see 'Chronology' (pp. 306–8), 'Social, Political and Legal Structures' (pp. 311–13) and 'Early Icelandic Literature' (pp. 317–21). Translations of Icelandic works not included in this volume are listed in Further Reading (pp. xlvi–l). And for the particular meaning of terms used in the sagas and the notes, see the Glossary on pp. 327–38.

first four sagas in this volume are customarily regarded as the classic sagas of poets, or skald sagas (Icelandic *skáldasögur*) – which is a modern, rather than medieval, grouping, but one of the most distinctive within the saga literature.[1] *Viglund's Saga*, though not usually counted within this group, has much in common with the sagas in it, and is included here as an intriguingly fresh variation on the theme of a poet's love in adversity.

Meanwhile, the sagas of poets belong to the wider grouping of the Sagas of Icelanders, which in turn is part of the remarkable flowering of vernacular prose narrative in medieval Iceland. The authors' purpose in writing, it seems, was to entertain, to preserve and shape traditions about the past, and through them to explore issues of concern to their own societies. The mainly thirteenth-century authors of the Sagas of Icelanders cast their discerning gaze back to the Christianization of Iceland *c.* 1000, and beyond to the settlement period, *c.* 870–930. This saw the migration of thousands of families to a virtually uninhabited island just below the Arctic Circle.[2] Its interior was, and is, lava desert and glacier, but there was also rich pastureland. Many or most of these people came from western Norway, but others came from the Norse settlements in the British Isles, especially Ireland, western Scotland and the Hebrides, and these brought Celtic slaves with them, probably in quite large numbers. Once established, the first Icelanders formed a kingless, if scarcely egalitarian, society in which law was sovereign, at least in theory, and local and national assemblies attempted to balance the needs of individuals, families and the wider community in the ongoing struggle for scarce economic resources and the no less precious commodities of honour and social status. This Icelandic 'Commonwealth' survived until the Icelanders accepted Norwegian rule in 1262–4.

Like the other Sagas of Icelanders, the sagas of poets are set mainly in the dispersed farmsteads of Viking Age Iceland and are intensely preoccupied with neighbourhood conflict, its violent outcomes, and the possibility of resolution. Their art is quasi-dramatic and apparently realistic, and designed more for reading aloud than for private contemplation. Brief, formal sketches of the main dramatis personae are given at their first appearance, but otherwise character and motive emerge through action and dialogue. A medieval Icelandic audience would also have made deductions about status, personality and kinship loyalties from genealogical information. There is a certain amount of stereotyping and idealization, but many of the main characters have a complex mix of flaws and virtues which is quite rare in European medieval literature. Despite the intricate action and often profuse descriptive detail, nearly everything in the sagas is functional, contributing to the implacable advance of the plot as conflict gathers to a – usually tragic – climax, to be followed by revenge or reconciliation, or both. The sagas are constructed from fully staged scenes with vivid action and well honed dialogue, which are flanked and connected by rapid summaries of essential information. The narrator's voice is occasionally heard, for instance when he switches threads, tracing one rival's movements then another's, but in general it is restrained, rarely judging the characters, imputing feelings or motives to them or indulging in showy rhetoric or scenic description for its own sake. The result is a spare, stark but vibrant prose that has been compared with the 'hard-boiled' style of Ernest Hemingway or some of the Old Testament narratives. Meanwhile, the intricacy and apparent impartiality of much saga narrative give these works an open-endedness that offers fascinating scope for interpretation of their meaning and aesthetic qualities.

The skalds who dominate the first three of these sagas, Kormak, Hallfred and Gunnlaug, are famously difficult characters (as literary personae, whether or not they were so in life), and their awkward temperaments are associated with their poetic gifts. They are powerful and promising men of distinguished parentage and striking but not conventionally handsome appearance; they are dynamic, obstreperous, hot-tempered and serpent-tongued. They can be as much of an aggravation to their friends as to their enemies, and the moderate nature of others in the saga, often including the hero's brother or the rival lover, provides a foil to the hero's perversity. The attractive Bjorn and Viglund stand out from these stereotypes. Although they compose verse, they are given neither the status of skald nor a difficult personality; in the saga of Bjorn these attributes are borne primarily by his perennial rival, Thord Kolbeinsson.

The eponymous heroes all fall into a passionate, lifelong attachment to a woman who becomes locked into marriage to another man, and it is this that most clearly distinguishes the sagas of poets from other Sagas of Icelanders. Passion, albeit largely unexpressed, flickers through certain other sagas: most famously *The Saga of the People of Laxardal*, in which Bolli returns to Iceland ahead of Kjartan and marries Kjartan's love, Gudrun, or *The Saga of the People of Eyri*, with its adulterous love triangle featuring Bjorn, Champion of the Breidavik People. In most sagas, however, male–female encounters are mainly linked to seductions or divorces which lead to litigation and hence function merely as nuts and bolts in the machinery of plot. Of the two works most often considered as sagas of poets but not included in this collection, *Egil's Saga* contains only an embryonic love story, and in *The Saga of the Sworn Brothers* the skaldship and philandering of Thormod play a relatively minor role, while his sworn brother Thorgeir disdains women altogether.

The protagonist's love is always returned in the sagas of poets, and although burgeoning love is usually reported rather than shown, we see, for instance, the spark of interest kindling between Kormak and Steingerd through glimpses and whisperings amidst the farmhouse partitions. However, Kormak apprehends from the outset that his love is doomed (ch. 3). Like that of his fellow skalds, it is a love that feeds on adversity and absence. Viglund apart, none of the poets marries his beloved or gains more than momentary happiness with her, while none of the principal marriages is motivated by love. The widowed Bersi the Dueller in *Kormak's Saga* (ch. 7) and the bachelor Gris in *The Saga of Hallfred* (chs. 3–4) are brought in as eligible suitors to resolve the dilemma presented by the poet's relationship with the woman. So too is Hakon in *Viglund's Saga* (ch. 15), though the plot there has a twist. Hrafn in *The Saga of Gunnlaug* (chs. 9–10) and Thord in *The Saga of Bjorn* (ch. 5) appropriate the woman pledged to the hero, in Thord's case by falsely rumouring his death, but it is not desire, or not desire alone, that drives them.

Unwelcome visits to a woman, whether single or married, bring dishonour to the whole family ('there is disgrace in it to us all', *Kormak's Saga*, ch. 20), and violence can break out between the poet-hero and any one of the defensive male circle around her. As hostilities develop, other parts of the complex dynamic of honour come into play, as public redress is demanded, through reprisals or compensation, for slanders, infringement of rights, injuries and killings. In three of the sagas of poets, the animosity between the poet-hero and the husband forms a particularly strong axis. Gunnlaug's intense rivalry with Hrafn, both as partner to Helga and as poet to kings, is so crucial to his saga that it is headed 'the saga of Gunnlaug and Hrafn' in one manuscript. The bulk of *The Saga of Bjorn* is similarly occupied by the prolonged and vicious verbal and physical conflict between Bjorn and Thord, and it is almost as much Thord's saga as Bjorn's. As for Kormak in his saga, he has two main opponents to spar with, since Steingerd is married twice. The first husband, Bersi, has such prominence that he threatens to take over the first part of the saga, while the second, Thorvald, shares the adversarial role with his more forceful brother Thorvard. In *The Saga of Hallfred* the husband Gris is also a joint antagonist, with his pagan friend Mar, but in this saga hostilities against these characters do not dominate. Finally, the male rivalries in *Viglund's Saga* are complex and diffused, and the husband plays a relatively minor role.

Sorcery, fate, the duplicity of the rival or the perversity of the hero are shown as reasons for the hero's failure to marry the beloved, but there are more general factors too, practical, social and temperamental. As Gunnlaug prepares to seek fame and adventure abroad, both his father and his intended father-in-law point out the incompatibility of this with his commitment to Helga (ch. 5). This is the practical dilemma facing many ambitious young Icelanders, and it is at the root of the tragedy in the sagas of Gunnlaug and Bjorn. Further, the male–female encounters take place in the context of social hierarchies as finely gradated and as nervously observed as those of Jane Austen's England, and the differing social standing of the families involved may well have been understood by medieval saga audiences as determining the failure of Kormak and Hallfred to marry the women they desire.[3] Looked at still another way, from the viewpoint of literary typology, it is also clear that a life of marital harmony, a mellow old age and death in bed are neither the stuff of saga nor the likely outcome for heroes who feel contempt as well as envy for the husbands' easy life and sexual felicity (e.g., *Kormak's Saga* verses 53, 55 and 57). These poets have kinship both with old-style heroes such as Sigurd/Siegfried of the Volsung and Ni(e)belung legends, and with the tragic lovers of Arthurian romance – Lancelot or Tristan.[4] For them, a life of action is the most important thing. Passionate love is possible, but only of a doomed or distant kind. Like their heroism, it will not be domesticated.

The problematic energies of the poet-heroes find an outlet and an arena abroad, and the amount of action overseas is a leading characteristic of the sagas of poets. The verbal brilliance and fighting strength that fuel slander and feud in Iceland win wealth and prestige abroad, in the service of princes and in raiding and trading.[5] The sagas of poets contain over two dozen appearances at royal courts, mainly within the wider Scandinavian-speaking world of Norway, Denmark, Sweden, Orkney and Dublin, though Gunnlaug's itinerary also takes in Russia and England. Some of the court visits are linked into the romantic plot, most notably in *The Saga of Gunnlaug,* while in the life of Hallfred there is a set of creative tensions, parallels and contrasts between his anguished love for an Icelandic beauty and his service of a Christian king of Norway. Others of the skalds' overseas adventures are less easy to account for, and some critics have felt that they detract from the taut advance of conflict and resolution, or that they sit uneasily with the love stories. However, the traditions concerning foreign adventures have their rightful place in the skalds' biographies, and they match – or rather, help to create – the restless character of the saga heroes.

So dominated are these sagas by male action and male aggression that one could see the female figures as nothing more than a commodity to be wrangled over by men, and love as little more than a pretext for rivalry. As Gunnlaug says of Helga, 'The woman was born to bring war between men' (verse 19). It is certainly true that the role of the female characters is defined and determined entirely by the men. The beautiful Oddny 'Isle-candle', though described as of strong personality, has a relatively slight role in *The Saga of Bjorn,* and it is only after bearing eight children by Thord that she discovers

for certain that her first love, Bjorn, is still alive (ch. 10). Hallfred's
Kolfinna, another fine woman, is as unable to determine her own fate
as the others: 'Leave the arranging to those with a right to decide,'
she tells him (ch. 4). Nevertheless, the erotic theme gives rise to a
gallery of fine female portraits, from the lovely Helga of the wistful
gaze and hair like burnished gold in *The Saga of Gunnlaug* to Kormak's
sharp-tongued Steingerd. Uniquely, Steingerd takes some initiative
in trying to seal a marriage with the poet (ch. 6), and insists on
travelling abroad, even taking an active part in a sea-battle, though
she is also kidnapped in a pirate attack (chs. 24–6). We also see
women participating in the honour culture of the men. The most
terrible example is the scornful fortitude with which Thordis in *The
Saga of Bjorn* responds when faced with the severed head of her son
(ch. 33). Thordis also stands as a reminder of the role of supporting
female characters – mothers or sisters, servants or sorceresses. Few
of them except the sorceresses are able to influence events by action
(Steinvor, for instance, is merely used by Bersi for his own violent
ends in *Kormak's Saga*, ch. 16), yet they form vital links in the plot, and
within dialogues they advise, comment or simply act as necessary
interlocutors. Similarly, although many of these women are stereo-
types, the more developed of them, such as Kormak's resourceful
mother Dalla, or the evil and neurotic Thorbjorg in *Viglund's Saga*,
add to the rugged appeal of the sagas.

NARRATIVE FRAMEWORK

There is sufficient common ground among the five sagas of poets to
amount almost to a shared narrative framework which, with certain
stretching of detail (especially in the case of *Viglund's Saga*), can be
summarized as follows:

1. Prelude (*Kormak's Saga*, *The Saga of Hallfred* and *Viglund's Saga*):
Adventure(s) of the skald's father in Norway, and his emigration to
Iceland; *The Saga of Bjorn* and *The Saga of Gunnlaug* begin in Iceland
with few preliminaries or none.

2. Introduction of the hero. He develops a mutual attraction for a woman in the neighbourhood, spending time at her farm.

3. This presents social difficulties: the father, mindful of the family honour and the economics of matrimony, wants a firm betrothal. A rival for the woman's hand appears now or later.

4. The hero voyages in Scandinavia and (often) the British Isles, engaging in trade or raiding, or spending periods in the service of rulers as warrior or court poet.

5. The beloved woman marries the rival, before or during the hero's absence abroad.

6. On return, the hero's bitter jealousy against his rival is enacted in aggression against him and his family and friends. This takes the form of some combination of:
– fights (single combat or with supporters)
– vitriolic verses (reciprocated or not)
– legal action.
His love for the woman finds expression in:
– love verses
– visiting, and sometimes sleeping with, her.

7. There may be further voyages abroad, containing adventures either related or unrelated to the love rivalry.

8. The hero dies, never having achieved lasting fulfilment of his obsessive love, nor having freed himself from it. Kormak and Hallfred meet accidental deaths in Scotland having effectively relinquished their claim to the beloved, but still haunted by her. Bjorn and Gunnlaug die fighting the rival. Viglund is the happy exception.

9. Epilogue/Aftermath: This is perfunctory in *Kormak's Saga*, *The Saga of Hallfred* and *Viglund's Saga*, while *The Saga of Gunnlaug* and *The Saga of Bjorn* have longish accounts of revenge and/or legal proceedings, ending with the focus on Helga and Thord respectively.

Despite so much common ground, each saga springs from a unique synthesis of historical moments with oral story and literary creativity, and the reader will find a wealth of subtle differences between them. The Plot Summaries on pp. 290–301 and the following discussions of themes and narrative art in each of the five sagas will, it is hoped, provide some starting-points.

THEMES AND NARRATIVE ART

Kormak's Saga

Kormak's first meeting with Steingerd (ch. 3) is neatly motivated and beautifully staged using the technique of 'limited viewpoint'. We see and hear the man and the woman each through the other's eyes and ears as they discuss what they see with a companion. The Icelandic farmhouse setting with its wood-stack, water-butt and sheep on the fellside frames the magnificent verses in which the 'beam from the eyelid-moon [eye] of the goddess of the golden torque [woman]' (v. 3) presages sorrow for them both. The fate of Kormak and Steingerd is set from the beginning, as is the saga's pungent combination of romance and realism.

Despite some fine episodes, and touches of telling characterization and dialogue, the saga has been seen by some critics as something of a structural disaster, an imperfectly designed vehicle for the verse quotations. There are many roughnesses in the prose narrative, duplicated incidents and materials not relevant to the main plot (such as Bersi's quarrels in chs. 15–16). Prose and verse are not always harmonized, while at some points it is clear that the prose is a rather heavy-handed attempt to explain an obscure item of poetic diction. However, the poet's obsession with the unattained beloved is an exceptionally strong thread which pulls the narrative together. The prelude inversely foreshadows Kormak's fate, since his father Ogmund wins the noble Helga by vanquishing a rival in a duel, and although Kormak's death is the result of a rash encounter with a Scottish giant and therefore externally unconnected with his love, his dying verses referring to Steingerd provide the connection. (The case of Hallfred is similar.)

The eighty-five verses in *Kormak's Saga* are remarkable in both number and quality. '*Cormac* [*Kormak*] without the verse would be like *Hamlet* without the Ghost', as W. G. Collingwood put it.[6] The sixty-four verses attributed to Kormak almost all relate to Steingerd or to the male rivalry she unintentionally occasioned, and they contain some of the most splendid expressions of love and spite in European literature. The fifteen verses spoken by Kormak's rival Bersi range from colourful belligerence to the frustrated indignity of old age.[7] However, poetry is not mentioned in the opening characterization of Kormak (ch. 2), and he is not portrayed in his known historical role as court poet to Earl Sigurd of Lade or King Harald Grey-cloak, although he serves the latter in the saga.

The hero's travels abroad are also less important than in the other sagas of poets. The saga is almost two-thirds over, and Steingerd is divorced and remarried, before Kormak sets sail (ch. 18). He makes two trips with his brother Thorgils, who is useful as an interlocutor and foil – a contrastive voice of moderation and reason. The first voyage occasions a sketchy account of the brothers' raiding expeditions and their part in a Norwegian triumph in Ireland, but its main effect is to show that no amount of travel and adventure will distract Kormak from his hopeless love (chs. 18–19). The second journey, however, has the unique feature of an encounter between the poet-hero, his resourceful beloved Steingerd and her second husband Thorvald, which presents an opportunity for racy rescues from Viking pirates as well as amusing arbitration by King Harald over the Icelanders' kisses and quarrels (chs. 24–6).

The concentration of the action in Iceland gives maximum opportunity for Kormak to press his attentions on Steingerd. Her reactions are variable, but he never gains fulfilment with her, even when they spend a night together, and his lingering kisses prove expensive. Even so, there is never an intense focus on the love triangle as such, as there is in *The Saga of Bjorn*. It is Kormak's complex and relentless quarrels with Steingerd's family and two successive husbands, and the embroilment of kinsmen and neighbours in these, that are in the spotlight. Kormak fights three of the six duels in the saga, and hostilities are conducted verbally as well as physically. A lull in the action is provided when Steingerd divorces Bersi and the narrative follows Bersi's quarrels over her dowry and other matters only minimally connected with Kormak. Meanwhile, Steingerd quietly marries Thorvald, providing Kormak with a new target for contempt.

Alongside the sublime poetic expressions of love and the serious concern with conflict, there flickers an almost picaresque quality in some incidents where the mercurial Kormak is subjected to various indignities – rowing after his rival in a leaky, overpriced boat, losing a duel for a mere scratch, and being capsized by his beloved (chs. 8, 10 and 25). He is the comic extreme of the hero with more courage than sense, and his family and supporters could all echo the seeress Thordis in saying that 'helping you will be far from easy' (ch. 22). Chapters 9–11, for instance, show Kormak wilfully abusing the magic sword Skofnung, and at his death 'people bewailed the fact that he should have acted so imprudently' (ch. 27). There is, however, a double layer of causation: human and supernatural. It is not only Kormak who believes that external forces blighted his union with Steingerd – that 'evil spirits or adverse destinies had prevented it from the start' (ch. 26) – but also the narrator, who attributes the cooling of his feelings to the sorceress Thorveig's spell (ch. 6). Indeed, sorcery and magic weapons and objects play an exceptionally strong part in this saga set a few decades before the formal acceptance of Christianity in Norway and Iceland. But is the supernatural machinery merely 'period' scenery, or part of the meaning of the saga? Are malign forces at work, or is the root of Kormak's tragedy within himself: in his restlessness, his romantic refusal to negotiate for his love, or his (possibly subliminal) reluctance to take a bride from a socially inferior family? The reader is left to wonder how the saga author meant his Christian audience to view the balance of fate and human responsibility.

The Saga of Hallfred Troublesome-poet

Here, as in *Kormak's Saga*, we watch a perverse hero making his way in an imperfect and unpredictable world: a headstrong poet who relishes freedom of action but four times finds himself in chains. In terms of plot, the saga is distinguished especially by the weight and diversity of the hero's adventures abroad, and the separation of these from the Icelandic love affair and its ramifications. It is almost as if there were two sagas, one entwined within the other.[8]

In the scenes set in Iceland, virtually everything that happens to Hallfred relates to his passion for Kolfinna. So too, obliquely, does the prelude set in the previous generation, and showing Ottar's and Avaldi's emigration from Norway to Iceland, for these oldest and closest of friends are to be the fathers of the two lovers, and of sons one of whom will kill the other because of the love affair. This is almost a reverse *Romeo and Juliet* plot, in which tragic discord arises in spite of interfamilial friendship, and if the lovers are star-crossed, their unhappy fate springs more from Hallfred's wilfulness than from external circumstances. Similarly, the episode in which the chieftain's son Ingolf woos Hallfred's sister Valgerd and composes verses about her anticipates and duplicates the main plot, emphasizing the social disruption caused by an unregulated liaison (chs. 2–3). Further, the determination of Ottar, father of Valgerd, to mount a legal action against his social superior, Ingolf's father Thorstein, may be seen as a piece of foolish hubris for which the penalty is heavy – Ottar's forced departure from the district.[9]

Hallfred's teenage romance is hardly under way before his defiance of social mores brings trouble. When, in a deftly staged scene, he sits Kolfinna on his knee and kisses her in full view of the party who have come to ask for her hand, he seems more intent on provocation than seduction (ch. 4), and the pattern of provocation and ensuing chase and skirmish repeats when the love plot resumes much later, in chs. 9–10. After a long absence, Hallfred spends a night at the shieling-huts with Kolfinna and slanders Gris, but this time with fatal consequences – first the unintended death of Einar Thorisson, and later the revenge killing of Hallfred's brother Galti.

Hallfred sails abroad with Kolfinna's name on his lips after her betrothal to Gris has been announced (ch. 5), and he thinks of her as he dies at sea off Iona (ch. 11), but otherwise, Hallfred's emotional energy is deployed elsewhere during his foreign travels. He is the only one of the skalds in these sagas to marry abroad, and his grief over his wife Ingibjorg's death is touching (ch. 9). It is, however, King

Olaf Tryggvason who forms the hub of Hallfred's wheeling fortunes overseas, and Olaf's centrality is emphasized by the fact that little is made of Hallfred's visits to four other rulers. The bond forms when the king, incognito, rescues Hallfred and his crew from a storm that is symbolic of the poet's perilous heathen state, and cajoles him into conversion to Christianity (ch. 5).[10] From then on Hallfred is driven by a desire to earn his liege's favour, though this is frequently at odds with the dictates of his own stubborn will. Inseparable from this is the parallel conflict between Hallfred's new religion and his residual paganism, which is treated with some sympathy and even benign humour, as in the account of Hallfred's minimalist Christian devotions (end of ch. 8).

The plot may be somewhat episodic and occasionally inept (some examples being mentioned in the notes), yet the saga has much to offer. There is some striking visualization and folk-tale atmospherics, for instance in Hallfred's 'mission' to Thorleif the Wise, or in the night-long trauma in which Onund, in spite of having been skewered by Hallfred's knife, pounds on the door of the forest refuge (chs. 6, 7). Further, a marvellous tissue of thematic strands emerges from individual episodes in the context of the whole saga. In Hallfred's approach to Thorleif the Wise, for instance, his physical disguise of beggar's garb and disfigured face is only the most obvious manifestation of a much larger theme of appearance and reality, and its verbal counterpart, Hallfred's dissembling speech, raises questions of truth and falsehood: ' "I'm just a pauper," [Hallfred] said, "I went to the king and he wanted to force his religion on me, but I ran away under cover, and before that killed one of the king's men. Now I want to ask you for some protection" ' (ch. 6). Though dishonest in purpose – a means to effect the blinding of Thorleif – Hallfred's claim to have killed one of Olaf's men is perfectly true, and his reference to a coerced conversion is at least half-true. He only pretends to seek protection here, but fabrication will turn into reality much later on when Thorleif the Wise saves his life (ch. 11). Thorleif, meanwhile, is almost Hallfred's alter ego, an embodiment of recalcitrant but not unattractive paganism. The Thorleif episode thus typifies the work as a whole, for this is a saga full of betrayals of trust, reversals, contradictions, disguises and other mismatches of appearance and reality. Hallfred exclaims at one point, 'Who will be true to me, then, if my father breaks faith?' (ch. 4);[11] he almost meets death at the hands of the confidence trickster Onund and the genial host Bjorn, and he is cheated by bereavement at the moment when a loving marriage and reconciliation with God and the king seem to guarantee happiness (chs. 7, 8 and 9). But good also comes from surprising quarters: not only from Thorleif, but also from Hallfred's rival Gris, who, when Hallfred backs out of a duel, is the only one to understand the reason (ch. 10).

The restless and complex narrative is in fact ideally suited to its central character, who is introduced as unreliable and unpopular, who has no real reason for not marrying his beloved, and who wins the nickname 'Troublesome-poet' (*vandræðaskáld*, literally 'skald of problems/troubles'). A kind of resolution is reached at the end of the saga, however. The two main narrative strands of Hallfred's fortunes at home and abroad are eventually united, for King Olaf's dream-borne moral authority also extends to Iceland, where he prevents Hallfred from going ahead with his duel against Gris. The religious contradictions are also dissolved in the last scenes. Storm-tossed and fatally injured by a swinging boom, Hallfred, in true pagan style, sees his fetch (the embodiment of his personal spirit) and bids farewell to her. His death follows swiftly, then the dream-inspired recovery of his body and the recasting of his gifts from King Olaf as ecclesiastical vessels. Seen from one point of view, this is an eccentric juxtaposition of literary motifs, but from another, it exemplifies the humane and synthesizing intelligence that pervades the work. The heroine does not come to hate her husband Gris, who is decent, though short on sexual charisma. Neither Gris nor Hallfred meets a violent end (though Hallfred does try to kill him), and Gris and Kolfinna, we presume, live unhappily ever after. The hero attracts trouble, and does some appalling things, including two partial blindings and five killings, not all justified. Yet at the bidding of Olaf Tryggvason he grudgingly accepts arbitration in place of a duel against Gris and forgoes revenge against Earl Eirik. He is not only buried on the Holy Isle of Iona but is also perpetuated in his son, who despite inheriting both his names – Hallfred and 'Troublesome-poet' – grows up to be successful and prolific. The implicit message seems to be that this specimen of erring humanity is redeemed in the end.

The Saga of Gunnlaug Serpent-tongue

In many ways the most shapely of these sagas, and hitherto the best known among English-speaking readers, *The Saga of Gunnlaug* combines an intensely focused version of the romantic plot with an unusually rich catalogue of court appearances by its poet-hero. There are few episodes or characters that could be counted as extraneous. The Norwegian sea-captain Bergfinn, for instance, enters the narrative only to interpret Thorstein's premonitory dream in a finely staged conversation, and is then 'out of the saga' (ch. 2).

The imaginative power of the love theme owes much to the portrayal of Helga the Fair, tinged as it is with new currents of romantic taste. She forms the passive centre of the saga, and her birth and death frame it. Her love for Gunnlaug is never in doubt. Unlike other saga heroines, she never affects cold resignation to her situation, but rests longing eyes on her unattainable lover and accepts both his poetry and his gift of the splendid cloak presented to him by King Ethelred (ch. 11). She gazes at the cloak as she dies in the arms of her second husband (ch. 13).

The overseas adventures of Gunnlaug are tightly integrated with the love story, for the tragic rivalry between Gunnlaug and Hrafn springs up at the court of the Swedish king, and only ends when they fight to the death overseas. Gunnlaug's audiences at court, meanwhile, range through the whole spectrum of the stereotypes offered by stories of this sort. The first is far from a triumph. Gunnlaug may bring to his audience with Earl Eirik excellent family connections and an introduction from the distinguished Skuli Thorsteinsson, but when he displays a boorish lack of tact that matches his homespun garb he is lucky to escape with his life (ch. 6). Later, the comically inexperienced Earl Sigtrygg Silk-beard in Dublin has to be counselled against rewarding him with two ships for his poetry, while the mighty King Olaf of Sweden keeps itinerant poets in their place (chs. 8, 9). Essentially though, Gunnlaug matures, even turning diplomat on one occasion (ch. 8), like some of the greatest skalds. On return to Iceland the question of Helga comes to the fore, and Gunnlaug's second set of voyages abroad appears as a muted and shortened refrain of the first. In his last two court visits, he is entirely preoccupied with resolving his quarrel with Hrafn (ch. 12).

The theme of male rivalry attains the greatest tragic dignity in this saga. It is heightened by the essentially admirable character sketch of Hrafn in ch. 5, and by the initial friendship of Gunnlaug and Hrafn, both skalds. Later, there is a poignant moment of fellow-feeling between them when they decide to lance the boil of enmity by fighting abroad (ch. 11). Despite that enmity, and despite the fact that the last sixteen verses of the saga arise from the yearning and strife caused by Helga, the saga contains almost no poetic invective.

The plot hinges on injured pride, for Hrafn's perfidious bid for Helga is made as he smarts from a publicly delivered slight about his person and poetry from his one-time friend Gunnlaug (ch. 9). Interestingly, Hrafn's second, fatal, act of treachery is motivated instead by despair over the failure of his marriage (ch. 12), but the hostility between the two men has a dynamic of its own. Gunnlaug's attentions to Helga after her marriage are enough to provoke Hrafn, but he deliberately adds to them by making as if to ride him down (ch. 11). Gunnlaug is susceptible to goading too, when two Norwegians' scoffing mimicry of the Icelanders stiffens his resolve to press on with the quarrel to its bitter end, and the saga mounts to a tragic climax with the tense pursuit to Dingenes and the heroics and anti-heroics of the fight there (ch. 12).

At the human level, the tragedy is a product of emotion, circumstance and individual choice: love and the desire for honour, the incompatibility of marriage and a successful career abroad (pointed out twice to Gunnlaug in ch. 5), and Gunnlaug's decision, apparently, to prolong his service of King Ethelred beyond strict necessity (ch. 10). Yet the saga also allows the possibility of a deterministic view, not least through the author's comment, 'and events had to take their course' (ch. 11), and it seems like a cruel trick of fate that Gunnlaug's arrival home exactly coincides with the marriage feast of Hrafn and Helga, ensuring maximum unhappiness for all (ch. 10).

The premonitory dream experienced by Thorstein in the opening of the saga may also suggest the limits of human choice (ch. 2). Two eagles fight to the death over a swan, who sorrows and then flies away with a gentle hawk, and this, in Bergfinn's interpretation, presages the tragedy that Thorstein's lovely daughter, as yet unborn, will unwillingly occasion. As a literary device, the dream is a graphic and compelling way of unifying the action through a pattern of anticipation and fulfilment, but it may also imply that the eventual outcome is not merely foreseen but predetermined. Despite Thorstein's 'dreams don't mean anything' (ch. 2) and his rejection of Bergfinn's interpretation, he makes spasmodic attempts to defy fate, always in vain.

Though skilled in evoking vivid scenes, the narrator of *The Saga of Gunnlaug* can be obtrusive, given to breaking in with pedantic source references, including a solemn assurance that 'learned men say' that Helga was the loveliest Icelandic woman ever (ch. 4). Equally intrusive but perhaps more meaningful is the distance created when the narrator draws attention to the temporal and cultural gulf between his own milieu and the world inhabited by his characters some two hundred and fifty years earlier. Dominating the landscape of the saga-writer's past is the adoption of Christianity in the year 1000, 'the best thing ever to have happened in Iceland' (ch. 5). Like other sagas whose events straddle the Conversion, including *Njal's Saga*, this one has to confront the question of its ethical impact. The saga is doubtless honest in the overall impression it gives that the Conversion stopped far short of the wholesale embrace of humility and forgiveness urged in the teachings of Christ. Duelling may have been made illegal, forcing Gunnlaug and Hrafn to settle their differences in mainland Scandinavia, but when Gunnlaug's family are insufficiently compensated for his death, the old ethic of satisfying honour by revenge prevails.

The Saga of Bjorn, Champion of the Hitardal People

This bleakly fascinating saga ends with Bjorn dead after a valiant defence against attackers who vastly outweigh him in numbers and viciousness. His antagonist Thord Kolbeinsson, after the glow of triumph fades, is left once more dissatisfied and humiliated. Relentlessly focused on the enmity of the two men and its impact on the wider Icelandic community, the saga contains only rather minimal versions of the other characteristic elements of the sagas of poets – the adventures abroad, the love affair, and the stereotyped skald figure in central position.

For once, the titular hero is handsome in both looks and behaviour. He engages in venomous poetic sparring matches with Thord, but he is not introduced as a skald. (Although the opening chapters are supplied from a text of *The Saga of St Olaf* to fill a gap in the *Saga of Bjorn* manuscript, they give quite a full account of Bjorn's early life.) Bjorn wins favour with Earl Eirik Hakonarson and King Olaf Haraldsson for his noble character and dashing feats of valour, not for poetry (chs. 2, 3, 9). His arena of action is wider, and his exploits more exotic than any in the sagas of poets, as he slays the champion Kaldimar in Russia and a flying dragon in England (chs. 4, 5). He takes home with him the sobriquet of 'Champion', and lives up to it, though the heroics demanded by everyday life in Iceland can be of a quieter kind: he is even glimpsed helping mother with the washing (ch. 11). Thord, by contrast, composes *drápur* (singular *drápa*, a formal eulogy with refrains) for Eirik and Olaf, and gains splendid rewards from Olaf, though he has to surrender some of these to Bjorn as compensation (chs. 7, 8). Unlike the other skald figures, Thord is no warrior. His puny physique (if the taunts against the 'little lad' are justified), cowardly manipulations and eloquent duplicity are the perfect antithesis to the mighty and glamorous Bjorn. However, neither antagonist has a monopoly of good behaviour. Bjorn's killing of Thorkel Dalksson, for example, technically justified but clearly excessive, gives Thord the chance to make the magnanimous gesture of compensating Dalk (ch. 20).

Bjorn's relationship with Oddny Isle-candle develops early and is smiled upon by 'many people' (ch. 1), but no narrative capital is made out of this trigger to the saga's action. Despite the assertion of her outstanding looks and character (ch. 1), the figure of Oddny is lightly drawn, just sufficient to explain the sexual jealousy that pervades the tense and claustrophobic winter that the members of the triangle pass together (chs. 12–14). Bjorn's claim to be the father of Kolli also declares an adulterous liaison with Oddny (verses 12, 29, ch. 32), but this happens off stage. Bjorn marries another woman, Thordis (the marriage itself presumably taking place in a section now lost), while it is only after Bjorn is dead and Oddny ill from grief that Thord regrets the loss of Oddny's love and aspires to any kind of pathos: 'It seemed to him a great disaster that had come to them and to Bjorn all together' (ch. 33).

The antagonism between Thord and Bjorn appears more fevered than their feelings for Oddny. Uniquely, it is established in the very first chapter of the (reconstructed) saga, when Bjorn, aged about twelve, opts to live with his older cousin Skuli Thorsteinsson in order to avoid unspecified 'aggression' with which Thord, some fifteen years his senior, harasses Bjorn and others. That this aggression consisted of homoerotic advances has been suggested, and although this cannot be proven, there is a highly charged strand of sexual insult in the dealings between the two men, which reaches its most graphic and public when Bjorn uses a carving and a verse to portray Thord as the passive partner in a homosexual act (ch. 17). The icon is more about aggression than sex, and the symbolic emasculation would have been understood as a metaphor for abject cowardice; it doubtless also functions as a displaced expression of the sexual rivalry over Oddny. Whether there is also an allusion to actual homoerotic behaviour is, again, uncertain.[12]

The running duel of poetic insults, lawsuits and plots which occupies chs. 10–26 is exceptionally long, complex and rather episodic, yet there is progress from verbal to physical strife, and momentum in the mounting severity and directness of Thord's attacks. There is also a neatness in the replication of similar incidents: both men suffer a humiliation involving an animal which the other mocks in verse, both harbour outlaws, and there are triplets of slayings by Bjorn and ambushes arranged by Thord.[13] The entry of Thorstein Kuggason into the saga in ch. 27, as he and his party take chilly refuge from the blizzard at Bjorn's farm, provides a narrative landmark, after which the pace slows while the action intensifies. Arbitration is tried and abandoned, then 'conflict' motifs, many of them paralleled elsewhere, build to a climax: premonitory dreams, a splendidly staged ambush including a farm-boy's description of the advancing enemies, a scene of understated tragedy across drawn weapons between Bjorn and his putative son Kolli, and the hero's last stand. His enemy dead, Thord displays pungent contrasts of behaviour – bitter callousness in his public flaunting of Bjorn's detached head, and patient tenderness towards the heartbroken Oddny (ch. 33).

The impact of violence ripples out from the Thord–Bjorn epi-centre to affect the whole community, and many others play a part, as bereaved relatives, inciters, assassins, conspirators, arbitrators or commentators, in adjusting the delicate controls that determine peace or strife. The saga becomes almost a casebook of provocations, conflicts, and attempts at resolution through out-of-court compen-sation, enforced redress, the legal penalties of lesser or greater out-lawry or fines, and blood revenge. Thorstein Kuggason articulates the idea that compensation and outlawry, but not blood revenge, are fitting expedients for Christian men who have been wronged (ch. 29); but there is no pretence that finding appropriate solutions is easy. After all, even wise arbitration from the saintly King Olaf of Norway failed to settle the feud between Thord and Bjorn (ch. 8). The saga risks anticlimax by a careful account of the legal proceedings following the death of Bjorn, closing at the point when 'interest in the affair began to die down'. Vivid events and strong or difficult characters are the lifeblood of saga narratives, but given the chance, moderation will eventually prevail and – in saga as in life – the community will go quietly about its business.

The most important feature of the action abroad is the role of King Olaf. His court is the stage for the quick souring of attempted friendship between Thord and Bjorn, while the close and admiring comradeship between the king and Bjorn intensifies the narrative bias towards the latter. Bjorn's acquisition, by accident commuted to gift, of cross-garters belonging to the king, and his wearing of them until he dies, become symbolic of their relationship and hence of Bjorn's standing, which is otherwise implausibly reduced once he returns to Iceland. The treatment of the royal gift as if a holy relic (chs. 9 and 32) gives Bjorn a share in Olaf's sanctity in a way reminiscent of the close of *The Saga of Hallfred*, and this King Olaf, like his namesake, Hallfred's patron Olaf Tryggvason, exerts a moral influence in the career of the Icelander. At the Branno islands, Bjorn spares Thord because he is the retainer of the sovereign whom Bjorn admires but has not yet met (ch. 7); and he leaves off raiding at the bidding of the king, who deems it a violation of God's law (ch. 9). He finds it less easy to abandon his vendetta against Thord. Christianity is not fully developed as a theme, but Bjorn's building of a church and composing of a drapa in honour of St Thomas mark him as, at least, religiously well intentioned. It is in this church that Bjorn's hacked body is laid to rest.

Viglund's Saga

The final saga in this volume is a splendid complement, even antidote, to the first four. Set earlier than they, in the reign of King Harald Fair-hair (up to *c.* 932), but written later (*c.* 1400), it contains much that is familiar. The distinctive features of the sagas of poets are present – a poet-hero and a plot involving frustrated love, travels abroad and male rivalry – and the narrative world is that of the Sagas of Icelanders. Chapter 7, for instance, opens, 'There was a man called Holmkel who lived at Foss', and continues with the expected genealogy and Icelandic place-names, and most of this detail is matched in that treasury of respected tradition, *The Book of Settlements* (ch. 77). Scenes such as the ball game, incitement and battle among the frozen hayricks in ch. 14 are also firmly in the idiom of the Sagas of Icelanders, and if occasional details such as a harp with gold and silver strings, an orchard or pastimes such as hunting transport us temporarily into a world of foreign romance, they are rarities in the saga and confined to the scenes set in Norway.

Nevertheless, the writer takes several steps in the direction of romance, not only offering a 'happy ever after' ending but also achieving it by patterns of character, motivation and plot that are often quite unlike those of the classic sagas of poets. Viglund is not a stereotypical skald. Rather, he is an idealized hero who occasionally speaks in verse. His suspiciously non-traditional name means 'Battle-mind', and supported only by his brother Trausti ('Trusty'), he prevails against twelve attackers, juggling deftly with shield and axe in order to dispatch one of his main rivals (ch. 16, cf. ch. 14). Viglund is also the ideal lover, and the enduring passion of Viglund and Ketilrid shines out from the saga, though with rare exceptions the author gives little ground to sentimentality. For a Kormak or Bjorn, the desire to humiliate the opposition seems even to outweigh desire for the woman, who is effectively lost to the hero. Viglund's priority, by contrast, is always to win Ketilrid, and his love poetry is unmixed with spite. Ketilrid's first husband, Hakon, is only a short-lived instrument of the malevolence of others. The saga hence lacks intense and sustained antagonism between the male rivals, becoming instead an elaborate illustration of the axiom that true love flourishes in adversity (ch. 12), and a demonstration of the possibility that goodwill and restraint can triumph. Indeed, Viglund is only intermittently centre-stage, and although his noble valour plays its part, there is the sense of a larger, rather schematic struggle going on around him. Those of goodwill (Viglund's father Thorgrim, brother Trausti and uncle Helgi, and Ketilrid's father Holmkel) are ranged against those driven by malice (Ketilrid's mother Thorbjorg, and brothers Jokul and Einar and their allies), while the process of the plot gradually brings the Norwegian party (Ketil, Gunnlaug and Sigurd) over to the side of harmony and reason.

In fact, of course, there are two situations of love in adversity, for in the extended Norwegian prelude, Viglund's father Thorgrim is in competition with Ketil of Raumarike, the favourite of King Harald, for his beloved Olof. The repercussions of Thorgrim's swashbuckling abduction of Olof interweave with the life of Viglund. The Norwegian Hakon, sent out by Ketil as a surrogate avenger against Thorgrim, also becomes the tool of spite against Thorgrim's sons, and the working-out of the plot involves the resolution of both sets of problems through action in Iceland and Norway.

The mainspring of the action in Iceland is the unexplained hostility of Thorbjorg to her daughter Ketilrid, unique in the Sagas of Icelanders and unusual in romance, though reminiscent of the wicked stepmothers of fairy-tale. It is shared by Ketilrid's brothers Jokul and Einar, who are also driven by envy of Thorgrim's standing in the neighbourhood. Even their horse Blackie is vicious, and Thorbjorg's friend Kjolvor uses witchcraft to try to drown Viglund and his brother (chs. 9, 12). Holmkel, devoted father to Ketilrid and staunch friend to Thorgrim, produces much of the narrative interest. He may appear not man enough to defy his wife and sons, but he wins the day for the young lovers by a deft stratagem which on the surface will appeal to his wife's malice. Suspense is maintained until the magnificent last scene where, rather in the manner of a comic opera, almost the entire cast gathers on stage to hear some startling revelations and witness no fewer than three happy unions.[14]

We are, then, after all in a rather different world, in terms of plot, character, morality and atmosphere, from that of the classic sagas of poets. There are many similarities to European romance literature: testing of the hero's virtue through trials and adventures, exploration of familial relationships, a partially exotic setting and a happy ending. The basic two-tiered plot, with son succeeding father as the central figure, is especially characteristic of bridal-quest romances.[15] This is not, then, a decadent outgrowth of the Sagas of Icelanders, but a transformation and hybridization of the genre by an author who clearly relished his literary freedom and used it to take a feud plot in an unusually optimistic direction. He ends his saga with a verse epilogue that explicitly waives his copyright, and thanks God 'if the story has been a pleasure'. For most readers, it undoubtedly will be.

POETRY

The power of words is a running preoccupation of the Sagas of Icelanders. Themselves a product of great verbal artistry, the sagas portray a culture in which praise, blame, vows, curses, slanders and taunting nicknames play a vital part in the social dynamics.[16] For most of the saga characters, personal and family honour are more important than life, and words, especially poetic words, are the makers or breakers of public reputation. No wonder, then, that the gift of poetry was both cherished and feared, and its mythological origins as the mead or drink of Odin frequently recalled, as when Bjorn declares 'I mix beer for Odin' in v. 32 of his saga.

Poets often figure among the dramatis personae of Icelandic sagas, and other characters not formally introduced as poets speak, on occasion, in verse. Even within this poetry-minded genre, though, the sagas of poets are remarkable for the way in which historical skalds have been placed centre-stage and elevated into literary stereotypes. Outstanding too is the amount and variety of verse quoted within them:[17] poetry of praise, slander and love, travelogue, and verses associated with combat. Without the verses, many of the episodes in these sagas, including several in *Kormak's Saga* and the whole central section of *The Saga of Bjorn*, would simply not be there.

Scandinavian rulers gave rich rewards for elaborate poetic eulogies in the form of the drapa, or the flokk (eulogy without refrains). Dozens of skalds are known to have composed at the courts of Scandinavia from the ninth to thirteenth centuries, for their names are catalogued in the *List of Poets* (*Skáldatal*), and after AD 1000 most of the court poets were Icelanders seeking fame, reward and a suitable outlet for their energy and talent. Many of them make appearances in the Icelandic or Norwegian Sagas of Kings or in short tales (*þættir*).

In Iceland, the social functions of poetry were quite different. Battle-verses mainly bragged of the speaker's own exploits, and poetry could be a potent tool of aggression. The laws encoded in the mainly thirteenth-century *Grágás* ('Grey Goose') imposed heavy penalties for poetic slander, or for poetry in praise of women, since this compromised their marriage prospects and constituted a threat to their menfolk. Hallfred ruefully notes that he has to compensate Gris for a 'scrap of verse' with the jingling gold he received from his royal patrons (v. 29). The cost is, moreover, not just financial. Verse obscenities in *The Saga of Bjorn* are paid for in one case with death, and Thord's erupting resentment at the imbalance in slander-verses reopens old wounds, and dashes all hopes of reconciliation (chs. 20, 29).

In both form and content, the poetry found in the sagas obeys fundamentally different laws from those of the prose, especially in respect of metre, diction and word order. Its central figurative device, the kenning, draws on myth, legend and the world of nature to express common concepts in striking and often riddling ways – 'man' as 'tree of treasure' or 'Odin of the sword', 'woman' as 'Freyja of jewellery', gold as 'blaze of the sea' or 'ship' as 'stallion of the waves' (see further, 'The Techniques of Skaldic Poetry', pp. 322–6). When inlaid within prose narratives, forming the prosimetrum composition so beloved of Icelandic writers as of others in medieval Europe,[18] the poetry therefore has a contrastive and decorative function, thrown into relief by the directness of the surrounding prose. Within the sagas of poets it also plays a dynamic role, either forming part of the action or dialogue (as when the protagonists hurl abuse at one another in a fight) or reflecting on events soon afterwards. Unlike much medieval poetry, it is not communal and utilitarian, promoting collective values, but rather it at least purports to express individual emotion. Even more than the dialogue, it reveals the interior state of characters, and hence complements the normally reticent prose narrative. Gris, for instance, not known for eloquence, is given a verse whose intertwining clauses capture eddies of feeling: pity for his swollen-eyed wife Kolfinna, mingled with suspicion and fury (*The Saga of Hallfred*, v. 25).[19] Nevertheless, love poetry as such is poorly represented, except in *Kormak's Saga*; and v. 28 of *The Saga of Hallfred*, with its marvellous image of Kolfinna like a gilded ship sailing between islands, is something of a rarity. More often, romantic longing is interlaced with hatred and scorn for the woman's husband (*The Saga of Hallfred*, vv. 18–19), or the poet torments himself by contrasting his present hardships, at sea or in battle, with the sensual comforts of the married couple, sometimes grossly imagined (*The Saga of Hallfred*, vv. 4 and 33). Then there is the poetry of sexual insult and pure spite, brought to grotesque perfection in the 'Grey-belly Satire' (*The Saga of Bjorn*, ch. 20).

The verse quotations may also have trained saga audiences in certain ways of interpreting the prose. The metaphors inherent in much of the poetic diction may have encouraged the perception that, for instance, treasure is both a material reality and a symbol of status and of social relations between lord and retainer or lover and beloved; seafaring is the outward expression of a restless and possibly erotically excited mind. Further, both skaldic poetry and saga narratives demand alertness and skilful anticipation of stereotypical patterns in their audiences. In the poetry, the elements of kennings and parts of clauses are often widely separated, while narrative patterns of anticipation and fulfilment or action and reaction abound in the saga narratives – and naturally so, given their preoccupation with feuds, vows, prophecies and omens. Viglund's conditional vow not to cut or wash his hair cues the audience to expect its fulfilment, for example (chs. 18, 23), while the appearance of Thorleif the Wise as the *deus ex machina* who rescues Hallfred fulfils a promise made long before (*The Saga of Hallfred*, chs. 6, 11).[20]

To what extent, we may ask finally, do the verses genuinely belong to their supposed creators? The small scraps from court poems, for instance Gunnlaug's almost idolatrous praise of King Ethelred (v. 3), are probably authentic, but the freestanding occasional verses on love and strife are extremely difficult to date. They have been viewed with some scholarly scepticism, on the evidence of their content, style, language or metre, but metrical evidence adduced by Kari Ellen Gade suggests that many of the 'Kormak' and 'Hallfred' verses may genuinely belong to the late tenth century or beginning of the eleventh,[21] though this does not of course prove that they were composed in the (often unlikely) circumstances depicted in the sagas. Most of the verses in *The Saga of Gunnlaug* and some in *The Saga of Bjorn* appear to be later, composed at some stage after the lifetime of the poets but before the composition of the saga prose, while those in *Viglund's Saga* may be the work of the saga-writer himself. Beyond this it is difficult to go – regrettably, since many questions about the historical basis of these sagas and about their literary development depend crucially on the age and role of the poetry.

THE SAGAS OF POETS AND HISTORY

'It reads like a novel, and yet it is a true story,' wrote Collingwood, introducing *Kormak's Saga* in 1902.[22] A hundred years later we might want to probe this by asking what kind of truth can be found in these sagas. Their unassuming artistry allows them to be read, up to a point, as realistic and historically credible, and in many ways their anonymous authors encourage this. The *Kormak's Saga* author, for instance, notes concerning the expedition to Permia that 'no other names of ships' commanders are recorded' (ch. 25), as though his account rested on firm evidence. Although this is hardly the case, there is a historical kernel to the sagas. Kormak, Hallfred, Gunnlaug and his rival Hrafn, and Thord Kolbeinsson from *The Saga of Bjorn*, were all famed as court poets. Their service of Nordic rulers is vouched for in the *List of Poets*, and courtly verses by Kormak, Hallfred and Thord are preserved outside the sagas of poets. The rulers whom the Icelanders visit are also, with one exception, verifiable and datable figures, stretching from Harald Fair-hair in the late ninth century to Earl Eirik in the early eleventh. Even when *The Saga of Bjorn* moves to the exotic location of Russia (ch. 12), the essentials of the situation are anchored into history. The early twelfth-century *Russian Primary Chronicle* records that a force of Scandinavian 'Varangians' *c.* 980 assisted a ruler called Valdimar in displacing his brother and rival for power (who is not, however, named Kaldimar as in the saga; nor are Bjorn's exploits confirmed).

However, the saga authors were not limited by historical actuality in a narrow sense, and their art has often been compared with that of the historical novelist. To take the depiction of the poets at foreign courts, the *Kormak's Saga* author either did not know, or more likely chose to ignore, the historical fact that Kormak was a court poet, while on the other hand it is highly improbable that all the court visits depicted in the sagas took place, or that the standing of Icelanders abroad was always quite so exalted as claimed. The author of *The Saga of Gunnlaug* in particular seems to have enjoyed elaborating on a well known theme, even inventing a ruler for his hero to visit (Earl Sigurd in Skarar, ch. 8). There is, however, a deeper kind of truth here, for the narratives seem to encode concerns of the authors' times, in this case ambivalent attitudes to Norway, the former homeland. On the one hand, there is gratitude to those Norwegian monarchs who spread Christianity throughout the Nordic lands, and a fascination with the court, with all its promise of advancement. On the other, the Norwegian throne is a threat to Icelandic self-esteem and ultimately to Iceland's independence. By the thirteenth century, the Viking battles were over, and the Norwegian state was consolidating itself along European lines. Its ambitions towards Iceland were promoted there by key Icelanders and this, combined with internal troubles and economic necessity, led in 1262–4 to Iceland renouncing its status as an independent commonwealth and pledging homage to the Norwegian king.

A similar interweaving of 'fact', 'imaginative reconstruction' and 'fiction' is apparent when we look at characters and events in Iceland. We can be fairly certain that many of the main saga characters existed, since they appear in the thirteenth-century *Book of Settlements*: Kormak, Thorgils, Steinar and Thorvald from *Kormak's Saga*; Illugi, Gunnlaug, Onund and Hrafn from *The Saga of Gunnlaug*, and Thord and Bjorn from *The Saga of Bjorn*, though the heroines do not. The kernel of *The Saga of Hallfred* is also found in the *Book of Settlements*: the marriage of Kolfinna Avaldadottir to Gris, and her brother Brand's killing of Galti Ottarsson because of Hallfred's slander.[23] Even the writer of the blithely fictitious *Viglund's Saga* may have used the *Book of Settlements*, since Ketil from Raumarike and Holmkel appear there.

How far the love rivalries at the core of these sagas represent historical reality is difficult to say, especially since so much depends on the evidence of the verses, whose dating is elusive. There is some external evidence, for example a couplet attributed to Kormak in the *Third Grammatical Treatise*. This addresses 'Thorkel' (the name of

Steingerd's father and brother in the saga) and mentions a female friend (*málvina*, literally 'confidante'), and this could encourage belief in Kormak's love for Steingerd. On the other hand it is disconcerting that Steingerd is not named in any source but *Kormak's Saga*, and we may have to admit that the historical truth is undiscoverable. Again, however, the sagas' truth lies not so much in factual information as in what they suggest about the culture and concerns of Icelandic society. The difficulties over the forming of marriages that they dramatize were social realities. The impulse of young men to seek their fortunes abroad must have come into conflict with commitments to Icelandic women; and adventurers and farmers offered very different prospects for economic stability and child-rearing to their potential brides. The legal penalties for poetry of scorn or love show that the poetry, the passions that inspired it, and the social disruption it caused, were also very real. And although the saga authors were recreating events at a distance of two centuries or more, everyday lives, religious observance apart, were probably not vastly different. Scenes of making hay, hunting seals, rounding up sheep on a hillside or struggling through a blizzard to the nearest farmhouse pictured their own hard lives. The fascination with genealogy, with legal process, and the effect of these on the standing of individuals within the community, also belong equally to both periods. Above all, the preoccupation with conflict and its resolution which runs through all the Sagas of Icelanders resonates with conditions in the thirteenth century, when, as documented in *Sturlunga Saga*, mounting strife between a small number of aristocratic families sucked whole districts into violence. The sagas can appear equivocal, placing a premium on moderation and forgiveness, yet admiring independence, tenacity and a heroic bravado driven by extreme sensitivity over personal and family honour. These tensions not only made for good stories, but were also still potent forces in contemporary society. The sagas thus present a version of real life that distils, isolates and schematizes certain situations and character traits. They are stories that help people to reflect on their lives, and in this respect they come very close to myth.

THE MAKING OF THE SAGAS OF POETS

The authors of the poets' sagas were clearly familiar with the localities in western Iceland in which their stories are set, and they may have had family connections with the main characters. *The Saga of Bjorn* and *The Saga of Gunnlaug* show an especially detailed knowledge of the Borgarfjord area. Beyond this, nothing is known for certain about the authors, though most were clearly knowledgeable about native traditions and foreign literature, and there has been speculation that some were trained clerics.

Whomever we should thank for the sagas in the form we have them, they are clearly not so much the product of an individual creative act as a result of long and complex evolution within local communities. None of the texts is an author's original, and they were certainly adapted as they went through various copyings. More fundamentally, the authors worked with a rich legacy of tradition: verses attributed to the poets and other characters, genealogical information, oral stories circulating locally and written materials of both Icelandic and foreign origin, all of which gradually assembled around the historical figures of the skalds, transforming them into legends. Also important were certain stereotyped situations and characters which must have provided templates for these storytellers and writers. The glamorous exploits of the champion Bjorn, his superbly laconic utterances and his valiant last stand are, for example, an amalgam of heroic motifs found widely elsewhere. Nevertheless, the authors would have had a good deal of freedom to select, shape and even invent materials according to their priorities and artistic skill. The following paragraphs review the kinds of source material available to the authors, then briefly survey what is known about the sources of the five sagas individually.

The most important single source of the prose narratives is the poetry cited within them. As noted above, it seems likely that the verses were inherited by the saga authors rather than fabricated by them, though the *Viglund's Saga* verses may, exceptionally, be contemporary with the prose. The variable success with which scenes have been built up round the verses depends on the expertise of the authors but probably also reflects the extent to which stories were already attached to the verses in local tradition. Sometimes there are teasing discrepancies between prose and verse or, as with the first two verses of *The Saga of Bjorn*, the prose contexts appear rather random. Sometimes, too, in a blatantly contrived way, the prose provides a brief narrative context and introduces an addressee whose sole purpose seems to be to prompt a verse (for instance, the encounter with the anonymous farm woman in *Kormak's Saga*, ch. 21). In some cases the stanzas concerned must originally have formed part of long verse sequences.[24] The first five verses of *Kormak's Saga* are among the numerous examples.

Oral tradition in prose, although by definition impossible to pin down, is another essential category of source material. This is especially true of *Kormak's Saga*, which is probably the earliest of the poets' sagas, *c.* 1220, and is one of the earliest of the Sagas of Icelanders. It hence has few known written sources (although a lost written saga about Kormak's rival Bersi has been postulated), and many of its incidents, racy but rough, could well be local stories only recently committed to writing by that time. Similarly, the central section of *The Saga of Bjorn*, which is somewhat episodic and apparently lacking in written sources, has also been seen as a set of imperfectly processed oral traditions.

The elusiveness of oral tradition has probably led to an over-concentration among scholars on the tracing of written sources, itself no straightforward task, especially because theories about relationships between written texts are strongly dependent on their dating, while the literary relationships themselves are a major part of the evidence for dating. What is certain, nevertheless, is that all these sagas grow to some extent out of a tradition of vernacular writing about the Icelandic past which goes back to the early 1120s and Ari Thorgilsson's *Book of the Icelanders*, and which has supplied both materials and literary models. Common to all the poets' sagas is an abundance of genealogical information, much of which, as noted above, may well derive from early versions of *The Book of Settlements*. All of them except *Viglund's Saga* also share material with *The Saga of the People of Eyri* (*Eyrbyggja saga*), although the exact relations are obscure. Their accounts of events overseas are probably also all partly indebted to various early Sagas of Kings, the sagas of (mainly) Norwegian kings that were composed from the later twelfth century onwards. Beyond this, the written sources differ from saga to saga, and a brief sketch of these follows.

Kormak's Saga and its relative independence from written sources have been mentioned above, but *The Saga of Hallfred*, though seemingly composed only slightly later in the thirteenth century, offers an interesting contrast, showing influence from a rich array of sources on both content and literary treatment. The characterization of the hero and the trajectory of the love affair are very clearly influenced by *Kormak's Saga*; and there is substantial overlap with another saga from northern Iceland, *The Saga of the People of Vatnsdal* (*Vatnsdæla saga*). *The Saga of Hallfred* hence belongs clearly with the Sagas of Icelanders, yet it also has kinship with the Sagas of Kings. Hallfred's legend grew up within that of King Olaf Tryggvason, and his saga is also indebted to semi-hagiographic lives of the king by Odd Snorrason (*c.* 1190), or perhaps more likely Gunnlaug Leifsson (before 1218/19); both were monks at Thingeyrar, close to the scenes of the saga. The dealings between skald and king may also be touched by stories about other court poets, especially Sighvat Thordarson, a devotee of another missionary king, Olaf Haraldsson. Influence from several other Icelandic writings, including lives of saints, kings, and earls of Orkney, has also been detected in the story of Hallfred.

In the case of *The Saga of Bjorn*, the interdependent problems of its date and its literary relations with other sagas are still more intractable than elsewhere. Some scholars have seen the saga as an earlier thirteenth-century product, and more or less independent of other Sagas of Icelanders, others as late thirteenth-century, and highly dependent; some reckon with later revision of an early saga.[25] Certainty is impossible, but it is clear that, as with *The Saga of Hallfred*, narratives about the Icelandic hero's dealings with a Norwegian missionary king must have been fundamental to the genesis of the saga. One of the few direct clues is a reference to one Runolf Dagsson (ch. 17), normally assumed to be Runolf Dalksson, a learned priest of the mid-twelfth century, who, it is suggested, may have written an account of Bjorn's association with King Olaf and his acts of devotion. The story of rivalry in love, meanwhile, seems to be principally based on the verses credited to the protagonists. The saga also has much in common with *The Saga of the People of Eyri*, but the exact nature of the relationship is elusive.

The author of *Gunnlaug's Saga*, writing, probably, towards the end of the thirteenth century, clearly drew inspiration from earlier sagas of poets. The opening portrait of Gunnlaug reads like a replica of that of Hallfred, Gunnlaug speaks a beautiful verse probably composed by Kormak, and his story often parallels that of Bjorn the Champion, whose saga is usually assumed to be the older of the two. Helga is of the family of the Myrar folk who are central to *Egil's Saga*, and the rivalry of Gunnlaug and Hrafn over her is mentioned there. The dream of her father, Thorstein Egilsson, meanwhile, seems to be influenced by more exotic sources (see note 4 to *Gunnlaug's Saga*).

The delightful hybrid that is *Viglund's Saga* was made possible by the talent of its author and by the fact that he was working as late as *c.* 1400, by which time an ample range of influences was available to Icelandic writers. Its exotic touches, polarized characterization and emphasis on entertainment rather than historical plausibility were inspired especially by foreign romance, which was mediated by Icelandic authors in the more fantastical branches of the saga literature – Chivalric Sagas and Legendary Sagas. Probably the greatest single influence was *Fridthjof's Saga*, in which the union of childhood sweethearts is obstructed by wicked brothers until after numerous adventures the hero wins his princess and reigns in Sweden.

The most contentious issue concerning the genesis of the poets' sagas is the degree of non-native influence on the erotic plots. It has been argued that the presentation of 'lovesick skalds' at the centre of whole sagas could only be explained by assuming influence from poems by, and stories about, Provençal troubadours, and from European romance, notably an early version of the story of the tragic adulterous love of Tristan and Isolde/Iseult (which was translated into Old Norwegian *c.* 1226).[26] In its extreme form, this theory has been refuted, not least because a tragic love triangle already existed in Nordic traditions about Sigurd/Siegfried and his doomed love for Brynhild/Brünhild(e);[27] these are traceable in the *Poetic Edda* and *The Saga of the Volsungs*. Nevertheless, there is little doubt that the sagas of poets were influenced by the 'bridal-quest' motif famous from the Tristan story, and affected by a general interest in romantic themes borne on literary breezes from the south.

The portrayal of the skalds seems, on the other hand, to be wholly or mainly of native origin. It reflects the status of poets and poetry in society, and may be coloured by the association of poets with the mercurial god Odin, though the additional possibility has been suggested that saga authors were familiar with the Aristotelian connection between melancholia and poetic frenzy, transmitted through medieval learned treatises.[28] A model for bringing Icelandic skalds to centre-stage, meanwhile, existed in the *þættir*, 'threads' or short tales woven into the Sagas of Kings, and one of these, the touching tale of Ivar Ingimundarson in the early thirteenth-century *Morkinskinna*, unites an Icelander's appearance at court with a brief bride-theft plot.[29] There is also a tantalizing sliver of evidence for a skald biography existing, at least in oral form, very early in the twelfth century, for according to ch. 10 of *The Saga of Thorgils and Haflidi*, in *Sturlunga Saga*, a saga about Orm 'skald of Barra' (the Hebridean island) was among the entertainments at a wedding in 1119. No such work survives, so its content and character are unknowable, but we are told that it both included verses and was rounded off with poems by its reciter, Ingimund, a priest and a 'good poet'.[30]

To conclude, each of the sagas of poets combines oral and written materials concerning lovesick skalds, feuds and foreign adventures into an individual vision of the past, and even if all their sources and influences were identifiable, it would hardly diminish the achievement of their creators. If the plot materials seem at times imperfectly coordinated, especially in *Kormak's Saga* and *The Saga of Hallfred*, it is partly due to the earliness of these rough diamonds within the saga-writing tradition. What their authors learned from the Sagas of Kings and other works fertilized the nascent Sagas of Icelanders, helping to launch the remarkable literary enterprise that was later to produce *The Saga of the People of Laxardal* and *Njal's Saga*. The sagas were unique in medieval Europe for their use of vernacular prose, and for their penetrating dramatization of the lives of non-aristocratic people in a remote and windswept corner of north-west Europe. They were read aloud to households gathered around fires and tallow lamps in the turf-built farmsteads of Iceland – audiences who were probably familiar with the places involved, and with descendants of the dramatis personae, as well as possessing the kind of cultural knowledge that is supplied for modern readers through notes and reference materials. The paradoxical achievement of the sagas is that their grounding in actual life in small pastoral communities gives them a universal and enduring appeal.

NOTES

1. For discussions of the grouping, see Russell Poole, pp. 1–24, and Margaret Clunies Ross, pp. 25–49, in *Skaldsagas. Text, Vocation and Desire in the Icelandic Sagas of Poets*, ed. Russell G. Poole (Berlin: De Gruyter, 2000). The phrase 'warrior-poets' is used in the title of this volume to avoid romantic or modern connotations about the character and role of the poet.

2. Historical sources, and a handful of place-names, point to the presence of a few Irish monks at the time of the Norse arrival in Iceland. They are said to have fled the island at the coming of pagans (*Book of the Icelanders* (*Íslendingabók*), ch. 1; *Book of Settlements* (*Landnámabók*), ch. 1).

3. See Torfi Tulinius in *Skaldsagas*, ed. Poole, pp. 201–5, a reading of *The Saga of Hallfred* which foregrounds matters of power and social status.

4. The love between the dragon-slayer Sigurd/Siegfried and the valkyrie Brynhild/Brünhilde seems predestined, but Sigurd's sworn brother Gunnar/Günther wins Brynhild by a trick, leaving Sigurd to marry Gunnar's sister Gudrun/Kriemhild. Brynhild goads Gunnar into having Sigurd killed, then herself commits suicide. The hero Tristan wins the beautiful Isolde for his sovereign King Mark, but through an unwitting misapplication of a love potion, Tristan and Isolde conceive a fatal passion for one another. Lancelot's adulterous love for Guinevere, King Arthur's queen, prevents him from seeing the Holy Grail and damages the fellowship of the knights of the Round Table. All these stories circulated in the British Isles, on the Continent and in Scandinavia in numerous versions.

5. The contrasting experiences of skalds at home and abroad are explored by Diana Whaley in *Skaldsagas*, ed. Poole, pp. 285–308.

6. W. G. Collingwood, *The Life and Death of Cormac the Skald* (London: Viking Club, 1902), p. 14.

7. The remaining verses, two attributed to Steinar, two to Narfi, one to Steingerd and one anonymous, serve a variety of purposes.

8. In another sense, too, it is as if there are two sagas of Hallfred, since there are two main versions: see Note on the Translations (p. lii).

9. See Torfi Tulinius in *Skaldsagas*, ed. Poole, p. 201.

10. See John Lindow, '*Akkerisfrakki*. Traditions concerning Óláfr Tryggvason and Hallfreðr Óttarsson vandræðaskáld and the problem of the Conversion', in *Sagas and the Norwegian Experience. 10th International Saga Conference* (Trondheim: Senter for Middelalderstudier, 1997), pp. 409–18. He and Marianne Kalinke, '*Stæri ek brag*: protest and subordination in *Hallfreðar saga*', *Skáldskaparmál* 3 (1997), 50–68, demonstrate ways in which the Conversion theme is supported by resonances with the literature of medieval Christendom.

11. Kalinke, '*Stæri ek brag*', points to the way that Hallfred's biological father Ottar, by whom he feels betrayed, is replaced by his spiritual mentor Olaf, who is the agent of his regeneration.

12. Jenny Jochens in *Skaldsagas*, ed. Poole, p. 331, suggests that the saga narrative as a whole 'carries the implication that [Bjorn and Thord] experience homosocial desire and have engaged in homosexual acts' (though not necessarily with each other); see also her 'Triangularity in the pagan North: The case of Bjǫrn Arngeirsson and Þórðr Kolbeinsson', in *Conflicted Identities and Multiple Masculinities: Men in the Medieval West*, ed. J. Murray (New York and London: Garland, 1999) pp. 111–34.

13. See Theodore M. Andersson, *The Icelandic Family Saga: An Analytic Reading* (Cambridge, Mass.: Harvard University Press, 1967), p. 136.

14. Part of *Viglund's Saga* was in fact made into an opera, *Thorgrim*, by Sir Frederic Hymen Cowen, to a libretto by Joseph Bennett, in 1890.

15. Marianne Kalinke, '*Víglundar saga* : an Icelandic bridal-quest romance', *Skáldskaparmál* 3 (1994), 119–43, has argued convincingly for the view that *Viglund's Saga* is essentially a bridal-quest romance transposed into a Norwegian–Icelandic setting.

16. See, e.g., Laurence de Looze's discussion of the importance of language in 'Poet, poem and poetic process in *Bjarnar saga Hítdœlakappa* and *Gunnlaugssaga ormstungu*', *Journal of English and Germanic Philology* 85 (1986), 479–93.

17. There are 85 verses in *Kormak's Saga* (one of them repeated), 33 in *The Saga of Hallfred*, 25 in *The Saga of Gunnlaug*, 39 in *The Saga of Bjorn* and 23 in *Viglund's Saga*.

18. On prosimetrum composition, see Preben Meulengracht Sørensen in *Skaldsagas*, ed. Poole, pp. 172–90, and Joseph Harris, 'The prosimetrum of Icelandic saga and some relatives', in *Prosimetrum: Cross-cultural Perspectives on Narrative in Prose and Verse*, ed. Joseph Harris and Karl Reichl (Cambridge: D. S. Brewer, 1997), pp. 131–63.

19. Prose and verse can yield images that are not only complementary but almost contradictory. Poole argues that the stanzas in *The Saga of Gunnlaug* promote an image of the hero as 'man of action' while the prose narrative shows him as indecisive, even as a stereotypical 'procrastinator' figure (*Skaldsagas*, pp. 125–71).

20. Interpretative strategies available to audiences familiar with skaldic composition are further explored by Torfi Tulinius in *Skaldsagas*, ed. Poole, pp. 191–217. He demonstrates how the concept of 'skaldic prose' can elucidate aspects of meaning as well as structure.

21. Kari Ellen Gade in *Skaldsagas*, ed. Poole, pp. 50–74.

22. Collingwood, *Cormac the Skald*, p. 3.

23. Ch. 183 in the Sturlubók version, ch. 150 in the Hauksbók. In one manuscript, and in *The Saga of the People of Vatnsdal*, the brother is Hermund, not Brand.

24. See Heather O'Donoghue, *The Genesis of a Saga Narrative: Verse and Prose in Kormaks Saga* (Oxford: Clarendon Press, 1991), and the essays by Edith Marold and Russell Poole in *Skaldsagas*, ed. Poole, pp. 75–124, 125–71.

25. For a summary of the debate, see Alison Finlay, *The Saga of Bjorn, Champion of the Men of Hitardale* (Enfield Lock: Hisarlik, 2000), xlvii–lii.

26. Bjarni Einarsson, *Skáldasögur: Um uppruna og eðli ástaskáldasagnanna fornu* (Reykjavík: Menningarsjóður, 1961) (English summary, pp. 280–99), and 'The lovesick skald: a reply to Theodore M. Andersson', *Mediaeval Scandinavia* 4 (1971), 21–41.

27. Theodore M. Andersson, 'Skalds and troubadours', *Mediaeval Scandinavia* 2 (1969), 7–41, and his essay in *Skaldsagas*, ed. Poole, pp. 272–84; and Alison Finlay in *Skaldsagas*, pp. 232–71. See n. 4 above on Sigurd and Tristan.

28. Margaret Clunies Ross, 'The art of poetry and the figure of the poet in *Egils saga*', in *The Sagas of Icelanders*, ed. John Tucker (New York: Garland, 1989), pp. 126–49, especially p. 132. Her point refers above all to *Egil's Saga*, but also to other skald biographies.

29. On the tale of Ivar in relation to the sagas of poets, see Andersson in *Skaldsagas*, ed. Poole, p. 273. John Lindow discusses the kinship between the sagas of poets and tales on the 'king and Icelanders' theme in *Skaldsagas*, pp. 218–31.

30. Harris explores the literary-historical implications of the lost *Orms saga* in 'The prosimetrum of Icelandic saga', pp. 134–5 and 152–6.

Further Reading

ICELANDIC SOURCES IN TRANSLATION

The Book of Settlements, trans. Hermann Pálsson and Paul Edwards (Winnipeg: University of Manitoba Press, 1972)

The Complete Sagas of Icelanders, including 49 Tales, ed. Viðar Hreinsson, 5 vols. (Reykjavík: Leifur Eiríksson Publishing, 1997)

Heimskringla: see *Snorri Sturluson*

Laws of Early Iceland [*Grágás*]: *Grágás*, trans. Andrew Dennis, Peter Foote and Richard Perkins (Winnipeg: University of Manitoba Press, 1980–99)

Njal's Saga, trans. Robert Cook (London: Penguin Books, 2001)

The Poetic Edda, trans. Carolyne Larrington (Oxford University Press, 1996)

Prose Edda: see *Snorri Sturluson*

The Saga of Fridthjof the Bold, trans. Eiríkur Magnússon and William Morris, in *Three Northern Love Stories and other Tales* (London: Ellis and White, 1875)

The Saga of Tristram and Ísönd, trans. Paul Schach (Lincoln: University of Nebraska Press, 1973)

The Saga of the Volsungs, trans. Jesse L. Byock (London: Penguin Books, 1999)

The Sagas of Icelanders: A Selection (London: Allen Lane The Penguin Press, 1997) Contains *Egil's Saga, The Saga of the People of Vatnsdal, The Saga of the People of Laxardal, The Saga of Hrafnkel Frey's Godi, The Saga of the Confederates, Gisli Sursson's Saga, The Saga of Gunnlaug*

Serpent-tongue, *The Saga of Ref the Sly*, *The Saga of the Greenlanders*, *Eirik the Red's Saga* and seven tales

Snorri Sturluson, *Edda* [*Prose Edda*], trans. Anthony Faulkes (London: Dent, 1987)

Snorri Sturluson, *Heimskringla*, trans. Lee M. Hollander (Austin: University of Texas Press, 1964)

Sturlunga Saga, trans. Julia McGrew and R. George Thomas (New York: Twayne, 1970–74)

See also 'Early Icelandic Literature', p. 317.

STUDIES OF THE SAGAS OF POETS

Andersson, Theodore M., 'Skalds and troubadours', *Mediaeval Scandinavia* 2 (1969), 7–41

Clunies Ross, Margaret, 'The art of poetry and the figure of the poet in *Egils saga*', in *The Sagas of Icelanders*, ed. John Tucker (New York: Garland, 1989), pp. 126–49

Collingwood, W. G., *The Life and Death of Cormac the Skald* (London: Viking Club, 1902)

De Looze, Laurence, 'Poet, poem and poetic process in *Bjarnar saga Hítdœlakappa* and *Gunnlaugssaga ormstungu*', *Journal of English and Germanic Philology* 85 (1986), 479–93

Einarsson, Bjarni, *Skáldasögur: Um uppruna og eðli ástaskáldasagnanna fornu* (Reykjavík: Menningarsjóður, 1961) English summary, pp. 280–99

—, 'The lovesick skald: a reply to Theodore M. Andersson', *Mediaeval Scandinavia* 4 (1971), 21–41

Finlay, Alison, 'Skalds, troubadours and sagas', *Saga-Book of the Viking Society* 24 (1995), 105–53

—, *The Saga of Bjorn, Champion of the Men of Hitardale* (Enfield Lock: Hisarlik, 2000)

Foote, P. G., ed., *Gunnlaugs saga ormstungu/The Story of Gunnlaug Serpent-Tongue*, trans. R. Quirk (London: Nelson, 1957) Useful introduction and notes

Hollander, Lee M., trans. and ed., *The Sagas of Kormak and the Sworn Brothers* (Princeton University Press, 1949) Useful introduction and notes

Jochens, Jenny, 'Triangularity in the pagan North: The case of Bjǫrn Arngeirsson and Þórðr Kolbeinsson', in *Conflicted Identities and Multiple Masculinities: Men in the Medieval West*, ed. J. Murray (New York and London: Garland, 1999), pp. 111–34

Kalinke, Marianne, '*Víglundar saga*: an Icelandic bridal-quest romance', *Skáldskaparmál* 3 (1994), 119–43

—, '*Stæri ek brag*: protest and subordination in *Hallfreðar saga*', *Skáldskaparmál* 3 (1997), 50–68

Lindow, John, '*Akkerisfrakki*. Traditions concerning Óláfr Tryggvason and Hallfreðr Óttarsson vandræðaskáld and the problem of the Conversion', in *Sagas and the Norwegian Experience. 10th International Saga Conference* (Trondheim: Senter for Middelalderstudier, 1997), pp. 409–18

O'Donoghue, Heather, *The Genesis of a Saga Narrative: Verse and Prose in* Kormaks Saga (Oxford: Clarendon Press, 1991)

Poole, Russell, 'Verses and prose in *Gunnlaugs saga ormstungu*', in *The Sagas of Icelanders*, ed. John Tucker (New York: Garland, 1989), pp. 160–84

Skaldsagas. Text, Vocation and Desire in the Icelandic Sagas of Poets, ed. Russell G. Poole (Berlin: De Gruyter, 2000) Contains essays on several aspects of the sagas of Kormak, Hallfred, Gunnlaug and Bjorn by: Theodore M. Andersson, pp. 272–84, Margaret Clunies Ross, pp. 25–49, Alison Finlay, pp. 232–71, Kari Ellen Gade, pp. 50–74, Jenny Jochens, pp. 309–32, John Lindow, pp. 218–31, Edith Marold, pp. 75–124, Preben Meulengracht Sørensen, pp. 172–90, Russell Poole, pp. 1–24 (Introduction) and 125–71, Torfi Tulinius, pp. 191–217 and Diana Whaley, pp. 285–308

Sveinsson, Einar Ólafur, 'Kormákr the poet and his verses', *Saga-Book of the Viking Society* 17 (1966), 18–60

THE SAGAS OF ICELANDERS:
LITERARY AND CULTURAL BACKGROUND

Andersson, Theodore M., *The Icelandic Family Saga: An Analytic Reading* (Cambridge, Mass.: Harvard University Press, 1967)

Clover, Carol J. and John Lindow, *Old Norse–Icelandic Literature: A Critical Guide* (Ithaca: Cornell University Press, 1985) Contains full bibliographies

Clunies Ross, Margaret, ed., *Old Icelandic Literature and Society* (Cambridge University Press, 2000) Essays by thirteen scholars on the major genres

Frank, Roberta, *Old Norse Court Poetry: The* Dróttkvætt *Stanza* (Ithaca: Cornell University Press, 1978)

Hallberg, Peter, *The Icelandic Saga*, trans. Paul Schach (Lincoln: University of Nebraska Press, 1962)

Harris, Joseph, 'The prosimetrum of Icelandic saga and some relatives', in *Prosimetrum: Cross-cultural Perspectives on Narrative in Prose and Verse*, ed. Joseph Harris and Karl Reichl (Cambridge: D. S. Brewer, 1997), pp. 131–63

Hastrup, Kirsten, *Culture and History in Medieval Iceland* (Oxford: Clarendon Press, 1985)

Jochens, Jenny, *Women in Old Norse Society* (Ithaca: Cornell University Press, 1995)

Kristjánsson, Jonas, *Edda and Saga: Iceland's Medieval Literature*, trans. Peter Foote (3rd edn, Reykjavík: Hið íslenska bókmenntafélag, 1997)

Magnusson, Magnus, *Iceland Saga* (London: Bodley Head, 1987)

Meulengracht Sørensen, Preben, *Saga and Society: An Introduction to Old Norse Literature*, trans. John Tucker (Odense University Press, 1993)

Miller, William Ian, *Bloodtaking and Peacemaking: Feud, Law, and Society in Saga Iceland* (University of Chicago Press, 1990)

Nordal, Guðrún, *Ethics and Action in Thirteenth-century Iceland* (Odense University Press, 1998)

Ólason, Vésteinn, *Dialogues with the Viking Age: Narration and Representation in the Sagas of the Icelanders*, trans. Andrew Wawn (Reykjavík: Heimskringla, 1998)

Pulsiano, Phillip and Wolf, Kirsten, eds., *Medieval Scandinavia: An Encyclopedia* (New York: Garland, 1993) Useful introductions and bibliographical guides to many relevant topics

Schach, Paul, *Icelandic Sagas* (Boston, Mass.: Twayne, 1984)

Sveinsson, Einar Ólafur, *The Age of the Sturlungs: Icelandic Civilization in the Thirteenth Century*, trans. Jóhann S. Hannesson (Ithaca: Cornell University Press, 1953)

Turville-Petre, E. O. G., *Myth and Religion of the North* (London: Weidenfeld and Nicolson, 1964)

A Note on the Translations

All five translations in the present volume are reprinted, with only minor alterations, from *The Complete Sagas of Icelanders*, edited by Viðar Hreinsson and published in five volumes by Leifur Eiríksson Publishing, Reykjavík in 1997:

Kormak's Saga, I, 179–224
The Saga of Hallfred, I, 225–53
The Saga of Gunnlaug, I, 305–33
The Saga of Bjorn, I, 255–304
Viglund's Saga, II, 411–41.

The editions and manuscripts on which the translations are chiefly based are as follows.

Kormak's Saga (*Kormáks saga*)

Edition: In *Vatnsdæla saga*, ed. Einar Ól. Sveinsson (Íslenzk fornrit 8, Reykjavík: Hið íslenzka fornritafélag, 1939), pp. 201–302. Manuscript: Möðruvallabók (AM 132 fol.), *c.* 1330–70; also fragments in AM 162 F fol. (*c.* 1350–1400).

The Saga of Hallfred Troublesome-poet (Hallfreðar saga)

The saga exists in two main versions. The text from the Möðruvalla-bók ('M') manuscript translated here is a continuous, independent saga, whereas a group of manuscripts (collectively 'O') present the saga in sections, woven into *The Greatest Saga of Olaf Tryggvason*. The M version gives more prominence to Hallfred's relationship with Kolfinna and its consequences, since it contains six more verses arising from it than O. Both versions appear to be based on an earlier one, which M has streamlined, sometimes at the price of coherence.

Edition: *Hallfreðar saga*, ed. Bjarni Einarsson (Reykjavík: Stofnun Árna Magnússonar á Íslandi, 1977); also in *Vatnsdæla saga* (as above), pp. 133–200, and *Íslendinga sögur og þættir*, ed. Bragi Halldórsson et al. (Reykjavík: Svart á hvítu, 1987), vol. 2, pp. 1194–1252. Manuscript: Möðruvallabók (AM 132 fol.), *c.* 1330–70; also AM 61 fol. and other manuscripts of *The Greatest Saga of Olaf Tryggvason*.

The Saga of Gunnlaug Serpent-tongue (Gunnlaugs saga)

Edition: *Íslendinga sögur og þættir* (as above), vol. 2, pp. 1166–93. Manuscript: Holm. perg. 18 4to, early fourteenth-century.

The Saga of Bjorn, Champion of the Hitardal People (Bjarnar saga Hítdælakappa)

Edition: In *Borgfirðinga sögur*, ed. Sigurður Nordal and Guðni Jónsson (Íslenzk fornrit 3, Reykjavík: Hið íslenzka fornritafélag, 1938), pp. 109–211. Manuscript: AM 551 D a 4to, seventeenth-century (but first four and a half chapters supplied from manuscripts of Snorri Sturluson's *Great Saga of St Olaf*).

Viglund's Saga (*Víglundar saga*)

Edition: In *Kjalnesinga saga*, ed. Jóhannes Halldórsson (Íslenzk fornrit 14, Reykjavík: Hið íslenzka fornritafélag, 1959), pp. 61–116. Manuscript: AM 551a 4to (*c.* 1500); also AM 510 4to (*c.* 1550).

The translators' aim in all cases has been to produce accurate and readable modern English versions of the original texts. This involves being as faithful as practicable to the spirit, style and detail of each saga, avoiding pedantic imitation of formal features but also resisting the temptation to 'improve' the originals. The *Complete Sagas* project as a whole also sought to reflect the homogeneity of the world of the Sagas of Icelanders, by aiming for consistency in the translation of certain essential vocabulary: for instance, terms relating to legal practices, social and religious practices, farm layouts or types of ships.

As is common in translations from Old Icelandic, the spelling of proper nouns has been simplified, both by the elimination of non-English letters and by the reduction of inflections. Thus 'Þórðr' becomes 'Thord', 'Björn' becomes 'Bjorn' and 'Egill' becomes 'Egil'. The reader will soon grasp that '-dottir' means 'daughter of' and '-son' means 'son of'. Place-names have been rendered in a similar way, often with an English identifier of the landscape feature in question (e.g. 'Holmfjall mountain', in which '-fjall' means 'mountain'). For place-names outside Scandinavia, the common English equivalent is used if such exists; otherwise, the Icelandic form has been transliterated. Nicknames are translated where their meanings are reasonably certain.

The translation of the skaldic poetry that appears in such profusion in the sagas of poets is particularly challenging, both because of obscurities and corruptions in the texts, and because its intricate metre, flexible word order and compressed and often riddling diction do not transpose well into English (see 'The Techniques of Skaldic Poetry', pp. 322–6). Translators are therefore faced with difficult choices between favouring fidelity to the meaning and style of the original, and producing English verses that are comprehensible and poetically satisfying, and the five translators who have contributed to this volume have adopted varying positions along the spectrum of good compromise.

SAGAS OF
WARRIOR-POETS

KORMAK'S SAGA

1 | King Harald Fair-hair[1] was ruling over Norway when the first
  | events of this saga took place. In those days there was a chieftain
in the land whose name was Kormak, from the Vik area of Norway,
powerful and of prominent family; he was a great warrior and had
been with King Harald in many battles. He had a son whose name
was Ogmund, a most promising person, who soon grew big and
strong. When he was of full age and mature, he went off raiding in
the summers and was with the king in the winters; he earned himself
a good reputation and great wealth.

One summer he set out on a raiding expedition to the west, where
a man named Asmund was active. Asmund was a great champion; he
had conquered many Vikings and warriors. The two men now heard
of each other, and messages passed between them; they met face to
face, appointed themselves a place of battle, and fought. Asmund had
a larger band of men than Ogmund, but did not marshal them all for
the battle. They fought for four days. Asmund's troops fell in great
numbers, and he himself fled; Ogmund had the victory and came
home with wealth and prestige.

Kormak declared that Ogmund would never win greater prestige
in raiding – 'and I will provide you with a wife,' he said, 'Helga, the
daughter of Earl Frodi'.[2]

'That's just what I want,' said Ogmund.

After that they made their way to Earl Frodi, who received them
warmly. When they stated their business, the earl responded well
and said that there was some cause for anxiety with regard to
Ogmund's dealings with Asmund, but nevertheless the marriage

arrangements went ahead, and Kormak and Ogmund returned home; a feast was prepared, and a great number of people attended that feast. Helga, the daughter of Earl Frodi, had a foster-mother who could foretell the future, and she came with her.

Asmund the Viking heard of this and went to visit Ogmund. He challenged him to a duel, and Ogmund accepted.

Helga's foster-mother used to feel men with her hand before they went into battle;[3] she did this to Ogmund before he left home, and declared that at no point would he be severely harmed. They both went then to the duel and fought. The Viking presented his side, but nothing could pierce him. Then Ogmund swiftly raised his sword, shifted it about in his hands, and struck off Asmund's leg. He took three marks of gold in duel ransom.

2 | At that time King Harald Fair-hair died and Eirik Blood-axe succeeded him. But Ogmund, who did not become friendly with Eirik or his queen Gunnhild, prepared his ship for sailing to Iceland. Ogmund and Helga had a son, whose name was Frodi. When the ship was almost ready, Helga fell ill and died, and so did Frodi, their son.

After that Ogmund and his followers sailed out to sea. Then Ogmund threw out his high-seat pillars;[4] and he and his company came to land in Midfjord, where his high-seat pillars had already arrived, and cast anchor there.

But in those days Skeggi from Midfjord held sway there; he rowed out to them and offered them a welcome into the fjord and their own choice of land. Ogmund accepted that, and measured out the ground for a building. It was believed that if the measuring-rod shrank, if it grew smaller, when a man measured more than once, then his situation would worsen; but it would improve if the rod showed an increase. After they had measured three times, the measuring-rod shrank.

Ogmund had houses built there on the stretch of gravel, and lived there from then on. He married Dalla, the daughter of Onund Sjoni (the Keen-sighted); their sons were Thorgils and Kormak. Kormak had dark curly hair and a fair complexion and was rather like his mother;[5] he was big and strong, and in temperament an impetuous man. Thorgils was taciturn and gentle.

When these brothers were full-grown, Ogmund died. Dalla kept the farm going with her sons, and it was Thorgils who took charge of the farm under the supervision of Skeggi of Midfjord.

3 | There was a man named Thorkel, who lived at Tunga; he was married and he and his wife had a daughter whose name was Steingerd; she was in Gnupsdal being fostered.

It happened one autumn that a whale came ashore on to Vatnsnes, and it was the property of the Dolluson brothers.[6] Thorgils offered Kormak the choice of going on up the mountain to look for sheep, or working on the whale. He chose to go up on the mountain with the farmhands.

There was a man named Tosti. He was an overseer whose job was to make arrangements for sheep searches, and he and Kormak went off together, until they came to Gnupsdal, where they spent the night; there was a large hall there, with fires made ready for the occupants.

In the evening Steingerd left her room, and with her was a slave-woman. They could hear the voices of the strangers in the hall.

The slave-woman said, 'Steingerd dear, let's take a look at the visitors.'

Steingerd said there was no need for that, but nevertheless she went to the door, stepped up on to the threshold, and looked over the wood stacked by the door;[7] there was a space between the bottom of the door and the threshold, and her feet showed.

Kormak saw that, and spoke a verse:

1.

Mighty love has filled my mind,
my troll-woman's fair breeze,　　　　　*troll-woman's breeze*: mind
a necklace-sleigh has just　　　　　　*necklace-sleigh*: woman
presented her instep to me.

7

The feet of that headdress-goddess   *headdress-goddess* (Gerd):[8] woman
will bring me grief more often
than now, yet of this maid
I otherwise know nothing.

Steingerd now sensed that she was being observed; she turned into the dark, narrow passage and looked out from under the carved beard of Hagbard.[9] The light now shone on to her face.

Then Tosti said, 'Kormak, do you see the eyes out there by the head of Hagbard?'

Kormak spoke a verse:

2.

The bright lights of both   *lights of cheeks*: eyes
her cheeks burned on to me
from the fire-hall's felled wood;
no cause of mirth for me in that.
By the threshold I gained a glimpse
of the ankles of this girl
of glorious shape; yet while I live
that longing will never leave me.

And again he spoke:

3.

The moon of her eyelash – that valkyrie   *moon of her eyelash*: her eye
of herb-surf, adorned with linen –   *herb-surf*: ale; its *valkyrie* (Hrist): woman
shone hawk-sharp upon me   who serves the ale
beneath her brows' bright sky;   *brows' sky*: forehead
but that beam from the eyelid-moon   *beam*: gaze
of the goddess of the golden torque   *goddess* (Frid) *of the golden torque*: woman
will later bring trouble to me
and to the ring-goddess herself.[10]   *ring-goddess* (Hlin): woman

Tosti said, 'She's starting to stare at you.'
Kormak said:

4.

The ring-laden linden of ale   *linden of ale*: woman
did not raise her eyes from me,
nor I hide my burning anguish;
I recall the ribbon-yearner   *ribbon-yearner*: woman
when she, the winner of board games
standing at the doorstep's prow   *doorstep's prow*: threshold
carved with Hagbard's image,
stared, necklace-laden, at me.

Now the women went into the hall and sat down.

Kormak heard them talking about his looks. The slave-woman declared him dark and ugly. Steingerd declared him good-looking and as fine as he could be in every respect, but added: 'There is just one fault – that the hair is curled on his forehead.'

Kormak spoke a verse:

5.

One fault in me she said she found,
the all-bright goddess of the fire   *sea-king's* (Ati's) *bench*: sea; its *fire*: gold;
of the sea-king's bench, in evening's shades –   *goddess* (Eir) of gold: woman
one fault, but just a small one.
The well-born goddess of hawk's land   *hawk's land*: arm (an image drawn
declared that on my brow my hair   from falconry); arm's *goddess*
was curled; I should have recognized   (Hlin): woman
that trait which women have.

The slave-woman said, 'The eyes are black, sister, and that doesn't go well.'

Kormak heard this and spoke a verse:

6.

Dark eyes I bring to meet with her,
the pretty vessel-ground,   *vessel-ground*: bearer of vessels, woman
and pale complexion; I appear
pallid to the goddess of sleeves;   *goddess* (Ilm) *of sleeves*: woman

yet, necklace-ground, I have at times   *necklace-ground*: woman
wooed maidens, in my flirting
with the goddess of rings –   *goddess* (Horn) *of rings*: womankind, women
as skilful as a man more handsome.

The men were there for the night. In the morning, when Kormak
got up, he went to a water-butt and washed; then he went to the
main room and saw no one there, but he heard human voices in an
inner room and turned in that direction: Steingerd was there, and
some women with her.

The slave-woman said to Steingerd, 'That good-looking man's
coming now, Steingerd.'

'He's certainly a brave-looking man,' Steingerd said. She was
combing her hair.

Kormak said, 'Will you lend me the comb?'

Steingerd handed it to him; she was the finest-haired of women.

The slave-woman said, 'You would have to pay a high price for a
wife with such hair as Steingerd has, or such eyes.'

Kormak spoke a verse:

7.

Those eyes of the ale-goddess,   *ale-goddess* (Saga): woman
I price one – in the body bright
of the goddess of the bed it lies –   *goddess* (Nanna) *of the bed*: woman
at three hundred silver pieces.
At five hundreds I price the hair
which she, flax-greedy goddess, combs;   *flax-greedy goddess* (Sif): woman
the goddess who polishes hoards of gold   *goddess* (Freyja) *who polishes gold*:
is fast growing costly.   woman

The slave-woman said, 'So you two have taken a liking to
each other; but you will surely put a high price on the whole of
her.'

Kormak spoke a verse:

8.

All told, I price the pine-tree   *pine-tree of wealth*: wearer of finery, woman
of wealth, who gives me anguish,
boldly with Iceland, with Denmark too,
and Germany beyond the sea.
The goddess in clothes with tiny clasps   *goddess* (Eir) *in clothes with clasps*:
is worth the land of the English   woman
and the Irish ground; I value
the wise valkyrie of sea-fire.   *sea-fire*: gold; its *valkyrie* (Gunn): woman

Tosti came in and asked Kormak to attend to something.
Kormak spoke a verse:

9.

Tired as you are, Tosti,
take my swift-paced horse to gallop
beneath you across vast moors;
strike the steed now with a whip!
More pleasant for me to be speaking
many a word with Steingerd
than chasing russet sheep
over distant mountain pastures.

Tosti said that Kormak was bound to find that more enjoyable. He
went off, while Kormak played a board game and enjoyed himself.
Steingerd said that he was more charitable with words than was
reported. He remained there throughout the day.

Then he spoke a verse:

10.

The goddess with waving head-sedge   *head-sedge*: hair; its *goddess* (Freyja):
brought me a clean hair-comb;   woman
that was good provision
for the poet, I remember.
Yet I was but little known
to that tree of the snakes' bed.   *snakes' bed*: gold; its *tree*: woman
I shall not cease to love
that goddess of wave-fire.   *wave-fire*: gold; its *goddess* (Eir): woman

Then Tosti returned from the mountain, and they went home.

After that Kormak made a habit of walking to Gnupsdal to visit Steingerd, and asked his mother to make him fine clothes, so that he might appear to Steingerd in the best possible light. Dalla said that, while there was quite a difference between the parties involved,[11] it was not certain that happiness would be the outcome if Thorkel of Tunga knew of this.

4 | Thorkel soon heard how matters stood, and it seemed to him that there was a prospect of dishonour to himself and his daughter if Kormak would not make the situation more definite. He sent for Steingerd, and she went home.

There was a man named Narfi living with Thorkel;[12] he was an impetuous and foolish man, and given to boasting, for all the pettiness of his character. Narfi said to Thorkel, 'If Kormak's visits here are not to your liking, I can quickly put things right.'

Thorkel agreed to that.

In the autumn Narfi was busy making blood sausages. It happened on one occasion that Kormak came to Tunga; he saw Steingerd in the kitchen. Narfi was standing by a pot, and when the boiling was done, he lifted up a sausage of suet and meat, thrust it in front of Kormak's nose, and said:

11.

As for the snakes of the cauldron,   *snakes of the cauldron*: sausages
Kormak, what do you reckon?

He added:

12.

What the son of Ogmund fancies
is suet,[13] preferably boiled.

And in the evening, when Kormak was preparing to go home, he saw Narfi, and remembered his taunts.

Kormak said, 'I think it will turn out sooner, Narfi, that I will strike

you than that you will determine my comings and goings.' Kormak
struck him a blow with the back of an axe and spoke:

13.
What do you know about food,
you ignorant, scythe-handling oaf?
There was no need for such cheek,
Narfi, from you towards me.

And again he spoke:

14.
A cow's inquisitive feeder
asked me how I liked pot-snakes;   *pot-snakes*: sausages
red round the eyelids he seems to me
from time spent at home in the kitchen.
I know that that grimy no-gooder,
that bruiser with filthy matted hair
– the one who manured the homefields –
was treated like a bitch and beaten.

5 | There was a woman named Thorveig, who was very skilled in
magic; she lived at Steinsstadir in Midfjord. She had two sons;
the elder was named Odd, and the younger Gudmund; they were a
boisterous pair.

Odd habitually visited Thorkel in Tunga and would sit talking to
Steingerd. Thorkel became very friendly with the brothers and incited
them to ambush Kormak. Odd said that was not beyond his strength.

It happened one day that Kormak came to Tunga; Steingerd was
in the main room, seated on a cross-bench. The sons of Thorveig
were sitting in the main room, and were all set to attack Kormak
when he entered; Thorkel had placed on one side of the doorway a
drawn sword, and on the other Narfi placed a scythe with a long
handle. And when Kormak came to the hall doorway, the scythe slid
down, and it met the sword, making a large notch in it. Then Thorkel
approached and said that Kormak was doing a great deal of harm;

ranting, he turned quickly into the main room and called Steingerd from it. He and Steingerd went out by another doorway, and he shut her up in one of the storage sheds, saying that she and Kormak would never see one another again.

Kormak entered the room, more swiftly than they expected, and they were startled. Kormak looked around and did not see Steingerd, but did see the brothers, stroking their weapons; he turned away quickly and spoke a verse:

15.

A meadow-chopper clashed	*meadow-chopper*: scythe
with the footstand of the giant	*footstand of the giant* (Hrungnir): shield;
that belonged to the hall-comer;	the giant Hrungnir stood on his shield
I had gone in to meet a goddess.	when he fought with the god Thor;
That will mean more to put up with	*hall-comer*: visitor
if he's threatening me now with trouble;	
but from Odin's work I'll cease not,	
whether it be verses or warfare.	

Kormak failed to find Steingerd, and spoke a verse:

16.

From the room the sweet stay-at-home vanished;	
my mind remains all the more keenly	
on the valkyrie of channel-fire;	*channel-fire*: gold; its *valkyrie* (Gunn): woman
what can now give the hall its sparkle?	
All around within the house	
I cast my brow's beams on her;	*brow's beams*: eyes
I am eager to find the goddess	
whose gift is to soothe and heal.	

After that Kormak went to the building that Steingerd was in, forced it open and spoke to her.

She said, 'You're acting incautiously in coming to talk to me, for the sons of Thorveig are intent on killing you.'

Then Kormak spoke:

17.

Sitting indoors and sharpening
swords is what they are doing:
my enemies, sons of one churl;
they will never be my slayers.
And if those two attack me
on my own, on an open plain,
it'll be like ewes seeking
the life of a savage wolf.

Kormak remained there throughout the day.

Thorkel now saw that this plan of his had come to nothing, so he
asked the sons of Thorveig to ambush Kormak in a certain valley
outside his hayfield wall. Then Thorkel said, 'Narfi is to go with the
two of you, but I'll stay at home and give you support if you need it.'

In the evening Kormak went away, and when he came to the
valley, he saw three men and spoke a verse:

18.

Sitting in wait and denying
to me the goddess of beads;   *goddess* (Gna) *of beads*: woman
those men have a hard task ahead
to keep the ribbon-goddess from me.   *ribbon-goddess* (Gna): woman
But the more they harbour envy
over my visits to her,
so much the more shall I love her,
that valkyrie of the sea's herb.   *sea's herb*: dulse; its *valkyrie* (Gunn): woman

Then the sons of Thorveig leapt up and attacked Kormak at
length. Narfi sneaked about on the fringes of the fighting. From where
he was, at home, Thorkel saw that it was a lengthy struggle for them,
and took up his weapons. At that moment Steingerd came out and
saw what her father was about; she seized him in her arms and he got
nowhere near to supporting the brothers. What happened in the end
was that Odd fell, and Gudmund was disabled; nevertheless, he too
died later. After this Kormak went home, and Thorkel saw to the
brothers' bodies.

Shortly afterwards Kormak went to see Thorveig and said he was thoroughly opposed to her living there at the fjord – 'You are to move away at a time to be appointed, and I wish to withhold all compensation for your sons,' he said.

Thorveig replied, 'There's nothing more likely than that you'll arrange things so that I'm compelled to flee from the district, with my sons unatoned for; but this is how I'll pay you back for it: you will never enjoy Steingerd's love.'

Kormak said, 'You will have no say whatever in that, you evil woman.'

6 | Then Kormak went to visit Steingerd, just as he did before.
    On one occasion, when they were discussing these events, she in no way expressed disapproval.

Kormak spoke a verse:

19.

Men lie in wait and deny
to me the sight of your face;
they have a hard fight ahead
with the serpents of the shield.   *serpents of the shield*: swords
For all the mighty rivers in the land
shall sooner flow uphill
than I shall forsake you, shining ground   *ground* (i.e. bearer) *of ale cups*: woman
of flame-gleaming ale-cups.   *flame-gleaming*: possibly with gold ornament

'Don't speak so much about it,' said Steingerd. 'There are many things that can happen to change the situation.'

Then Kormak spoke a verse:

20.

Which valkyrie's champion,   *valkyrie's* (Hrund's) *champion*: warrior
oh goddess of the veil,   *goddess* (Hlin) *of the veil*: woman
would you choose for your husband?
Your soothing looks bode brightly.

Steingerd spoke:

21.

Ring-breaker, though he were blind,	*Ring-breaker:* generous man
it's to Frodi's brother I'd bind me.	*Frodi's brother:* Kormak
For then the gods and the fates	
would despite all be treating me well.	

Kormak said, 'Now you've made the right choice; I have often visited you here.'

Steingerd now asked Kormak to cultivate her father's friendship and obtain the promise of her hand in marriage, and for Steingerd's sake Kormak gave Thorkel gifts. After that many people were involved in the matter, and what happened in the end was that Kormak asked for Steingerd's hand, and she was betrothed to him and the wedding was arranged, and things stayed quiet for a while. Now messages passed between them, and these came to include certain disagreements about money matters; and it turned out strangely that, after the marriage was decided on, Kormak's feelings about it cooled, and this was because Thorveig worked a spell so that they would not be able to enjoy each other's love.

Thorkel of Tunga had a grown-up son whose name was Thorkel, and he was known as the Tooth-gnasher; he had been abroad for a while. This summer he came to Iceland and stayed with his father.

Kormak did not attend the wedding as had been arranged, and time passed. Steingerd's kinsmen considered it dishonourable that he should break off this engagement, and they sought a solution.

7 | There was a man named Bersi who lived at Saurbaer, a wealthy man, a decent person, and powerful; he was a fighting man and a dueller. He had been married to Finna the Fair, but by then she was dead. Their son was named Asmund; he was young in years, but precocious. Bersi's sister was named Helga; she was unmarried, accomplished, and a woman of firm character. She was in charge of Bersi's housekeeping after Finna's death.

On the farm named Muli lived Thord Arndisarson, whose wife was Thordis, the sister of Bork the Stout; they had two sons who were both younger than Asmund Bersason.

There was a man named Vali, whose farm was named Valastadir. That farm is situated a short distance from Hrutafjord.

Thorveig the Sorceress went to see Bersi the Dueller and told him of her difficulties; she said that Kormak was forbidding her to stay in Midfjord. Bersi bought land for her north of Hrutafjord, and she lived there for a long time afterwards.

On one occasion, when Thorkel of Tunga and his son were talking about Kormak's breach of promise, it seemed to them that it was deserving of vengeance.

Narfi said, 'I see the solution that will serve: let's go to the western districts with some goods, and approach Bersi in Saurbaer; he is without a wife. Let's get him involved in the affair; he is a great support to us.'

They adopted this course of action, and kept going until they came to Saurbaer.[14] Bersi received them well. In the evening they happened to be talking a lot about women as desirable matches. Narfi spoke, saying that there was no match as desirable as Steingerd, and added, 'Many people say, Bersi, that she would suit you.'

Bersi said, 'I'm told that there's bound to be a drawback there, even though the match is a good one.'

Narfi said, 'If people fear Kormak, they don't need to, because he's made a point of dissociating himself from this affair.'

And when Bersi heard that, he raised the matter with Thorkel the Tooth-gnasher and asked for Steingerd's hand. Thorkel answered positively and betrothed his sister to Bersi. They were to go north, eighteen of them together, to attend the wedding. Thord Arndisarson went north with Bersi.

There was a man named Vigi, a big, strong man and skilled in magic; he was a kinsman of Bersi, and he accompanied him. They had great confidence in Vigi, who had a farm in Holm. Those who went upon this journey were selected with great care. And when they arrived in the north at Thorkel's, they proceeded to the wedding feast straight away, so that no news got around the district about this matter. All this was done very much against Steingerd's wishes.[15] Vigi the Shape-shifter inquired into the affairs of every man who came to the farm or left it; he sat outermost in the main room, sleeping by the hall doorway.

Steingerd had Narfi called to her, and when they met, she said, 'I would like it, kinsman, if you could tell Kormak of the plan concocted here; I would like you to take this message to him.'

So Narfi left secretly, but by the time he had travelled a short distance, Vigi came after him, and asked him to turn back and not to engage in any plots. They returned together, and the night passed. In the morning Narfi tried again but advanced a shorter distance than the previous evening, for Vigi waylaid him and drove him back, showing no mercy.

When the wedding was over, the guests made ready to leave; Steingerd had gold and valuables with her. They then rode at a fairly easy pace to Hrutafjord.

Narfi went off, once Steingerd and the others had left, and came to Mel. Kormak was building a wall and beating away at it with a rammer. Narfi held a shield before him as he rode, affecting a grand air, while at the same time letting his eyes move in all directions like those of a hunted animal. There were a few men up on the wall with Kormak when he arrived; the horse Narfi was riding then backed. Narfi was girt with a sword.

Kormak spoke: 'What news, Narfi? What sort of company did you people have last night?'

Narfi said, 'Not much news, but we had plenty of guests.'

Kormak said, 'Who were the guests?'

Narfi said, 'Bersi the Dueller was there with seventeen followers, attending his own wedding.'

Kormak asked, 'Who was the bride?'

'Bersi received Steingerd, Thorkel's daughter, in marriage,' said Narfi. 'She sent me here, when she and the rest had left, to tell you the news.'

Kormak said, 'You're always saying evil things.'

Kormak leapt at Narfi and struck a blow on his shield, and Narfi, when the shield was thus borne towards him, was scratched on the chest; he fell from horseback, and the horse galloped away with the shield. Thorgils, Kormak's brother, said he had gone too far in what he had done; Kormak said it was fair enough. Narfi, having been stunned, came round and they talked together.

Thorgils asked, 'What was the placing of the guests at the wedding feast?'

Narfi told him.

'Did Steingerd know about this in advance?' asked Thorgils.

Narfi replied: 'Not until the very same evening, when people had arrived at the feast.'

Narfi told of his dealings with Vigi and declared that Kormak would find it easier to whistle in vain for Steingerd and to incur disgrace by his behaviour than to fight against Bersi.

Then Kormak spoke a verse:

22.
Try this for a change: holding tight
to your horse as well as your shield.
You will soon feel the touch
of my club upon your ear.
Never speak again of a banquet,
though you hear of seven a day!
Barrow-breaker, you'll comb your hair   *Barrow-breaker*: despoiler of tombs,
over a bump on your head.   robber

Thorgils asked about the formal agreement between Bersi and Steingerd. Narfi said that Steingerd's kinsmen were now free of all responsibility in this marriage, however it turned out, but that the father and son were supposed to be answerable for the wedding feast.

8 | Kormak took his horse and weapons and all his saddle-trappings. Thorgils asked, 'What are you going to do now, brother?'

Kormak spoke a verse:

23.

Bersi has taken away
my betrothed and earned the anger
of the one who asks for wine
from the chooser of the slain.   *chooser of the slain*: Odin; his *wine*: poetry
He has taken her who loved me
of all men the most; I have lost
the sad woman, the maid that I kissed
on most days all day long.

Thorgils said, 'It's not a good idea to go after Bersi, for he will have got home before you and his party meet; but I'll go with you.'

Kormak said he would go and would wait for no one; he at once mounted his horse and did all in his power to make it gallop. Thorgils soon mustered some men; in the end there were eighteen of them altogether. They caught up with Kormak on the Hrutafjord ridge, by which time Kormak had exhausted his horse. They went ahead to Thorveig's farm, and saw then that Bersi had boarded Thorveig's boat.

Thorveig said to Bersi, 'I would like you to accept a small gift from me; it will be a good friend to you.'

It was an iron-bordered targe.[16]

Thorveig said she thought Bersi would be not much wounded if he carried this protection. 'It is, however, worth little,' she added, 'in comparison with the fact that you have brought me here, where I can live permanently.'

Bersi thanked her for the gift, and then they parted. Thorveig got people to damage all those boats that were on land, because she knew in advance of the arrival of Kormak and his companions. Kormak and his company then arrived, and asked Thorveig for a boat. She said she would do them no service free of charge, adding, 'There's a wretched boat here in the boat-shed that I value for hiring purposes at half a mark.'

Thorgils said that two ounces would be reasonable, but Kormak said that conflict over such a matter was totally unbecoming. Thorgils then said that he would prefer to ride round the coast of the fjord.

Kormak had his way, and they went in the boat; but when they had got a short distance from land, the boat filled with water under them, and it was all they could do to get back to the coast from which they had come.

'You deserve punishment and not payment, you evil woman,' said Kormak.

Thorveig said it was just a little trick. After that Thorgils paid her the silver.

Kormak spoke a verse:

24.

I'm busy, god of Odin's	*Odin's* (Ygg's) *garments*: armour; their *god* (Ull):
garments, with Odin's drink	warrior; *Odin's* (Svolnir's) *drink*: poetry
for the rosy goddess of the laundry-	*goddess* (Sif) *of the laundry-beater*:
beater – busy as the beater at the spring.	woman
Many candles of Draupnir's dew	*Draupnir's* (a magic ring's) *dew*: gold; its
will cost a pretty price;	*candles*: precious articles
for three ounces that ship	
from Thorveig shall be hired.	

Bersi quickly got himself a horse and rode homewards.

Kormak saw that there was likely to be some distance between him and Bersi, and spoke a verse:

25.

So far, I declare, has the goddess	
of the hand's fire gone	*hand's fire*: gold; its *goddess* (Freyja): woman
from the hollow of my hawk's plain	*hawk's plain*: hand
(earlier I trusted that woman)	
that I shall fight to gain	
the prop of gold that blazes	*prop of* (sea's) *gold*: woman (whose hand he will
where the ship glides; I fed	win); or possibly, a warrior (whom he will beat
ravens on human flesh.	in battle)

They now took their horses and rode round the coast of the fjord, and came to Vali, and asked about Bersi. Vali said that Bersi had arrived at Muli[17] and assembled an army of men, and added, 'There are a good many of them.'

'We're too late, then,' said Kormak, 'if they've got men to join them.'

Thorgils asked Kormak to let them turn back; he thought the situation would bring them little honour. Kormak said he wanted to see Steingerd. Vali went with them, and they came to Muli. Bersi was there to meet them, with quite a crowd.

They talked together, Kormak maintaining that Bersi had cheated him with the abduction of Steingerd, and saying, 'We now wish to take the woman with us, as well as compensation for the dishonour.'

Then Thord Arndisarson said, 'We are ready to offer Kormak terms, but Bersi's the man with control over the woman.'

Said Bersi, 'There's no hope of Steingerd going with you, but I will offer Kormak my sister in marriage; I would consider him well married, with Helga as a wife.'

Thorgils said, 'That's a handsome offer; let's think about it, brother.'

Kormak hesitated.

9 | There was a woman of evil character named Thordis; she lived at Spakonufell (Prophetess hill) on Skagastrond; she knew about Kormak's movements in advance.

She came that day to Muli and answered for Kormak in this case, speaking as follows: 'Don't offer him a harlot, for this woman is a fool and suited to no man worthy of the name; and his mother won't be happy at so evil a fate befalling him.'

Thord said, 'Get away, you wicked witch', adding that Helga would undoubtedly prove a woman of firm character.

Kormak said, 'The statement must have been made because it is true; I will in no way consider this marriage.'

Thorgils said, 'Little luck will come our way from heeding the words of this she-devil and not accepting this offer.'

Then Kormak said, 'I challenge you to a duel, Bersi, in a fortnight's time in Leidholm in Middalir.' That place is now called Orrustuholm (Battle islet).

Bersi said he would come, declaring that Kormak was choosing the less honourable option.

Afterwards Kormak went to look around the farm for Steingerd, found her, and told her he felt that she had let him down in wishing to marry another man.

Steingerd said, 'You were the cause of things going wrong before, Kormak; but still, this was in no way done at my instigation.'

Then Kormak spoke a verse:

26.

Bright linen-goddess, you think   *linen-goddess* (Gefn): woman
my promise to meet you was broken;
yet I made my steed breathless
for your sake alone.
Ring-goddess, I would twice rather   *ring-goddess* (Eir): woman
ride my horse to death than you should be
given to another; it's little
that I spared that charger of mine.

Then Kormak and his companions went homewards. Kormak told his mother how things had gone. Dalla said, 'Not much luck will come to us from the way your fate's turning out, since you've refused the best of matches there. It's also a most unpromising business, fighting with Bersi; he is a great warrior and has good weapons.'

Bersi owned the sword named Hviting – a sharp sword – and a healing-stone went with it; he had borne that sword in many mortally dangerous situations.

Dalla said, 'Which weapon will you use to withstand Hviting?'

Kormak said he would use a large, sharp axe. Dalla considered it advisable to find Skeggi of Midfjord and ask for the sword Skofnung.[18] After that Kormak went to Reykir and told Skeggi the state of the case, asking him to lend him Skofnung.

Skeggi said he was unwilling to do so, and declared that the two of them were unlike in temper, making the point that 'Skofnung is slow, but you are headstrong and rash.'

Kormak rode off, not best pleased, came home to Mel and told his mother that Skeggi did not want to lend him the sword. Skeggi often gave Dalla guidance with his advice, and they were good friends.

Dalla said, 'He'll lend the sword, even if it takes him some time to yield it up.'

Kormak said that it was inappropriate – 'if,' as he put it, 'he does not withhold the sword from you, but withholds it from me'.

Dalla said Kormak was an aggressive person. Some days later Dalla asked Kormak to go to Reykir, saying, 'Skeggi will lend the sword now.'

Kormak met Skeggi and asked for Skofnung.

'You'll find it difficult to manage,' said Skeggi. 'A pouch goes with it, but you are to leave it alone. The sun is not to shine on the pommel of the sword hilt, and you are not to wield the sword unless you're getting ready for combat; but if you do find yourself on a battlefield, sit by yourself and draw it there, hold out the sword blade in front of you and blow on it; then a little snake will crawl out from under the hilt.[19] Turn the sword sideways and make it possible for him to crawl back under the hilt.'

Kormak said, 'What will you sorcerers think of next?'

Skeggi said, 'Well, that's exactly what will happen.'

Afterwards Kormak rode home and told his mother how things had gone, saying that her wishes seemed to carry great weight with Skeggi. He showed her the sword and tried to draw it, but it did not budge from the scabbard.

Dalla said, 'You're too self-willed, my son.'

Kormak then placed his feet against the hilt and tore off the pouch, whereupon Skofnung howled in response and again did not budge from the scabbard.

The time of the appointed meeting now drew near. Kormak rode off, taking fifteen men with him; Bersi likewise rode to the duelling-ground with as many men. Kormak got there first, and told Thorgils that he wanted to sit by himself. Kormak sat down and took the sword off, not caring whether the sun shone on the hilt of Skofnung, with which he had earlier girt himself, outside his clothes, and which he now wished to draw – but he could not do so until he stepped on the hilt and the little snake came out. Things were in no way handled as they should have been, and the spell of the sword was broken; it came out of the scabbard howling.

10 | After that Kormak went to join his men. Bersi and his followers had arrived by then and many other people had come to see the encounter. Kormak picked up the targe for Bersi and struck on it, and fire rose from it.

A cloak was now taken and spread under their feet.

Bersi said, 'You, Kormak, challenged me to a duel, and in return I offer you single combat; you are a young man with but little experience, and there is difficulty involved in a duel, but none whatever in single combat.'[20]

'You won't fight one bit better in single combat; I am willing to risk this and to maintain equal status with you in everything,' said Kormak.

'Have it your own way,' retorted Bersi.

The duelling laws had it that the cloak was to be five ells square, with loops at the corners, and pegs had to be put in of the kind that had a head at one end. They were called tarses, and he who made the preparations was to approach the tarses in such a way that he could see the sky between his legs while grasping his ear lobes and uttering the invocation that has since been used again in the sacrifice known as the tarse sacrifice. There were to be three spaces marked out around the cloak, each a foot in breadth, and outside the marked spaces there should be four strings, named hazel poles;[21] when that was done, what you had was a hazel-poled stretch of ground. You were supposed to have three shields, but when they were used up, you were to go on to the cloak, even if you had withdrawn from it before, and from then on you were supposed to protect yourself with weapons. He who was challenged had to strike. If one of the two was wounded in such a way that blood fell on to the cloak, there was no obligation to continue fighting. If someone put just one foot outside the hazel poles, he was said to be retreating, or to be running if he did so with both. There would be a man to hold the shield for each one of the two fighting. He who was the more wounded of the two was to release himself by paying duel ransom, to the tune of three marks of silver.

Thorgils held the shield for his brother, and Thord Arndisarson for Bersi. Bersi struck first and split Kormak's shield, and Kormak struck at Bersi in the same way. Each of them rendered three of the other's shields useless by striking at them. Then it was for Kormak to strike, so he struck at Bersi, and Bersi drew Hviting in response. Skofnung took the point off Hviting in front of the ridge along the middle of the blade, and the sword point fell on to Kormak's hand, and he got a scratch on his thumb. His thumb joint was split, and blood fell on to the cloak. After that people interceded between them and did not want them to fight any more.

Then Kormak said, 'This is no great victory that Bersi has gained from my mishap, even if we do part.'

And as Skofnung moved downwards it hit the targe,[22] and a hole was nicked in Skofnung, and fire leapt from the targe, Thorveig's Gift.

Bersi claimed duel ransom, and Kormak said that the money would be paid to him. They parted on those terms.

II | There was a man named Steinar, the son of Onund Sjoni[23] and the brother of Dalla, Kormak's mother. He lived at Ellidi, and was an unruly type.

Kormak rode there from the duelling-ground to visit Steinar, his kinsman. He told of his activities, and Steinar expressed disapproval.

Kormak said he intended to leave the country – 'and I leave the paying of Bersi to you'.

Steinar said, 'You're no great hero, but the money will be paid if it has to be.'

Kormak was there for some nights; his hand, which had no bandages on, swelled up a good deal.

After this encounter Bersi the Dueller went to visit his brothers, and they asked Bersi how the duel had gone; he told it as it had happened. They said that the two heroes in question had struck rather small blows, and that Bersi had won as a result of Kormak's mishap. Bersi met Steingerd, and she asked how it had gone.

He spoke a verse:

27.

The holding-god of the helmet	*holding-god* (Ull) *of the helmet*: warrior
had to pay me in duel ransom	(Kormak)
three marks; that fighting pine	*fighting pine*: man, warrior
may indeed be called bold-minded.	
Never will the shield-storm's stirrer	*shield-storm*: battle; its *stirrer*: warrior
(skilled though he be in the tempest	
of the valkyrie's treasure)	*valkyrie's* (Skogul's) *treasure*: weapons; their
challenge me again; I beat him.	*tempest*: battle

Steinar and Kormak rode away from Ellidi, in the direction of Saurbaer. They saw a body of men riding to meet them, and among them was Bersi. He greeted Kormak and asked how the wound was doing. Kormak said that no special remedies were needed.

Bersi said, 'Would you like me to cure you, even though I'm the cause of it? And then the harm it will do you will be only short-lived.'

Kormak refused the offer and said he wished always to be on bad terms with him.

Then Bersi spoke a verse:

28.

You'll remember a battle; the one	
when you challenged me to the loud voice	*loud voice of the valkyrie* (Hild):
of the valkyrie; gladly to a spear-thing	battle, duel; *spear-thing*: battle
I go; I've been to another.	
With my slender sword I clove	
a shield in Kormak's hands;	
yet that same shield-god no longer	*shield-god* (Frey): warrior
would duel on the cloak.	

With that they parted.

After this Kormak went home to Mel to see his mother. She cured his hand; but the wound became ugly and the infected flesh around it swelled up. Kormak and his friends sharpened the nick that was in Skofnung, and the more often it was sharpened, the bigger it became.

Then he went to Reykir, threw Skofnung at Skeggi's feet and spoke a verse:

29.
To you, Skeggi, I've had to bring
a sword with broken edge;
the weapon did not bite; indeed,
the victory was theirs.
Not mine the blame for the journey
that I made to engage in a spear-thaw   *spear-thaw*: battle
over a maiden noisily guarded
by the quarrelling of swords.   *quarrelling of swords*: battle

Skeggi said, 'It turned out as I expected.'
Kormak then returned homewards to Mel. He spoke a verse:

30.
I've gone on to a duelling-isle
(and I thought I'd have better luck!)
to fight the forest-lair's dweller,   *forest-lair's dweller*: bear (Bersi means
the bear of the hand-stone.   'bear'); *hand-stone*: gold; its *bear*: man
The famous fist-wand failed me   *fist-wand*: sword
when it broke in my hand;
the inciter of men to slaughter   *inciter of men to slaughter*: combatant
has suffered many a setback.

And when they met, Dalla and Kormak, he spoke a verse:

31.
It was hardly a strong-edged slaying-wand   *slaying-wand*: sword
that Skeggi gave me for battle;
that snake was not supple as it struck   *snake*: sword
from the shore of the shield-strap's land.   *shield-strap's land*: shield; its
Skofnung made a healthy job   *shore*: rim
of cutting Hviting in two
from the hilt; I've chipped a hole
in the shield-strap's staff, now shortened.   *shield-strap's staff*: sword

And again he spoke:

32.

Of little gain in combat	
my staff of slaughter proved	*staff of slaughter*: sword
when I hewed shield-rims; the hand's	
sharp-toothed bear charged into battle.	*hand's bear*: sword
There was clamour when the bruin of blood,	*bruin of blood*: sword
unwilling for truce, left its lair,	*its lair*: scabbard
its slender scabbard, on its way	
to the dwellings of the sea-king.	*dwellings of the sea-king* (Ati):[24] shield

And again he spoke:

33.

I'd gone on two mornings, goddess,	*goddess* (Gefn): woman
on foot, to a meeting as arranged;	
what I'm left of the linen-pole's favour	*linen-pole*: woman
is no more than a bastard's inheritance.	*bastard's inheritance*: virtually
I expect, linen-land, that I shall	nothing; *linen-land*: woman
be staying at home on the third;	
very much on my mind	
is the goddess of sleeves.	*goddess* (Ilm) *of sleeves*: woman

After this Kormak went one day to Reykir, and he and Skeggi talked together; Skeggi considered that the duel had turned out shabbily.

Then Kormak spoke a verse:

34.

Don't blame me, god of the helmet,	*god* (Frey) *of the helmet*: warrior
if I am late in bringing	
the serpent of blood to you	*serpent of blood*: sword
(my poetry before you I bear),	
for fate takes the men of axe-storms	*axe-storms*: battle
under its arm, its hawk-slopes;	*under its arm*: under control; *hawk-slopes*: arm
your sword has been at work	
in the noisy beating of blades.	*beating of blades*: battle

And again he spoke:

35.

God of the clash of Odin's griddle,	*Odin's* (Gaut's) *griddle*: shield; its *clash*:
I thought I was thrusting my sword,	battle; the battle's *god* (Frey): warrior
with its greed for blood, ever nearer	
to where the blood-tracks meet;	*blood-tracks*: veins; where they *meet*: heart,
but the launcher of the sea's horse	breast; *sea's horse*: ship; its *launcher*: man
could not bite with murderous mouth	*murderous mouth*: possibly, the sword
the mate of the pounding sea:	*mate*: Steingerd's husband
my mind is set on her.	

12 | In the winter games took place in Saurbaer, and both Asmund
Bersason and the sons of Thord Arndisarson were there; they
were younger and weaker than Asmund. Asmund was not good at
curbing his strength, and the sons of Thord often came home blue
and bloody. This displeased Thordis, their mother, who asked Thord
to raise the matter with Bersi, Asmund's father, so that he might
consider paying compensation on his behalf. Thord said he was
unwilling to do so.

She said, 'I'll find Bork then, my brother; but the outcome will be
just as bad.'

Thord asked her not to do that, saying, 'I would rather talk about
it with Bersi', and at her entreaty he met Bersi and raised the matter
of compensation.

Bersi said, 'You're too greedy for money, and it hardly seems
honourable to carry on like this; I doubt if you'll become destitute as
long as I don't run short.'

Thord went home, and there was a coolness between them over
the winter.

Spring wore on to the time of the Thorsnes Assembly, and Bersi
now felt sure that Thordis had been behind the claim that Thord put
to him. People now made preparations to attend the assembly. It was
the custom with Thord and Bersi to ride to the assembly together,

and Bersi rode from home and came to Muli, but Thord had already left.

Bersi said, 'Thord has departed from custom in not waiting for me.'

Then Thordis answered: 'It was you that made things go wrong, and this is a small revenge, if a greater one is not on the way.'

Bersi and Thordis had words, and Bersi said that her advice would have evil results. Bersi and his companions rode away.

Bersi said, 'Let us turn ahead to the fjord and get ourselves a boat; it's a long way to ride by the inner road.'

There they obtained a boat, which was Thord's property; they continued on their way, arrived at the assembly when most people had arrived already, and went to the booth of Olaf Peacock from Hjardarholt. Bersi was his thingman. There were many people in the booth, and no space was found for Bersi, who was used to sitting next to Thord – but that space was occupied; in it sat a large and strong-looking man in a bearskin cloak with a mask over his face. Bersi stood in front of him, but the space was not given up. Bersi asked this man his name, and was told that he was named variously Glum or Skuma.[25]

Bersi spoke a verse:

36.
Who's that wretch on the men's bench,
fearsome-looking in bear's fur?
Beneath their shoulders our kinsmen
nurse a wolfish disposition.
This man is made in the image
of Steinar, though Glum or Skuma
he is named; for a fight in the morning
we surely shall be meeting.

'– and there's no sense in your concealing your name, bearskin-cloak man,' said Bersi.

'That's true enough,' said Steinar, 'and I have money to pay you on Kormak's behalf, if necessary, but first I challenge you to a duel. It may be that you'll then gain two marks or else lose both.'

Then Bersi spoke:

37.

The duel-challenge has been issued,
desirers of the darts' shower,   *darts' shower*: battle; its *desirers*: warriors
engaged as you are in battle –
that causes me no distress.
I'm a seasoned battle-raiser
letting loose the valkyrie's storm;   *valkyrie's* (Hlokk's) *storm*: battle
I never suffer anxiety for
the steeds of the spear-river.[26]   *spear-river*: blood; its *steeds*: wolves, hungry
                                              for carnage

'– but it is clear that you kinsmen intend to destroy me. It's as well for you, Steinar, to find out whether my goodwill carries any weight; and your arrogance might be put down.'

Steinar replied: 'We will not bring about your death, but we would appreciate your recognizing your limits.'

Bersi consented to the duel, went into a side-booth and remained there.

One day there was a call for people to go swimming. Steinar spoke to Bersi: 'Do you want to try out your swimming against me, Bersi?'

He said, 'I have given up swimming, but I'll come along.'

Bersi worked hard at the swimming, breasting the water; he was wearing a healing-stone round his neck. Steinar lunged at him and tore the stone from him along with the pouch it was in,[27] threw it into the water and spoke a verse:

38.

A long time I lived;
I let the gods take charge;
never did I have
hose of moss-brown hue;
never did I bind
a bag to my neck,
full of herbs; however,
I have my life still.[28]

After that they swam ashore. The trick that Steinar played on Bersi was at Thord's instigation, so that the duel would go worse for Bersi. Thord walked along the fjord when the tide went out, found the healing-stone and kept it.

Steinar owned the sword that was named Skrymir.[29] It was never dirty, nor troublesome to handle.

On the day appointed for the duel, Thord and Steinar left their booth, and Kormak came to the assembly. Olaf Peacock provided Bersi with back-up for the duel. Thord Arndisarson was accustomed to holding the shield for Bersi, but that did not happen on this occasion. Bersi nevertheless went to the duelling-ground; the name of his shield-bearer is not recorded. Kormak was to hold the shield for Steinar. Bersi had the targe Thorveig's Gift, and each of the two had three shields. Then Bersi hacked two of Steinar's shields, but Kormak held on to the third. Bersi struck at Steinar, but Hviting stuck fast in the iron rim of Steinar's shield. Kormak raised the shield, and in that moment Steinar struck at Bersi, hitting the shield rim with his sword, which glanced off the shield and on to Bersi's buttocks and slid down along his thighs to the hollows of his knees, so that it stuck in the bone, and Bersi fell.

Steinar said, 'Now the money is paid for Kormak.'

Bersi sprang up then and struck at Steinar and split the shield, and the sword point entered Steinar's chest. Thord rushed up and pushed Steinar away.

Thord said, 'Now I've paid you back for the injury to my sons.'

After that Bersi was carried to his booth and his wounds were bandaged. Thord went back to the booths.

When Bersi saw him, he spoke a verse:

39.
Earlier you gave me your company,
god of battle, when the gaping wolf   *god* (Njord) *of battle* (Hlokk): warrior
of Odin's door sped from my hand   *Odin's door*: shield; its *wolf*: angry sword
on to opposing shields.
It is still so that the widow
of Odin's clouds wishes to help   *Odin's* (Jalk's) *clouds*: shields;
                                                      their *widow*: valkyrie

34

with the killing; oh murderous god   *murderous god* (Frey)
of the targe, how fickle you are.   *of the targe* (shield): warrior

And again he spoke:

40.
To trees of the fire of battle   *fire of battle* (Gunn): sword; its *trees*: warriors
I seemed, when I was younger,
skilful in the valkyrie's snowstorm;   *valkyrie's* (Hlokk's) *snowstorm*: battle
long ago was that related.
Now my kinsmen wish to cover me
with earth, I in no way deny it;
this is what I have got for going
to Saurbaer, that flat land.

Thord said, 'It was not your death, but your dishonour that we brought about on this occasion.'

Then Bersi spoke a verse:

41.
At this meeting kinsmen have failed me;
the hope of joy diminishes;
in speaking to people of this,
I do so straight from the heart;
trusty friends are hard to come by.
By a corpse the raven was always
made happy; by threats of men
I too am undistressed.

After this Bersi was brought home to Saurbaer, and he lay wounded for a long time.

To return to Kormak and Steinar: about the time that Bersi was carried to the booth, Steinar said to Kormak:

42.
Four and a further eight
hewers of the valkyrie's gates   *valkyrie's* (battle-Syr's) *gates*: shields;
I caused to feel the edge   their *hewers*: warriors
of bright-polished Skrymir – do you hear?

Now at last the offerer   *waterfalls of Bestla's* (Odin's mother's) *kin*, i.e. liquid
of the waterfalls of Bestla's kin   of Odin: poetry; its *offerer*: poet (Steinar)
has felled Bersi with a lightning-flash   *wound-wasps*: arrows; their *sweat*: blood;
of wound-wasps' sweat.   *lightning-flash* of blood: sword

Steinar said, 'It is my wish that you should now own Skrymir,
Kormak, because I expect this duel to be my last.'

After that the friends parted; Steinar went home, but Kormak went
to Mel.

13 | To return to Bersi: his wounds healed slowly.

     It happened on one occasion that many people came to see
him, and the talk was of the encounter and how it had gone.

Then Bersi spoke a verse:

43.
You held me beneath sword's edges
and were strong enough, god of the snake's plain,   *snake's plain*: gold;
but you were protecting another;   its *god* (Ygg): warrior; *another*: (variant
now necessity gives rise to verses;   reading: others)
thus go a battle-tree's counsels,   *battle-tree*: warrior
but some over less grow angry;
at this point it seems to me, Thord,
that our friendship has come to an end.

Afterwards Thord visited Bersi in bed and brought him the heal-
ing-stone. Then Thord cured Bersi, and their friendship took hold;
they maintained it well thereafter.

As a result of these events Steingerd conceived a dislike for Bersi
and wished to divorce him.[30]

When she was ready to leave, she went to Bersi and said, 'You
were first known as Bleary-eye-Bersi, and then as Bersi the Dueller,
but now you may in truth be called Arse-Bersi', and she declared
herself separated from him.

Steingerd went north to her relatives, met her brother Thorkel, and asked him to recover her possessions, her bride-price and dowry, saying that she did not wish to be married to a maimed Bersi. Thorkel in no way condemned this and promised to go and deal with it; but the winter passed, and Thorkel's journey was delayed.

14 | Later, in the spring, Thorkel Tooth-gnasher went to see Bersi the Dueller to recover Steingerd's property. Bersi said that the predicament he was in seemed grave enough, even if both parties had a good deal to put up with – 'and the property will not be returned,' he added.

Thorkel said, 'I challenge you to a duel on Orrustuholm off Tjaldanes.'

Bersi said, 'That will seem a small matter to a warrior such as yourself, but nevertheless I promise you I'll come.'

They came to the duelling-ground, and the duel went ahead. Thord Arndisarson held the shield for Bersi, and Vali for Thorkel. And when two shields were destroyed, Bersi invited Thorkel to take the third. Thorkel did not wish to do so. Bersi had a shield, and a sword that was long and sharp.

Thorkel said, 'The sword you have, Bersi, is longer than the laws allow for.'

'That will not be so,' said Bersi, taking up Hviting and wielding it with both hands; he dealt Thorkel his death-blow.

Then Bersi spoke:

44.
Tooth-gnasher I have now slain,
my killings are now thirty-one;
and my own teeth I show in a grin;
let men bear these words from the slaying.   *rowing-bench steeds*: ships;
The god of the rowing-bench steeds   their *god* (Ull): man, Bersi;
will come to all the better a realm;   *all the better a realm*: the hereafter

though ageing, he'll more often stain
with gore the swan of the blood's seat. *blood's seat*: corpse; its *swan*: raven

After that Vali challenged Bersi to a duel. Bersi spoke a verse:

45.
The duel-challenge has been issued,
desirers of the darts' shower, *darts' shower*: battle; its *desirers*: warriors
engaged as you are in battle –
that causes me no distress.
In sending the valkyrie's storm *valkyrie's* (Hlokk's) *storm*: battle
to the battle-sweller, men take pleasure. *battle-sweller*: warrior
I never lose heart in hewing
on the banks of the duelling-isle.

When the fighting was to take place, Thord arrived and spoke to
Bersi and Vali: 'People will think it highly unfortunate if valiant men
go killing each other off for no reason; I am offering to settle things
between you.'

They agreed to that.

Thord said, 'Vali, the most hopeful prospect of reconciliation
seems to me for Bersi to marry your sister; you're bound to get
honour from that.'

Bersi agreed to that, and the Brekka land was to be Thordis's
dowry; thus he and Vali became related by marriage. After this Bersi
had a fortification built around his farm, and he stayed there for many
years in peace and quiet.

15 | There was a man named Thorarin, who was the son of Alf; he
lived to the north, in Thambardal, a valley leading off from
Bitra. He was a big, strong man, known as Thorarin the Mighty; he
had for a long time been going on voyages and was so successful in
doing so that he could choose wherever he liked as a port of call. He
had three sons; one was named Alf, the second Loft, and the third
Skofti. Thorarin was a most unruly person, and his sons were similar
in temperament: they were as rowdy as could be.

There was a man named Odd; he lived at Tunga, which is in Bitra. His daughter, whose name was Steinvor, was a good-looking and accomplished woman; she was known as the Slender-legged. Living with Odd were many fishermen. There was a man named Glum who worked at the fishing camp and was an ill-tempered, unpleasant person.

It happened once that Odd and Glum were discussing who were the greatest in the district.[31] Glum considered Thorarin the top man, but Odd declared Bersi the Dueller to be better in all respects.

Glum said, 'What can you produce in evidence of that?'

Odd said, 'Are they really all that alike, Bersi's heroism and Thorarin's thefts?'

They discussed this to the point at which they got angry and laid wagers.

Then Glum went and told Thorarin, who became very angry, and spoke threateningly to Odd. Then Thorarin went and took Steinvor away from Tunga without the consent of Odd, her father, and declared that he, Odd, would not be free from danger if he took exception to this; and Thorarin and she came home to Thambardal. So it went on for a while.

After this Odd went to find Bersi the Dueller, told him how things had turned out, and asked him for support in going to fetch Steinvor and avenging this insult.

Bersi said that this conversation had been uncalled for and asked Odd to go home and not get involved in any of it. 'Nevertheless,' he added, 'I promise you my protection.'

When Odd had gone, Bersi made ready to leave home. He rode fully armed, girt with Hviting and taking three spears, and came to Thambardal towards the end of the day when the women were leaving their room. Steinvor saw Bersi, and went to meet him and told him of her difficulties.

'You get ready to leave with me,' he said, and she did so.

Bersi said he did not wish his journey to Thambardal to be to no purpose, and turned to the doorway where people were sitting by the long fires. Bersi knocked on the door, and a man came to answer it, giving his name as Thorleif. Thorarin, recognizing Bersi's voice, ran out with a large whittling knife and thrust at him with it. Bersi saw this, drew Hviting, and at once dealt him his death-blow. After this Bersi leapt into the saddle, placing Steinvor on his knee, took his spears, which Steinvor had been keeping for him, and rode into a nearby forest, where he left the horse and Steinvor in a particular hiding place and asked her to wait for him; then he went to the scarp over which the main track ran and established himself there.

All was not quiet in Thambardal. Thorleif ran and told Thorarin's sons that he was lying dead in the doorway. They asked who was responsible, and Thorleif told them. Then they pursued Bersi, making for the ascent by the shortest route, intending to head him off; but he was already there. And when they came near to him, Bersi aimed a spear at Alf, piercing him through; then Loft aimed a spear at Bersi, who warded it off with the shield, from which it rebounded; and then Bersi aimed at Loft, piercing him to death, and at Skofti with the same result. When that was over, the brothers' household servants arrived; Thorleif turned back towards them, and they all went home together.

16 | Then Bersi went to fetch Steinvor and mounted his horse and came home before people had risen from bed. They asked about Bersi's travels, and he told them. Thord asked Bersi, when they met, about their encounter, and how it had gone.

Then Bersi spoke a verse:

46.

One feeder of wolves suffered death   *feeder of wolves*: warrior
in Thambardal: Thorarin the Mighty
fell flat on his face in front
of the speaker of wise verses.
People suffered ruin of life;
Loft fell, as did Alf and Skofti;
those four, father and sons, earned
death's doom; I faced them alone.

After this Odd went home, but Steinvor stayed with Bersi, which displeased Thordis. Bersi's fortification was rather the worse for wear by then, but now he had it repaired. It is said that no compensation was forthcoming for these men. So time passed.

On one occasion, when Thordis and Bersi were talking together, Bersi said, 'I've had the idea of offering to foster a child for Olaf Hoskuldsson.'

She said, 'I'm not too keen on that; it seems to me a great responsibility, and by no means certain to add to our honour.'

'It is also a sure source of protection; after all, I've had many quarrels with people, and I'm not getting any younger,' said Bersi.

He went to meet Olaf and offered to foster the child for him; Olaf accepted this gratefully and Bersi brought Halldor home with him and gave him to Steinvor to foster. This displeased Thordis, who embezzled the money involved. Bersi was now beginning to age fast.

It also happened on one occasion that Bersi's thingmen came to see him; he was sitting on his own, and his food was served sooner than other people's. Bersi had porridge, but the others had cheese and curdled milk.

Then Bersi spoke a verse:

47.

Morsels of food I chopped	
for the wound-sea's black-feathered bird;	*wound-sea*: blood; its *bird*: raven
thrice ten times and five this happened:	
I was well known for slaying of men.	
May the trolls have my life if I never	
again tint a sharp sword;	
may the mail-coat's trees dispatch	*mail-coat's trees*: warriors; their *breaker*:
their breaker to his mound.	warrior (me) (the last part of the verse is
	defective)

Halldor said, 'So, my foster-father, you still intend to kill a man.'

Bersi said, 'I see one deserving case.'

Thordis allowed her brother Vali use of the land at Brekka. Bersi got his farmhands to work at home and to have no dealings with

Vali. It displeased Halldor that Bersi did not manage his own property.

After that Bersi spoke a verse:

48.
Both of us lie
on a bench together,
Halldor and I,
unable to move;
youth does this to you,
and old age to me;
you've hope of better things,
but I, none at all.[32]

Halldor said, 'I don't like Vali.'
Bersi spoke a verse:

49.
I know that arrogant Vali
uses our home-fields for grazing;
the troublesome helmet-wearer
wants to tread us under foot.
I've often been angered by less
when I've repaid wrath to the trees
of the waves' bright fire. I reddened   *waves' fire*: gold; its *trees*: men
the wound-serpent on the mailcoat-wearer.   *wound-serpent*: sword

And again he spoke:

50.
The god of the forearm's rock   *forearm's rock*: gold; its *god* (Ull): man, Bersi
has become decrepit with age;
I must suffer much from the busy
gods of the spear-meadow.   *spear-meadow*: shield: its *gods* (Gautar): warriors
Though shield-trees may shape for this poet   *shield-trees*: warriors
a cold time in the grave, I'll rather
redden the helmet's storm's wand   *helmet's storm*: battle; its *wand*: sword
in a duel than suffer fear.

42

Halldor said, 'In spirit you're hardly ageing yet, my foster-father.'

Steinvor and Bersi talked together. Bersi said to her, 'There are plans to be made, and we need your advice.' She declared it her duty to give whatever advice she could.

'You're to get into a disagreement with Thordis over a milk-can and hold on to it until the two of you spill the milk. Then I'll come up and side totally with her, and then you're to go to Vali and pour out your woes.'[33]

This went just as Bersi had planned, and she went to Vali saying that things had not gone smoothly for her; she asked Vali to accompany her along the cliff, and he did so.

When Vali wished to turn back, Halldor and Bersi confronted him. Bersi had a halberd in one hand and a stick in the other, but Halldor had Hviting. When Vali saw them he turned to oppose them and struck at Bersi. Halldor got at Vali from behind and used Hviting on his leg tendons. Then Vali moved briskly in response and turned to oppose Halldor, whereupon Bersi stuck the spear between his shoulders, and that was his death-wound. Then they set up his shield by his feet and his sword at his head, and spread his homespun cloak over him; and after that they mounted their horses and rode around five farms, declaring themselves responsible for the slaying; and then they rode home. People now went and prepared Vali for burial, and the place where he was killed has since been called Valafall (Vali's fall).[34] Halldor was twelve years old when this event took place.

17 | There was a man named Thorvald who was the son of Eystein and was known as Thorvald Tintein. He was a wealthy and skilled man, and a poet, but lacked firmness of character. His brother, whose name was Thorvard, lived up north at Fljot. They had many relatives, known as the Skidi clan;[35] their following was slight.

Thorvald Tintein asked for Steingerd's hand in marriage, and she was granted to him with the consent of her kinsmen and with no protest from her. This was in the same summer that Steingerd left Bersi. Kormak heard this news but acted as if he knew nothing about it. Shortly before, Kormak had moved his goods on to a ship, as he and his brother planned to go abroad together.

One morning early, Kormak rode from the ship, went to see Steingerd and talked to her, asking her to make him a shirt.[36] She said there was no need of his coming and that Thorvald and his kinsmen would not let it go unavenged.

Kormak spoke a verse:

51.

One thing I can't bear to think of,
Caring fir-tree of gold,   *fir-tree of gold*: woman
is why you should be given in marriage
to a tinkerer with tin.
Silk-goddess, I can scarcely   *Silk-goddess* (Nanna): woman
show my teeth in a grin since your father
promised you, famed as you are,
to a character so base.

Steingerd said, 'There's no doubting the hostility of such a remark, and I'll tell Thorvald how you have slandered him; no one can tolerate such behaviour.'

Then Kormak spoke:

52.

Bright goddess of the splendid head-cloth,   *bright goddess* (Hlin) *of the head-*
you have no need to threaten me,   *cloth*: beautiful woman
with the scorn of Skidi's family;
I can give back as good as I get.
I'll compose on the showerer of spears
such slander as will make stones float;
it's an evil end for Eystein's sons
that I've now set in train.[37]

After that they parted with no friendliness, and Kormak went to the ship.

18 | When the brothers put out from their place of anchorage, a walrus surfaced beside the ship. Kormak fired a weighted staff at it, hitting the animal, so that it sank. People thought they recognized Thorveig's eyes when they saw it.[38] The animal did not surface from then on; and it was reported of Thorveig that she was dangerously ill, and people say that she died as a result.

Then they sailed out to sea and came to the Norwegian coast. In those days Hakon, Athelstan's foster-son, was ruling in Norway. The brothers went speedily to visit the king, who received them well; they were held in high honour there over the winter. The following summer they went raiding and performed many remarkable feats. There was a man in partnership with them whose name was Sigurd, a German, and well born. They made raids far and wide.

One day, when they had gone ashore, eleven men came upon the brothers and attacked them; and the encounter ended with the two brothers overcoming the eleven. After that they went back to their ships, and their fellow Vikings, who thought they must have lost them, now rejoiced that they were returning with victory and wealth. On this journey the brothers won great renown.

Summer now drew to a close, and winter approached. They wished then to steer towards Norway, but ran into cold weather; the sail was covered with hoar-frost. The brothers were always extremely active.

Then Kormak spoke a verse:

53.

Skardi, we must shake the hoar-frost *Skardi*: (probably 'hare lip'): Thorgils
from the ship's tent; the poet's dwelling
is all too cold, the mountains
are cowled with the fjord's helmet. *fjord's helmet*: ice
I'd wish there were no better place
for the wielder of the metal-threader; *wielder of the metal-threader*: tinsmith,
he's too lazy to leave his bright i.e. Thorvald Tintein
goddess of the serpent's bed. *serpent's bed*: gold; its *goddess* (Gna): Steingerd

Thorgils said, 'You're always mentioning her, but you wouldn't marry her when the opportunities were there.'

Kormak said, 'That had more to do with the spell-casting of evil spirits than with my fickleness.'

Now they sailed close to some crags, and took in the sails to counter the great danger involved.

Kormak said, 'It would be good if Thorvald Tintein were here alongside us.'

Thorgils said, with a smile, 'It's altogether likely that he's having a better time than we are today.'

'Then things aren't as they should be,' said Kormak.

Shortly afterwards they reached Norway.

19 | While they had been away, there had been a change of rulers. Hakon was deceased, and Harald Grey-cloak[39] had come in his place. They made friends with the king, who was sympathetic to their interests. They went with him to Ireland, and fought battles there.

On one occasion, when they had gone ashore with the king, a great force opposed him, and when they came to blows, Kormak spoke a verse:

54.

For myself I fear death but little,
though shield may be laid against shield
(the gold-rich guardian of land   *guardian of land*: king
need not fault the sweller of praise),   *sweller of praise*: poet, myself
for as long, Skardi, as I remember
the skerry-land's tree in the north,   *skerry-land*: sea; its *tree*: woman
Thorkel's daughter. That sickness,
benchmate, gives me sharp pain.

Thorgils said, 'You never enter upon a trial of courage without Steingerd always coming into your mind.'

Kormak said, 'That's indeed something I've hardly yet forgotten.'

This was a great battle, in which King Harald won a glorious victory; his men pursued the enemy as they fled. The brothers were positioned both together; nine men then turned against them, and they fought for a while.

Kormak spoke a verse:

55.

Hardened as we are, Skardi,
we shall swiftly deprive
nine foes of life; loyal sword-driver,
let us two be their slayers,
while the thin-faced gold-thread goddess,   *gold-thread goddess* (Njorun):
the woman who once loved me,   woman
goes at home to an ornate bed
with a wretch whom the gods find loathsome.

Thorgils said, 'That's what you most often end up talking about.'

Their battle ended with the brothers gaining the victory, and the other nine falling; for that they received great praise from the king, and many other honours. The brothers were always with the king on military expeditions. Then Thorgils noticed that Kormak never slept much, and asked the reason.

Then Kormak spoke a verse:

56.

The surf roars, steep cliffs rise
from the edge of the sea-king's blue realm;   *sea-king's* (Haki's) *blue realm*: sea
to the water's domain glides the din
of the sea that encircles islands.
Much more sleepless than you
I am made by the wave-gleam's valkyrie;   *wave-gleam*: gold; its *valkyrie*
yet if, having slept, I awaken,   (Hild): woman
it's the bead-decked goddess I'll miss.   *bead-decked goddess* (Gefn): woman

– 'I can tell you this, brother, that I'm giving notice of my travelling to Iceland.'

Thorgils said, 'You have many problems to contend with, brother, and I don't know at this stage how things will turn out.'

When the king learned of Kormak's eagerness to depart, he called Kormak to him and said he was acting unwisely and tried to dissuade him from the journey, but it was of no use; he embarked on the voyage. As they put out to sea they ran into a bitter wind and heavy seas, and the sail-yard broke.

Then Kormak spoke a verse:

57.
For me it's not as if a slave
were breaking Tintein's dung-sledge;
the coward's afraid of hardships;
he's made timid by such turmoil.
Now the sail-yard of the channel-steed   *channel-steed*: ship
has been mended in Solundarsund;
may all the brave-hearted staves   *staves of the showering spears*: warriors
of the showering spears hear this!

They put out to sea and suffered harsh weather, and on one occasion, when there had been a particularly heavy sea, people got wet.

Then Kormak spoke a verse:

58.
Little he knows, the cowardly tin-biter,
fearful of seafaring
(the goddess decked with beads   *goddess* (Ilm) *decked with beads*: woman
blocks my contentment).
Where did the wave with blazing crest
offer warmth to men's arms
as it sweeps across their heads?
He has a woman to visit.

They had a rough passage and at last came to land in Midfjord. They cast anchor near to land, and looking up at the coastline saw where a woman was riding. Kormak recognized Steingerd, and had a boat launched and rowed to shore; he left the boat quickly, got himself a horse, and rode to meet Steingerd. When they met, Kormak leapt from his horse's back, took her from hers, and set her down beside him. The horses left them, the day drew to its close, and darkness began to fall.

Steingerd said, 'It's time to look for our horses.'

Kormak said that there would be little need to do so, but he looked around and saw the horses nowhere; they had in fact straggled into the bed of a brook that was a short distance from where they were sitting. Now night approached, and they started walking and came to a small farm, where they were received and granted such hospitality as they needed. During the night they slept on separate sides of a screen.

Then Kormak spoke a verse:

59.

Goddess of arm's fires, we repose	*arm's fires*: gold; their *goddess* (Hlin):
on either side of a screen;	woman
the mighty fates have their way,	
and are hostile; I see it clearly.	
Yet whenever we share a bed,	
we have not a care in the world,	
so dear are you, sea-goddess,	*goddess* (Freyja) *of the sea*: woman;
to the sword of the love-hair's island.[40]	*love-hair's island*: vagina or mons Veneris; its *sword*: (my) penis

Steingerd said it would be better if their paths did not cross again. Kormak spoke a verse:

60.

Famous goddess of the horn-froth's	*horn-froth*: ale; its *fjordland*: ale-horn;
fjordland, you and I	*goddess* (Freyja) of the ale-horn: woman
slept together, hale and hearty,	
in a house, for five grim nights;	
and every one of those raven's lives	*raven's lives*: nights
I lay there, thinking of little,	
deprived of the locking embrace	
on the ship of the fire-kettle's gables.	*ship of the fire-kettle's gables*: bed

Steingerd said, 'It's over; don't speak of it.'
Kormak spoke a verse:

61.

Stones will stand poised to float
as boldly as grains on water,
and lands be submerged (I remain
unfavoured by the youthful wealth-staff), *wealth-staff*: wearer of finery,
huge mountains, of high renown,   woman
will shift to the depths of the sea
before a wealth-pole as beauteous *wealth-pole*: wearer of finery, woman
as Steingerd will be born.[41]

Steingerd said she did not want his mockery.
Kormak spoke a verse:

62.

For a long time, necklace-goddess, *necklace-goddess* (Gefn): woman
a vision has assailed me
in my dreams – unless I make
my self-deceit the more –
that at last your shoulder-branches, *shoulder-branches*: arms
wealth-goddess, valkyrie, lie *wealth-goddess* (Frigg) and *valkyrie* (Hrund):
on that land of mine, whose slopes woman; *slopes . . . where the hawk alights*:
are where the hawk alights. arm; its *land*: shoulder

Steingerd said, 'That is not to happen, if I have any say in the
matter; you dissociated yourself from the arrangements between us
in the one way that meant that you could have no hope of that.'

Now they slept the night through. In the morning Kormak made
ready to leave, sought out Steingerd, and took a gold ring from his
hand, meaning to give it to her.

She said, 'May the trolls take every bit of you, and your gold ring.'
Kormak spoke a verse:

63.

Unlucky was the time I offered
the driving blizzard of crucibles *blizzard of crucibles*: ring or rings
to the scarf-tree – that day was not *scarf-tree*: scarf-wearer, woman
fortunate for such a deed.

But the gentle goddess of gold	*goddess* (Njorun) *of gold*: woman
made my finger-rings over to trolls	
and me too – the goddess of wealth	*goddess* (Fylla) *of wealth*: woman
wishes no riches of mine.	

Kormak rode off, not best pleased with Steingerd, and even less with Tintein. He rode home to Mel, was there for the winter, and found food and lodgings for his merchant companions near the ship.

20 | Thorvald Tintein lived to the north, in Svinadal, but Thorvard his brother lived in Fljot. During the winter Kormak travelled northwards to Svinadal to visit Steingerd, and when he came into Svinadal he dismounted and went into the main room. Steingerd was sitting on a cross-bench, and Kormak sat down beside her; but Thorvald was sitting on a bench, and there beside him was Narfi.

Narfi spoke to Thorvald: 'Aren't you to have any say in where Kormak sits? This sort of situation is intolerable.'

Thorvald said, 'I'll put up with it; there seems to me no disgrace in Kormak and Steingerd talking together.'

Narfi said, 'Well, it's a bad business.'

Shortly afterwards the brothers Thorvald and Thorvard met; Thorvald told him of Kormak's arrival there. Thorvard said, 'Do you find such a thing bearable?'

He said that no harm had come of it so far, but added that he was displeased at Kormak's arrival.

Then Thorvard said, 'Let me remedy the situation, even if you don't dare to, for there is disgrace in it to us all.'

The next thing was that, when Thorvard came into Svinadal, the two brothers and Narfi actually hired a tramp to recite a verse so that Steingerd would hear it, and to say that Kormak had composed it, though there was no truth in the assertion. They said that Kormak had taught it to a woman named Eylaug, a kinswoman of his.

This was the verse:

64.

I would have wished Steingerd,
that mighty goddess, as an old   *mighty goddess* (Eir): woman(?)
and proud mare for mating
– and myself a stud-stallion.
Then I'd have leapt on the back
of that valkyrie of threads   *valkyrie* (Thrud) *of threads*: woman
whose fiery hole's wall   *fiery hole*: vulva
halts the battle-erect spears.   *spears*: penises

Steingerd now grew very angry, to the point that she did not wish to hear Kormak's name mentioned. Kormak heard of this and went to visit Steingerd; he tried for a long time to get a response from her.

At last the reply emerged that she was displeased at his composing slanderous poetry about her, which, she added, 'has now been spread around the whole district'. Kormak said that he had done no such thing.

Steingerd said, 'Your denial would be a lot more convincing if I had not heard it.'

Kormak said, 'Who recited it for you to hear?'

She said who recited it – 'and you needn't anticipate any further conversation with me, if this turns out to be true,' she added.

Kormak rode off to look for this prankster and found him; and he now had to tell the truth. Kormak grew very angry and set upon Narfi and killed him. He intended such a fate also for Thorvald, who, however, beat a hasty retreat, cowering in shame; people got between them and separated them.

Kormak then spoke a verse:

65.

That human spawn, wealth's meeter,   *human spawn*: degenerate descendant
will proceed to threaten me   of men; *wealth's meeter*: man
with the scorn of Skidi's family;
I can give back as good as I get.
I'll compose on the showerer of spears
such slander as will make stones float;

it's an evil end for Eystein's sons
that I've now set in train.[42]

News of this spread around the district, and nothing but bad feeling
developed between them. The brothers Thorvard and Thorvald
talked boastfully, which displeased Kormak.

21 | After this Thorvard sent word from Fljot that he wished to
fight against Kormak. He fixed a place and a time, saying that
he now wished to avenge the slander and other insults.[43] Kormak
agreed to that, and when the day came he went to the appointed
place, but neither Thorvard nor any of his men had arrived there.
Kormak did, however, meet a woman there on the farm; she greeted
him, and they asked each other for news.

She said, 'What is your errand, or who are you waiting for?'
Kormak spoke a verse:

66.

Late in coming from Fljot
to our sword-fight is he who feeds
the kin of Odin's destroyer, *kin of Odin's* (Unn's) *destroyer*: wolves (Odin
and who sent me word from the north; is killed at the doom of the gods
what that crazy sword-polisher needs by the wolf Fenrir); *he who*
is to plant in himself a heart, *feeds* wolves: warrior; *sword-polisher*: man
albeit of clay;[44] but worse still
is the necklace-valkyrie's husband. *necklace-valkyrie*: woman, Steingerd

Kormak said, 'Now I challenge Thorvard to a duel again, if he
considers himself in possession of his own courage; let him be the
object of every man's contempt if he doesn't turn up.'

Then Kormak spoke a verse:

67.

Let me not be forced into silence
by scoundrels; I'm being charged
for a daughter's gift;[45] but still
I'll keep paying Odin his due. *Odin's* (Gauti's) *due*: poetry

Word of this will soon reach	*Odin's* (?Throp's) *rain*: battle (?); its *staves*:
the arraigned staves of Odin's rain;	warriors; *arraigned*: i.e. punished with
I'll win fame, unless file-mongers	lampoons; *file-mongers*: tinsmiths (such as
should chance to cheat me of life.	Thorvald Tintein)

Then the brothers initiated an action against Kormak for slander. Kormak's kinsmen acted as his spokesmen, but he would allow no offer to be made to the brothers, who, he declared, were worthy of derision and not of honour. He declared himself in no way unprepared for them, unless they tricked him. Thorvard had not kept the duelling appointment that Kormak offered him, and Kormak said that derision had been brought down upon them as a natural result and that it was fitting for them to suffer such derision.

Time now passed until the Hunavatn Autumn Meeting, and both parties went to it.

On one occasion, when they met – Thorvard and Kormak – Thorvard said, 'We have many different kinds of score to settle with you, and on that account I challenge you to a duel here at the meeting.'

Kormak said, 'Then you must be more up to it than in the past; you've always shrunk from confrontation.'

'The risk is to be taken nonetheless,' said Thorvard. 'We're not tolerating such dishonours any longer.'

Kormak said there was nothing to keep him there and went home to Mel.

22 | There was a man named Thorolf who dwelt at the foot of Spakonufell; his wife was Thordis the Prophetess, who was mentioned before. They were both there at the meeting. Many people considered themselves well protected with her around. Thorvard turned to her and asked her for help against Kormak and gave her money to that end; Thordis now equipped him for the duel at her own discretion.

Kormak told his mother his intention, and she asked whether he thought any good would come of it.

'Why ever not?' said Kormak.

Dalla said, 'It won't go well for you the way things are, because Thorvard will be unwilling to fight unless magic is involved. What I think is advisable is that you should see Thordis the Prophetess, since treachery is what you're up against.'

Kormak said, 'I'm not too keen on that.' Nevertheless he went to see Thordis and asked her for help.

She said, 'You've come too late. Weapons won't hurt him now, but I won't withhold support from you. Stay here tonight and submit yourself to magic, and I'll fix it that iron weapons won't harm you either.'

So Kormak stayed the night there.

When he awoke, he noticed that someone's hand was feeling under the blanket close to his head. He asked who was there, and whoever it was turned away in the direction of the outer door, but Kormak followed and saw that it was Thordis there. By then she had reached the place where he and Thorvard were supposed to fight, and she was holding a goose. Kormak asked what the idea was. She put the tame goose down and said, 'Why couldn't you stay quiet?'

Then Kormak lay down and kept himself awake, eager to find out what Thordis was up to. She made three visits, and on each occasion he wondered what she was doing.

On the third occasion, when Kormak came out, she had slaughtered two geese and let their blood run together into a bowl, and by then she had taken the third goose and was about to slaughter it.

Then Kormak said, 'Where's this all leading, foster-mother?'

Thordis said, 'It's going to prove all too true, Kormak, that helping you will be far from easy. It was my intention now to avert the evil destinies that Thorveig had cast upon you and Steingerd; the two of you might have enjoyed each other's love if I had slaughtered the third goose without anyone knowing about it.'

Kormak said, 'I don't believe in such things' – and spoke a verse:

68.
Silver ounces I gave at the duel;
twice the maid did her slaughtering,
making the god of treasure   *god* (Tyr) *of treasure*: warrior, i.e. Thorvard
easier for me to overcome.

Thus blood will come of the blood
of two geese; never offer that
to a poet, the accomplished
brewer of Odin's ale.   *Odin's ale*: poetry

They now went to the duelling-ground. Thorvard gave the prophetess more money, and received in return the sacrifice she performed. Kormak spoke a verse:

69.
The trolls, it is true, have much
trodden this chariot that carries   *sea-king's* (Ati's) *land*: sea; its *fire*: gold;
the fire of the sea-king's land; that man   *chariot* (i.e. bearer) of gold: woman
believes another man's wife!
Now I expect that the seeress –
hoarse voice and all – will cause harm
as we go to the battlefield's reddening.   *battlefield's reddening*: duel
Why should we blame her for that?

Thordis spoke: 'I'll fix it so that you're not recognized.'
Kormak gave a hostile response to this and said that she would cause nothing but harm; he wanted to pull her out into the doorway and see her eyes in the sunlight.[46] His brother Thorgils forbade him to do so, saying that it would serve no purpose.

Steingerd said she wished to go to the duel, and that was what happened.

When Kormak saw her, he spoke a verse:

70.
I've gone on to the duelling-ground
for your sake a second time,
goddess who bears a bonnet;   *goddess* (Eir) *who bears a bonnet*: woman
what can shake our love for each other?
Two fights now I've started
over you, goddess of the wave;   *goddess* (Var) *of the wave*: woman
my beloved ought then to be nearer
to me, I'd have thought, than to Tintein.

Then they fought, and Kormak's sword did not cut at all. They had a lengthy exchange of blows, and neither sword would cut. In the end Kormak struck at Thorvard's side. It was a mighty blow, with numbing effect, and Thorvard's ribs broke, so that he could fight no longer; and with that they parted.

Kormak saw a bull standing nearby and killed it.[47] He had become hot, and took the helmet off his head, and spoke a verse:

71.
I've gone on to the duelling-ground,
pine-tree of the arm's rock;   *arm's rock*: jewellery; its *pine-tree* (i.e. wearer):
you are not to forbid me   woman
to fight on a third occasion.
This time I won't be reddening
a blood-reed in the gory river.   *blood-reed*: weapon, sword
Blunt, I declare – and with blood –
has the sorceress rendered my sword.

He wiped the sweat from his body on a flap of Steingerd's mantle.
Kormak spoke a verse:

72.
Because I often seem quarrelsome,
I must wipe myself on a mantle-flap;
tribulation is what I earn,
pine-tree of gold, from you.
So let the dung-bearer, deserving   *dung-bearer*: man
of death, slink away to his seat.
It's me, the purveyor of poetry,
that Steingerd has plunged into sorrow.

Kormak now asked Steingerd to leave with him. She said she would be the one to decide who accompanied her, and they parted, neither one of them at all pleased. Thorvard was brought there and she bandaged his wounds.

Kormak was now always meeting Steingerd.

Thorvard recovered slowly, and when he was able to rise to his feet he went to see Thordis and asked her what would be the best way for him to recover. She said, 'There's a certain hillock a short way from here, in which elves live. You are to take the bull that Kormak killed, redden the surface of the hillock with the bull's blood, and make the elves a feast of the meat;[48] then you'll recover.'

After that Thorvard and his associates sent word to Kormak that they wished to buy the bull. He said he did not wish to deny them the purchase of it, but would take for it the ring belonging to Steingerd. They came to collect the bull, handed over the ring to Kormak, and dealt with the bull as Thordis had instructed.

Kormak spoke a verse:

73.

When you bring home the meat
reddened from the sacrifice,
the flax-goddess who loved me   *flax-goddess* (Gefn): woman
will ask the wound-stick's desirer: *wound-stick*: weapon; its *desirer*: warrior
Where is the fire-tempered ring?
That indeed is no small misfortune.
Has that dark youth, the poet, the son
of Ogmund, been given it?

It turned out as Kormak guessed it would: that Steingerd was displeased at their having parted with the ring.

23 | After that Thorvard recovered speedily. When he felt he was on the mend, he rode to Mel and challenged Kormak to a duel. Kormak said, 'You're slow to tire of this matter, but I accept.'

Now they went to the duel.[49] Thordis met Thorvard now as before, but Kormak in no way sought her protection. She made Kormak's sword blunt, so that it did not cut at all; but Kormak nevertheless struck such a mighty blow at Thorvard's shoulder that the shoulder-blade broke, and his arm at once ceased to be of any use to him. As a result of these injuries he could no longer fight and was obliged to pay another ring as a ransom by which to release himself after the duel.

Then Thorolf of Spakonufell ran up and struck at Kormak.

Kormak parried the blow, and then spoke a verse:

74.

The reddener of shields let — *reddener of shields*: warrior, i.e. Thorolf
a rusty sword fumble around me;
let him snort, most wretched of men;
of Odin's drink I'm the handler. — *Odin's* (Fjolnir's) *drink*: poetic mead;
Well out of my way did you keep — its *handler*: poet
the trappings of that twanging shower, — *twanging shower*: battle: its *trappings*:
you husband of a seeress; — (your) armour
that attack gave cause for scorn.

Kormak now slaughtered a sacrificial bull according to custom and said, 'We're in a bad position, having to suffer your aggression as well as Thordis's magic' – and he spoke a verse:

75.

A cowardly crone blunted
the blaze of the shield-wave for me — *shield-wave*: blood; its *blaze*: sword
when swords clashed; I'm letting
the blade-hound bite on the back. — *blade-hound*: sword
The sword availed not when I thought
to attack the helmet-wearer;
he received, spineless wretch that he is,
rather heavy blows as a keepsake.

After that each of the two sides went home, neither of them best pleased.

24 | The ship belonging to Kormak and his brother was laid ashore in Hrutafjord during the winter. In the spring, some merchants came to look at it, and the brothers proposed to take their ship abroad. When they were ready, Kormak went to meet Steingerd, and before they parted, Kormak gave Steingerd two kisses, in a long, drawn-out way. Tintein was not prepared to tolerate this. Friends of both parties now intervened in the question of Kormak paying compensation. Kormak asked what they were requesting.

Thorvald said, 'Those two rings that I lost earlier.'[50]
Then Kormak spoke a verse:

76.

I had to pay with a ring
both times I embraced the bright
brooch-bearer with my brown arms;   *brooch-bearer*: woman
you people paid money before.
Two costlier kisses never
came the way of the gold-leafed tree   *gold-leafed*: gold-adorned
of the sword; indeed I am   *tree of the sword*: warrior
cheated of cheerful encounters.

And when Kormak had reached the ship, he spoke a verse:

77.

I'll have my verse sent off
to Svinadal, to the goddess   *goddess* (Rind) *of neck-adornments*: woman
of neck-adornments, before
we go on board the ship.
Let all my words reach the ears
of the valkyrie of the ribbon;   *valkyrie* (Skogul) *of the ribbon*: woman
I love the goddess of the brooch   *goddess* (Saga) *of the brooch*: woman
at least twice as much as myself.

Kormak now went abroad, and with him went his brother Thorgils.
They came to the king's court, and were well received there.

It is told that Steingerd asked Thorvald Tintein to travel abroad
with her.[51] He said that that was not advisable, but nevertheless could
not refuse her. They embarked on the journey and crossed the sea,
and some Vikings attacked them with the intention of robbing them
and taking Steingerd away. Kormak got to hear of this and went there
and gave them support, with the result that they held on to all their
property. Then they came to the king's court.

It happened one day, when Kormak was walking in the street, that
he saw Steingerd sitting in a ladies' chamber. He went there, sat next
to her, spoke to her and gave her four kisses. Thorvald noticed this
and drew his sword, whereupon some women intervened; and then

King Harald was sent for. The king said that it would be a difficult business seeing to matters between Thorvald and Kormak – 'but I'll bring about a reconciliation between the two of you,' he insisted.

They consented to that.

The king said, 'Let one kiss be made up for by the fact that Kormak gave you support when you landed, and in place of another comes the fact that Kormak rescued Steingerd;[52] but for two of the kisses let two ounces of gold be paid.'

Kormak spoke the same verse as was written before:

76.

I had to pay with a ring
both times I embraced the bright
brooch-bearer with my brown arms; *brooch-bearer*: woman
you people paid money before.
Two costlier kisses never
came the way of the gold-leafed tree *gold-leafed*: gold-adorned
of the sword; indeed I am *tree of the sword*: warrior
cheated of cheerful encounters.

One day, when Kormak was walking in the street, he saw Steingerd, turned towards her and asked her to walk with him. She refused. Then Kormak snatched her to him, and she called for help. The king happened to be nearby and came up, thinking this behaviour looked strange; he extricated her from Kormak and spoke to him shortly. The king was indeed angry, but Kormak nevertheless remained at the court, and was soon on friendly terms with the king; so things were quiet over the winter.

25 | The following spring, King Harald went off on a journey to Permia[53] with a great following. Kormak commanded a ship on that expedition, and Thorvald another one; no other names of ships' commanders are recorded. And when they sailed near each other in a certain sound, Kormak struck at Thorvald's ear with his ship's tiller, and Thorvald fell from the helm of his ship, stunned. Kormak's ship veered aside when it lost its tiller. Steingerd, who had

been sitting next to Thorvald, took hold of the helm and steered at the broadside of Kormak's ship.

Kormak saw this and spoke a verse:

78.

He who came much closer
to the beautiful woman than I
took a blow from the ski of the helm   *ski of the helm*: tiller
in the middle of the hat's perch.   *hat's perch*: head
Eystein's heir is stumbling   *Eystein's heir*: Thorvald
in the ship's prow; Steingerd,
don't steer on to me, however
arrogantly you may act.

The ship capsized under Kormak and his men, but they were quickly rescued as there were many people there. Thorvald recovered, and they proceeded on their voyage. The king offered his services as arbitrator in the matter, and they consented to that. The king judged as equal the blow to Thorvald and the insult to Kormak.

They made land in the evening. The king and his men were seated at a meal. Kormak was sitting relatively near to the door in the tent and drinking with Steingerd out of the same vessel, and while he was doing so, a man stole a cloak-pin from Kormak as a joke, after he had taken his cloak off; and when he was about to put it on, the pin was missing.

Kormak leapt up and ran after the man with the spear that he called Vig,[54] cast it after him, missed, and spoke a verse:

79.

A young lad stole a cloak-pin
from me, as I drank the health
of an upstanding maid; let's share
the pin like two young boys.
My spear has been well shafted;
at stones I'm forced to cast it,
for I missed the man, my target,
and tore up only moss.

After this they journeyed to Permia, and from there back home to Norway.

26 | Thorvald Tintein prepared his ship for a voyage to Denmark, and Steingerd accompanied him. A little later the brothers Kormak and Thorgils travelled in the same direction and came to the Branno islands late in the evening. They saw Thorvald's ship afloat ahead of them. Thorvald himself was there, and there were some men with him, but they had been robbed of all their property, and Steingerd had been taken away by Vikings. Leading those Vikings was Thorstein, son of the Asmund – known as Ash-sides[55] – who had fought against Ogmund, the father of Kormak and Thorgils.

Now Thorvald and Kormak met, and Kormak asked if things had not gone smoothly.

He said, 'Things have certainly not gone as well as they might have done.'

Kormak asked, 'What has happened? Is Steingerd gone?'

Thorvald said, 'Steingerd is indeed gone, along with all our property.'

Kormak spoke: 'Why don't you go after them, then?'

Thorvald said, 'We haven't got the manpower.'

Kormak said, 'Are you admitting that you're not up to it?'

Thorvald said, 'We haven't the strength to fight against Thorstein, but if you have the manpower to do so, see what you can gain for yourself.'

Kormak said, 'We'll go, then.'

During the night the brothers commandeered a boat and rowed to the Viking ship. They boarded Thorstein's ship. Steingerd was on the raised afterdeck, having been offered in marriage to a man, but most of the company were ashore, by the cooking fires. Kormak demanded a report of events from the cooks,[56] and they told him everything the brothers wanted to know. They boarded the ship by the stern gangway. Thorgils pulled the bridegroom out to the side of the ship, and there Kormak killed him. Thorgils plunged into the water with Steingerd and swam to land. When Kormak was near land, some eels attacked him, slithering over his hands and feet, so that he was pulled down.

Kormak spoke a verse:

80.

Wielders of shield-snakes in battle:	*shield-snakes*: swords
the denizens of the canal	*denizens of the canal*: eels
attacked me in ample numbers,	
in hordes, as I crossed the shallows.	
I would long have been remembered	
as a tree of battle-ice, brandishing	*battle-ice*: sword; its *tree*: warrior
Odin's door, had I fallen there:	*Odin's* (Gaut's) *door*: shield
I saved a maiden from harm.	

Kormak made for land and conveyed Steingerd to Thorvald. Thorvald now asked Steingerd to go with Kormak, saying that he had pursued her like a man. Kormak said that was his wish. Steingerd said that she was not going to exchange one knife for another. Kormak also said that that was in no way fated to come about; evil spirits or adverse destinies had prevented it from the start, he said.

Kormak spoke a verse:

81.

Goddess of the arm's girdle,	*arm's girdle*: armband or ring; its *goddess*
don't bother to strive for the pleasure	(Hlin): woman
of this man; sleep next to your husband;	
you do little for my fortune.	
You should lie closer to that rogue,	
goddess of the ancient headdress,	*goddess* (Frigg) *of the ancient headdress*:
than to me; I've made Aurrek's potion	woman; *Aurrek*: a dwarf or a giant;
for you as well as for him.	his *potion*: poetry

Kormak asked Steingerd to go with her husband.

27 | Then the brothers returned to Norway, but Thorvald Tintein made his way to Iceland. The brothers went raiding in Ireland, Wales, England and Scotland and were thought to be the most excellent men. It was they who established the stronghold named Scarborough.[57] They went ashore in Scotland and performed many great feats, and had a large band of men; in that band there was none to compare with Kormak in strength and courage.

On one occasion, after they had been raiding, Kormak was pursuing the enemy as they fled, but his troops had gone to the ship. Then a giant whom the Scots worshipped as an idol[58] came out of a forest in pursuit of Kormak, and a bitter struggle ensued. Of the two, Kormak was the weaker; the giant had more of a troll's strength. Kormak felt for his sword, but it had slipped from its scabbard. He stretched out his hand for it and struck the giant his death-blow. The giant gripped Kormak's sides so firmly, however, that his ribs broke, and Kormak fell with the dead giant on top of him, and could not get up. His men, meanwhile, went to look for him; they found him, and brought him to their ships.

Then Kormak spoke a verse:

82.
It was not as if I had a woman
such as Steingerd in my embrace
when I pitted my strength as a wrestler
against a steerer of rigging-steeds;   *rigging-steeds*: ships
I'd be drinking ale in the high seat
in Odin's hall,[59] had Skrymir
given me help; swiftly
I'll say this to comrades.

Kormak's wounds were then attended to, and the ribs had been broken on both sides. Kormak said there was no need to treat him. He lay wounded for a while, and people bewailed the fact that he should have acted so imprudently.

Kormak spoke a verse:

83.

Anger was always my policy
(after all, I was famed once for killing),
sea-goddess, so that the sword   *sea-goddess* (Rind): woman
would forestall my dying of sickness.
In no way can I escape it;
other staves of the battle-snake surely   *battle-snake*: sword; its *staves*
must die in their beds; on my heart   (i.e. bearers): warriors
weighs heavy the pain of death.

And he spoke another verse:

84.

Your husband, fair-armed wise woman,
was not with me this morning in Ireland;[60]
reddened indeed was the sword
in the course of fighting for gold-hoards,
when the cutting-staff of the valkyrie,   *valkyrie's* (Hlokk's) *cutting-staff*: sword
drawn as it was from the scabbard,
sang round my cheek, goddess,   *goddess* (Saga): woman
and hot blood fell on beak of raven.

And now Kormak's life began to ebb away.
Then he spoke a verse:

85.

The dew of deep wounds poured   *dew of deep wounds*: blood
like rain from the stroke of the sword;
with splendid companions I carried
a sword stained with blood to battle.
Each one of the gods of the sword   *god* (Thund, i.e. Odin) *of the sword*:
bore a broad-bladed blood-wand, but I,   *warrior*; *blood-wand*: sword;
goddess of the hands' golden fire,   *hands' fire*: gold; its *goddess* (Gerd): woman
will have to die in bed.

Kormak said that he wished to pass on his property and his
followers to his brother Thorgils; he was the one he would most like
to benefit from them, he said. Then Kormak died, and Thorgils

commanded his followers, and was for a long time engaged in raiding.

And there this saga ends.

Translated by Rory McTurk

THE SAGA OF HALLFRED
TROUBLESOME-POET

1 | There was a man called Thorvald, who was nicknamed the
Discerning. He lived on the island of Ylf in Halogaland, and
was married to a woman called Thorgerd Hallfredardottir.[1] She had
a brother called Galti. He was a powerful man and lived in Sogn.
Thorvald's sons were Ottar and Thorkel Silver; Thorkel was illegiti-
mate. There was a man called Ingjald who also lived there on the
island. He had a son called Avaldi. Ottar was being fostered by
Ingjald.

There was a Viking called Sokki, a big man and vicious to deal
with. He went far and wide on plundering raids, and he was a friend
of the sons of Gunnhild, who ruled Norway at that time. He came
by night to Thorvald's farm, telling his men that a fine haul would
fall into their hands, since a wealthy man lived there: 'So we'll attack
the farm with fire.'[2]

And this they did.

Thorvald went to the door and asked who was responsible for the
fire. Sokki gave his name.

'What have we done to deserve this?' said Thorvald. 'I don't
remember doing you any harm.'

Sokki said, 'We Vikings don't work like that. We're after your life
and goods.'

'They're in your power for now,' said Thorvald.

Now the Vikings attacked the farm with fire and weapons, and the
outcome was that Thorvald burned inside with fifteen others, though
some escaped from the fire. The Vikings took all the loot they could
manage. Some of Sokki's men went to Ingjald's farm and set fire to

the buildings there. He went to the door and asked for his people to be allowed out, but there was no possibility of this.

Then Ingjald went to the boys Ottar and Avaldi and said, 'It's probable that my share of life is over; but I'd very much like to get you out from the fire, so that you can enjoy a longer destiny. I'm going to hurry you out of a secret entrance, and you should be given chance enough to avenge this if your lot improves.'

They answered that the will would be there, 'though we don't see any chance for us as things stand'.

Then they were hurried out of a secret entrance, and they managed to get away under cover of the smoke and run out across the island; and because of the roaring and the surging of the fire, and because they were not yet doomed, they escaped, and made their way to a farmer who lived there on the island.

Ottar said, 'Will you ferry us to the mainland?'

The farmer recognized them and ferried them across. They landed where a herring-boat lay, and its crew was from Vagan in the north. The boys said they were destitute, and obtained work on board. They sailed south until they reached Sognefjord.

Then the boys said they wanted to go up the fjord – 'we have kinsmen here'.

The skipper said, 'As you wish, then, and you won't be worse off here than when we took you on. You have worked well, and you will soon have bigger things to do.'

With that they parted. Late in the day they reached the home of Galti, Ottar's uncle, and sat down near the door. Galti came up to them and asked who they were. Ottar gave their names truthfully.

'Then it is natural that you came here,' said Galti. 'Now, find a seat.'

They stayed there in great favour for seven or eight years, and grew to be accomplished men. Ottar fought at Fitjar where King Hakon fell;[3] and the sons of Gunnhild took power.

One day Galti said, 'It seems to me, Ottar, that you take the lead as between you two foster-brothers, and I expect you will become a man of great deeds. But now such a time has come in Norway that I dare not keep the two of you here with me. Now I want to give you some trading goods, so that you can sail west to England, and see how that succeeds.'

Ottar said he was willing to trust his advice. Galti had sold their lands for movable goods. Now the foster-brothers Ottar and Avaldi left the country, heading west to England, and acquired wealth for themselves. They spent three or four years sailing between Norway and England, and became very wealthy. They then went to the Orkneys, where they were highly regarded by worthy men.

After a time Ottar said to Avaldi, 'I have a mind to buy a cargo ship for Iceland and move there. But I would want us to avenge our fathers before we leave for good.'

Avaldi said it was up to him. Then they bought themselves a sound ship, hired a crew, and sailed to Norway. They came up Sognefjord to Galti and told him their plans.

Galti said, 'Things are turning out well. Sokki is anchored a short way from here, and at night he sleeps ashore in a loft. I will get you a man who knows all about it, and whom Sokki will least suspect.'

2 | Now Ottar and Avaldi left their ship, and the man, who was called Stein, went with them. Late in the evening they approached the farm where Sokki and his brother Soti slept at night. Stein went alone to the farm and quickly got into conversation with Soti and the others, and drank with them all evening. Then when they started for bed, up in the loft, Stein sent Ottar and Avaldi a signal. Soti and his men were seven in all. They came into the loft and were about to undress. Then Ottar and his comrade burst in, and straight away he thrust his sword into Sokki beneath his coat of mail, and so up into the gut, so that Sokki fell dead at once. Avaldi swung at Soti with his sword, cutting off his buttocks. Then the three ran out, letting the darkness protect them. They reached their ship and at once set out to sea, with a favouring wind. Their venture was reckoned to have turned out quite heroically.

Gunnhild heard this and said it was a blow that she had not laid eyes upon the men who had slain and shamed her friends.

'And yet I know,' she said, 'who did this.'

Ottar and Avaldi steered into the Blonduos estuary in the north of Iceland. All the land there had been settled by then, so Ottar bought land at Grimstungur in Vatnsdal from a man called Einar, giving him the trading vessel for it. Ottar established a farm. Avaldi stayed with Ottar for the first winter, then in the spring he bought land at Hnjuk in Vatnsdal. He married a woman called Hild, daughter of Eyvind Sorkvir. They had a daughter called Kolfinna. She was a fine woman, and very fond of show.

There was a man called Olaf who lived at Haukagil. He was a wealthy man, and was married to a woman called Thorhalla, who was the daughter of Aevar the Old. They had a daughter called Aldis, and she was an outstanding woman. Ottar asked to marry her and gained her, together with a large dowry. They had a son called Hallfred, and a second called Galti. Their daughter was called Valgerd, and she was a most beautiful woman.

Olaf of Haukagil fostered Hallfred, and he was well cared for there. He soon grew big, strong and manly, with rather heavy brows and an ugly nose, but with handsome chestnut hair. He was a good poet, though rather given to slander, and changeable. He was not popular.

Thorstein Ingimundarson was chieftain in Vatnsdal at that time. He lived at Hof and was considered the greatest man in the district. He was popular and very well respected. Ingolf and Gudbrand were his sons. Ingolf was the most promising man in the north. This verse was composed about him:

I.

All the girls longed
to go with Ingolf,
the ones who were fully grown.
'Poor me,' said the lass too little.
'I too,' declared the crone,
'shall go with Ingolf,
as long as two teeth
stick in my upper gum.'[4]

An autumn feast[5] was held at Grimstungur, together with ball games. Ingolf came to the games, and many people with him from down the valley. The weather was fine and the women were sitting outside watching the play. Valgerd Ottarsdottir was sitting up on the slope nearby, and other women with her. Ingolf was in the game, and the ball flew up towards them. Valgerd caught the ball and let it slip under her cloak, saying that the one who had thrown it should fetch it. Ingolf had thrown it. He told the others to play on, but he sat down beside Valgerd and talked with her all day.

3 | Now the games were over and all those not going to the feast went home. Afterwards, Ingolf took to visiting Grimstungur to talk with Valgerd.

Ottar spoke to Ingolf, saying, 'I'm not pleased by your visits, and you must have heard that I don't put up with offence or dishonour. You can marry her if you wish.'

Ingolf said he would decide for himself where he went, whatever Ottar said. He added that the way things were in the valley,[6] he wouldn't take orders from anyone. After that Ottar went to Thorstein and asked him to control his son so that he did not have to take any dishonour from him, 'for you are a wise man, and well intentioned'.

Thorstein said, 'Certainly he's acting like this against my will, and I will promise to speak to him'; and at that they parted.

Thorstein spoke to Ingolf: 'Your ways are different from ours when we were young. You make laughing-stocks of yourselves, although you stand to be chieftains. Leave off your flirting with Ottar's daughter.'

Ingolf said he would mend his ways, since Thorstein asked it, and to begin with he left off his visits. But then Ingolf composed a love poem about Valgerd.[7]

Ottar was furious at that and went to see Thorstein again, saying that great offence was being done to him: 'Now I ask you to allow me to summons your son, for I'm not inclined to let matters rest.'

Thorstein said, 'That's not wholly advisable, but I won't forbid you.'

Then Jokul, Thorstein's brother, spoke up, for he was present. 'Hark at that for an outrage! You mean to summons us kinsmen here in our own district. You'll get no joy of that.'

Jokul lived up at Tunga in Vatnsdal. Thorstein, however, showed his goodwill further by appointing men to arbitrate between them at the Hunavatn Assembly, and he offered surety for his son. Thorstein asked Ottar to agree to his judging the matter of the poem and the whole dispute between them. People urged this on Ottar, and it was settled that Thorstein alone should arbitrate.

Then Thorstein spoke: 'My verdict on this will be swift. I will pronounce for both sides, however you like it. I award half a hundred of silver to Ottar, but he must sell his lands and move out of this district.'

Ottar said he had not expected such injustice would be done him. Thorstein said he had not given any less consideration to his interests, given the temperaments of both parties, and after that Ottar moved south into Nordurardal, settling initially at Ottarsstadir.

By this time Hallfred Ottarsson was a man of nearly twenty. He set his heart on Kolfinna Avaldadottir, but Avaldi was not pleased about that. He wanted him to marry his daughter, but Hallfred did not want to take a wife. Avaldi went to see his friend Mar, who lived at Masstadir, and told him his troubles.

He answered, 'There's a solution to this: I will get someone to ask to marry her. There's a man called Gris Saemingsson. He is a friend of mine, and lives at Geitaskard in Langadal' – he had travelled abroad as far as Constantinople and won great honour there[8] – 'he is a wealthy man, and popular.'

4 | Now Mar sent word to Gris, and he came to Masstadir.
Mar said, 'I have thought of a wife for you. You should ask for the hand of Kolfinna Avaldadottir. There is no lack of money there, and she is a good match, though I am told that Hallfred Ottarsson is always talking with her.'

This was before Ottar moved south.

Now Mar and Gris came to Avaldi's – there were seven of them in all. They left their spears outside; Gris had a spear inlaid with gold. Now they sat discussing the matter, and Mar spoke up on Gris's behalf.

Avaldi said Mar's guidance should decide the issue, 'if it is what you want, and you won't be turned down'.

At that moment Hallfred came, and a companion with him, and they saw the spears. Hallfred said, 'Somebody's made a long journey here. You look after our horses, and I will go to Kolfinna's room'; and this he did.

He sat down beside her and asked what was going on: 'But I'm not going to be pleased, because they must be asking for your hand, and I don't believe any good will come of it.'

Kolfinna said, 'Leave the arranging to those with a right to decide.'

He said, 'I see you already think more of this new suitor of yours than of me.'

Hallfred sat her on his knee outside by the wall of Kolfinna's room, and talked with her in full view of anyone coming out. He drew her towards him, and there were a few kisses.

Now Gris and the others came out.

He said, 'Who are these sitting by the wall of the room and behaving so intimately?'

Gris was rather dim-sighted and blear-eyed.

Avaldi answered, 'It's Hallfred and my daughter Kolfinna.'

Gris said, 'Do they usually do this?'

'It often happens,' said Avaldi, 'but you will have to deal with this trouble, now she's betrothed to you.'

Gris answered, 'It's obvious that he wants to make trouble with me, for such things are done out of arrogance.'

Now Gris and his men went to their horses.

Then Hallfred said, 'You need to know, Gris, that you will have me for an enemy if you intend this match for yourself.'

Mar said, 'Your words on this matter will carry no weight, Hallfred, and it's for Avaldi to decide about his daughter.'

Then Hallfred spoke a verse:

2.

The anger of the busy
bucket-sinker, a true pansy,   *bucket-sinker*: man (a jibe about either
all-heathen, is about   farmwork or pagan ritual)
as terrible to my eyes
as if, fair-sized, outside,
worst of all when guests arrive,
(I swell the poetry)[9] at the pantry-door
an aged pantry-dog fretted.

'And I don't care, Mar the Sacrificer,' said Hallfred, 'what you have
to say.'

Mar said that if he composed insults about him he would react
strongly. Hallfred said he would decide his words for himself. Then
he spoke a verse:

3.

The caring-trees of shield-snakes   *shield-snakes*: swords; their *caring-trees*:
are set on asking the hand   men
(dread this causes the poet)
of Avaldi's only daughter.
Slowly will it happen
(so do men plan for her)
that my breeze of Surt's bride   *Surt*: fire-giant; his *bride*: giantess;
turns from serene Kolfinna.   her *breeze*: mind, thought

Hallfred then rode away; he was angry.

Mar said, 'Let's ride after them', and this they did.

There were nine of them in all, for Avaldi had supplied them with
two men.

Olaf, Hallfred's foster-father, grew suspicious at the movements
of Gris and Mar. He at once sent for Ottar, and when they met, Olaf
told him that Hallfred would be in need of men.

To turn to Hallfred, the two men rode off, with the nine after
them.

Hallfred saw them riding in pursuit and said, 'Let's not run any
further.'

They had reached the side of a hillock by then. They took their stand there and heaved up stones. Now Gris and the others caught up and attacked them, but they defended themselves most manfully. Even so, it turned out as the saying goes, that nothing can beat numbers, and Hallfred and his companion were captured and bound.

Next, Gris said, 'There are men riding after us – no fewer than thirty of them – and it may be a short-lived victory.'

Gris and his men turned back and rode off at a gallop and across the river, to where there was a defile in the bank, and a good vantage ground. There they came to a halt.

Ottar and his men then reached the river. Gris greeted Ottar and asked what he wanted.

Ottar said, 'Where is my kinsman Hallfred?'

Gris replied, 'He is bound, but not killed, beside the hill where we had our fight.'

Ottar said, 'You've dealt dishonourably with him; but will you give me the sole judgement in this?'

Gris said he would honour his words completely, and so they made peace and parted, leaving things at that.

Ottar now rode back to the track, found Hallfred and released him and his companion. Ottar said, 'This venture has not turned out honourably, kinsman.'

Hallfred said he could not commend it, 'and I don't care how you frame the settlement, father, as long as Gris doesn't get Kolfinna'.

Ottar said, 'Gris is to marry the woman, since he trusts me in this, but you, kinsman, are to go abroad and seek greater honour for yourself.'

Hallfred said, 'Who will be true to me, then, if my father breaks faith? Now the first thing to happen will be that I will challenge Gris to a duel as soon as I see him.'

Now Ottar rode home, and Hallfred to Haukagil. Olaf felt it had turned out badly and that Hallfred could not be trusted to keep the settlement, so he sent word to Ottar that he thought trouble was likely. Then word came to Hallfred that his father was ill and had asked to see him to make arrangements for his property.

Hallfred came and at once Ottar had him seized and fettered –

'Now there are two choices: one is to stay in fetters, the other, to let me alone decide things on your behalf.'

Hallfred said, 'Well, you don't deal half-heartedly with me, but it's better that you should decide, than that I should sit here in fetters.'

Then the fetters were taken off Hallfred.

Mar held the marriage feast for Gris and Kolfinna at his home, and she went with Gris back to his farm at Geitaskard. There was no great love for Gris on her part.

Olaf of Haukagil strongly urged his kinsman Hallfred to go abroad: 'I will give you money so that you can make your way among good men.'

His father too urged him strongly to go abroad. Ottar concluded the settlement between him and Gris and awarded a hundred of silver to Hallfred.[10] Hallfred would not accept it and said, 'I see your love for me, father. Your decision will stand, but I have a feeling that the trouble between him and myself will last a long time.'

It was a year later that Ottar moved south to Nordurardal.

5 | That summer Hallfred went south to the river Hvita, and when he reached the ship he spoke a verse:

4.

Eager am I yet, though our prow
be battered by breakers
(the river-stallion speeds on),   *river-stallion*: ship
to kiss Kolfinna,
for I love the well-born stave
of Endil's eel-land   *Endil*: sea-king; his *eel-land*: sea;
almost more now than if she,   *stave* of the sea: woman
so fine, were pledged to me.

Hallfred sailed out to Norway. He sought an audience with Earl Hakon the Powerful, who ruled Norway at that time. He went before him and greeted him. The earl asked who he was. He said he was an Icelander, 'and my mission is this, my lord, that I have composed a poem about you and wish for a hearing'.

The earl said, 'You seem like a man who deals boldly with rulers. You have that look about you, and you will indeed have a hearing.'

Hallfred recited the poem – it was a drapa[11] – and performed it magnificently. The earl thanked him and gave him a great axe inlaid with silver, and fine clothes, and invited him to stay with him over the winter. Hallfred accepted the offer. In the summer Hallfred sailed to Iceland, making land in the south, and by that time he owned great wealth. After that he spent several years travelling, and never came to northern Iceland.

Now one summer when he had arrived from Iceland he and his companions were anchored off Agdenes. There they met and spoke with people, asking the news. They were told that a change of ruler had come about in Norway. Earl Hakon was dead, and Olaf Tryggvason had come in his stead with a new religion and new laws.

Then the shipmates agreed to swear a vow that they would give a large sum of money to Frey if they got a wind to Sweden, or to Thor or Odin if they reached Iceland.[12] But if they had no wind out to sea, the king should decide matters. They got no wind out at all, and were forced to sail into Trondheim, heading into the harbour called Flagde. Many longships were moored there.

A great gale blew up from the sea overnight, so that the anchors would not hold. Then one of the crew on the longships said, 'These men on the trading ship are in a bad place, and it's not safe, for the gale is right where they're lying. We'll row out to them.'

They boarded a boat, thirty of them, and one was sitting in the bow. And as they reached the trading ship, the one sitting in the bow shouted, 'You're badly positioned, and there are dangerous waters just here. We'll help you to move.' He was large in build.

Hallfred said, 'What is your name?'

He said, 'I'm called Anchor-fluke.'[13]

And as they were speaking, the anchor-cable sheared in two, but the man sitting in the prow at once threw himself overboard and dived for the cable in the storm, catching it straight away. Then the anchor was pulled up.

Hallfred spoke this half-verse:

5.

Let's move our anchor-cables.
Sea-spray beats on the vessel.
The rope is straining rather.
Where is Anchor-fluke?

The man in the cloak[14] replied:

6.

I've found a green-cloaked fellow
to go after the cable;
he hauls at the anchor-rope.
Here is Anchor-fluke.

They rowed ahead of the ship into a safe anchorage. The merchants did not know who this man was, but later they were told it was the king himself who had helped them. After that they steered in to Lade. King Olaf was there, and he was told that these men must be heathens, newly arrived from Iceland. He summoned them to an audience, and when they arrived the king preached the faith to them and urged them to throw off the heathen ways and evil superstitions and to believe in the true God, creator of heaven and earth.

Hallfred answered the king's speech: 'Not without making a bargain, my lord, will I accept the religion you are preaching.'

The king said, 'What do you mean?'

He answered, 'You must never turn me away from you, whatever evil befalls me.'

The king said, 'You have a look about you as though there is little you would flinch at and much you could do to your credit.'

Then Hallfred went away, wanting to speak with the king again.

Later the king asked where the Icelander was and ordered men to go for him. Now Hallfred came before the king a second time, and the king said, 'Accept baptism now and what you asked will be done. But what is your name?'

He said he was called Hallfred.

'You are a determined man, and a brave one, and you must serve the devil no longer.'

Hallfred said, 'I have another request, my lord: that you should be my sponsor in baptism.'

The king said, 'You ask so much that there's no dealing with you.'

Then the bishop said, 'Do as he asks. God will do more for your sake, the more you do to strengthen God's Christendom.'

After this the king stood sponsor to Hallfred in baptism, and then he entrusted him to Thorkel Beak, his brother, and to Jostein,[15] and had them teach him holy doctrine. Hallfred vouches for this in a poem he composed about King Olaf:

7.

I gained as godfather one
who of all men (I vouch for this)
beneath the burden of Nordri's kin[16]
in the north was the greatest.

6 | Now Hallfred stayed with the king for a time. He composed a flokk about him and asked for a hearing. The king said he did not wish to hear it.[17] Hallfred said, 'You must decide that, but I will lose the doctrine you had taught to me, if you will not hear the poem, for the doctrine you had me learn is no more poetic than the poem I have composed about you.'

King Olaf said, 'Truly, you should be called Troublesome-poet;[18] but the poem will be heard.'

Hallfred performed the poem magnificently, and it was a drapa. And when it was finished the king said, 'This is a good poem. Now, accept from me a decorated sword. But you will have trouble managing it, because no sheath comes with it, and you must keep it for three days and three nights without harm coming to anyone.'

Then Hallfred spoke a verse:

8.

I know the wide-domained king
gave the adorner of verse
a naked sword, not grudging,
for his skiff of Austri's son.   *skiff of Austri's son*: poetry

83

The hilt of the war-hardener,   *war-hardener*: sword
the king's gift,[19] seems richly wrought;
the fierce lord favoured me with a blade;
a weapon I have earned.

Hallfred managed to take good care of the sword. He praised the gods a great deal and said it would turn out badly for people if they abused them. On one occasion he spoke this verse in the king's hearing:

9.

It was different in former days, when
I made fine sacrifices to the mind-swift
(change has come to the fortunes of men)
Lord of Hlidskjalf himself.   *Hlidskjalf*: Odin's high seat

The king said, 'A hateful verse. Now, make amends.'
Hallfred spoke again:

10.

The whole race of men to win
Odin's grace wrought poems
(I recall our forefathers'
exquisite works);
so with sorrow – for well the poet
was pleased with Vidrir's rule –   *Vidrir*: Odin
I kindle hate for the first husband
of Frigg, now I serve Christ.   *Frigg*: Odin's wife

Then the king said, 'You are extremely fond of the gods, and that is unworthy of you.'
Then Hallfred spoke a verse:

11.

I am neutral, cheerer of heroes, towards
the name of the raven-rite's priest,   *raven-rite's priest*: Odin, whose sacred
of him who repaid men's praise   creatures include the raven
with fraud, from heathen times.

The king said, 'There's no improvement here; now recite a verse to make atonement.'

Hallfred spoke a verse:

12.

Against me Frey and Freyja   *Njord*: a god, father of the fertility deities
(last year I left off Njord's deceit;   *Frey and Freyja*, his *deceit* seems to
let fiends ask mercy of Grimnir)[20]   stand for the old religion as a whole.
will bear fury, and the mighty Thor.
From Christ alone will I beg all love
(hateful to me is the Son's anger;
under the father of earth He holds
famous sway) and from God.

Then the king said, 'This is well recited, and better than not. Now, compose some more.'

Hallfred spoke a verse:

13.

It's the creed of the sovereign   *sovereign of Sogn* (i.e. Sogn in
of Sogn, to ban sacrifices.   Norway): King Olaf Tryggvason
We must renounce many
a long-held decree of norns.   *norns*: female beings who determine human fate
All mankind casts Odin's words
to the winds. Now I am forced
to forsake Freyja's kin
and pray to Christ.[21]

There was a man from Oppland called Ottar, and Kalf was the name of his brother. They were followers of the king, valiant men and highly regarded by him. They were jealous of Hallfred and felt he was too much in favour with the king. And one evening as they were drinking they started a serious quarrel. The king was present, and he judged their argument in Ottar's favour, since he saw that he would not come off well in a wrangle with Hallfred; then he left. And afterwards a battle of words flared up between them, which ended with Hallfred springing up and striking Ottar his death-blow with the axe Hakon's Gift.

Kalf and the men with him seized Hallfred and put him in fetters, for it was the law that a man who killed another in the king's chamber should be executed.[22] Next they went to the king and said that it was clear now what kind of man Hallfred was, and that he must be meaning to pick off all the king's men; and they defamed him as much as they could until the king ordered him to be executed the next morning. Kalf was pleased at that.

Now the following day they led him out to be executed.

Hallfred said, 'Where is the king?'

They answered, 'What's that to you? You are already condemned to death.'

Then Hallfred said, 'Is the man I wounded dead?' They said he was.

Hallfred said, 'If there is anyone here to whom I have been of service, let him repay it by taking me to where the king is, for I want to thank him for my time here.'

Then it turned out as the saying goes, that everyone has a friend among enemies, for there were some there who acknowledged that he had been of service to them, and they took him to where the king was, and his bishop.

And as Hallfred came towards them he said, 'Remember, my lord, what you promised – never to turn me away, so do not break faith with me. Another thing is that you are my godfather.'

Bishop Sigurd said to the king, 'Let him have the benefit of these things.'

'So be it,' said the king, and ordered him to be released straight away. This was now done, and Kalf was most displeased.

Now Hallfred stayed with the king's followers and swiftly got himself into favour, and although the king was colder towards him than before, he paid compensation for the killing on his behalf.

It happened one day that Hallfred went before the king and fell at his feet. The king noticed that he was shedding tears and asked what moved him so much.

He said, 'Your anger weighs upon me, and I want to be free of it.'

The king said, 'So be it. You will go on a mission for me after Christmas, and we will be reconciled, if you succeed in the venture. Now, have you got the sword I gave you?'

'Indeed I have, my lord, and it has never been sheathed.'

The king said, 'It is quite fitting for the Troublesome-poet to own the troublesome treasure. Now, would you be able to mention "sword" in every line of a verse?'

Hallfred said, 'I will try, if you wish, and I will do anything to get free of your anger.'

The king said, 'Then speak it now.'

At that Hallfred spoke a verse:

14.

One sword among swords
has made me sword-rich.
For brandishing Njords of swords   *Njords* (gods) *of swords*: warriors
sword-plenty now there'll be.
There would be no sword-problem
(I'm worthy of three swords)
if there were a sward-strip,[23]
a sheath for that sword.

The king thanked him and said that he showed great skill in his poetry, and gave him a sheath, very finely made.

'And even if it should happen,' said the king, 'that you incur a fine for not attending a meal or church, you will be pardoned more readily than others.'

Hallfred thanked the king.

One time it happened that the king asked where Hallfred was.

Kalf said, 'He must be keeping up his habit of sacrificing in secret – he has a Thor amulet[24] made out of walrus ivory in his money-bag, and you are being badly duped by him, my lord, when you don't have him properly put to the test.'

The king ordered Hallfred to be called to him at once to answer for himself. Hallfred arrived.

The king said, 'Are you guilty of the charge against you, that you make sacrifices?'

'It's not true, my lord,' said Hallfred. 'Let my money-bag be searched now.[25] I'd have had no chance for trickery here, even if I had wanted it.' Now nothing was found in his possession to prove this. 'This is deadly slander,' said Hallfred, 'and it will be the worse for Kalf if I can get hold of him. He brought me to the point of death once before.'

The king said, 'You two cannot be in the same place, and Kalf must return to his estate. As for you, Hallfred, you must go on a mission for me to Oppland, to Thorleif the Wise. He refuses to accept Christianity, and you must kill or blind him. He is the grandson of Thorleif Horda-Karason. I will grant this my luck,[26] and you can take however many men you wish.'

Hallfred said the venture was ignoble, 'but everything will be done as you wish. I want your uncle Jostein to go with me, and those of my fellow retainers that I choose, so that we are twenty-four in all.'

'Do as you please,' said the king, 'though I have sent men to Thorleif before and they have not carried out my wishes.'

After this Hallfred and his companions left the king, riding until they reached a forest which was close to Thorleif's farm. They dismounted from their horses in a clearing. Then Hallfred said, 'You must wait for me here until the third day dawns, and then set out back if I don't return.'

Jostein offered to go with him, but he did not want that. Hallfred then put on beggar's gear. He had colour put on his eyes, and turned his eyelids back, which changed his appearance greatly. He had a long bundle on his back, and in it was his sword King's Gift. Now he walked up to Thorleif's farm and to the mound on which he was sitting.[27] This was early in the day.

Thorleif greeted him and asked who he was.

'I'm just a pauper,' he said. 'I went to the king and he wanted to force his religion on me, but I ran away under cover, and before that killed one of the king's men. Now I want to ask you for some protection.'

To this Thorleif said little, but he asked a great deal about countries and harbours. Hallfred acquitted himself knowledgeably in all this.

Thorleif said, 'Was there perhaps a man called Hallfred with the king?'

He answered, 'I heard tell of him, and rarely to the good.'

Thorleif said, 'That man is always appearing to me in dreams, though that is nothing remarkable. But there will be men coming here from the king soon, and this Hallfred is the kind of man that I can't fathom out at all from the rumours. Well, whatever happens next, luck has left me.'

Then Thorleif suspected who the man was and made to stand up, but Hallfred grabbed at him and pushed him down, for he was far stronger. They rolled down the mound, and Hallfred got on top. He set his heel in Thorleif's eye and jerked the eye out of him.

At that Thorleif said, 'The king's luck is with you. I have long worried about you, and now it has happened, and I know that you are carrying out the king's command to blind or kill me. But now I want to ask you to grant me the other eye, and I will give you a knife and belt, both of them fine treasures. And I will come to your aid if the chance arises – and you're not unlikely to need this.'

Hallfred said he did not want to disobey the king's command and take fine treasures from him for it. He said he would rather take it upon himself to grant him the other eye. Thorleif thanked him, and they parted at that.

Hallfred went to his men and there was a joyful reunion. Thorleif went home to his farm and told no one of the injury until they were far away.

Hallfred and the others rode on their way until the route passed by Kalf's. Then Hallfred said, 'This evil man must be put to death.'

Jostein said, 'Don't do that – let us not mix good luck with bad.'

Hallfred answered, 'Justice has not been done. An excellent man has been maimed, but that scum of a man lives.' And he took hold of him and jabbed his eye out. Kalf moaned at that. Hallfred said, 'Once more you're showing your cur's spirit.' Then they made their way back, and came to the king as he sat over a board game. They greeted him. The king asked the news, and Hallfred told the whole story.[28]

The king said, 'You have done well. Now, show me the eye.'

Then Hallfred brought out Kalf's eye.

The king said, 'Where did you get such an eye?'

'This is Thorleif's eye.'

'No,' said the king, 'you must have done more than I ordered you.'

Then he showed him Thorleif's eye.

The king said, 'This is his eye, but the job is still no more than half done.'

Hallfred said, 'Now I have paid Kalf for having poked me with a spear-point as he was leading me to my death', and now he told everything as it had happened.

The king said, 'Now will you go to Thorleif again?'

Hallfred said, 'I'm not willing to go there, but I will go to Kalf and put his other eye out.'

The king said the matter should rest there. After that Hallfred received honour from the king.

7 | It happened once when Hallfred was in the presence of the king, that he said, 'I would like leave to sail on a trading voyage east to Eyrar this summer.'

The king said, 'That will not be refused you. But I have a feeling you won't be less eager to return to me than you are to leave, and a great deal will happen to you.'

Hallfred said, 'Well, that risk will have to be taken.' Then he set out. He had heard that Earl Sigvaldi was a great ruler. Hallfred obtained an audience with him and told him he had composed a poem about him.

The earl asked, 'Who are you?'

He told him.

'Are you the poet of King Olaf?'

'That's so,' said Hallfred, 'and I would like to have a hearing.'

The earl said, 'Why shouldn't that be to my honour if it pleases King Olaf?'

Hallfred recited the poem, and it was a flokk. The earl thanked him for the poem and gave him a gold arm-ring weighing half a mark, and invited him to stay there with him.

Hallfred thanked him for the invitation – 'but I must go to Sweden first'.

The earl told him he should decide.

That same autumn Hallfred went east to Vik, and was shipwrecked there on the east shore of Oslo Fjord, and lost a great amount of goods. From there Hallfred went to Kungalv and stayed a while.

Now one day when Hallfred was walking in the market a man came towards him. They greeted one another and Hallfred asked who he was.

He said he was called Audgisl and was travelling east from England, 'and I am not short of money. But is this Hallfred Troublesome-poet?'

That was so, he said.

'I have heard,' said Audgisl, 'that you have lost your goods. Now will you strike a bargain with me, to travel east to Vastergotland with me and stay over the winter, and I will give you ten marks of silver for your company. For I'm told your company is worth the price.'

Hallfred said he was willing. The route was perilous,[29] and many used to turn back. Hallfred and his companion had five pack-horses and one each for riding. They now went east into the forests, and one day they noticed a man coming towards them. They asked who he was; he replied that he was called Onund.

He was large in build and said he would be willing to travel with them, if they gave him some fee – 'I know all the routes around here.' Audgisl said he was not keen on him and that he did not know what sort of a fellow he was. Hallfred argued for taking him on, so they did, and he was to have twelve ounces of silver. Hallfred was then at his peak, but Audgisl was elderly.

Now they followed the track. Onund led throughout the day, and by evening they reached a wayside hut.

Then Hallfred said, 'Now we have three jobs. You, Onund, will collect wood – you have a big axe. Audgisl will make the fire, and I will fetch water.'

Then Onund said, 'It will be best to collect plenty of wood for the hut, because there'll be a lot of people coming here needing firewood.'

Hallfred said that was well spoken.

Then Audgisl said, 'I'd prefer to get the water, and you make the fire, Hallfred.'

'We'll do that, then,' he said.

Then Hallfred kindled the fire, while Onund fetched his load, and they each did their allotted job. It seemed to Hallfred that the others were being slow. He was crouching down to the fire and had slung his belt round his neck. There was a large knife attached to it, as men commonly had at that time, and the knife was lying on his back. Now Onund came in with his load. He sprang suddenly at Hallfred, and struck at him two-handed with the axe, but it hit the knife on the belt.

Now Hallfred grabbed at his legs and called out to God, saying, 'Help me, White Christ,[30] if you are so mighty as King Olaf says. Don't let this man overpower me.'

Then Hallfred got to his feet from under him, with the help of God and the luck of King Olaf. Next he pulled Onund up and hurled him down with such a crash that he lay unconscious, and the axe flew out of his hand. Hallfred had a small short-sword, which he drew, and at that moment Onund came round.

Hallfred asked, 'Have you killed Audgisl?'

He said it was so. Then Hallfred put the short-sword through him and dragged him out of the hut, then barred it firmly. And in the night Onund battered against the door, but Hallfred leaned against it from inside, and this went on until daybreak. In the morning Hallfred found Audgisl dead by the stream and took his knife and belt from him, and kept them with him. He attended to Audgisl's body according to the custom. He saw now that Onund must have been a criminal who killed people for their money, and the hut was laden with money and goods.

Hallfred then spoke a verse:

15.

I nourished on my white coins
– since I never wished to betray   *wealth-bestower*:
the wealth-bestower – the wielder   man, i.e. (ironically) Onund
of the raven-wine's flame.   *raven-wine*: blood; its *flame*: sword;
I was as good to the feeder   its *wielder*: warrior, Onund
of the battle-gull as I knew how,   *battle-gull*: raven; its *feeder*: warrior, Onund
but the shearer of sword-fire   *sword-fire*: (a corrupt kenning for) weapon; its
served mortal treachery on me.   *shearer*: warrior, Onund

92

Then he rode east to the mountains and came upon dangerous tracks.

8 | One day at evening Hallfred heard timber being cut, and rode towards the sound. There was a clearing ahead of him, and a man was there chopping wood. He was burly, with a red beard[31] and heavy brows, and rather villainous-looking. The man greeted him. Hallfred asked who he was.

He said he was called Bjorn – 'Come and stay with me.'

He accepted this.

Bjorn was most hospitable towards him. The farmer slept in one bed closet, and Hallfred in another. He was suspicious of Bjorn, and stood up behind the hangings with King's Gift drawn. At the same moment Bjorn thrust a weapon into the bed, so Hallfred struck him his death-blow. The mistress of the house called the men to get up and seize this criminal. The men threw clothes over Hallfred's weapon, and he was caught and bound.

Then word was sent to a man called Ubbi. He had a brother called Thorir, who was chieftain in those parts. He had a daughter called Ingibjorg. It was she to whom Audgisl had been married, and she was a most outstanding woman.

Now men came to an assembly to judge Hallfred. Thorir came, and Ubbi and Ingibjorg, and they agreed that Hallfred should be offered as a sacrifice. He went up to Ingibjorg and greeted her, saying that he had valuables with him which Audgisl had sent her.[32]

She said, 'I recognize the valuables.'

He told her the whole story, and spoke a verse:

16.

So fiercely have I paid back
(the Balder of the wound-snake fell   *wound-snake*: sword; its *Balder* (a god):
in the roar of shields; we are bereft   man, warrior; *roar of shields*: battle
of the ring-hurler) my hurts,   *ring-hurler*: (generous) man, Audgisl
that I made him lie praise-stripped,
the Balder of the reddened shield   *Balder of the reddened shield*: man, warrior,

(thus I avenged us both),   Onund
dead beside Audgisl.

Ingibjorg questioned him carefully about what had happened.
Hallfred spoke:

17.
In fury I pushed down
the cur-spirited launcher   *fish-trail*: sea; its *flame*: gold; *launcher* of gold:
of fish-trail's flame   (generous) man, i.e. (ironically) Onund
– I laid hands on the cur.
That sender of Hlokk's blizzard-skis   *Hlokk's* (valkyrie's) *blizzard*: battle; its
will not again confront   *skis*: arrows; their *sender*: man, warrior, Onund
(I reddened Odin's blizzard-blaze)   *Odin's* (Ygg's) *blizzard*: battle; its *blaze*:
folk with treachery.   (gleaming) sword

Ingibjorg said, 'I see that you must be telling the truth. Now you
must come home with me.'

Hallfred went home with her, and was stiff from the bonds. She
had food served to him. Thorir and Ingibjorg sent men up to the
mountains and found evidence there of everything Hallfred had said.
It was a great haul of money that was brought away from there. It
was agreed by all the men of the region that Hallfred should take the
money Onund had had, and they held him in great respect.

Hallfred set his heart on Ingibjorg and asked to marry her.

She said, 'Not everything would be taken care of then, for you are
a Christian and a foreigner here. But you should go to see my father
if this is what you want.'

He did so, and put his suit before Thorir, and they easily settled
the matter. And so it came about that Hallfred married Ingibjorg, and
he loved her deeply. They had a great fortune, and Hallfred enjoyed
great honour there. It was his main act of piety that he used to blow
the sign of the cross over his drink before drinking, but he prayed
little.

One time he said to Ingibjorg, 'I am planning to visit Olaf, king of
the Swedes, and to deliver a poem that I have composed for him.'

She said she expected he would want to hear the praise-poem.

9 | That summer Hallfred made his way to Sweden. He went to visit the king and greeted him. The king asked who he was; he told his name.

The king said, 'Your name is widely known, and you are the poet of excellent men.'

'I have composed a poem about you, and would like to have a hearing.'

The king agreed to this. Then he performed the poem. The king invited Hallfred to stay with him and gave him fine gifts.

Hallfred said that he had a farm and a wife in his tributary land, 'and I want to return there'.

The king wished him a good journey.

Hallfred came home to his wife, and remained there two years, but in the third year it happened one night that he dreamed that King Olaf[33] came to him, looking angry and saying he had cast his Christian faith right away – 'Come with your family to see me.'

Hallfred was gasping heavily when he awoke. Ingibjorg asked what he had been dreaming. He told her. 'But how would you feel about it? Are you at all willing to come with me? I have many good things to repay you, and I could reward you best by your adopting the faith.'

She said, 'It's to be expected that you would long to go there, and I understand that this religion must be far superior, and I will go with you.'

They had a son called Audgisl, who was two years old at the time. They went to visit King Olaf, and he welcomed Hallfred warmly, though he rebuked him severely and ordered a priest to shrive him.

Ingibjorg then gave birth to a son, and the boy was called Hallfred, his father giving him his own name. Then Ingibjorg was baptized, and both her sons.

King Olaf then said to Hallfred, 'Now you must atone to God for having been long among heathens and having lapsed badly from the faith.'

He said he earnestly wished to, and composed Uppreistardrapa,[34] a fine poem.

*

That winter Ingibjorg died, and this Hallfred felt as a terrible loss. In the spring he told the king that he longed to see Iceland.

The king said it should be as he wished. 'I have found you to be an excellent man. But the point will come when you will wish you were here with me, given the temperament you have. Now you must accept these treasures from me: a costly cloak, an arm-ring and a helmet, for it is uncertain whether we will meet again. Do not part with the treasures,' said the king, 'for they must go with you to church, or lie beside you in your coffin if you die at sea.'

The ring weighed three ounces. Hallfred was deeply moved by the parting with the king.

Audgisl, Hallfred's son, went east to his grandfather Thorir. For his son Hallfred, he found a good foster-home. Then Hallfred launched out to sea, and steered his ship into the estuary of Kolbeinsaros after the assembly. He said to his shipmates, 'My way lies south across the heath, to visit my father, and the twelve of us will ride together.'

Now the ship was hauled ashore, and they rode off twelve together, and turned west into Langadal. They were all in coloured clothing,[35] and they headed for Gris's shielings. Kolfinna was there, and other women with her. There were other shielings there; they lay in Laxardal, between Langadal and Skagafjord.

Kolfinna's shepherd told her that twelve men were riding towards the shieling, all in coloured clothing. She answered, 'They mustn't know the way.'

He said, 'They ride as if they know it, though.'

Now the men reached the shielings. Kolfinna welcomed Hallfred warmly and asked the news.

He answered, 'There's little news, but it can be told at leisure. We want to stay the night here.'

She answered, 'I'd prefer you to ride to the farmhouse, and I'll give you a guide.'

He said he wanted to stay there.

'I'll give you food,' she said, 'if that's all you want.'

Now they dismounted from their horses, and in the evening when they had eaten Hallfred said, 'For my part I mean to sleep with Kolfinna, and I give my comrades leave to do as they wish.'

There were other shielings there, and it is said that every one of them found himself a woman for the night.

Now when Hallfred and Kolfinna got into bed, he asked what kind of love there was between her and Gris. She said all was well. Hallfred said, 'It may be so, but it seems otherwise to me from the verses you have composed about Gris.'

She said she had not composed any.

He said, 'I've only been here a short time, and I have heard the verses.'

'Let me hear,' said Kolfinna, 'what kind of verse-making this is that's credited to me.'

18.

There streams from Gris
on to the bright slope of arm's ice   *arm's ice*: silver; its *bright slope*: lady, i.e.
(Hlin suffers anguish beside him)   Kolfinna; *Hlin*: the goddess Frigg,
hot sweat, most rank;   here Kolfinna
and gloomily the Ran   *Ran* (sea-goddess) *of eiderdown*: woman, Kolfinna
of eiderdown droops beside him
– the bright lady's nature
I praise – like a swan swimming.[36]

'That's no remedy for anything, and it's amazing that someone with your courage wants to utter such a thing.'

Hallfred said, 'I've heard another one too.'

19.

He lumbers (like a fulmar
swimming) to his bed,
the shearer of fjord-flame   *fjord-flame*: gold; its *shearer*: (generous or wealthy)
(herring-stuffed on the foam-path),   man, Gris; *foam-path*: sea
before he, beguiler of scythes,   *beguiler of scythes*: farmer, man
unlovely, dares to slide
(with the Gunn of lace he's not swift   *Gunn* (valkyrie) *of lace*: woman,
into bed) under the blankets.   Kolfinna

Kolfinna said, 'Gris wouldn't make verses about you, and it would be more fitting for you not to be so hostile to him, for one never knows where a person might turn up.'

Hallfred spoke this verse:

20.

Scarcely will the white fellow stride,
helmet-slicing, by the pantry
(he will go without the Eir   *Eir* (goddess) *of coins*: woman, Kolfinna
of coins), nor the grey dog Strut,
though the scythe-shover,
unlovely, has a wide milking-shed
(the sword-plain's keeper enjoys   *sword-plain*: shield, its *keeper*: warrior or
his livestock)[37] and a long sheep-pen.   man, Gris

Kolfinna was offended at that. Hallfred spoke another verse:

21.

Kolfinna said she felt
(I make more verse about this matter;
they say the sage lady is irked)
that foul words came from the poet.
But still from the young woman
it seems to the wealth-strewer   *wealth-strewer*: (generous) man, here Hallfred
(I am eager to fashion poetry)
that a precious fragrance issues.

The shepherd rode away during the night and told Gris what was going on, and he rode out with twenty men. Early in the morning Hallfred and his men made ready to leave, and before he mounted his horse he spoke this verse:

22.

Little would I care though I
(the tree of the foam-land's stallion   *foam-land's stallion*: ship; its *tree*:
has taken risks for the lady)   man, Hallfred
were slaughtered in the splendid one's arms,

98

if I managed to sleep embraced
by the Sif of the gown-chest.   *Sif* (goddess) *of the gown-chest*: woman, Kolfinna
I cannot confine my too-great grief
for the bright linden of the lock.   *linden* (tree) *of the lock*: woman, Kolfinna
                                      (locks and keys being female attributes)

Then he leapt on to his horse and smiled. Kolfinna said, 'Why are
you smiling now?'

He spoke a verse:

23.

This I know not: what will be
on the lips of the ocean-glow's post   *ocean-glow*: gold; its *post*: woman,
(I let my love flow out   Kolfinna
to the Unn of wave's day),   *wave's day* (i.e. brightness): gold; its *Unn* (?water
if the rejoicers in giant-stories,   goddess): woman
sterling men, find out   *giant-stories*: gold; its *rejoicers*: men
(off the hog's son Gris I flayed   *flay a goatskin*[38] *off a hog*: dupe
a goatskin) what makes me grin.

Hallfred wanted to give Kolfinna the cloak King's Gift,[39] but she
would not accept it. And before they rode away he spoke this
verse:

24.

Home come the caring-Naumas
of sea-blaze (the ladies' looks   *sea-blaze*: gold; its *caring-Naumas*
are splendid) from the shielings,   (goddesses): women
sleek-haired each one.
I renounce my responsibility,
ruffled as the Syn of the ale-bench   *Syn* (goddess) *of the ale-bench*:
may be – let each man take   woman, Kolfinna
his lady unto himself.

After that they rode away.

10 | Now Gris arrived at the shielings. Kolfinna was in low spirits.
   | Gris saw that, and spoke a verse:

25.

Now it seems to me, stave   *stave of skirts*: woman
of skirts, that there has been
(I see a stir in the district)
some bustle while I was away.
Strangers here have worked
(the woman walks swollen-faced;
the handsome girl dries
her eyes) a grievous scorn.

There with Gris was Einar, son of Thorir Thrandarson.[40] Gris
wanted to ride off in pursuit, but Kolfinna urged against it, saying it
was not certain that he would gain by that. Still, Gris wanted to ride
after them. They rode on past Audolfsstadir to the river Blanda. By
then Hallfred and the others had reached the middle of the river.
Gris shot a spear at Hallfred, but he caught it in mid-air, and shot it
back at Gris. Einar tried to ward it off with his axe, but the spear
pierced Einar's chest and he fell dead. Gris said Hallfred was running.
He said he would not go further than out of the river, and told them
to attack, but Gris did not ride against him. Then the people urged
that Hallfred should compensate Gris for all the dishonour he had
done him. Hallfred asked what he was demanding.

Gris answered, 'I would be satisfied if I had both the arm-rings,
Earl's Gift and King's Gift.'[41]

Hallfred replied, 'Something else will happen before that', and at
this they parted.

Hallfred rode south to his brother's, for his father had died by
then, and he stayed the winter there. And in the spring as he was
travelling north a blizzard started up ahead of them. Hallfred said it
was a storm raised by sorcery. They rode along Vatnsdal to the point
where an enclosure lay ahead of them, and twenty men sprang out
from behind it. It was Mar of Masstadir who had come there. He
sprang out at Hallfred, and Hallfred at once struck at him, but Mar

parried with a sacrificial trough and was not wounded.[42] Hallfred
then rode out of the gate to the enclosure.

Mar shouted, 'Let's attack them.'

Hallfred spoke a verse:

26.

The self-deluding sinker	*sinker of treasures*: man, here Mar
of treasures is set on assailing me	
(I face the fellow's threats,	
think each day of the splendid lady).	
For the bragging Balder of the	
carrion-maker, it would be less bother	*carrion-maker*: sword; its *Balder* (god):
(this is my surmise) to lick	man, Mar
the inside of his sacrificial trough.	

With that they parted.

There was a man called Hunrod who lived at Moberg. Gris was
one of his thingmen. Thorkel Scratcher lived at Hof at that time, for
Ingolf was dead.

That winter Hallfred composed verses about Gris, and when Gris
heard about this, he went to see Hunrod and asked his advice, 'for
Hallfred is hardening towards me in pure hatred'.

Hunrod said, 'What I urge you to do is this: prepare a case and
summons Hallfred to the Hunavatn Assembly.'

Gris did this. He rode south in the spring to Hreduvatn lake, for
Galti and Hallfred were living there then.

Gris summonsed Hallfred to the Hunavatn Assembly for the
killing of Einar; and after he and his men had left, Galti said to
Hallfred, 'What's your intention concerning this case?'

He answered, 'I intend to ask my aunt's husband Thorkel for support.'

They rode north in the spring, thirty men in all, and stayed at Hof.
Hallfred asked Thorkel what support he could have from him.
Thorkel said he would back him in the case if some kind of honour-
able terms were offered.

Now people arrived at the assembly, and during the assembly
Hallfred and Galti went to Thorkel's booth to ask how the case
would go.

He replied, 'I will offer to arbitrate if you and the other side are willing, and if so I will try to make a settlement.'

Now they went out of the booth. Brand Avaldason, Kolfinna's brother, was leaning against the wall of the booth, and he struck Galti his death-blow as he came out.

Hallfred told Thorkel of the killing. Thorkel went with him to Gris's booth and told him to give the man up, 'or else we will break up the booth'.

Then Hild, Brand's mother, rushed to the doorway, asking what Thorkel wanted. He told his business. Hild said, 'You weren't thinking of killing my son when I swept you under the fold of my cloak and saved your life after the killing of Glaedir, when Thorgils and Thorvald were out to kill you.'

Thorkel said, 'That's in the past now. The women can leave the booth, and we're going to look for the man.'

Brand had covered himself with a woman's hood, and that way managed to escape without being discovered. Thorkel said he must have gone to Hunrod's booth.

Then Hallfred said, 'I doubt now whether I can rely on any support and so I challenge Gris to a duel.'

Gris said he had made a challenge like that before.

Then Hallfred spoke a verse:

27.
Then at last my love
for Kolfinna will be proven
to the strife-snatchers   *strife-snatchers*: warriors, men
in the steel-maid's slander,   *steel-maid's* (valkyrie's) *slander*: battle
if, rash, on the river-bank,
the steerer of the launcher-steed   *launcher-steed*: ship; its *steerer*: man
(I am content to have it so)
sets me against Gris.

Gris was holding the sword the emperor of Byzantium had given him.

Hallfred saw Kolfinna walking one day. He spoke a verse:

28.

It seems to me, as I gaze
at the Gunn of filmy head-dresses,   *Gunn* (valkyrie) *of head-dresses*: woman,
as though there sailed the ship-roads   Kolfinna; *ship-roads*: sea
a ship between two islands;
and, looking at the Saga   *Saga* (goddess) *of seams*: woman, Kolfinna
of seams in the throng of women,
as though, adorned, there glided
a vessel with gilded tackle.

The night before they were to fight, Hallfred was sleeping in his bed. He dreamed that King Olaf appeared to him, and he felt overjoyed, and yet afraid.

The king said, 'Sleep is upon you, though it will feel as though you were awake. You are set on a wrongful course in fighting Gris in such a bad cause, and he has prayed, asking God that whichever of you has the better cause should gain the victory. Take my advice – accept with thanks that there should be no duel, and pay compensation.And in the morning when you are dressed, go out to the hillock beside the assembly-place, where the tracks meet. You will see some men riding. Get into conversation with them, and it may be that after that you will feel there is something more important than a duel with Gris, and don't pay any heed even if he thinks you are afraid.'

Hallfred woke and considered what had happened to him, and told the man next to him. He answered, 'Now you're scared of the hog,[43] and it would have been better to have accepted a fair settlement before, when he favoured it, but now your enemies will reckon that you daren't fight.'

Hallfred said, 'Anyone who wants to reckon so, can. I will take King Olaf's advice – it will turn out best for me.'

In the morning he went out to the hillock, and saw some men riding towards him in coloured clothing. He asked them for news, and they told of the fall of King Olaf.[44] Hallfred started as though he had been hit by a stone, and at once walked back to his booth in great sorrow, and lay straight down on his bed.

Then Gris's men said that his behaviour was unmanly. Gris answered, 'It is not that way at all. I had less honour from the emperor of Byzantium, yet it struck me as the greatest news when I lost my sovereign. Love for a liege lord burns hot; and it is well that I will not be fighting against the king's luck. I still want Thorkel to arbitrate, as was the plan.'

Thorkel said, 'I will now take on the case for Hallfred and make a settlement between the two of you.'

Hallfred agreed to this.

'This is my judgement,' said Thorkel, 'that the killing of Einar should offset the killing of Galti, with the visit to Kolfinna offsetting the difference in rank between the two men. But for the Gris-verses Hallfred must give Gris something of great value.'

Then Hallfred spoke a verse:

29.
Wealth at an evil time
I have most worthily gained
(with jingling gold the king
and earl have ennobled me)
if for a scrap of verse
I have to pay a fool's fine
to the gourmet Gris, and cannot
possess the wide ocean's tree.   *wide ocean's tree*: woman, Kolfinna (a non-standard kenning)

Thorkel told him to stop his verse-making, 'and hand over some treasure, even if it's not one of the king's gifts'.

Then Hallfred handed him the arm-ring Sigvaldi's Gift, and at that they parted.

II | After that Hallfred went south across the heath and put the farm into the hands of his sister Valgerd, then went abroad from Kolbeinsaros and made land in the Orkneys. From there he went to Norway and, reaching Sognefjord during the Winter Nights, he inquired about the fall of King Olaf. He then composed the Olafsdrapa,[45] and this refrain is from it:

30.
All the lands of the north are desolated
by the death of the king.
All peace is confounded by the fall
of the flight-shunning son of Tryggvi.

He felt so deeply about the fall of King Olaf that he took no pleasure in anything, and he planned to go south to Denmark or east to Sweden. They were lying at anchor in a secluded creek, when Hallfred heard that Earl Eirik was not far inland from there. He fell on the idea of killing the earl, even though he might be killed instantly himself.

But in the night he dreamed that King Olaf appeared to him, saying, 'This is an ill-conceived plan you have in mind. Instead, compose a drapa about the earl.'[46]

The following morning Hallfred went to the farm where Earl Eirik was staying and into the main room where the earl was drinking. Hallfred was recognized, seized, and taken to the earl. The earl wanted to have him put to death for having mutilated Thorleif the Wise, and ordered him to be fettered. But as the fetters were brought towards him he lunged and grabbed them from the man who was trying to put them on him, and swung them at his head so that he at once fell dead. The earl ordered him to be killed immediately so he could not do any more harm.

An aged man got up from one of the outer benches and went before the earl, asking him to grant Hallfred his life; it was Thorleif the Wise.[47]

Then the earl said, 'It is completely unwarranted for you to ask for him to be spared, or don't you remember that he mutilated you?'

Thorleif answered, 'I wish Hallfred to be spared, my lord.'

The earl said it should be as he wished.

Thorleif took Hallfred into his following.

He said to Hallfred, 'Do you want me to arbitrate between the earl and you?'

Hallfred said he wanted that very much.

'Then you must compose a poem about the earl and have it done within three nights.'[48]

And when the three nights had passed Hallfred declaimed the poem, and this is the opening of it:

31.
You are worthy to hear an ode,
war-valiant one, wrought for you.

The earl rewarded him well for the poem, 'but I don't want to keep you here with me, because of King Olaf Tryggvason'.

Thorleif invited Hallfred to his home, and he went there. Thorleif proved an excellent friend to him.

The following summer Hallfred sailed out to Iceland and steered his ship into Leiruvog on the south coast. At that time Onund[49] was living at Mosfell. Hallfred owed half a mark of silver to a farmhand of Onund, and responded to him rather harshly. The farmhand came home and told of his trouble. Hrafn said the chances were that he would come off the worse in any dealings with Hallfred, and the following morning Hrafn rode to the ship, intending to shear the cables and prevent Hallfred and his men from sailing. After that people intervened to reconcile them. The farmhand was paid twice as much as he was owed, and at that they parted.

The summer after that Hallfred and Gunnlaug Serpent-tongue travelled together as far as Melrakkasletta. By that time Hrafn had married Helga. Hallfred told Gunnlaug how things had fared between him and Hrafn.[50]

Hallfred spent a long time travelling, but took no pleasure in anything after the fall of King Olaf. He went to Sweden to visit his son Audgils, and see to his property. He intended to settle there.

When Hallfred was nearly forty he intended to go to Iceland to collect his money. His son Hallfred was with him then. They had a rough passage. Hallfred did his share of the bailing, but was very ill, and one day as he left off bailing he sat down on the boom, and at that moment a huge wave flung him down into the ship with the boom on top of him.

Then Thorvald[51] said, 'Are you in difficulty, brother?'

He spoke a verse:

32.
The boom hammered me,
storm-battered, on heart and side.
So badly have the breakers
scarcely struck at you.
Still more is my ship hammered;
I am soaked through.
The spray-flecked billow
will not pity its poet.

They realized how ill he was and took him aft in the ship and tended him and asked how he felt. He spoke this verse:

33.
The lady of linen drapes
will wipe her soft brow
(the beauty won great renown,
unrivalled) with her white hand,
if the trees of the battle-wall   *battle-wall*: shield; its *trees*: warriors, men
must launch me over the gunwale
dead – in times past I brought grief
to the young beauty.

Then they saw a woman following the ship. She was tall and dressed in a mail-coat. She walked on the waves as if on land. Hallfred looked and saw that it was his fetch.

Hallfred said, 'I declare myself finally parted from you.'

She said, 'Will you take me on, Thorvald?'

He said he would not.

Then the boy Hallfred said, 'I'll take you on', at which she disappeared.

Then Hallfred said, 'To you, my son, I want to give the sword

King's Gift, but the other treasures are to lie in the coffin beside me if I die.'

A little later he died and was laid in a coffin, with his treasures beside him – the cloak, helmet and arm-ring – and then it was all launched overboard. The coffin washed up on the Holy Isle (Iona)[52] in the Hebrides, where the abbot's serving-lads found it. They broke open the coffin and stole the goods, and sank the body in a deep bog.

That same night the abbot dreamed that King Olaf appeared to him.

He looked angry and said that he had wicked servants – 'They have broken up my poet's ship and stolen his goods, and bound a stone about his neck. Now get the true story from them, or else strange things will befall you.'

Now the servants were caught, and they confessed and were allowed to go free. Hallfred's body was carried to the church and buried with honour. A chalice was made from the arm-ring, an altar-cloth from the cloak, and candlesticks from the helmet.

Thorvald and the others reached Iceland and went to Ottarsstadir, where they stayed over the winter. Thorvald went abroad in the summer, but Hallfred took over the farmstead at Ottarsstadir. He was nicknamed Troublesome-poet.[53] He was a man of great standing, and accomplished, and many people are descended from him.

And here the saga of Hallfred ends.

Translated by Diana Whaley

THE SAGA OF GUNNLAUG
SERPENT-TONGUE

This is the saga of Hrafn and of Gunnlaug Serpent-tongue, as told by the priest Ari Thorgilsson the Learned, who had the greatest knowledge of stories of the settlement and other ancient lore of anyone who has lived in Iceland.[1]

I | There was a man named Thorstein. He was the son of Egil, the son of Skallagrim, the son of the hersir Kveldulf from Norway. Thorstein's mother was named Asgerd. She was Bjorn's daughter. Thorstein lived at Borg in Borgarfjord. He was rich and a powerful chieftain, wise, tolerant and just in all things. He was no great prodigy of either size or strength, as his father, Egil, had been. Learned men say that Egil was the greatest champion and duellist Iceland has ever known and the most promising of all the farmers' sons, as well as a great scholar and the wisest of men. Thorstein, too, was a great man and was popular with everyone. He was a handsome man with white-blond hair and fine, piercing eyes.

Scholars say that the Myrar folk – the family descended from Egil – were rather a mixed lot. Some of them were exceptionally good-looking men, whereas others are said to have been very ugly. Many members of the family, such as Kjartan Olafsson, Killer-Bardi and Skuli Thorsteinsson, were particularly talented in various ways. Some of them were also great poets, like Bjorn, the Champion of the Hitardal people, the priest Einar Skulason, Snorri Sturluson and many others.[2]

Thorstein married Jofrid, the daughter of Gunnar Hlifarson.

Gunnar was the best fighter and athlete among the farmers in Iceland at that time. The second best was Gunnar of Hlidarendi, and Steinthor from Eyri was the third. Jofrid was eighteen years old when Thorstein married her. She was a widow, having previously been married to Thorodd, the son of Tunga-Odd. It was their daughter, Hungerd, who was being brought up at Borg by Thorstein. Jofrid was an independent woman. She and Thorstein had several children, although only a few of them appear in this saga. Their eldest son was named Skuli, the next Kollsvein and the third Egil.

2 | It is said that, one summer, a ship came ashore in the Gufua estuary. The skipper was a Norwegian named Bergfinn, who was rich and getting on in years. He was a wise man. Farmer Thorstein rode down to the ship. He usually had the greatest say in fixing the prices at the market, and that was the case this time. The Norwegians found themselves lodgings, and Thorstein himself took the skipper in, since Bergfinn asked him if he could stay at his house. Bergfinn was rather withdrawn all winter, but Thorstein was very hospitable to him. The Norwegian was very interested in dreams.

One spring day, Thorstein asked Bergfinn if he wanted to ride with him up to Valfell. The Borgarfjord people held their local assembly there in those days, and Thorstein had been told that the walls of his booth had fallen in. The Norwegian replied that he would indeed like to go, and they set out later that day, taking a servant of Thorstein's with them. They rode until they arrived at Grenjar farm, which was near Valfell. A poor man named Atli, a tenant of Thorstein's, lived there. Thorstein asked him to come and help them with their work, and to bring with him a turf-cutting spade and a shovel. He did so, and when they arrived at the place where the booths were they all set to work digging out the walls.

It was a hot, sunny day, and when they had finished digging out the walls, Thorstein and the Norwegian sat down inside the booth. Thorstein dozed off, but his sleep was rather fitful. The Norwegian was sitting beside him and let him finish his dream undisturbed. When Thorstein woke up, he was in considerable distress. The

Norwegian asked him what he had been dreaming about, since he slept so badly.

'Dreams don't mean anything,'[3] Thorstein answered.

Now when they were riding home that evening, the Norwegian again asked what Thorstein had been dreaming about.

'If I tell you the dream,' Thorstein replied, 'you must explain it as it really is.' The Norwegian said that he would take that risk.

Then Thorstein said, 'I seemed to be back home at Borg, standing outside the main doorway, and I looked up at the buildings, and saw a fine, beautiful swan up on the roof-ridge. I thought that I owned her, and I was very pleased with her. Then I saw a huge eagle fly down from the mountains. He flew towards Borg and perched next to the swan and chattered to her happily. She seemed to be well pleased with that. Then I noticed that the eagle had black eyes and claws of iron; he looked like a gallant fellow.

'Next, I saw another bird fly from the south. He flew here to Borg, settled on the house next to the swan and tried to court her. It was a huge eagle too. As soon as the second eagle arrived, the first one seemed to become rather ruffled, and they fought fiercely for a long time, and I saw that they were both bleeding. The fight ended with each of them falling off the roof-ridge, one on each side. They were both dead.[4] The swan remained sitting there, grief-stricken and dejected.

'And then I saw another bird fly from the west. It was a hawk. It perched next to the swan and was gentle with her, and later they flew off in the same direction. Then I woke up. Now this dream is nothing much,' he concluded, 'and must be to do with the winds, which will meet in the sky, blowing from the directions that the birds appeared to be flying from.'

'I don't think that's what it's about,' said the Norwegian.

'Interpret the dream as seems most likely to you,' Thorstein told him, 'and let me hear that.'

'These birds must be the fetches of important people,' said the Norwegian. 'Now, your wife is pregnant and will give birth to a pretty baby girl, and you will love her dearly. Noble men will come from the directions that the eagles in your dream seemed to fly from, and will ask for your daughter's hand. They will love her more intensely than is reasonable and will fight over her, and both of them will die as a result. And then a third man, coming from the direction from which the hawk flew, will ask for her hand, and she will marry him. Now I have interpreted your dream for you. I think things will turn out like that.'

'Your explanation is wicked and unfriendly,' Thorstein replied. 'You can't possibly know how to interpret dreams.'

'You'll see how it turns out,' the Norwegian retorted.

After this, Thorstein began to dislike the Norwegian, who went away that summer. He is now out of the saga.

3 | Later in the summer, Thorstein got ready to go to the Althing. Before he left, he said to his wife, Jofrid, 'As matters stand, you are soon going to have a baby. Now if you have a girl, it must be left out to die, but if it is a boy, it will be brought up.'

When the country was completely heathen, it was something of a custom for poor men with many dependants in their families to have their children exposed.[5] Even so, it was always considered a bad thing to do.

When Thorstein had said this, Jofrid replied, 'It is most unworthy for a man of your calibre to talk like that, and it cannot seem right to you to have such a thing done.'

'You know what my temper is like,' Thorstein replied. 'It will not do for anyone to go against my command.'

Then he rode off to the Althing, and Jofrid gave birth to an extremely pretty baby girl. The women wanted to take the child to Jofrid, but she said that there was little point in that, and had her shepherd, whose name was Thorvard, brought to her.

'You are to take my horse and saddle it,' Jofrid told him, 'and take this child west to Egil's daughter Thorgerd at Hjardarholt. Ask her to bring the child up in secret, so that Thorstein never finds out about it. For I look upon the child with such love that I really have no heart to have it left out to die. Now, here are three marks of silver which you are to keep as your reward. Thorgerd will procure a passage abroad for you out there in the west, and will give you whatever you need for your voyage overseas.'

Thorvard did as she said. He rode west to Hjardarholt with the child and gave it to Thorgerd. She had it brought up by some of her tenants who lived at Leysingjastadir on Hvammsfjord. She also secured a passage for Thorvard on a ship berthed at Skeljavik in Steingrimsfjord in the north, and made provision for his voyage. Thorvard sailed abroad from there, and is now out of this saga.

Now when Thorstein came back from the Althing, Jofrid told him that the child had been exposed – just as he said it should be – and that the shepherd had run away, taking her horse with him. Thorstein said she had done well, and found himself another shepherd.

Six years passed without this coming out. Then one day Thorstein rode west to Hjardarholt, to a feast given by his brother-in-law Olaf Peacock, who was then the most respected of all the chieftains in the west country. Thorstein was warmly welcomed at Hjardarholt, as might be expected.

Now it is said that, one day during the feast, Thorgerd was sitting in the high seat talking to her brother Thorstein, while Olaf was making conversation with other men. Three girls were sitting on the bench opposite them.

Then Thorgerd said, 'Brother, how do you like the look of those girls sitting opposite us?'

'Very well,' he replied, 'though one of them is by far the prettiest, and she has Olaf's good looks, as well as the fair complexion and features we men of Myrar have.'

'You are certainly right, brother, when you say that she has the complexion and features of the Myrar men,' Thorgerd said, 'but she has none of Olaf Peacock's looks, since she is not his daughter.'

'How can that be,' Thorstein asked, 'since she's your daughter?'

'Kinsman,' she answered, 'to tell you the truth, this beautiful girl is your daughter, not mine.' Then she told him everything that had happened, and begged him to forgive both her and his wife for this wrong.

'I cannot blame you for this,' Thorstein said. 'In most cases, what will be will be, and you two have smoothed over my own stupidity well enough. I'm so pleased with this girl that I count myself very lucky to have such a beautiful child. But what's her name?'

'She's named Helga,' Thorgerd replied.

'Helga the Fair,' mused Thorstein. 'Now you must get her ready to come home with me.'

And so she did. When he left, Thorstein was given splendid gifts, and Helga rode home to Borg with him and was brought up there, loved and cherished by her father and mother and all her relatives.

4 | In those days, Illugi the Black, the son of Hallkel Hrosskelsson, lived at Gilsbakki in Hvitarsida. Illugi's mother was Thurid Dylla, the daughter of Gunnlaug Serpent-tongue. Illugi was the second-greatest chieftain in Borgarfjord, after Thorstein Egilsson. He was a great landowner, very strong-willed, and he stood by his friends. He was married to Ingibjorg, the daughter of Asbjorn Hardarson from Ornolfsdal. Ingibjorg's mother was Thorgerd, the daughter of Skeggi from Midfjord. Ingibjorg and Illugi had many children, but only a few of them appear in this saga. One of their sons was named Hermund and another Gunnlaug.[6] They were both promising fellows, and were then in their prime.

It is said that Gunnlaug was somewhat precocious, big and strong, with light chestnut hair, which suited him, dark eyes and a rather ugly nose. He had a pleasant face, a slender waist and broad shoulders. He was very manly, an impetuous fellow by nature, ambitious even in his youth, stubborn in all situations and ruthless. He was a gifted poet, albeit a somewhat abusive one, and was also called Gunnlaug Serpent-tongue. Hermund was the more popular of the two brothers and had the stamp of a chieftain about him.

When Gunnlaug was twelve years old, he asked his father for some wares to cover his travelling expenses, saying that he wanted to go abroad and see how other people lived. Illugi was reluctant to agree to this. He said that people in other countries would not think highly of Gunnlaug when he himself found that he could scarcely manage him as he would wish to at home.

Soon after this, Illugi went out early one morning and saw that his outhouse was open and that half a dozen sacks of wares had been laid out in the yard, with some saddle-pads. He was very surprised at this. Then someone came along leading four horses; it was his son Gunnlaug.

'I put the sacks there,' he said. Illugi asked why he had done so. He said they would do to help cover his travelling expenses.

'You will not undermine my authority,' said Illugi, 'nor are you going anywhere until I see fit.' And he dragged the sacks back inside.

Then Gunnlaug rode off and arrived down at Borg that evening. Farmer Thorstein invited him to stay and he accepted. Gunnlaug told Thorstein what had happened between him and his father. Thorstein said he could stay as long as he liked, and he was there for a year. He studied law with Thorstein and everyone there thought well of him.

Gunnlaug and Helga often amused themselves by playing board games with each other. They quickly took a liking to each other, as events later bore out. They were pretty much the same age. Helga was so beautiful that learned men say that she was the most beautiful woman there has ever been in Iceland. She had such long hair that it could cover her completely, and it was radiant as beaten gold. It was thought that there was no equal to Helga the Fair throughout Borgarfjord or in places further afield.

Now one day, when people were sitting around in the main room at Borg, Gunnlaug said to Thorstein, 'There is still one point of law that you haven't taught me – how to betroth myself to a woman.'

'That's a small matter,' Thorstein replied, and he taught Gunnlaug the procedure.

Then Gunnlaug said, 'Now you should check whether I've understood properly. I'll take you by the hand and act as though I'm betrothing myself to your daughter Helga.'

'I don't see any need for that,' Thorstein said.

Then Gunnlaug grabbed his hand. 'Do this for me,' he said.

'Do what you like,' Thorstein said, 'but let those present here know that it will be as if this had not been said, and there must be no hidden meaning to it.'

Then Gunnlaug named his witnesses and betrothed himself to Helga. Afterwards, he asked whether that would do. Thorstein said that it would, and everyone there thought it was great fun.

5 | There was a man named Onund who lived to the south at Mosfell. He was a very wealthy man, and held the godord for the headlands to the south. He was married, and his wife was named Geirny. She was the daughter of Gnup, the son of Molda-Gnup who settled at Grindavik in the south. Their sons were Hrafn, Thorarin and Eindridi. They were all promising men, but Hrafn was the most accomplished of them in everything. He was a big, strong man, extremely good-looking and a good poet. When he was more or less grown up, he travelled about from country to country and was well respected wherever he went.

Thorodd Eyvindarson the Wise and his son Skafti lived at Hjalli in Olfus in those days. Skafti was Lawspeaker[7] in Iceland at that time. His mother was Rannveig, the daughter of Gnup Molda-Gnupsson, and so Skafti and the sons of Onund were cousins. There was great friendship between them, as well as this blood tie.

Thorfinn Seal-Thorisson was then living out at Raudamel. He had seven sons, and they were all promising men. Their names were[8] Thorgils, Eyjolf and Thorir, and they were the leading men in that district.

All the men who have been mentioned were living at the same time, and it was about this time that the best thing ever to have happened in Iceland occurred: the whole country became Christian and the entire population abandoned the old faith.

For six years now, Gunnlaug Serpent-tongue, who was mentioned earlier, had been living partly at Borg with Thorstein and partly at Gilsbakki with his father Illugi. By now, he was eighteen years old, and he and his father were getting on much better.

There was a man named Thorkel the Black. He was a member of Illugi's household and a close relative of his, and had grown up at Gilsbakki. He came into an inheritance at As in Vatnsdal up in the north, and asked Gunnlaug to go with him to collect it, which he did.

They rode north to As together and, thanks to Gunnlaug's assistance, the men who had Thorkel's money handed it over to them.

On their way home from the north, they stayed overnight at Grimstungur with a wealthy farmer who was living there. In the morning, a shepherd took Gunnlaug's horse, which was covered in sweat when they got it back. Gunnlaug knocked the shepherd senseless. The farmer would not leave it at that, and demanded compensation for the blow. Gunnlaug offered to pay him a mark, but the farmer thought that was too little.[9] Then Gunnlaug spoke a verse:

1.

I offered the middle-strong man,	
that lord of lodgings, a mark;	*lord of lodgings*: man
you'll receive a fine silver-grey wire	*silver-grey wire*: piece of silver
for the one who spits flame from his gums.	*flame from . . . gums*: blood
It will cause you regret	
if you knowingly let	
the sea-serpent's couch	*sea-serpent's couch*: gold
slip out of your pouch.	

They arranged that Gunnlaug's offer should be accepted, and when the matter was settled Gunnlaug and Thorkel rode home.

A little while later, Gunnlaug asked his father a second time for wares, so that he could travel abroad.

'Now you may have your own way,' Illugi replied, 'since you are better behaved than you used to be.'

Illugi rode off at once and bought Gunnlaug a half-share in a ship from Audun Halter-dog. The ship was beached in the Gufua estuary. This was the same Audun who, according to *The Saga of the People of Laxardal*, would not take the sons of Osvif the Wise abroad after the killing of Kjartan Olafsson, though that happened later than this.

When Illugi came home, Gunnlaug thanked him profusely. Thorkel the Black went along with Gunnlaug, and their wares were loaded on to the ship. While the others were getting ready, Gunnlaug was at Borg, and he thought it was nicer to talk to Helga than to work with the traders.

One day, Thorstein asked Gunnlaug if he would like to ride up to his horses in Langavatnsdal with him. Gunnlaug said that he would, and they rode together until they arrived at Thorstein's shielings, which were at a place called Thorgilsstadir. Thorstein had a stud of four chestnut horses there. The stallion was a splendid creature, but was not an experienced fighter. Thorstein offered to give the horses to Gunnlaug, but he said that he did not need them, since he intended to go abroad. Then they rode over to another stud of horses. There was a grey stallion there with four mares; he was the best horse in Borgarfjord. Thorstein offered to give him to Gunnlaug.

'I don't want this horse any more than I wanted the others,' Gunnlaug answered. 'But why don't you offer me something I will accept?'

'What's that?' Thorstein asked.

'Your daughter, Helga the Fair,' Gunnlaug replied.

'That will not be arranged so swiftly,' he said, and changed the subject.

They rode home, down along the Langa river.

Then Gunnlaug spoke: 'I want to know how you will respond to my proposal.'

'I'm not taking any notice of your nonsense,' Thorstein replied.

'This is quite serious, and not nonsense,' Gunnlaug said.

'You should have worked out what you wanted in the first place,' Thorstein countered. 'Haven't you decided to go abroad? And yet you're carrying on as if you want to get married. It wouldn't be suitable for you and Helga to marry while you are so undecided. I'm not prepared to consider it.'

'Where do you expect to find a match for your daughter if you won't marry her to Illugi the Black's son?' Gunnlaug asked. 'Where in Borgarfjord are there more important people than my father?'

'I don't go in for drawing comparisons between men,' Thorstein parried, 'but if you were such a man as he is you wouldn't be turned away.'

'To whom would you rather marry your daughter than me?' Gunnlaug asked.

'There's a lot of good men around here to choose from,' Thorstein replied. 'Thorfinn at Raudamel has seven sons, all of them very manly.'

'Neither Onund nor Thorfinn can compare with my father,' Gunnlaug answered, 'considering that even you clearly fall short of his mark. What have you done to compare with the time when he took on Thorgrim Kjallaksson the godi and his sons at the Thorsnes Assembly by himself and came away with everything there was to be had?'

'I drove away Steinar, the son of Onund Sjoni[10] – and that was considered quite an achievement,' Thorstein replied.

'You had your father, Egil, to help you then,' Gunnlaug retorted. 'Even so, there aren't many farmers who would be safe if they turned down a marriage bond with me.'

'You save your bullying for the people up in the hills,' Thorstein replied. 'It won't count for much down here in the marshes.'

They arrived home later that evening, and the following morning Gunnlaug rode up to Gilsbakki and asked his father to ride back to Borg with him to make a marriage proposal.

'You are an unsettled fellow,' Illugi replied. 'You've already planned to go abroad, yet now you claim that you have to occupy yourself chasing after women. I know that Thorstein doesn't approve of such behaviour.'

'Nevertheless,' Gunnlaug replied, 'while I still intend to go abroad, nothing will please me unless you support me in this.'

Then Illugi rode down from Gilsbakki to Borg, taking eleven men with him. Thorstein gave them a warm welcome.

Early the next morning, Illugi said to Thorstein: 'I want to talk to you.'

'Let's go up on to the Borg[11] and talk there,' Thorstein suggested.

They did so, and Gunnlaug went along too.

Illugi spoke first: 'My kinsman Gunnlaug says that he has already spoken of this matter on his own behalf; he wants to ask for the hand of your daughter Helga. Now I want to know what is going to come of this. You know all about his breeding and our family's wealth. For our part, we will not neglect to provide either a farm or a godord, if that will help bring it about.'

'The only problem I have with Gunnlaug is that he seems so unsettled,' Thorstein replied. 'But if he were more like you, I shouldn't put it off.'

'If you deny that this would be an equal match for both our families, it will bring an end to our friendship,' Illugi warned.

'For our friendship's sake and because of what you've been saying, Helga will be promised to Gunnlaug, but not formally betrothed to him, and she will wait three years for him. And Gunnlaug must go abroad and follow the example of good men, and I will be free of any obligation if he doesn't come back as required, or if I don't like the way he turns out.'

With that, they parted. Illugi rode home and Gunnlaug rode off to his ship, and the merchants put to sea as soon as they got a fair wind. They sailed to the north of Norway, and then sailed in past Trondheim to Nidaros,[12] where they berthed the ship and unloaded.

6 | Earl Eirik Hakonarson and his brother Svein were ruling Norway in those days. Earl Eirik was staying on his family's estate at Lade, and was a powerful chieftain. Skuli Thorsteinsson was there with him: he was one of the earl's followers and was well thought of.

It is said that Gunnlaug and Audun Halter-dog went to Lade with ten other men. Gunnlaug was dressed in a grey tunic and white breeches.[13] He had a boil on his foot, right on the instep, and blood and pus oozed out of it when he walked. In this state, he went before the earl with Audun and the others and greeted him politely. The earl recognized Audun, and asked him for news from Iceland, and Audun told him all there was. Then the earl asked Gunnlaug who he was, and Gunnlaug told him his name and what family he came from.

'Skuli Thorsteinsson,' the earl asked, 'what family does this fellow come from in Iceland?'

'My lord,' he replied, 'give him a good welcome. He is the son of the best man in Iceland, Illugi the Black from Gilsbakki, and, what's more, he's my foster-brother.'[14]

'What's the matter with your foot, Icelander?' the earl asked.

'I've got a boil on it, my lord,' he replied.

'But you weren't limping?'

'One mustn't limp while both legs are the same length,' Gunnlaug replied.

Then a man named Thorir, who was one of the earl's followers, spoke: 'The Icelander is rather cocky. We should test him a bit.'[15]

Gunnlaug looked at him, and spoke:

2.

One of the train's
a particular pain;
be wary of trusting him:
he's evil and black.

Then Thorir made as if to grab his axe.

'Leave it be,' said the earl. 'Real men don't pay any attention to things like that. How old are you, Icelander?'

'Just turned eighteen,' Gunnlaug replied.

'I swear that you'll not survive another eighteen,' the earl declared.

'Don't you call curses down on me,' Gunnlaug muttered quite softly, 'but rather pray for yourself.'

'What did you just say, Icelander?' the earl asked.

'I said what I thought fit,' Gunnlaug replied, 'that you should not call curses down on me, but should pray more effective prayers for yourself.'

'What should I pray for, then?' asked the earl.

'That you don't meet your death in the same way as your father Earl Hakon did.'[16]

The earl turned as red as blood, and ordered that the fool be arrested at once.

Then Skuli went to the earl and said, 'My lord, do as I ask: pardon the man and let him get out of here as quickly as he can.'

'Let him clear off as fast as he can if he wants quarter,' the earl commanded, 'and never set foot in my kingdom again.'

Then Skuli took Gunnlaug outside and down to the quay, where there was a ship all ready for its voyage to England. Skuli procured a passage in it for Gunnlaug and his kinsman Thorkel, and Gunnlaug entrusted his ship and the other belongings he did not need to keep with him to Audun for safe-keeping. Gunnlaug and Thorkel sailed off into the North Sea, and arrived in the autumn at the port of London, where they drew the ship up on to its rollers.

7 | King Ethelred, the son of Edgar, was ruling England at that time. He was a good ruler, and was spending that winter in London. In those days, the language in England was the same as that spoken in Norway and Denmark, but there was a change of language when William the Bastard conquered England. Since William was of French descent, the French language was used in England from then on.[17]

As soon as he arrived in London, Gunnlaug went before the king and greeted him politely and respectfully. The king asked what country he was from. Gunnlaug told him – 'and I have come to you, my lord, because I have composed a poem about you, and I should like you to hear it'.

The king said that he would. Gunnlaug recited the poem expressively and confidently. The refrain goes like this:

3.
The whole army is cowed
by England's great king, as by God:
at Ethelred's feet all bow down,
menfolk and martial king's clan.

The king thanked him for the poem and, as a reward, gave him a cloak of scarlet[18] lined with the finest furs and with an embroidered band stretching down to the hem. He also made him one of his followers. Gunnlaug stayed with the king all winter and was well thought of.

Early one morning, Gunnlaug met three men in a street. Their leader was named Thororm. He was big and strong, and rather obstreperous.

'Northerner,'[19] he said, 'lend me some money.'

'It's not a good idea to lend money to strangers,' Gunnlaug replied.

'I'll pay you back on the date we agree between us,' he promised.

'I'll risk it then,' said Gunnlaug, giving Thororm the money.

A little while later, Gunnlaug met the king and told him about the loan.

'Now things have taken a turn for the worse,' the king replied. 'That fellow is the most notorious robber and thug. Have nothing more to do with him, and I will give you the same amount of money.'

'Then your followers are a pretty pathetic lot,' Gunnlaug answered. 'We trample all over innocent men, but let thugs like him walk all over us! That will never happen.'

Shortly afterwards, Gunnlaug met Thororm and demanded his money back, but Thororm said that he would not pay up. Then Gunnlaug spoke this verse:

4.

O god of the sword-spell,	*sword-spell*: battle; its *god* (Modi): warrior
you're unwise to withhold your wealth	
from me; you've deceived	
the sword-point's reddener.	*sword-point's reddener*: warrior, who reddens the
I've something else to explain –	sword's point with blood
'Serpent-tongue' as a child	
was my name. Now again	
here's my chance to prove why.	

'Now I'll give you the choice the law provides for,' said Gunnlaug. 'Either you pay me my money or fight a duel with me in three days' time.'

The thug laughed and said, 'Many people have suffered badly at my hands, and no one has ever challenged me to a duel before. I'm quite ready for it!'

With that, Gunnlaug and Thororm parted for the time being. Gunnlaug told the king how things stood.

'Now we really are in a fix,' he said. 'This man can blunt any weapon just by looking at it. You must do exactly as I tell you. I am going to give you this sword, and you are to fight him with it, but make sure that you show him a different one.'

Gunnlaug thanked the king warmly.

When they were ready for the duel, Thororm asked Gunnlaug what kind of sword he happened to have. Gunnlaug showed him and drew the sword, but he had fastened a loop of rope around the hilt of King's Gift and he slipped it over his wrist.

As soon as he saw the sword, the berserk said, 'I'm not afraid of that sword.'[20]

He struck at Gunnlaug with his sword, and chopped off most of his shield. Then Gunnlaug struck back with his sword King's Gift. The berserk left himself exposed, because he thought Gunnlaug was using the same weapon as he had shown him. Gunnlaug dealt him his death-blow there and then. The king thanked him for this service, and Gunnlaug won great fame for it in England and beyond.

In the spring, when ships were sailing from country to country, Gunnlaug asked Ethelred for permission to do some travelling. The king asked him what he wanted to do.

'I should like to fulfil a vow I have made,' Gunnlaug answered, and spoke this verse:

5.

I will most surely visit
three shapers of war *shapers of war*: kings
and two earls of lands,
as I promised worthy men.
I will not be back
before the point-goddess's son *point-goddess* (Gefn): valkyrie; her
summons me; he gives me *son*: Ethelred
a red serpent's bed to wear. *serpent's bed*: gold

'And so it will be, poet,' said the king, giving him a gold arm-ring weighing six ounces. 'But,' he continued, 'you must promise to come back to me next autumn, because I don't want to lose such an accomplished man as you.'

8 | Then Gunnlaug sailed north to Dublin with some merchants.
At that time, Ireland was ruled by King Sigtrygg Silk-beard, the son of Olaf Kvaran and Queen Kormlod. He had been king for only a short while.[21] Straight away, Gunnlaug went before the king and greeted him politely and respectfully. The king gave him an honourable welcome.

'I have composed a poem about you,' Gunnlaug said, 'and I should like it to have a hearing.'

'No one has ever deigned to bring me a poem before,' the king replied. 'Of course I will listen to it.'

Gunnlaug recited the drapa, and the refrain goes like this:

6.
To the troll-wife's stallion   *troll-wife's stallion*: wolf
Sigtrygg feeds carrion.

And it contains these lines as well:

7.
I know which offspring,
descendant of kings,
I want to proclaim
– Kvaran's son is his name;
it is his habit
to be quite lavish:
the poet's ring of gold
he surely won't withhold.

8.
Let the sovereign
eloquently explain
if he's found phrasing neater
than mine, in drapa metre.[22]

The king thanked Gunnlaug for the poem, and summoned his treasurer.

'How should I reward the poem?' he asked.

'How would you like to, my lord?' the treasurer said.

'What kind of reward would it be if I gave him a pair of knorrs?' the king asked.

'That is too much, my lord,' he replied. 'Other kings give fine treasures – good swords or splendid gold bracelets – as rewards for poems.'

The king gave Gunnlaug his own new suit of scarlet clothes, an embroidered tunic, a cloak lined with exquisite furs and a gold bracelet which weighed a mark. Gunnlaug thanked him profusely and stayed there for a short while. He went on from there to the Orkney islands.

In those days, the Orkney islands were ruled by Earl Sigurd Hlodvesson. He thought highly of Icelanders. Gunnlaug greeted the earl politely and said that he had a poem to present to him. The earl said that he would indeed listen to Gunnlaug's poem, since he was from such an important family in Iceland. Gunnlaug recited the poem, which was a well constructed flokk. As a reward, the earl gave him a broad axe, decorated all over with silver inlay, and invited Gunnlaug to stay with him.

Gunnlaug thanked him for the gift, and for the invitation, too, but said that he had to travel east to Sweden. Then he took passage with some merchants who were sailing to Norway, and that autumn they arrived at Kungalf in the east. As always, Gunnlaug's kinsman, Thorkel, was still with him. They took a guide from Kungalf up into Vastergotland and so arrived at the market town named Skarar. An earl named Sigurd, who was rather old, was ruling there.[23] Gunnlaug went before him and greeted him politely, saying that he had composed a poem about him. The earl listened carefully as Gunnlaug recited the poem, which was a flokk. Afterwards, the earl thanked Gunnlaug, rewarded him generously and asked him to stay with him over the winter.

Earl Sigurd held a great Yule[24] feast during the winter. Messengers from Earl Eirik arrived on Yule eve. They had travelled down from Norway. There were twelve of them in all, and they were bearing gifts for Earl Sigurd. The earl gave them a warm welcome and seated them next to Gunnlaug for the Yule festival. There was a great deal of merriment. The people of Vastergotland declared that there was no better or more famous earl than Sigurd; the Norwegians thought that Earl Eirik was much better. They argued about this and, in the end, both sides called upon Gunnlaug to settle the matter. It was then that Gunnlaug spoke this verse:

9.

Staves of the spear-sister,	*spear-sister*: valkyrie; her *staves*: warriors
you speak of the earl:	
this old man is hoary-haired,	
but has looked on tall waves.	
Before his billow-steed	*billow-steed*: ship
battle-bush Eirik, tossed	*battle-bush*: warrior
by the tempest, has seen	
more blue breakers back in the east.	

Both sides, but particularly the Norwegians, were pleased with this assessment. After Yule, the messengers left with splendid gifts from Earl Sigurd to Earl Eirik. They told Earl Eirik about Gunnlaug's assessment. The earl thought that Gunnlaug had shown him both fairness and friendliness, and spread the word that Gunnlaug would find a safe haven in his domain. Gunnlaug later heard what the earl had had to say about the matter. Gunnlaug had asked Earl Sigurd for a guide to take him east into Tiundaland in Sweden, and the earl found him one.

9 | In those days, Sweden was ruled by King Olaf the Swede, the son of King Eirik the Victorious and Sigrid the Ambitious, daughter of Tosti the Warlike. He was a powerful and illustrious king, and was very keen to make his mark.

Gunnlaug arrived in Uppsala around the time of the Swedes' Spring Assembly. When he managed to get an audience, he greeted the king, who welcomed him warmly and asked him who he was. He said that he was an Icelander. Now Hrafn Onundarson was with the king at the time.

'Hrafn,' the king said, 'what family does this fellow come from in Iceland?'

A big, dashing man stood up from the lower bench, came before the king and said, 'My lord, he comes from the finest of families and is the noblest of men in his own right.'

'Then let him go and sit next to you,' the king said.

'I have a poem to present to you,' Gunnlaug said, 'and I should like you to listen to it properly.'

'First go and sit yourselves down,' the king commanded. 'There is no time now to sit and listen to poems.'

And so they did. Gunnlaug and Hrafn started to chat, telling one another about their travels. Hrafn said that he had left Iceland for Norway the previous summer, and had come east to Sweden early that winter. They were soon good friends.

One day when the assembly was over, Hrafn and Gunnlaug were both there with the king.

'Now, my lord,' Gunnlaug said, 'I should like you to hear my poem.'

'I could do that now,' the king replied.

'I want to recite my poem now, my lord,' Hrafn said.

'I could listen to that, too,' he replied.

'I want to recite my poem first,' Gunnlaug said, 'if you please.'

'I should go first, my lord,' Hrafn said, 'since I came to your court first.'

'Where did our ancestors ever go with mine trailing in the wake of yours?' Gunnlaug asked. 'Nowhere, that's where! And that's how it's going to be with us, too!'

'Let's be polite enough not to fight over this,' Hrafn replied. 'Let's ask the king to decide.'

'Gunnlaug had better recite his poem first,' the king declared, 'since he takes it badly if he doesn't get his own way.'

Then Gunnlaug recited the drapa he had composed about King Olaf, and when he had finished, the king said, 'How well is the poem composed, Hrafn?'

'Quite well, my lord,' he answered. 'It is an ostentatious poem, but is ungainly and rather stilted, just like Gunnlaug himself is in temperament.'

'Now you must recite your poem, Hrafn,' the king said.

He did so, and when he had finished, the king asked: 'How well is the poem put together, Gunnlaug?'

'Quite well, my lord,' he replied. 'It is a handsome poem, just like Hrafn himself is, but there's not much to either of them. And,' he continued, 'why did you compose only a flokk for the king, Hrafn? Did you not think he merited a drapa?'[25]

'Let's not talk about this any further,' Hrafn said. 'It might well crop up again later.' And with that they parted.

A little while later, Hrafn was made one of King Olaf's followers. He asked for permission to leave, which the king granted.

Now when Hrafn was ready to leave, he said to Gunnlaug, 'From now on, our friendship is over, since you tried to do me down in front of the court. Sometime soon, I will cause you no less shame than you tried to heap on me here.'

'Your threats don't scare me,' Gunnlaug replied, 'and I won't be thought a lesser man than you anywhere.'

King Olaf gave Hrafn valuable gifts when they parted, and then Hrafn went away.

Hrafn left the east that spring and went to Trondheim, where he fitted out his ship. He sailed to Iceland during the summer, and brought his ship into Leiruvog, south of Mosfell heath. His family and friends were glad to see him, and he stayed at home with his father over the winter.

Now at the Althing that summer, Hrafn the Poet met his kinsman Skafti the Lawspeaker.

'I should like you to help me ask Thorstein Egilsson for permission to marry his daughter Helga,' Hrafn said.

'Hasn't she already been promised to Gunnlaug Serpent-tongue?' Skafti answered.

'Hasn't the time they agreed passed by now?' Hrafn countered. 'Besides, Gunnlaug's so proud these days that he won't take any notice of that or care about it at all.'

'We'll do as you please,' Skafti replied.

Then they went over to Thorstein Egilsson's booth with several other men. Thorstein gave them a warm welcome.

'My kinsman Hrafn wants to ask for the hand of your daughter Helga,' Skafti explained. 'You know about his family background, his wealth and good breeding, and that he has numerous relatives and friends.'

'She is already promised to Gunnlaug,' Thorstein answered, 'and I want to stick to every detail of the agreement I made with him.'

'Haven't the three winters you agreed between yourselves passed by now?' Skafti asked.

'Yes,' said Thorstein, 'but the summer isn't gone, and he might yet come back during the summer.'

'But if he hasn't come back at the end of the summer, then what hope will we have in the matter?' Skafti asked.

'We'll all come back here next summer,' Thorstein replied, 'and then we'll be able to see what seems to be the best way forward, but there's no point in talking about it any more at the moment.'

With that they parted, and people rode home from the Althing. It was no secret that Hrafn had asked for Helga's hand.

Gunnlaug did not return that summer. At the Althing the next summer, Skafti and Hrafn argued their case vehemently, saying that Thorstein was now free of all his obligations to Gunnlaug.

'I don't have many daughters to look after,' Thorstein said, 'and I'm anxious that no one be provoked to violence on their account. Now I want to see Illugi the Black first.'

And so he did.

When Illugi and Thorstein met, Thorstein asked, 'Do you consider me to be free of all obligation to your son Gunnlaug?'

'Certainly,' Illugi replied, 'if that's how you want it. I cannot add much to this now, because I don't altogether know what Gunnlaug's circumstances are.'

Then Thorstein went back to Skafti. They settled matters by deciding that, if Gunnlaug did not come back that summer, Hrafn's and Helga's marriage should take place at Borg at the Winter Nights, but that Thorstein should be without obligation to Hrafn if Gunnlaug were to come back and go through with the wedding. After that, people rode home from the Althing. Gunnlaug's return was still delayed, and Helga did not like the arrangement at all.

10 | Now we return to Gunnlaug, who left Sweden for England in the same summer as Hrafn went back to Iceland. He received valuable gifts from King Olaf when he left. King Ethelred gave Gunnlaug a very warm welcome. He stayed with the king all winter, and was thought well of.

In those days, the ruler of Denmark was Canute the Great, the son of Svein.[26] He had recently come into his inheritance, and was continually threatening to lead an army against England, since his father, Svein, had gained considerable power in England before his death there in the west. Furthermore, there was a huge army of Danes in Britain at that time. Its leader was Heming, the son of Earl Strut-Harald and the brother of Earl Sigvaldi. Under King Canute, Heming was in charge of the territory that King Svein had previously won.

During the spring, Gunnlaug asked King Ethelred for permission to leave.

'Since you are my follower,' he replied, 'it is not appropriate for you to leave me when such a war threatens England.'

'That is for you to decide, my lord,' Gunnlaug replied. 'But give me permission to leave next summer, if the Danes don't come.'

'We'll see about it then,' the king answered.

Now that summer and the following winter passed, and the Danes did not come. After midsummer, Gunnlaug obtained the king's permission to leave, went east to Norway and visited Earl Eirik at Lade in Trondheim. The earl gave him a warm welcome this time, and invited him to stay with him. Gunnlaug thanked him for the offer, but said that he wanted to go back to Iceland first, to visit his intended.

'All the ships prepared for Iceland are gone now,' said the earl.

Then a follower said, 'Hallfred Troublesome-poet was still anchored out under Agdenes yesterday.'[27]

'That might still be the case,' the earl replied. 'He sailed from here five nights ago.'

Then Earl Eirik had Gunnlaug taken out to Hallfred, who was glad to see him. An offshore breeze began to blow, and they were very cheerful. It was late summer.

'Have you heard about Hrafn Onundarson's asking for permission to marry Helga the Fair?' Hallfred asked Gunnlaug.

Gunnlaug said that he had heard about it, but that he did not know the full story. Hallfred told him everything he knew about it, and added that many people said that Hrafn might well prove to be no less brave than Gunnlaug was. Then Gunnlaug spoke this verse:

10.

Though the east wind has toyed
with the shore-ski this week   *shore-ski*: ship
I weigh that but little –
the weather's weaker now.
I fear more being felt
to fall short of Hrafn in courage
than living on to become
a grey-haired gold-breaker.[28]   *gold-breaker*: man

Then Hallfred said, 'You will need to have better dealings with Hrafn than I did. A few years ago, I brought my ship into Leiruvog, south of Mosfell heath. I ought to have paid Hrafn's farmhand half a mark of silver, but I didn't give it to him. Hrafn rode over to us with sixty men and cut our mooring ropes, and the ship drifted up on to the mud flats and looked as if it would be wrecked. I ended up granting Hrafn self-judgement, and paid him a mark.[29] That is all I have to say about him.'

From then on, they talked only about Helga. Hallfred heaped much praise on her beauty. Then Gunnlaug spoke:

11.

The slander-wary god
of the sword-storm's spark   *sword-storm*: battle; its *spark*: sword; *god* (Thund)
mustn't court the land of the cloak,   *of the* sword: warrior (Hrafn); *land of the*
snow-covered with linen.   *cloak*: woman

134

For when I was a lad,   *forearm's fire*: ring; its *headlands*: fingers; *played* on the
I played on the headlands   fingers: was her favourite (*or* caressed her)
of the forearm's fire
with that land-fishes' bed-land.   *land-fishes*: snakes; their *bed*: gold;
    gold-*land*: woman

'That is well composed,' Hallfred said.

They came ashore at Hraunhofn on Melrakkasletta a fortnight before winter, and unloaded the ship.

There was a man named Thord, who was the son of the farmer on Melrakkasletta. He was always challenging the merchants at wrestling, and they generally came off worse against him. Then a bout was arranged between him and Gunnlaug, and the night before, Thord called upon Thor to bring him victory. When they met the next day, they began to wrestle. Gunnlaug swept both Thord's legs out from under him, and his opponent fell down hard, but Gunnlaug twisted his own ankle out of joint when he put his weight on that leg, and he fell down with Thord.

'Maybe your next fight won't go any better,' Thord said.

'What do you mean?' Gunnlaug asked.

'I'm talking about the quarrel you'll be having with Hrafn when he marries Helga the Fair at the Winter Nights. I was there when it was arranged at the Althing this summer.'

Gunnlaug did not reply. Then his foot was bandaged and the joint reset. It was badly swollen.

Hallfred and Gunnlaug rode south with ten other men, and arrived at Gilsbakki in Borgarfjord on the same Saturday evening that the others were sitting down to the wedding feast at Borg. Illugi was glad to see his son Gunnlaug and his companions. Gunnlaug said that he wanted to ride down to Borg there and then, but Illugi said that this was not wise. Everyone else thought so too, except Gunnlaug, but he was incapacitated by his foot – although he did not let it show – and so the journey did not take place. In the morning, Hallfred rode home to Hreduvatn in Nordurardal. His brother Galti, who was a splendid fellow, was looking after their property there.[30]

11 | Now we turn to Hrafn, who was sitting down to his wedding feast at Borg. Most people say that the bride was rather gloomy. It is true that, as the saying goes, 'things learned young last longest', and that was certainly the case with her just then.

It so happened that a man named Sverting, who was the son of Goat-Bjorn, the son of Molda-Gnup, asked for the hand of Hungerd, the daughter of Thorodd and Jofrid. The wedding was to take place up at Skaney later in the winter, after Yule. A relative of Hungerd's, Thorkel the son of Torfi Valbrandsson, lived at Skaney. Torfi's mother was Thorodda, the sister of Tunga-Odd.

Hrafn went home to Mosfell with his wife Helga. One morning, when they had been living there for a little while, Helga was lying awake before they got up, but Hrafn was still sleeping. His sleep was rather fitful, and when he woke up, Helga asked him what he had been dreaming about. Then Hrafn spoke this verse:

12.

I thought I'd been stabbed
by a yew of serpent's dew   *serpent's dew*: blood; its *yew* (twig): sword
and with my blood, O my bride,
your bed was stained red.
Beer-bowl's goddess, you weren't   *beer-bowl's goddess* (Njorun): woman
able to bind up the damage
that the drubbing-thorn dealt to Hrafn: *drubbing-thorn*: sword
linden of herbs, that might please you.   *linden* (tree) *of herbs*: woman

'I will never weep over that,' Helga said. 'You have all tricked me wickedly. Gunnlaug must have come back.' And then Helga wept bitterly.

Indeed, a little while later news came of Gunnlaug's return. After this, Helga grew so intractable towards Hrafn that he could not keep her at home, and so they went back to Borg. Hrafn did not enjoy much intimacy with her.

Now people were making plans for the winter's other wedding. Thorkel from Skaney invited Illugi the Black and his sons. But while

Illugi was getting ready, Gunnlaug sat in the main room and did not make any move towards getting ready himself.

Illugi went up to him and said, 'Why aren't you getting ready, son?'

'I don't intend to go,' Gunnlaug replied.

'Of course you will go, son,' Illugi said. 'And don't set so much store by yearning for just one woman. Behave as though you haven't noticed, and you'll never be short of women.'

Gunnlaug did as his father said, and they went to the feast. Illugi and his sons were given one high seat, and Thorstein Egilsson, his son-in-law Hrafn and the bridegroom's group had the other one, opposite Illugi. The women were sitting on the cross-bench, and Helga the Fair was next to the bride. She often cast her eyes in Gunnlaug's direction, and so it was proved that, as the saying goes, 'if a woman loves a man, her eyes won't hide it'. Gunnlaug was well turned out, and had on the splendid clothes that King Sigtrygg had given him. He seemed far superior to other men for many reasons, what with his strength, his looks and his figure.

People did not particularly enjoy the wedding feast. On the same day as the men were getting ready to leave, the women started to break up their party, too, and began getting themselves ready for the journey home. Gunnlaug went to talk to Helga, and they chatted for a long time. Then Gunnlaug spoke this verse:

13.
For Serpent-tongue no full day
under mountains' hall was easy   *mountains' hall*: sky
since Helga the Fair
took the name of Hrafn's Wife.
But her father, white-faced
wielder of whizzing spears,
took no heed of my tongue
– the goddess was married for money.   *goddess* (Eir): woman

And he spoke another one, too:

14.

Fair wine-goddess, I must reward   *wine-goddess* (Gefn): woman, Helga
your father for the worst wound –
the land of the flood-flame steals joy   *flood-flame*: gold; its *land*: woman
from this poet – and also your mother.
For beneath bedclothes they both
made a band-goddess so beautiful: *band-goddess*: woman wearing garments
the devil take the handiwork   with woven bands, Helga
of that bold man and woman!

And then Gunnlaug gave Helga the cloak Ethelred had given him,
which was very splendid. She thanked him sincerely for the gift.

Then Gunnlaug went outside. By now, mares and stallions – many
of them fine animals – had been led into the yard, saddled up and
tethered there. Gunnlaug leapt on to one of the stallions and rode at
a gallop across the hayfield to where Hrafn was standing. Hrafn had
to duck out of his way.

'There's no need to dodge, Hrafn,' Gunnlaug said, 'because I don't
mean to do you any harm at the moment, though you know what
you deserve.'

Hrafn answered with this verse:

15.

Glorifier of battle-goddess,   *battle-goddess* (Saga): valkyrie; her *glorifier*: warrior
god of the quick-flying weapon,   *god* (Ull) *of the . . . weapon*: warrior
it's not fitting for us to fight
over one fair tunic-goddess.   *tunic-goddess* (Fulla): woman
Slaughter-tree, south over sea   *Slaughter-tree*: warrior, Gunnlaug
there are many such women,
you will rest assured of that.
I set my wave-steed to sail.   *wave-steed*: ship

'There may well be a lot of women,' Gunnlaug replied, 'but it
doesn't look that way to me.'

Then Illugi and Thorstein ran over to them, and would not let
them fight each other. Gunnlaug spoke a verse:

16.

The fresh-faced goddess
of the serpent's day   *serpent's day* (i.e. brightness): gold; its *goddess* (Eir): woman
was handed to Hrafn for pay –
he's equal to me, people say –
while in the pounding of steel   *pounding of steel*: battle
peerless Ethelred delayed
my journey from the east – that's why
the jewel-foe's less greedy for words.   *jewel-foe*: generous man, Gunnlaug

After that, both parties went home, and nothing worth mentioning happened all winter. Hrafn never again enjoyed intimacy with Helga after she and Gunnlaug had met once more.

That summer, people made their way to the Althing in large groups: Illugi the Black took his sons Gunnlaug and Hermund with him; Thorstein Egilsson took his son Kollsvein; Onund from Mosfell took all his sons; and Sverting the son of Goat-Bjorn also went. Skafti was still Lawspeaker then.

One day during the Althing, when people were thronging to the Law Rock and the legal business was done, Gunnlaug demanded a hearing and said, 'Is Hrafn Onundarson here?'

Hrafn said that he was.

Then Gunnlaug Serpent-tongue said, 'You know that you have married my intended and have drawn yourself into enmity with me because of it. Now I challenge you to a duel to take place here at the Althing in three days' time on Oxararholm[31] (Axe River Island).'

'That's a fine-sounding challenge,' Hrafn replied, 'as might be expected from you. Whenever you like – I'm quite ready for it!'

Both sets of relatives were upset by this, but, in those days, the law said that anyone who felt he'd received underhand treatment from someone else could challenge him to a duel.

Now when the three days were up, they got themselves ready for the duel. Illugi the Black went to the island with his son, along with a large body of men; and Skafti the Lawspeaker went with Hrafn, as did his father and other relatives. Before Gunnlaug went out on to the island, he spoke this verse:

17.

I'm ready to tread the isle
where combat is tried
– God grant the poet victory –
a drawn sword in my hand;
into two I'll slice the hair-seat   *hair-seat*: head
of Helga's kiss-gulper;   *Helga's kiss-gulper*: her lover, Hrafn
finally, with my bright sword,
I'll sever his head from his neck.

Hrafn replied with this one:

18.

The poet doesn't know
which poet will rejoice –
wound-sickles are drawn,   *wound-sickles*: swords
the edge fit to bite leg.
Alone and a widow, the young girl,
the thorn-tray, will hear from the Thing   *thorns*: brooch-pins; their
– though bloodied I might be –   *tray*: woman
news of her man's bravery.

Hermund held his brother Gunnlaug's shield for him; and Sverting, Goat-Bjorn's son, held Hrafn's. Whoever was wounded was to pay three marks of silver to release himself from the duel. Hrafn was to strike the first blow, since he had been challenged. He hacked at the top of Gunnlaug's shield, and the blow was so mightily struck that the sword promptly broke off below the hilt. The point of the sword glanced up and caught Gunnlaug on the cheek, scratching him slightly. Straight away, their fathers, along with several other people, ran between them.

Then Gunnlaug said, 'I submit that Hrafn is defeated, because he is weaponless.'

'And I submit that you are defeated,' Hrafn replied, 'because you have been wounded.'

Gunnlaug got very angry and said, all in a rage, that the matter had not been resolved. Then his father, Illugi, said that there should not be any more resolving for the moment.

'Next time Hrafn and I meet, father,' Gunnlaug said, 'I should like you to be too far away to separate us.'

With that they parted for the time being, and everyone went back to their booths.

Now the following day, it was laid down as law by the Law Council that all duelling should be permanently abolished. This was done on the advice of all the wisest men at the Althing, and all the wisest men in Iceland were there. Thus the duel that Hrafn and Gunnlaug fought was the last one ever to take place in Iceland. This was one of the three most crowded Althings of all time, the others being the one after the burning of Njal and the one following the Slayings on the Heath.[32]

One morning, when the brothers Hermund and Gunnlaug were on their way to the Oxara river to wash themselves, several women were going to its opposite bank. Helga the Fair was one of them.

Then Hermund asked Gunnlaug, 'Can you see your girlfriend Helga on the other side of the river?'

'Of course I can see her,' Gunnlaug replied. And then he spoke this verse:

19.
The woman was born to bring war
between men – the tree of the valkyrie   *tree of the valkyrie* (Gunn): warrior
started it all; I wanted her   (perhaps Hrafn, but more probably Thorstein)
sorely, that log of rare silver.   *log of silver*: woman
Henceforward, my black eyes
are scarcely of use to glance
at the ring-land's light-valkyrie,   *ring-land*: hand; its *light*: ring; *valkyrie*
splendid as a swan.   (Gunn) of the ring: woman

Then they went across the river, and Helga and Gunnlaug chatted for a while. When they went back eastwards across the river, Helga stood and stared at Gunnlaug for a long time. Then Gunnlaug looked back across the river and spoke this verse:

20.

The moon of her eyelash – that valkyrie	*moon of her eyelash*: her eye
of herb-surf, adorned with linen –	*herb-surf*: ale; its *valkyrie* (Hrist): woman
shone hawk-sharp upon me	
beneath her brows' bright sky;	*brows' sky*: forehead
but that beam from the eyelid-moon	*beam*: gaze
of the goddess of the golden torque	*goddess* (Frid) *of the golden torque*: woman
will later bring trouble to me	
and to the ring-goddess herself.[33]	*ring-goddess* (Hlin): woman

After this had happened, everyone rode home from the Althing, and Gunnlaug settled down at home at Gilsbakki. One morning, when he woke up, everyone was up and about except him. He slept in a bed closet further into the hall than were the benches. Then twelve men, all armed to the teeth, came into the hall: Hrafn Onundarson had arrived. Gunnlaug leapt up with a start, and managed to grab his weapons.

'You're not in any danger,' Hrafn said, 'and you'll hear what brings me here right now. You challenged me to a duel at the Althing last summer, and you thought that the matter was not fully resolved. Now I want to suggest that we both leave Iceland this summer and travel to Norway and fight a duel over there. Our relatives won't be able to stand between us there.'

'Well spoken, man!' Gunnlaug replied. 'I accept your proposal with pleasure. And now, Hrafn, you may have whatever hospitality you would like here.'

'That is a kind offer,' Hrafn replied, 'but, for the moment, we must ride on our way.'

And with that they parted. Both sets of relatives were very upset about this, but, because of their own anger, they could do nothing about it, and events had to take their course.

12 | Now we return to Hrafn. He fitted out his ship in Leiruvog. The names of two men who travelled with him are known: they were the sons of his father Onund's sister, one named Grim and the other Olaf. They were both worthy men. All Hrafn's relatives thought it was a great blow when he went away, but he explained that he had challenged Gunnlaug to a duel because he was not getting anywhere with Helga; one of them, he said, would have to perish at the hands of the other.

Hrafn set sail when he got a fair breeze, and they brought the ship to Trondheim, where he spent the winter. He received no news of Gunnlaug that winter, and so he waited there for him all summer, and then spent yet another winter in Trondheim at a place named Levanger.

Gunnlaug Serpent-tongue sailed from Melrakkasletta in the north with Hallfred Troublesome-poet. They left their preparations very late, and put to sea as soon as they got a fair breeze, arriving in the Orkney islands shortly before winter.

The islands were ruled by Earl Sigurd Hlodvesson at that time, and Gunnlaug went to him and spent the winter there. He was well respected. During the spring, the earl got ready to go plundering. Gunnlaug made preparations to go with him, and they spent the summer plundering over a large part of the Hebrides and the Scottish firths and fought many battles. Wherever they went, Gunnlaug proved himself to be a very brave and valiant fellow, and very manly. Earl Sigurd turned back in the early part of the summer, and then Gunnlaug took passage with some merchants who were sailing to Norway. Gunnlaug and Earl Sigurd parted on very friendly terms.

Gunnlaug went north to Lade in Trondheim to visit Earl Eirik, arriving at the beginning of winter. The earl gave him a warm welcome, and invited him to stay with him. Gunnlaug accepted the invitation. The earl had already heard about the goings-on between Gunnlaug and Hrafn, and he told Gunnlaug that he would not allow them to fight in his realm. Gunnlaug said that such matters were for the earl to decide. He stayed there that winter, and was always rather withdrawn.

Now one day that spring, Gunnlaug and his kinsman Thorkel[34] went out for a walk. They headed away from the town, and in the fields in front of them was a ring of men. Inside the ring, two armed men were fencing. One had been given the name Gunnlaug, and the other one Hrafn. The bystanders said that Icelanders struck out with mincing blows and were slow to remember their promises. Gunnlaug realized that there was a great deal of contempt in this, that it was a focus for mockery, and he went away in silence.

A little while after this, Gunnlaug told the earl that he did not feel inclined to put up with his followers' contempt and mockery concerning the goings-on between himself and Hrafn any longer. He asked the earl to provide him with guides to Levanger. The earl had already been told that Hrafn had left Levanger and gone across into Sweden,[35] and he therefore gave Gunnlaug permission to go, and found him two guides for the journey.

Then Gunnlaug left Lade with six other men, and went to Levanger. He arrived during the evening, but Hrafn had departed from there with four men the same morning. Gunnlaug went from there into Veradal, always arriving in the evening at the place where Hrafn had been the night before. Gunnlaug pressed on until he reached the innermost farm in the valley, which was named Sula, but Hrafn had left there that morning. Gunnlaug did not break his journey there, however, but pressed on through the night, and they caught sight of each other at sunrise the next day. Hrafn had reached a place where there were two lakes, with a stretch of flat land between them. This area was named Gleipnisvellir (Gleipnir's plains). A small headland called Dingenes jutted out into one of the lakes. Hrafn's party, which was five strong, took up position on the headland. His kinsmen, Grim and Olaf, were with him.

When they met, Gunnlaug said, 'It's good that we have met now.'

Hrafn said that he had no problem with it himself – 'and now you must choose which you prefer,' he said. 'Either we will all fight, or just the two of us, but both sides must be equal.'

Gunnlaug said that he would be quite happy with either arrangement. Then Hrafn's kinsmen, Grim and Olaf, said that they would not stand by while Gunnlaug and Hrafn fought. Thorkel the Black, Gunnlaug's kinsman, said the same.

Then Gunnlaug told the earl's guides: 'You must sit by and help neither side, and be there to tell the story of our encounter.' And so they did.

Then they fell to, and everyone fought bravely. Grim and Olaf together attacked Gunnlaug alone, and the business between them ended in his killing them both, though he was not himself hurt. Thord Kolbeinsson[36] confirms this in the poem he composed about Gunnlaug Serpent-tongue:

21.

Before reaching Hrafn,
Gunnlaug hacked down Grim
and Olaf, men pleased
with the valkyrie's warm wind;   *valkyrie's* (Gondul's) *warm wind*: battle
blood-bespattered, the brave one
was the bane of three bold men;
the god of the wave-charger   *wave-charger*: ship; its *god* (Ull): seafarer, man
dealt death out to men.

Meanwhile, Hrafn and Thorkel the Black, Gunnlaug's kinsman, were fighting. Thorkel succumbed to Hrafn, and lost his life. In the end, all their companions fell. Then the two of them, Hrafn and Gunnlaug, fought on, setting about each other remorselessly with heavy blows and fearless counterattacks. Gunnlaug was using the sword Ethelred had given him, and it was a formidable weapon. In the end, he hacked at Hrafn with a mighty blow, and chopped off his leg. Yet Hrafn did not collapse completely, but dropped back to a tree stump and rested the stump of his leg on it.

'Now you're past fighting,' Gunnlaug said, 'and I will not fight with you, a wounded man, any longer.'

'It is true that things have turned against me, rather,' Hrafn replied, 'but I should be able to hold out all right if I could get something to drink.'

'Don't trick me, then,' Gunnlaug replied, 'if I bring you water in my helmet.'

'I won't trick you,' Hrafn said.

Then Gunnlaug went to a brook, fetched some water in his helmet and took it to Hrafn. But as Hrafn reached out his left hand for it, he hacked at Gunnlaug's head with the sword in his right hand, causing a hideous wound.

'Now you have cruelly deceived me,' Gunnlaug said, 'and you have behaved in an unmanly way, since I trusted you.'

'That is true,' Hrafn replied, 'and I did it because I would not have you receive the embrace of Helga the Fair.'

Then they fought fiercely again, and it finished in Gunnlaug's overpowering Hrafn, and Hrafn lost his life right there. Then the earl's guides went over and bound Gunnlaug's head wound. He sat still throughout and spoke this verse:

22.

Hrafn, that bold sword-swinger,	
splendid sword-meeting's tree,	*sword-meeting*: battle; its *tree*: warrior
in the harsh storm of stingers	*stingers*: spears; spears' *storm*: battle
advanced bravely against me.	
This morning, many metal-flights	*metal-flights*: thrown weapons
howled round Gunnlaug's head	
on Dingenes, O ring-tree	*ring-tree*: man
and protector of ranks.	*protector of ranks*: leader of an army, warrior

Then they saw to the dead men, and afterwards they put Gunnlaug on his horse and brought him down into Levanger. There he lay for three nights, and received the full rites from a priest before he died. He was buried in the church there. Everyone thought the deaths of both Gunnlaug and Hrafn in such circumstances were a great loss.

13 | That summer, before this news had been heard out here in Iceland, Illugi the Black had a dream.[37] He was at home at Gilsbakki at the time. He dreamed that Gunnlaug appeared to him, covered in blood, and spoke this verse to him. Illugi remembered the poem when he woke up, and later recited it to other people:

23.

I know that Hrafn hit me
with the hilt-finned clang-fish   *hilt-finned ... mailcoat*: sword (with a hilt for
of the mailcoat,   fins) which clangs when striking a mailcoat
but my sharp edge bit his leg
when the eagle, corpse-scorer,   *corpse-scorer*: eagle, which carves up corpses
drank the mead of warm wounds.   with its beak; *mead of wounds*: blood
The war-twig of valkyrie's thorns *valkyrie's* (Gunn's) *thorns*: warriors; their
split Gunnlaug's skull.   *war-twig*: sword

On the same night, at Mosfell in the south, it happened that Onund dreamed that Hrafn came to him. He was all covered in blood, and spoke this verse:

24.

My sword was stained with gore,
but the Odin of swords   *Odin* (Rognir) *of swords*: warrior, i.e. Gunnlaug
sword-swiped me too; on shields
shield-giants were tried overseas. *shield-giants*: enemies of shields, i.e. swords
I think there stood blood-stained
blood-goslings in blood round my brain.   *blood-goslings*: ravens
Once more the wound-eager wound-raven
wound-river is fated to wade.   *wound-river*: blood

At the Althing the following summer, Illugi the Black spoke to Onund at the Law Rock.

'How are you going to compensate me for my son,' he asked, 'since your son Hrafn tricked him when they had declared a truce?'

'I don't think there's any onus on me to pay compensation for him,' Onund replied, 'since I've been so sorely wounded by their encounter myself. But I won't ask you for any compensation for my son, either.'

'Then some of your family and friends will suffer for it,' Illugi answered. And all summer, after the Althing, Illugi was very depressed.

People say that during the autumn, Illugi rode off from Gilsbakki with about thirty men, and arrived at Mosfell early in the morning. Onund and his sons rushed into the church, but Illugi captured two of Onund's kinsmen. One of them was named Bjorn and the other Thorgrim. Illugi had Bjorn killed and Thorgrim's foot cut off.[38] After that, Illugi rode home, and Onund sought no reprisals for this act. Hermund Illugason was very upset about his brother's death, and thought that, even though this had been done, Gunnlaug had not been properly avenged.

There was a man named Hrafn, who was a nephew of Onund of Mosfell's. He was an important merchant, and owned a ship which was moored in Hrutafjord.

That spring, Hermund Illugason rode out from home on his own. He went north over Holtavarda heath, across to Hrutafjord and then over to the merchants' ship at Bordeyri. The merchants were almost ready to leave. Skipper Hrafn was ashore, with several other people. Hermund rode up to him, drove his spear through him and then rode away. Hrafn's colleagues were all caught off-guard by Hermund. No compensation was forthcoming for this killing, and with it the feuding between Illugi the Black and Onund was at an end.

Some time later, Thorstein Egilsson married his daughter Helga to a man named Thorkel, the son of Hallkel. He lived out in Hraunsdal, and Helga went back home with him, although she did not really love him. She could never get Gunnlaug out of her mind, even though he was dead. Still, Thorkel was a decent man, rich and a good poet. They had a fair number of children. One of their sons was named Thorarin, another Thorstein, and they had more children besides.

Helga's greatest pleasure was to unfold the cloak Gunnlaug had given her and stare at it for a long time. Now there was a time when Thorkel's and Helga's household was afflicted with a terrible illness, and many people suffered a long time with it. Helga, too, became ill but did not take to her bed. One Saturday evening, Helga sat in the fire-room, resting her head in her husband Thorkel's lap. She sent for the cloak Gunnlaug's Gift, and when it arrived, she sat up and spread it out in front of her. She stared at it for a while. Then she fell back into her husband's arms, dead. Thorkel spoke this verse:

25.

My Helga, good arm-serpent's staff,	*arm-serpent*: gold bracelet; its *staff*:
dead in my arms I did clasp.	woman
God carried off the life	
of the linen-Lofn, my wife.	*linen-Lofn* (goddess): woman
But for me, the river-flash's poor craver,	*river-flash*: gold; its *craver*: man
it is heavier to be yet living.[39]	

Helga was taken to the church, but Thorkel carried on living in Hraunsdal. As one might expect, he found Helga's death extremely hard to bear.

And this is the end of the saga.

Translated by Katrina C. Attwood

THE SAGA OF BJORN,
CHAMPION OF THE
HITARDAL PEOPLE

1 | Now some account is to be given of the Icelanders who lived
   | in the days of King Olaf Haraldsson, and became his intimate
friends. The first of these to be mentioned was an excellent man,
Thorkel Eyjolfsson, who married Gudrun Osvifsdottir.[1] At that time
Thorkel was engaged in trading voyages, and he was always highly
esteemed at King Olaf's court when he was abroad.

In those days Thord Kolbeinsson lived at Hitarnes in Iceland. He
was a considerable poet, and did much to maintain his own reputation.
He was always held in respect by important men abroad because of
his skill as a poet. Thord was a follower of Earl Eirik Hakonarson
and was much esteemed by him. Thord was not very popular with
people in general, because he seemed to be mocking and spiteful to
everyone he considered himself a match for.

A man called Bjorn, son of Arngeir and of Thordis, daughter of
Thorfinn the Strong and of Saeunn, daughter of Skallagrim, grew up
with Skuli Thorsteinsson at Borg.[2] Bjorn soon grew to be tall and
powerfully built, manly and handsome. Like many others, Bjorn had
been a victim of Thord's mockery and aggression. It was for this
reason that he lived with his cousin Skuli while he was young, for he
seemed better off there than with his father on account of Thord
Kolbeinsson's aggression. I will not go into the small quarrels that
occurred between Thord and Bjorn before Bjorn came to Skuli,
because they have no bearing on this saga. Skuli treated Bjorn well
and held him in great regard, for, with his wisdom, he saw what a
distinguished member of the family he would grow up to be. Bjorn
was very contented with his lot while he was with Skuli.

Thorkel, son of Dufgus the Wealthy of Dufgusdal, lived on Hjorsey island off the coast of Myrar. Thorkel was a wealthy man and a householder of good standing. He had a daughter called Oddny, an exceptionally beautiful woman with a strong personality. She was known as Oddny Isle-candle. Bjorn made a habit of visiting there, and always sat talking with Oddny Thorkelsdottir, and they felt attracted to each other. It was said by many people that it would be an equal match if Bjorn were to get her for his wife, for he was a most impressive man, and well bred.

2 | When Bjorn had been living with his cousin Skuli for five years, a ship entered the mouth of the river Gufua. The ship was owned by Norwegians. Skuli rode to the ship and at once invited the merchants to stay with him, for it was his custom frequently to give lodgings to merchants, and to keep up firm friendships with them; so three of them went to stay with him as soon as they had drawn up their ship. Bjorn was very attentive to these merchants, accompanying them and doing them services, and they were well pleased with him.

Bjorn went to see Skuli and asked him to send him abroad with the merchants. Skuli responded favourably to this, saying, as was true, that many men had achieved success who were less mature than he was, and he said that he would provide Bjorn with whatever he considered he needed. Bjorn thanked him for his generous help, both on this occasion and in the past. Then Bjorn arranged his passage with these merchants. Skuli and his father gave him ample funds for the trip, so that he was well equipped to keep company with men of substance. Nothing worth telling happened during the merchants' stay; they went to the ship when spring came, made ready, and so lay by for a fair wind.

Then Bjorn rode to Borg to see Skuli, and when they met, Bjorn told him that he wanted nothing other than to win Oddny Thorkels-dottir before he went away. Skuli asked him whether he had spoken to her about this at all. Bjorn said he had indeed.

'Then let us go,' said Skuli, and so they did.

They came to Hjorsey, and went to see Thorkel and his daughter

Oddny. Then Bjorn began to speak, and asked to marry Oddny. Thorkel received this well, and referred the decision to his daughter; and because Bjorn was already known to her, and they had come to love each other dearly, she consented.[3] Then the betrothal took place at once, and she was to stay pledged for three years; and even if Bjorn should be back in the country in the fourth year but unable to come and confirm the betrothal, she must still wait for him, but if he did not come back from Norway after an interval of three years, Thorkel was to give her in marriage elsewhere if he wished. Bjorn was also to send people to Iceland to confirm the betrothal if he could not come himself. Skuli put forward on Bjorn's behalf money equal to all that Thorkel possessed, besides the bride-price for his daughter Oddny.

They parted on these terms, and Skuli went with Bjorn to the ship, and then Skuli said, 'When you get to Norway, Bjorn, and meet my friend Earl Eirik, carry to him my greeting and a message from me asking him to receive you. I would like to think that he will do that; take him this ring as a token, for then he cannot blind himself to what I wish.'

Bjorn thanked Skuli for all the kindness he had shown him since he came to live with him, and then they parted. That was towards the end of the days of Earl Eirik.

They sailed early in summer; their journey was accomplished smoothly, and they arrived in Norway. Bjorn at once went to see Earl Eirik and bore Skuli's greetings and token to him.

The earl responded graciously and said he would gladly grant his request – 'and you will be welcome, Bjorn'.

Bjorn said that he was very eager for that. He joined the earl's court and stayed with him, well entertained.

3 | Early that same summer, a ship came from Norway into Straumfjord. Thord Kolbeinsson rode to the ship and learned that the merchants meant to return to Norway in the same season, and so he bought a share in the ship and made known his departure abroad. Thord had a kinsman in Denmark called Hroi[4] the Wealthy. He lived in Roskilde and owned a house there; Thord was the heir

to all his property. Now he made ready for the journey abroad, and they were ready late. It became known at the earl's court that Thord had come to Norway from Iceland on the ship that had made the crossing both ways that summer, and also that he was the ship's skipper, and meant to present a poem to the earl. The earl asked Bjorn whether he had any acquaintance with Thord.

Bjorn said that he knew Thord well and that he was a good poet – 'and the poem that he recites will be splendid'.

The earl said, 'Do you think it advisable, Bjorn, that I should hear the poem?'

'I think so indeed,' said Bjorn, 'for it will honour you both.'

And soon afterwards Thord came to see the earl and greeted him politely. The earl responded graciously and asked who he was.

He said he was called Thord and was an Icelander, 'and I would like you to hear the poem that I have made about you'.

The earl agreed to that. Thord recited the poem, which was a drapa, and a fine poem. The earl was pleased with it and invited him to stay with him over the winter, and Thord accepted, and was well entertained; he and Bjorn both spent that winter with the earl.

There were people at court who reported to the earl that they were no friends, Bjorn and Thord. And on one occasion it is said that the earl called Thord before him and asked whether Bjorn was known to him, and why Skuli should have sent this man to him.

And Thord said that Bjorn was the most intrepid man, 'and known to me for his good qualities; Skuli sent you this man because he had no other kinsman better fitted for it'.

'That must be true,' said the earl.

Thord said, 'Have you asked at all how old a man Bjorn is?'

'No,' said the earl.

Thord said, 'He is eighteen years old now. There are many brave men here with you, and Bjorn will take the part of those who are the most daring.'

The earl was pleased to hear this. Thord did not let it be seen that all had not always been well between him and Bjorn. And one day during the winter Thord went to Bjorn and asked him to drink with him.

'We are now lodging where nothing else becomes us than to be on good terms; the only disagreement between us has been of little consequence, so let us be friends from now on.'

Bjorn agreed to this; so time went on till Yule. And on the eighth day of Yule, Earl Eirik made payment to his men for their service, as is the custom of rulers in other countries. He gave Bjorn a gold ring weighing half a mark, to reward his bravery and that of his kinsman Skuli; to Thord he gave a sword, a fine treasure, in payment for his poem.

It happened again, one evening that winter, that Thord spoke to Bjorn; they were both drunk then, especially Bjorn: 'What do you mean to do when spring comes? Do you mean to go to Iceland?'

'I'll not go out this summer,' said Bjorn, 'for I mean to ask Earl Eirik for leave to go raiding, to win money and fame, if I can.'

Thord answered, 'That seems unwise to me: with much honour and glory gained already, to take such risks now! Much better, come out to Iceland with me in the summer to your noble relatives, and confirm your betrothal.'

Bjorn repeated, 'I will not go back this summer.'

Thord answered, 'Your behaviour seems to me unwise, to leave the country with a great deal of money, not knowing whether you will come back or not.'

'Nothing ventured, nothing gained,' said Bjorn, 'and I will go raiding.'

Thord said, 'Then send to Oddny, your betrothed wife, the ring the earl gave you; leave it in my hands. For she will be even more sure of your love and fondness for her if you send her such a treasure; you will be still more in her thoughts than before, and she will be slower to forget you. But if you come out to Iceland, as I hope you will, then you will get the ring and the woman and the whole sum of money that was promised to you with her. And the truth is,' said Thord, 'that there is no such match in Iceland as Oddny.'

Bjorn said, 'It is true, as you say, Thord, that Oddny is a most outstanding woman, and a fine match for me in every way, and if you had treated me as well when we were in Iceland as you do now, I would do everything you ask; but I hardly think it is for me to trust you, and it would be said that I had kept a loose grasp on the earl's gift if I let the ring pass into your hands.'

Thord told him to confirm his betrothal. Bjorn said that he had appointed men to see to that – 'and you, Thord, tell the truth about my movements when you get to Iceland. But I think I have not tested myself in enough enterprises, or explored widely enough the customs of good men, and if I go to Iceland at once, I will not be inclined to travel again so soon after my marriage.'

Thord promised to do as he asked: 'But the reason I asked for treasures was to confirm my account; you have no need to suspect me, Bjorn, for I will be true to you.'

'Well, I will risk it,' said Bjorn, 'this once. But if you cheat me, I'll never trust you again in all my life.'

Then Bjorn gave the ring, the earl's gift, into Thord's hands, and told him to take it to Oddny. Thord promised to do this, and spoke very fairly to Bjorn and solemnly vowed to be true to him and discharge his errand well. He and Bjorn ended their conversation for the present. And when Bjorn was sober, he thought he had said quite enough to Thord and trusted him overmuch.

Then the winter drew to an end, and Thord made ready his ship. He and Bjorn met and spoke again.

'Remember, Thord,' said Bjorn, 'what we have said, and do my business well.'

Thord made fair promises about that, and they parted on reasonable terms. Nobody knew exactly what had been said between Thord and Bjorn.

People say that Thord was fifteen years older than Bjorn. The drapa he made about Earl Eirik is called 'Bag-Shaking'.[5] Thord put to sea early in the summer, and it was during the Althing that he sailed into the mouth of the Gufua river. He rode straight to the assembly, and his arrival caused a stir, for he was well able to tell all the news. He carried out Bjorn's errand well that time, saying that he, Bjorn, would come to confirm the betrothal with Oddny, and giving her the ring; but he said that Bjorn had made over the betrothal to him if Bjorn himself died, or did not come back to Iceland.

4 | The same summer that Thord went to Iceland, Bjorn went before the earl and asked for permission to go seafaring in the Baltic. The earl told him to go if it suited him. Then Bjorn went with some merchants east into Russia to see King Valdimar. He stayed there over the winter on good terms with the king. He made a good impression on men of rank, for all were pleased with his manners and character.

It was said that while Bjorn was in Russia with King Valdimar, it happened that an overwhelming army invaded the country, and commanding it was the champion called Kaldimar,[6] mighty and powerful, a close relative of the king, a notable warrior skilled in feats of arms, and a man of great daring. King Valdimar and the champion had been considered to have an equal claim to the kingdom, but the champion had not achieved power because he was the younger, and so he went raiding to win himself advancement; and now there was no such warrior as famous as he in the eastern lands at this time.

But when King Valdimar heard of this, he sent men with proposals for peace to his kinsman, offering him safe conduct and possession of half the kingdom. But the champion said he alone must rule the kingdom, and if the king would not agree, he would challenge him to a duel, or else they must do battle with all their troops. Neither choice seemed good to Valdimar; he was not willing to lose his troops, but said that he was not in the habit of duelling, and he asked his supporters what was advisable; and he was counselled to gather his troops and do battle. And within a short time a large company and crowd assembled there, and Valdimar advanced against the champion. Then the king offered to get someone to fight in single combat on his behalf, and the champion agreed to this on the condition that he alone should have control of all the kingdom if he brought down that man, but if he, the champion, fell, then the king should have control of his kingdom as before. Then the king entreated his men to undertake the duel for him, but they were not eager to do this, for whoever was to fight against the champion seemed doomed to die. The king promised his friendship and other honours to anyone who would undertake it, but no one was willing.

Bjorn said, 'Here I see everyone responding very cravenly to his lord's need. But I left my country because I wanted to win fame for myself. There are two possible outcomes: one, to win victory courageously, unlikely though that may be against such an opponent; the second, to die bravely and nobly, and that is better than to live with shame, not daring to win honour for one's king, and so I will undertake to fight against Kaldimar.'

The king thanked Bjorn. Then the duelling laws were proclaimed. The champion had the sword that was called Maering,[7] a most excellent and valuable weapon. They fought both fast and furiously, and the outcome was that the champion was brought down and killed by Bjorn, while Bjorn was wounded almost mortally. From this Bjorn won great fame and honour from the king. Then a tent was pitched over Bjorn, for he was considered too ill to be moved, while the king went back to his kingdom. Bjorn and his companions stayed in the tent, and when his wounds were beginning to heal, he spoke a verse:

1.

The elegant arm-goddess,   *arm-goddess* (Lofn): woman
Isle-candle, would gladly
– skilful verse I'm speaking –
sleep here as my lover,
if the linen-clad lady
learned that I was near her;
I win fame, three warriors
with me under canvas.

Later Bjorn was carried back to the king with great honour. The king gave him all the armour the champion had owned, including the sword Maering. Because of this, Bjorn was called 'champion' after that, and named after his district. Over the summer Bjorn lay wounded, and the following winter he stayed in Russia, and he had then been abroad for three years. After that he went to Norway. And when he got there, all the ships bound for Iceland had left, for it was late in the summer.

5 | The second summer, before what has just been related, Thord learned from merchants on the Hvita river that Bjorn had been wounded, and he bribed them to say that he was dead, and they did so. Then Thord spoke openly of Bjorn's death, saying he had been told of it by men who had sprinkled earth on his grave. No one was able to contradict this, and Thord seemed unlikely to lie. Then Thord went to Hjorsey and asked to marry Oddny. Her relatives were unwilling to marry her to him before the time agreed between them and Bjorn had elapsed, but they said that if nothing was heard of Bjorn when the ships came out that summer, they would be able to discuss it. Then the ships came out, and they could not give news of Bjorn, for he had not arrived in Norway before they put to sea. Then Thord pressed his suit, and Oddny was given to him in marriage.

But when Bjorn's crew was ready to put to sea, a ship sailed in from the sea towards them. Bjorn and his men took a boat and rowed out to the ship, wanting to learn the news, for the ship had come from Iceland. They told of Oddny's marriage, and when Bjorn knew of that, he did not want to go to Iceland.[8]

That winter Bjorn went to Earl Eirik's court and stayed with him, and as their ship lay off Hamarseyri, Bjorn composed a verse:

2.

The hero has pleasured
Hrist of the hand-fire.   *hand-fire*: gold; its *Hrist* (valkyrie): woman
Isle-candle's bunching buttocks
beat hard on the mattress,
while we strive to stiffen
the supple oar (with reason:
I bid the boat-prop's ski   *boat-prop's ski*: ship
be moving) on the gunwale.

Bjorn was held in as much esteem as before by the earl.

The next summer Bjorn went west to England, and won much esteem there, and stayed for two years with King Canute the Great. It happened, when Bjorn was accompanying the king, and sailing with his company in southern seas, that a dragon flew over the king's company and attacked them and tried to snatch one of the men. Bjorn was standing nearby and covered the man with his shield, but the dragon clawed almost through it. Bjorn then gripped the dragon's tail with one hand, while with the other he struck behind the wings, and the dragon was severed, and fell down dead. The king gave Bjorn a large sum of money and a fine longship; with this he sailed to Denmark. Then he entered into partnership with Audun Back-flap,[9] a man from Vik, but partly Danish by birth. Audun had been outlawed from Norway. He brought two ships into the partnership with him, and they went raiding east of Sweden, harrying during the summer and spending the winter in Denmark. This was their occupation for three years.

6 | It is now to be told that Thord stayed on his farm in Hitarnes for a while, and people held that Oddny was now better married than had been intended before, in terms of money, birth and other honours; and their love for each other was moderate. They had eight children – five sons and three daughters. Thord had then sold to merchants the ship he had owned and sailed when on his travels.

Bjorn was now raiding so as to win himself wealth and honour. He was a friend of Earl Eirik, and with him were those men who were mentioned before. He had little longing for Iceland now that he knew the news from there, and how Thord had treated him. And during the time when Bjorn was out of the country, there was a change of rulers in Norway. After Earl Eirik, his son Earl Hakon succeeded to the throne. Svein, Earl Eirik's brother, ruled his own part of the country as before, and so it went on for two years. After that St Olaf[10] came into the country and captured Hakon in Saudungssund, and he swore oaths of allegiance to King Olaf and then left the country. Olaf fought against Earl Svein off Nesjar on Palm Sunday, and Svein took flight. Then Olaf ruled the whole country and became its king. Now the news travelled to other countries that Earl Eirik and Earl Hakon had left the country. Bjorn and his men learned of the change of ruler, and heard that many good reports were going around about this king, as he deserved.

At this time that excellent man Thorkel Eyjolfsson was engaged in trading. He was greatly honoured by King Olaf. Thorkel was also a friend of Thord Kolbeinsson.

7 | It is now reported that Thord Kolbeinsson heard the news that Hroi the Wealthy, his mother's brother, was dead; Thord was his heir. Then he bought a ship, meaning to go abroad to claim the property. It is said that during his journey he sought a meeting with King Olaf. He was well received; he told the king the circumstances of his journey. Thorkel was there then and put forward a good case to the king for Thord's getting his property. The king had a letter written for him to his friends in Denmark and set his seal on it. With Thord then were the sons of Eid, Thord and Thorvald,[11] and Kalf the Ill-willed travelled with them too. Thord composed a drapa about King Olaf; then he went and recited it himself, and received from the king a gold ring, a silken tunic trimmed with lace, and a fine sword. Thord asked secretly whether people knew anything of Bjorn. He was told that he was raiding with a large company. Thord had a small ship; some men from Vik were on board with him – there were nearly thirty men altogether on the ship.

He reached Roskilde in Denmark that summer and got much of the property, although large chips had been pared from it. They left the south as summer was drawing to a close, and his course lay through the Branno islands.[12] This is a group of many islands, not much inhabited at that time. There were hidden creeks in them, and they were always exposed to raiders. There was also some woodland on the islands.

Meanwhile Bjorn was travelling from one harbour to another, and arrived late one day where two points of the Branno islands jutted forward; one is called Thraelaeyri, the other Oddaeyri. There Bjorn placed his ships. That same evening Thord reached the island and moored his ship there for the night. Then two men came forward on the island and asked who owned the ship. One man, ready of tongue and rather reckless, said that it was Thord Kolbeinsson's.

Thord said, 'You are too quick to talk. Say that Thorar the Far-traveller owns the ship.'

And so he did.

The man on the island said, 'Do as you please, lie or tell the truth.'

These men turned back. They were in fact Bjorn's men; he was anchored on the other side of the island with nine ships.

Thord said when they had gone, 'These must have been spies for somebody, and I will go on to the island and see if I can learn anything.'

Bjorn spoke to Audun when the men came back and told him about Thord: 'I thought I recognized from their report the ship that Thord must own. Our meeting is fitting.'

Thord said, when the men who had gone on to the island with him had come back, that he thought he could tell that Bjorn was not far away. 'Now I want you to say that I have stayed behind in Denmark because I could not get the property otherwise, if it turns out, as I expect, that Bjorn is not far away and is coming here. Meanwhile, I will save myself.'

Kalf the Ill-willed said, 'That will be a good plan if you aren't found, but otherwise you will suffer great shame. I would rather we defended our lives and goods as long as we can.'

'The other plan is wiser,' said Thord. 'Everyone else will be spared, except me.'

He went up on to the island and crouched in a bush under a bank and watched the ship. He had a cloak on over his clothes. Then Bjorn told his men to arm themselves and visit the merchants. He said that what had first been said was true, that Thord Kolbeinsson was the skipper. They did as Bjorn told them and went aboard the cargo ship, where the crew seemed to be without a leader; Bjorn asked who was in charge of the ship. They were not very pleased by Bjorn's arrival, but put forward their story as Thord had told them to.

Bjorn did not believe it and decided to search the island: 'The island is small, and we will find him if he is here.'

First they searched the ship without finding him; then they went over the island. Almost two hundred men took part in the search.

And when Bjorn and his men came to where Thord was sitting, he jumped up and hailed Bjorn heartily.

'So you are here, Thord,' said Bjorn, 'and not in Denmark. But why must you crouch so low? Now tell us the news from Iceland, for it is long since we last met.'

'I can tell a great deal of news,' said Thord.

'Where were you in the winter?'

Thord answered Bjorn and said, 'With the king in Norway.'

Bjorn said, 'Whereabouts in the country was the king?'

'He was in the north,' said Thord, 'and when spring came he went east to Vik, and he must be there now.'

Bjorn said, 'What is the latest news you can tell from Iceland?'

'Skuli's death,' said Thord, 'but your father and foster-father are still alive.'[13]

Bjorn said, 'It is grave news that Skuli is dead. But is it true that you married Oddny, Thorkel's daughter, not long after we parted?'

Thord said that was true.

Bjorn said, 'How faithful a friend did you think you were being to me?'

Thord replied, 'I didn't know that she had to wait for you for more than three years.'

Bjorn said, 'Such quibbling won't work for you now, for I already know the whole truth about this.'

Thord offered him compensation.

'It would be a better idea,' said Bjorn, 'for you to be put to death, and for things to be at an end between us.'

The end of it was that Bjorn spared their lives, but took their goods from them and the knorr as well; then he stripped Thord of valuables, and made his situation as humiliating as possible. Thord begged to keep the goods, but did not succeed. Then Bjorn made Thord and all his companions get into the boat from the knorr, with their clothes, and so cross to the mainland.

And before they parted, Bjorn spoke. 'Thord,' he said, 'you have been dealt some shame and dishonour and loss, although still less than you deserve in every way. Now go to the Orkneys without staying long in Norway, while I go and see the king. I honour him so

165

much, although I have never seen him, that I am not going to kill you because you were his guest this winter. But wherever I meet you from now on you will never be safe, unless things turn out very differently from the way I expect.'

Then Thord got into the boat, and so did the men of Vik, who wanted to go to their properties; they took their weapons. Then they went to the king and told him the news of the robbery and of the accusations against Thord.

8 | After this Bjorn had a conference with his partner Audun, and said that he wanted to go and see King Olaf: 'I don't want to have his anger hanging over me for robbing merchants.'

Audun said he would go with him, for homesickness was urging him to settle down in Norway. Then they went to see the king, leaving behind most of their men as well as the goods and the ships. They reached the king's presence three days later than Thord and his companions. Bjorn went in a company of twelve into the hall when the king was sitting at drink, while fifty men stayed behind by the ships. Bjorn went before the king and greeted him politely. The king asked who he was. He gave his name.

The king said, 'Is this not your enemy at law, Thord?'

And he said that it was indeed. The king said that he was a bold man to have dared to come into his presence, and ordered that Bjorn and his men be seized and put in irons. Bjorn said that that would be easy to do, but that he considered himself to be hardly without a case against Thord. The king said it was easy for Vikings to pick quarrels with merchants when they coveted their goods. Bjorn then spoke, starting from the beginning, about his dealings with Thord, and the case that he considered he had against Thord Kolbeinsson. The king asked Thord whether it was as Bjorn said. Thord said that he had heard of Bjorn's death as a fact before he married the woman.

'However, that has turned out not to be true,' said the king, 'and it seems to me that Bjorn has a strong case against Thord. Now, are you both willing for me to arbitrate between you?'

They both agreed to that, and a truce was imposed. And then the king assigned the woman, with all her possessions, to Thord, and to Bjorn an equal amount of property from what he had taken from Thord. The sum was reckoned to include Oddny's inheritance from her father. The dishonour of the theft of goods and that of the taking of the woman were to be considered equal. Bjorn was to have a tunic of precious cloth and a ring to compensate for the one Thord had taken along with Oddny. Thord was to keep the sword the king had given to him; and the king said it would be the better for the man who kept this settlement well. All the property Thord had there except the ship went to Bjorn, but each of the merchants was to get back the goods Bjorn had taken from him.

Thord stayed with the king over the winter, and so did Kalf and Eid's sons, but Bjorn went east into Vik with Audun and his men, for whom Bjorn had got pardon from the king, and they stayed there for the winter; but the next summer he went back to King Olaf and stayed with him for the next two years. But Thord went to Iceland that summer and did not mention his dealings with Bjorn, or anything that had happened in the east. King Olaf gave Thord a cargo of wood for his ship, and Thord sailed out here to Iceland and home to his farm.

9 | Now Bjorn stayed with the king. And on one occasion as the king and Bjorn were chatting, Bjorn said, 'I know, my lord, that the men who slandered me to you about my meeting with Thord will have mentioned what my chief reason was for not killing Thord and his men.'

The king said, 'I was not told that.'

Bjorn said, 'I must tell you that I honoured you so greatly, although I had never seen you, that I spared the lives of Thord and all his crew because he had been your guest for the winter – and so he would have discovered, if we had met when you were not involved, or when it would not have offended you.'

The king said, 'Now let us hear this from the men who told us the story, for we have found them to be good men; they will tell the truth.'

Then this was done, and they acknowledged that Bjorn had said that it was because of the king that he would not kill Thord and his companions. The king was now even more impressed than before, since Bjorn had spared Thord for his sake. There were men with the king who knew of the dealings between Bjorn and Thord; they had been with Earl Eirik, and they told the king about that. There had been witnesses to all that Bjorn had deposed.

The king said, 'Now it is just that Thord's crew should have sworn oaths which by my jurisdiction have earned them their property, and Thord his safety.'

Bjorn said that he thought it likely he would not have spared Thord except for the king's sake.

'You will be more my friend from now on than before,' said the king, but he added that nothing would befit them now but to keep to the settlement he had made between them.

'And I would wish,' said the king, 'that you give up raiding. Though you feel it suits you well, God's law is often violated.'

Bjorn said that it should be so, and that he was eager to remain with him.

The king replied, 'You are much to my liking, but we are not fated to spend long together, for my friend Thorkel Eyjolfsson is expected here, and he would soon be at odds with you because of Thord. It would be wise to set out for Iceland.'

It came about that Bjorn was present that autumn with the king at several feasts. They were on terms of great harmony, and Bjorn received fine gifts from him. Something happened at one feast when Bjorn was accompanying the king: many luxuries were always accorded to the king, as was fitting, and a bath in a tub was prepared for him, for there is no other kind of bath in Norway.[14] The king and his men went into the bath, and everyone left his clothes on the ground; a tent was pitched over the bath. It was customary then for men to wear cross-garters, which were like belts, laced up from the shoe to the knee. The better men and the nobility always wore them, and the king and Bjorn did the same. And when Bjorn went for his clothes before the others, his garments were beside the king's, and Bjorn did not realize until everyone was dressed that he had exchanged cross-garters with the king. He told him at once of his mistake, but the king let it rest, and said that the one he was wearing was no worse.

Bjorn always wore this cross-garter around his leg for as long as he lived, and with it he was buried. And much later, when his bones were taken up and moved to another church, that same cross-garter remained uncorrupted[15] around Bjorn's leg-bone, although everything else was decayed. It is now the cincture of a set of mass vestments at Gardar on Akranes.

Then the next winter Bjorn stayed in Norway, and King Olaf gave him a finely made cloak and promised him his friendship, calling him a fine and intrepid fellow.

10 | It is now to be told that in spring Bjorn made ready his ship for Iceland. Other ships were also making ready for Iceland, and they arrived there earlier than Bjorn's. King Olaf sent word with these men that Thord was to abide faithfully by the settlement with Bjorn if he came to Iceland, saying he was obliged to do so because of the negotiations that had already taken place. That summer Bjorn landed at Bordeyri in Hrutafjord, with a large amount of property, having achieved great renown and accomplishments. They carried their gear ashore and pitched their tent.

But elsewhere it is related that one evening Oddny began to speak thus to her husband Thord: 'Have you heard any news, Thord?'

'None,' he said, 'but you must have mentioned this because you have heard some.'

'Your guess is close to the truth,' she said; 'I have heard what seems like news to me. I am told of the coming of a ship into Hrutafjord, and on it is Bjorn, who you said was dead.'

Thord said, 'Maybe you think that news.'

'It certainly is news,' she said, 'and now I see more clearly what sort of marriage I have made. I thought you a good man, but you are full of lies and deceit.'

'It is said,' replied Thord, 'that there is compensation for everything.'

'I suspect,' she said, 'that he will have arranged his own compensation.'

'Believe whatever suits you,' he said. Now the talk between them was dropped.

Arngeir and Ingjald[16] went to the ship to meet Bjorn; there was a joyful meeting between them there, and they invited Bjorn to stay with them, saying they were glad to see him, and that it had been long since they met. He said that he would go to his father's. Then the ship was drawn up as the summer advanced, and Bjorn went home to his father's. Many were delighted at Bjorn's homecoming, for there had been so much mystery about his fate, and whether he was alive or not; one had said it was a lie, another that it was true, and now it was made clear which had been right.

Bjorn was warmly welcomed when he came home. His foster-father gave him the dog V—,[17] for he had admired it before. His father gave him a stallion called Hviting, pure white in colour, and two white foals with it. These were splendid possessions.

11 | Now it is said that Thord asked Oddny whether she thought it a good idea to invite Bjorn to stay, saying that he did not want people going back and forth between them slandering them to each other; 'and in this way I want to test Bjorn's mood and his faith with me'.

She argued against it, saying it was a bad plan on account of the gossip that was already going around. Thord said he would not be dissuaded, and went into Hitardal to Holm. He rode alone in a black cloak. A mountain stands behind the farmstead at Holm, and a ridge comes down from the mountain right up to the buildings. Bjorn and his mother were busy that day, spreading out the linen[18] that had been washed to dry.

She broke into speech: 'There is a man riding there,' she said, 'in a black cloak, looking very like Thord Kolbeinsson – it is him, too, and his business would be best left undone.'

'Not so,' said Bjorn.

Thord came up. They greeted each other and exchanged news.

Then Thord said, 'My business here is to learn whether you mean to hold to the settlement which the king made between us. Neither of us should now have any debts left unpaid to the other, and it is worthy of regard that a wise man has mediated between us; but it was in my mind for a while that we would not be reconciled.'

Bjorn said they had no choice but to keep to the settlement they had agreed to.

Thord said, 'I have got what seems the better half of the bargain, and now I will show that I want us to be wholly reconciled. I want to invite you to be my guest for the winter, and I will entertain you well; and I was hoping that you would accept this.' With fine words Thord went on.

Thordis said, 'It will be seen that I'm not very easily swayed by talk. Bear in mind, Bjorn, that the more fairly Thord speaks, the more falsely he thinks, so don't you trust him.'

Then Arngeir came up and asked what they were talking about. Thord told him.

'It seems to me,' said Arngeir, 'that anyone who encourages this is a better friend to them, if it makes them more reconciled than they were. I will urge Bjorn to go, and Thord will fulfil what he promises.'

And there was some difference of opinion between husband and wife.

Bjorn said, 'I had planned to stay with my father; many will think this invitation odd, because of people's gossip.'

Thord spoke again and said that Bjorn would be breaking faith with him if he did not accept the invitation. And then Bjorn promised to visit there for a while, but said that he would stay with his father first. Thord rode home and told Oddny where he had gone that day, saying that he had settled the business as he had intended.

'Which business is that?' she asked.

He said that he had invited Bjorn to stay, and that he had done it to make amends to her.

'I believe,' she said, 'that you are lying now if ever you were.'

Thord said, 'One oath broken doesn't destroy all others.'[19]

Then they dropped the subject.

12 | Now Bjorn made ready for his stay with Thord, and went to
   | Hitarnes with three valuable animals, two stallions and his dog.
He rode one horse and led the other. He left his goods behind at
Holm. Thord welcomed him and made him sit down beside him,
and gave his people particular instructions to treat him well. They
promised this readily, but most thought it odd that Bjorn should be
staying there. However, time passed, and all seemed to be well
between them.

It is said that early in winter Thord came to talk to Oddny and
asked how the work was to be organized.

'We have much on hand,' he said, 'and we need everyone to be
useful in some way.'

An island lies in the Hitara river, abundantly stocked for both
seal-hunting and egg-gathering, and with fields of hay and crops.

'Now both men and women are going there to stack corn,' he said,
'but you are to stay at home, because the sheep will be driven in
during the day, and you must be here to see to the milking, though
you don't usually do it.'

She said, 'Then I can see just the man to shovel dung from the
sheep-pens; that's what you are to do.'

'You're wrong to say that,' said Thord, 'for I take more care of our
farm than you do', and he flew into a rage and struck her cheek with
his right hand.

Bjorn was close at hand and heard what they said, and spoke a
verse:

3.
The lady bids the lily-white
lad muck out the byres;
wise wearer of Rhine-fire,   Rhine-fire: gold; its *wearer*: woman
the woman, speaks not wrongly.
The fine girl, Hlokk of the fire *Rokkvi*: a sea-king; of his *fishing bank*: sea; its
of the fishing bank of Rokkvi, fire: gold; *Hlokk* (valkyrie) of gold: woman
called Isle-candle, bids me
come to the porch, quickly.

Thord went to work, but Oddny did not milk the sheep, nor did Thord muck out the pens. Thord was not pleased with the verse Bjorn had spoken, but all was quiet at first.

Some time later, it is said, Thord came in and saw that Bjorn was talking to some women. It was during the evening, and Bjorn was joking with them. Thord spoke this verse:

4.
Out you must go!
I don't enjoy
your saucy games
with servant-girls.
You sit each evening
when I come in
as well-off as I.
Out you must go!

Bjorn said, 'You must want to have more of the same metre as before',[20] and spoke a verse in reply:

5.
Here I'm staying
speaking verses
loudly, amusing
your lady in style.
We will not get
a word of blame;
my heart is honest.
Here I'm staying.

What happened next was that one evening a little later, Thord came in, treading quietly, wanting to know what was going on. He heard people's voices and thought he recognized Bjorn and Oddny speaking to each other, and he stood listening, trying to overhear their conversation. Bjorn realized this, and told Oddny that Thord was listening to what they said. Oddny took this very badly, and went away panting with anger, while Bjorn spoke a verse:

6.
Panting, the much-praised
imperious Isle-candle
tries to tell me something;
her talk best pleases me.
But eavesdropping on the words
of Jord of the ale-horn   *Jord* (goddess) *of the ale-horn*: woman
is a little lad who lingers,
lurking at a distance.

Thord was not at all pleased with Bjorn over this verse-making, but still things were quiet, and each kept his own counsel. It happened one evening when they were in the sitting-room that Thord took Oddny on his knee and was affectionate to her, wanting to see how it would affect Bjorn. He kissed her, and followed this with a verse:

7.
From Bjorn – Bjorn will remember –
the bracelet-Grund, proud lady,   *bracelet-Grund* (goddess): woman
from the hands of Hitardal's
hero has slipped now.
Fate deemed me for a wife
the fir-tree with her headband;   *fir-tree with headband*: woman
that rogue won't win the slender
woman – the gain is mine.

'It's true,' said Bjorn, 'that I had to forgo my marriage, but there have been exchanges between us that I expect you will also be slow to forget', and he spoke a verse:

8.
Our meeting you'll remember,
my crew with your people
there by Thraelaeyri once;[21]
Thord, you'll not forget it.

Money, and much booty,
meekly you abandoned,
bearing, for all your boasting,
the baser part, as always.

There was not long to wait before he spoke this verse:

9.

You'll recall, your cap's land	*cap's land*: head
keenly you shook, noble	*shook*: i.e. in fear
little lad, on the hillside;	
less harm I endured.	
And from the wind-steed speeding	*wind-steed*: ship
swift as legs could take you	
you ran, in raging temper,	
robbed of all but panic.	

And still Bjorn felt he had not fully repaid Thord for reminding
him of their quarrel, and bragging that he had got the woman while
Bjorn had had to let her go, and he spoke another verse:

10.

I think vengeance has been done	
for making the brooch-bed your bride.	*brooch-bed*: woman
Your honour now only	
ebbs, Thord, and dwindles	
since by a bridge you grovelled	
in Branno islands, to dodge me,	
under a bank, dishonoured,	
on Oddaeyri, you braggart.	

Then there was quiet, but both were even less satisfied than before.
On one occasion Bjorn spoke this verse:

11.

Lily-white lad, though stripped of
luck and wealth in Solund
– I've often been in battle –
envy you avoided,

when I, my talents tested,
seized from you, boastful poet
– richly repaid for cunning
was the wretch – ship and cargo.

Thord did not like the verse, as was to be expected, and new coldness and discord developed between them. One evening, it is said that Bjorn sat beside Oddny, and added insult to injury by speaking this verse to Thord:

12.

The tree of gauzy garments,	*tree of gauzy garments*: woman
goddess of wealth, who wakened	*goddess* (Rind) *of wealth*: woman
me, will confirm fully	
her fearful husband's guessing,	
if soon the spirited lady's	
son by bush of sea-sun	*sea-sun*: gold; its *bush*: man, i.e. the poet
is born – I've promised perfect	
proof – in my image.[22]	

Only then did their verse-making cease, and they had nothing more to do with each other.

13 | It is said that one evening Thord came to speak to Oddny: 'You and many others tell me,' he said, 'that Bjorn is a fine man, but in some ways this doesn't seem so to me. He puts his dog alongside us under the table, but I have never had to do with dogs before. He will give this up if the portions are rationed.'

She said, 'Are you going to try this then, and find out what happens?'

'This is how we will arrange it,' he said. 'A share of bread will be buttered for each man, and let's see whether he gives the dog some of his. But on top of this,' said Thord, 'his two horses have been here all winter, and he coaxes my men into feeding them. It's petty of him to wheedle them into providing for his horses.'

But when the manner of serving was changed, Bjorn fed the dog no less than before, while both Thord and Bjorn had less to eat, and the servants threatened to run away because of the way the food was being served. It was not long before Thord remarked to Oddny that he did not mean to starve any longer for Bjorn's dog, and that the plan was not working; the old way of serving had to come back. This was done, and the servants were well pleased, but Bjorn acted as if he did not notice. Often Thord complained to Oddny about how ungrateful he thought Bjorn was, and how stubborn he had been over the incident. And once when they were discussing this, Thord spoke a verse:

13.
Calm were sixteen servants,
smoothly ran our household,
each bow-wielder, wealth-Hlin,   *bow-wielder*: warrior, man
was at heart untroubled,   *wealth-Hlin* (goddess): woman
till one haughty attacker   *attacker of treasure*: (generous) man
of treasure only lately
managed to make uproar
among our house's people.

There they all stayed throughout the winter in little harmony, and it was rather against Oddny's will. At first Thord had promised Bjorn that his horses would either be taken out to pasture in Hitarnes[23] or else be foddered at home. Bjorn had chosen to have them sent out, but the matter was dropped and nothing was done. Kalf the Ill-willed came to Hitarnes and asked Thord how he liked his winter guest, and whether it was his fault that more of the best hay had gone bad than his horses had eaten. Then they went to look at the hay, and it seemed to have been badly treated. Thord was angry, and told Oddny that Bjorn had bribed the servants to trample his hay in the dirt to spoil it.

She said in reply that Bjorn would not have had any part in allowing his horses to be treated differently from the others – 'and you make sure that you keep all your promises to him faithfully'.

After that Thord had Bjorn's horses taken away out to Hitarnes, where they had good pasture. And then Thord's grumbling about Bjorn's horses ceased, and things could be considered quiet for a while.

14 | It is said that one evening Thord and Bjorn were sitting on the
hall bench, when a quarrel arose between them. Then Thord
spoke a verse to Bjorn:

14.

Out you must go!
Grain you sold me
red to look at,
rye you called it.
But when people
put it in water,
it turned to ashes.
Out you must go!

Bjorn said in return,

15.

Quiet I'll stay.
I came in autumn,
paid full prices
for foul old suet.
A cloak you gave me
gaping with tatters,
elegant, furry;
Quiet I'll stay.[24]

It was easy to see that Thord thought his outlay great, with nothing
good in return. Bjorn repaid him like this because he thought that
Thord's invitation had been insincerely offered and meanly
honoured, and deserved only ill in return; and they were both more
aggrieved than before.

During the winter, Thord, Oddny and the serving-woman who
helped them off with their clothes[25] all slept in a separate apartment.
It happened one evening that Oddny came late to bed, and Thord
gave her no room in the bed. She climbed up over the side of the bed
and tried to get under the covers beside him, but this was not possible,
and so she stayed sitting up. Then Bjorn spoke a verse:

16.

The Ull of battle-Gefn's arrow,	*Gefn*: a goddess (Freyja); *battle-Gefn*: valkyrie;
ugly faults concealing,	valkyrie's *Ull* (a god): man, warrior (*arrow* is
stretches out and covers	slightly redundant)
the gold-island's whole couch,	*gold-island*: woman
so Njorun of the sea-steed's hill	*sea-steed*: ship; its *hill*: sea; *Njorun*
stays freezing on its corner	(goddess) of the sea: woman
– I have no praise for the plight	
of the mild necklace-Thrud.	*necklace-Thrud* (goddess): woman

Oddny ordered them not to make verses about her, saying that she had said nothing about this. Now from this time on, for the rest of the winter and until the summer began, they did not speak to each other.

Oddny had proposed to Bjorn during the winter that one of her and Thord's daughters should be his in her place, since he had not married her as had been intended. And one evening Bjorn recalled that, and sat the girls on his knee, and spoke this verse:

17.

Two maids and their fond mother	
the mangler of poetry	*mangler of poetry*: Thord
honours with affection;	
always I trust her speaking.	
In her place I prize them still more;	
praise always to the necklace-wearing	
Grund I give; to the sea-fire's	*necklace-wearing Grund* (goddess): woman
guardian that's not shaming.	*sea-fire*: gold; its *guardian*: man

And then as summer approached, Bjorn decided to make ready to leave. It is said that when he was about to leave at the end of his stay, he gave Oddny the cloak that had been Thord's,[26] and they spoke fondly to each other. And when he was quite ready, he rode to the outhouse where Thord was with Kalf the Ill-willed, who had just arrived. Bjorn told Thord that he was now ready to go, and meant to end his stay. Thord said he was pleased to hear it, and the sooner the better.

Bjorn said he had known that for a long time. 'This is how it has been,' he said . . .[27]

15 | Now it must first be related that Thord Kolbeinsson went out to look over his shore. He came upon a seal in a hole in the ice; the tide had gone out underneath it, and the seal was surrounded by ice and could not get away. It occurred to Thord that if he went home for his weapons, the tide would have come back up before he returned, and then he would not be able to catch the seal. He did not want that to happen, so he made an attempt and managed to bring down the seal. But this caused an accident, for the seal bit him in the thigh, giving Thord an injury. Thord went home and had the seal butchered, but decided to keep the bite secret; he did not succeed in this, for the wound grew so much worse that he had to take to his bed. Bjorn was not seldom at the farm at Vellir, and the story became known there, and people had plenty to say about the cause of Thord's injury, and Bjorn spoke a verse:

18.

The wealth-warder lies wounded,   *wealth-warder*: (miserly) man
wise men here have heard it;
scratched by a seal, the pallid
suet-gobbler's injured.
When waves come rushing roughly
on rocks, like a pebble
the sluggard goes skimming
smartly over the mudflats.

Thord learned about this and heard the verse quoted, and thought it very bad, but typical of Bjorn's behaviour. Thord made no reply to it at first, and all was quiet.

16 | Now it is to be told that Bjorn's farmhand Thorgeir spoke to him one evening, saying that they did not have as much hay as was needed for the animals he had to care for, and he asked Bjorn to go and look at the fodder to see whether he thought it would last. Bjorn did as he was asked. They went off and arrived at the byres, and Thorgeir stepped in first because he knew the way better. But a cow had borne a calf, and Thorgeir tripped over the calf as it lay on the floor, and cursed. Bjorn told him to throw the calf up into the stall, but Thorgeir said that the lower the monster lay the better, and would not touch it. Then Bjorn picked up the calf from the floor and threw it into the stall.

Home they went then, and Thorgeir told his friends how Bjorn had picked up the calf from the floor and thrown it up into the stall – 'but I wouldn't touch it'.

There were guests there who heard Thorgeir's story. And not much later these same people visited Thord at Hitarnes and told him about it. He spoke, saying that Bjorn had got enough people, both men and women, to see to such things so that there should be no need for him to act as midwife to the cows, and he spoke a verse:

19.
Why must you, O mighty
mud-dweller, keep casting
(though a seal has scratched me)
scorn on my wounding?
You'll be sorry, soldier,
at sight of shield shaking,
you clutched a twisted calf beneath
a cow's tail, dung-encrusted.

People thought it wise that this verse should not be spread about, but it was not kept secret, and it reached Bjorn's ears. He thought it a malicious verse, and he was not willing to let things rest. In the summer, Bjorn rode to Hitarnes with sixty men and issued a summons to Thord for the verse, as he claimed the law allowed.[28] Friends of both said that this case should not be taken to the Althing; they should, rather, come to terms within the district. But this could not be done; Thord would not make a settlement before the Thing was held. They came to terms at the Thing, and Thord had to pay a hundred of silver for the verse.[29] Bjorn proposed to the Law Council that either of them who recited anything in the hearing of the other should forfeit his immunity. Those whose task it was to judge approved that, and it was considered more likely then that they would bespatter each other less with foul language; and with that they went home. Then things could be considered quiet.

17 | It is further related that something appeared on the boundary mark of Thord's harbour that hardly seemed a token of friend-ship. It represented two men, one of them with a black hat on his head. They were standing bent over, one facing the other's back. It seemed to be an indecent encounter,[30] and people said that the position of neither standing figure was good, and yet that of the one in front was worse. Then Bjorn spoke a verse:

20.

Here stand the helmsmen
of harbour landing-places,

...

...

suited is the stalwart
spear-pointer for this work.   *spear-pointer*: man[31]
The weapon-wielder's anger   *weapon-wielder*: man
weighs on Thord foremost.

Thord thought it a malicious deed and a disgrace that a scorn-pole was raised on his land, and he held Bjorn responsible for it. He thought it none the better for the verse Bjorn had composed, and so the following spring he rode out to Bjorn with sixty men, and summonsed him to the Althing for raising the scorn-pole and for the verse. Again their friends said that they should come to terms at home rather than take such an ugly case to the Althing. Bjorn was not willing to do this, so they went to the Thing and settled the case there. Bjorn had to pay three marks of silver for the raising of the scorn-pole and for the verse. Then they went home and the case was considered closed. Now all was calm for two years, so that nothing is added to the story.

18 | The third summer, at the time of the Althing, a ship came to Eyrar, and on it were two kinsmen of Thord, brothers from Vik; one was called Ottar, the other Eyvind. They were related to Thord on his father's side. Both liked to throw their weight about. They sent word asking Thord to come and meet them, for they had heard of his splendid way of life, and meant to take up lodgings with him. And when Thord heard of their coming, he rode south to Eyrar, welcomed his kinsmen, and invited them to stay with him. They went home with him. The exchanges between Thord and Bjorn had not been so little spoken of that these men had not already heard them discussed, and rumour had it that Thord most often had the worst of it. They were dissatisfied with that, for they were over-bearing men, and said that it was clear to them that Bjorn was not as formidable as all that, although it was said that no one could get a fair deal from him. They urged Thord not to rest content with matters as they stood.

The local men often made trips out on to Snaefellsnes for stores of fish or other things that could be bought there. So it happened that Bjorn went out along the coast to Saxahvol to Arnor, his uncle by marriage, to buy fish. He was made welcome there.

Bjorn's aunt Thorhild spoke to him about his coming.

'The truth is, Bjorn,' she said, 'that you are a mighty man, but you also have a high opinion of yourself. Maybe you think me outspoken, but I think it's unwise to travel with only one other man when you have so many enemies. Men have come into the district who have often chosen not to be losers, and they know that Thord has often had the worst of it against you; it may be that they will want to put that right. I have a son here called Thorfinn. I offer him to you for your support, although there is board and lodging enough for him at home. I am glad you have come now, but would have been even happier if you had brought with you twelve men as good in a fight as Thorfinn, or even more. They would all have been made welcome, and you would have been less open to sudden attack from your enemies.'

Bjorn said, 'Thank you for your offer and your goodwill. I will agree to Thorfinn's coming with me, but I don't know that there is any need to travel with a large company.'

Bjorn stayed there three nights, and was well entertained.

Thord Kolbeinsson heard that Bjorn had left home and gone out to Saxahvol. He found himself some business out on the coast and went to Beruvikurhraun in a party of twelve. His kinsmen Ottar and Eyvind were among them. And when they got there, Thord told them what was behind the expedition. He said that he meant to lie in wait there for Bjorn, who was due to come out of Saxahvol, and intended to kill him.

His kinsmen answered that it was cowardly for twelve men to lie in wait for two, and that they would not have come out with him if they had known of this. They offered Thord the choice of ambushing Bjorn himself with two men, or else the two brothers would lie in wait for him: 'Now we reckon that although Bjorn himself may be a fine fighter, it will be balanced out, because we expect that his companion will be less skilled in a fight than either of us. But we will never lie in wait for him if there are twelve of us.'

Thord said, 'Time enough to talk like that when we have proved whether or not we need this troop to deal with Bjorn. But I can see that you are bold men, especially in your own opinion. Since you have given me the choice, as you said before, you lie in wait for him, and we will ride away.'

They agreed to that.

Thord turned away then, so that he was not involved with the brothers in their ambush of Bjorn, and he thought it looked most promising.

Now about Bjorn it must be told that he made ready to leave his uncle Arnor's.

Then the mistress of the house came up and said, 'It's my advice that Bjorn shouldn't go over Beruvikurhraun from here with fewer than twelve men, for I have dreamed that Thord will ambush you there, cunning as he is.'

'He won't do that,' said Bjorn; 'he will do it closer to his own farm, if he does intend it.'

Then Bjorn rode off, the three of them leaving the yard together.

As soon as they had gone, Thorhild said to her husband Arnor, 'If any harm comes to Bjorn today, you and I will not share a bed tonight.'

And at her urging, Arnor set out in a band of nine men, and followed the others to the lava field.

Bjorn greeted him gladly, and said, 'You are quick to ride after me, uncle.'

'The reason,' he replied, 'is that you seem slow to invite me, so now I am inviting myself.'

'So be it,' said Bjorn, and then they dismounted and led the horses over the lava field, for they had a long train of laden horses to take with them. Bjorn and Arnor went in front. Bjorn had a barbed spear in his hand and a helmet on his head. He was girt with a sword, with a shield at his side. Arnor Cross-stick had a sword in his hand, holding it over his shoulder by the middle of the haft. They followed the path over the lava field.

The brothers saw that there were more men coming than they had expected Bjorn to have with him. They thought their expedition would be a failure if it turned out not to be Bjorn and they had taken flight, so they waited. Bjorn and his men approached rapidly and came upon them before they were aware of it. Eyvind, the elder brother, made an assault on Bjorn, striking at him with a broad axe. It hit his helmet and glanced off, and the spike at the back of the axe caught his shield-strap. Bjorn was wounded in the chest and, secondly, in the leg, but neither was a serious wound. Ottar struck at Arnor's head, cutting off the ear and cheekbone, but the blow was halted by the sword he was carrying on his shoulder. Bjorn threw his shield from him on to the lava field and struck at Eyvind, and that was his death-blow. Both brothers fell there. Then Bjorn spoke this verse:

21.

The woman-presser, wasteful	*woman-presser*: man
of words, who tends the oxen,	
has no clue where I, the hero	
who long held sway in battle,	
felled the battle-shirt birches	*battle-shirt birches*: men
– blade cut leg-bone in two;	
the finisher of food	*finisher of food*: glutton
for fighting has no stomach.	

Then uncle and nephew bound their wounds and buried the brothers on the lava field. Then they declared them to have forfeited their immunity, as the law prescribed, on the grounds of assault and ambush. But Thord Kolbeinsson was not far away, and saw what was happening. It did not seem a good opportunity to attack them, since there were so many of them, so he went home and was not involved in the incident. He was asked when he got home where he had been for so long, and Thord spoke a verse in reply:

22.

Whispering goslings we twelve	*whispering goslings*: (feathered) arrows
whetted on Beruhraun,[32]	
Leifi's path, leaf-littered;	*Leifi's* (giant's) *leaf-littered path*: lava field
loosers of tears were silent.	*loosers of tears*: warriors, men
Swiftly the stone I trod,	
then saw the splendid dandy	
in war-gear – the heroes wished	
to have[33] the hardy men.	

And then Thord spoke another verse:

23.

Of Bjorn, I know, one battle-tale	
the Balder of shield-thorns bears,	*shield-thorns*: swords; their *Balder* (god):
of me another; the user	warrior
of snake's bed thinks he's useful,	*snake's bed*: gold; its *user*: man

for the scourge of sword-playing Ulls
is the slayer of two more;

sword-playing Ull (god): warrior

to Hogni's storm-trees, silence
would have seemed better.

Hogni: a legendary hero; his *storm-trees*:
warriors

Then Arnor went home and recovered from his wounds. Bjorn went home too, together with more men than had set out with him. And that day Bjorn made this verse:

24.

Here's news I hope that Thord
hears, the tree of battle,

tree of battle: warrior, man

who from the sword-bestower
south by sea went skipping,

sword-bestower: warrior

that where we met alone, two
warriors sank before the
sinker of the sea's horses,
supplying food to the raven.

sea's horses: ships; their *sinker*: warrior

Bjorn quickly recovered from his wounds and things were quiet after that. There was no suit taken up for the brothers. Thord had them taken to church for burial.

19 | People say that Kalf the Ill-willed lived for several years in Hraunsdal, as was said before, but after that Bjorn leased Holm to him while Bjorn and his father were both living at Vellir. Below Vellir is Grettisbaeli (Grettir's Lair), where Grettir stayed in a cave during the winter that he spent with Bjorn while he was living at Vellir. They went swimming down the river and were reckoned to be equally strong. At Vellir Bjorn had a church built and consecrated in God's name to St Thomas the Apostle, about whom Bjorn composed a fine drapa. So Runolf Dagsson[34] said.

Bjorn had given up the farm at Holm because he thought it too difficult to keep up two farms, although he had done so for some years when he first took over his father's farm. But later he had built up enough livestock, and he was not short of anything he needed for the running of the two farms. Then he and his wife lived at Holm, and Arngeir at Vellir with his wife. Kalf and Bjorn had not been friends some time before when Kalf had been in Thord's company and counsels, and had seemed rather ill-disposed, but later, when he and his son were living on Bjorn's land and they had financial dealings with each other, they struck up a friendship.

Now it happened that Kalf bought himself land west of Hitardal heath, at a place called Selardal. There are two farms there, and the other is called Hurdarbak. A man called Eid lived there; he and his wife had two sons, one called Thord, the other Thorvald. Their farm adjoined Kalf's in Selardal. And the next autumn, when Kalf had moved out from Holm west to Selardal, Kalf's son Thorstein went south over the heath, to Hitarnes, to see Thord. He was well received, and announced his business; he wanted to buy a load of seal meat.

Thord said, 'Why doesn't your friend Bjorn let you have what you need, you who have been his friends?'

Thorstein said, 'He doesn't have a big enough catch.'

Thord said, 'Are you certain of his friendship with you? I remember that he publicly declared property owing from you last summer at the Althing. He must mean to charge you with theft in such a way as to have you outlawed before you realize it, so that he can get the land you are farming for himself. It will suit him to own as much land to the west of the heath as to the east or south.'

Thorstein said that he had heard nothing of this.

'Now that,' said Thord, 'is because you are men who don't see below the surface, more given to big talk than to using your wits, and before you realize what has happened he will checkmate you out of your property. You don't know about your kinsman Dalk's plan, for you still wanted to associate with Bjorn, but Dalk and I came to an agreement about your dealings, and wanted to get rid of Bjorn before he outlawed you. But you seem to me likely to strike hard, and you must be very strong. There would be good luck and a fine reputation in it for you if you got him put out of the way by pulling a faster trick, and then you could get the support of influential people.'

Thorstein believed this.

Thord said that he should have what he had come for, just as he asked, 'and I will take nothing in exchange but friendship, for you must go into Holm on your way home and say that you will come back later and claim the barren sheep; and tell your father nothing about this when you get home'.

Then Thorstein went away with his load, and did as Thord instructed. He went to Holm and spoke to Bjorn, saying that he would come back later and claim the sheep that he and his father had kept there. After that Thorstein went home and took the load to his father. And not long afterwards, he went south over the heath, reaching Holm late in the day when people were sitting by the fires. Thorstein knocked on the door, and Bjorn went out and greeted him and invited him to stay.

He said that he was intending to go further, down to Husafell to see his kinsman Dalk, and asked Bjorn to see him to the path, 'and we must make arrangements so that I can get my sheep in the morning and drive them home'.

Then Bjorn went out of the yard with him, but had a suspicion that he was not speaking his mind about his true business, for he was thoughtful and very pale. As they came to the lava field, Bjorn said that he would turn back. Thorstein had a wood-axe, a sharp one on a long shaft, in his hand, but he was lightly clothed. It occurred to Bjorn that he had been to Thord before he came west. He saw that Thorstein was pale, and suspected that he had come as an assassin. He recoiled a little from him, giving him an opening. Thorstein quickly showed what was weighing on his mind; he raised the axe, meaning to drive it into Bjorn's head, but Bjorn ran in under the blow, for it was just what he had expected. He took hold of Thorstein by the waist and lifted him up against his chest. Thorstein lost his grip on the axe, which fell. Then Bjorn flung him down, not gently, so that there was little need to do more, then grasped his windpipe and strangled him until he was dead,[35] for Bjorn had no weapon with him. Bjorn covered his body there in the lava field, and then went home. His servants asked him where he and Thorstein had parted. He spoke a verse:

25.

The son himself of sword-god Kalf	*sword-god*: warrior
I know from life I banished	
– fearless men spoke fiercely –	
felled on red Klifsjorfi.	
I slew him without wielding	
weapons of Thund's tempest.	*Thund*: Odin; his *tempest*: battle
Fatal that fall was to the caster	
of Nid's fire, the warrior.	*Nid*: a river; its *fire*: gold; *caster* of gold: man

Bjorn slept through the night, but in the morning he got up and went at once with his servants to where he had buried Thorstein, named witnesses and declared him to have forfeited his immunity according to the law.

Then he rode west over the heath to Kalf and offered him compensation for his son, not because it was deserved, but rather for the sake of their friendship, and because they had once lived on his land and still had financial dealings with him.

'But I know,' said Bjorn, 'that it must have been Thord's idea for Thorstein to attack me.'

Kalf said he was willing to accept compensation if he could name the terms himself, but not otherwise. Bjorn said this was not possible, and that Kalf was being unreasonable, since Bjorn was offering him compensation for a man whose immunity was forfeit. Then he rode away. Bjorn had now killed three men on Thord's account, and had contrived that no compensation was due for any of them according to law.

20 | In spring, Bjorn went to drive his wethers up from Vellir along the side of the valley where the Husafell farm lies. He had his farmhands with him. They saw smoke from charcoal-burning in the wood[36] and heard men's voices, so they listened to what they were saying. Thorkel Dalksson and his farmhand were talking about the quarrel of Thord and Bjorn and about the verses that they flung at each other, and they disagreed a great deal about it; the farmhand

sided rather with Bjorn, and Thorkel with Thord. And the point of their argument was that they were wrangling over which had recited more abusive verses about the other.

Not long before, Bjorn had composed a satire against Thord, and that was well enough known to some people. The substance of it was that Arnora, Thord's mother, had eaten a kind of fish that Bjorn called a 'grey-belly';[37] he claimed that it had been found on the shore, and that from eating it she had become pregnant with Thord, so that he was not of wholly human descent on both sides. And this is part of the satire:

26.
A fish came to land
with the flood on the sand,
a lump-sucker seeming,
slimy flesh gleaming.
She-wolf of the gown   *she-wolf of the gown*: greedy woman
gulped grey-belly down,
poisoned; you'll see
bad things in the sea.

27.
Her belly increased
below her breast
so the oak of the girdle   *oak of the girdle*: woman
walked with a waddle,
sore in the womb,
swelled like a balloon.

28.
A boy was born.
She had to warn
the man wealth-winning;
the birth was beginning.

Fondly eyeing
the dog-biter, lying,   *dog-biter*: man who bites like a dog (or eats dogs?)
his eyes she thought
brave as a she-goat.[38]

The farmhand said that he thought Thord had come off badly both from the verses and in other ways, and that he had heard nothing as bad as the Grey-belly Satire that Bjorn had composed against Thord.

But Thorkel said that the Kolla-verses[39] that Thord had composed against Bjorn were much more abusive.

The farmhand said he had never heard these: 'Do you know the verses?'

'I think it's not unlikely that I know them, but I don't care to repeat them, for it is prohibited; it was declared that anyone who recited them in Bjorn's hearing would forfeit his immunity;[40] and there's no need for it, even if he doesn't hear.'

'There's no harm in it for you,' said the farmhand. 'I'm very curious, and Bjorn will not hear now.'

They argued about it for a long time, Thorkel refusing and the farmhand pressing him, saying there was no one to do anything about it now. Finally Thorkel allowed himself to be persuaded and recited the verses.

Then Bjorn leapt out at them and said there was more work to be done than teaching the Kolla-verses. 'Didn't you remember that anyone reciting the verses would forfeit his immunity, or didn't you care?'

Thorkel said he supposed Bjorn must have been hanging about eavesdropping – 'and that's not like you,' he said. 'But I don't think you are such a king among men that you won't let people pass in peace before you', and he said he did not wish for that.

Bjorn said, 'I'll not be king over anyone else if not over you', and struck him his death-blow.

The farmhand went home and told Dalk the news. He mourned his son greatly, and thought he was unlikely to get compensation; however, he had chosen up till now to keep out of the quarrels of Bjorn and Thord. Bjorn now went home, and kept a large number of men around him straight after the killing. Dalk went to see Thord Kolbeinsson and told him of the killing and its cause. Thord thought that he himself had been largely responsible, and he paid Dalk compensation and took over the case for the prosecution, independently of any settlement that might be reached, while Dalk was to support Thord in the prosecution as much as he could.

And later that spring, Dalk sought terms of settlement from Bjorn, who answered favourably and did not refuse to pay compensation. After that Thord prepared a case against Bjorn for the Thing. And when people came to the Thing, Thord tried to present the prosecution for the killing, but Bjorn was able to defend his case, putting forward the plea that it had been declared that anyone who recited the verses in his hearing was to forfeit his immunity. He said that he had heard Thorkel reciting, and had killed him for that offence. This defence was accepted, and Thord's prosecution was rendered invalid.

21 | It happened one summer when Kolli the Elegant was a child, that Bjorn came to the Autumn Meeting when the boy, some few years old, was running about there, showing promise of growing into a very handsome man. Bjorn asked whose son the boy was, and in reply someone told him that it was Thord Kolbeinsson's son Kolli. Bjorn spoke a verse:

29.

I saw the sprig of dusky	*steeds of the bay*: ships; their *sprig*: sailor, (here) boy
steeds of the bay running	
by the battle-tree, eyes	*battle-tree*: man
blazing, in my likeness.	
Chasers of channel-fire say	*channel-fire*: gold; its *chasers*: men
the child does not know	
the lord of trees that are launched	*lobster's path*: sea; its *trees*: ships; their
on the lobster's path: his father.	*lord*: sailor, man

No alteration was made in Kolli's paternity, though Bjorn sometimes seemed to be referring in his verses to what likelihood he thought there was of this.

22 | One winter it was said that Bjorn had some full outlaws living
with him, and got them to build a fortification around his farm.
And for this same harbouring of outlaws Thord prosecuted Bjorn,
hoping to get redress, if he could, for Bjorn's invalidation of the last
case against him.[41] He expected that this time he would be more
successful in his suit. Bjorn answered to the charge at the Althing,
admitting that Thord now had the law on his side and was speaking
the truth. He said that he did not intend to deny the charge in this
case and that he would pay compensation for the offence. They
came to terms about it and Bjorn paid the amount imposed by the
settlement.

It happened some time later that Thord Kolbeinsson sheltered
two full outlaws and got them lodgings in Hraunsdal with Steinolf,
the husband of Thorhalla Gudbrand's daughter. Bjorn heard about
this, set out from home and rode up to Steinolf's shieling, meeting
in Grjotardal a man called Eirik, who lived there. Bjorn gave him a
knife and a belt as a bribe to tell him when the outlaws who were
staying with Steinolf left for their ship. He promised to do that, and
kept watch from then on. Thord meant to give them some money
and get them abroad, thinking that this was the best way to get
them off his hands. And Bjorn had learned that this was what was
intended.

Now the time came when they set off for the ship. They made
ready in the evening and travelled by night. When Eirik became
aware of this he rode up to Holm and told Bjorn, who acted at once
and rode after them. Their path lay out over the Hitara river. Bjorn
pursued them hotly and caught up with them during the night before
they crossed the river, and it can quickly be told that Bjorn killed
them both, then dragged them under a crag and covered their bodies.
He took home the sum of money they had been carrying. The horses
they were travelling with belonged to Thord. And late that night
Bjorn rode out from home, taking the horses with him. He came to
Hitarnes so early that people had not yet got up, and there Bjorn set
loose the horses the outlaws had been using.

Then he met Thord and said, 'I must tell you that I have killed the outlaws you have taken into your hands. If you have any objection, you had better stand up and avenge them.'

Thord said, 'You have earned the name Champion.'

Bjorn said, 'What is the christening gift to be?'

Thord said he was to keep the money he had taken from the outlaws. Now they parted, for the time being, and Bjorn rode home. Again the rumour went round that this had not been to Thord's credit, and seemed to have gone heavily against him.

23 | Now it is to be told that on one occasion Bjorn and Thord held a horse-fight near Fagriskog, and they arrived before most of the local people. Then Thord was asked to entertain people, and he did not refuse. To begin with he recited the verses he called 'Beam of Day', which he had composed about Bjorn's wife Thordis; the lady herself he always called 'Light of Lands'.[42] Bjorn listened to the entertainment in a good spirit, but made it clear that he did not need to be asked to entertain them or to make a riposte. When Thord had finished Bjorn began, and entertained the company with the verses he called 'Isle-candle Verses'. And when this was finished, Thord asked his sons Arnor[43] and Kolli how they liked this entertainment.

Arnor said, 'I certainly do not like it, and this is not to be borne.'

Kolli said, 'I don't find that. I think the balance is even, since one poem counters the other.'

Then things were quiet. The local people arrived and were entertained according to plan, and it is not mentioned that any further developments took place there. But once again Thord was more dissatisfied than before.

It is also said that they held an entertainment and horse-fight on another occasion. Bjorn attacked strongly, driving one of the horses on with a stout goading-stick in his hand. Thord was sitting on horseback, riding behind the circle of men watching the fight. And when Thord came closest to the circle, he thrust at Bjorn with the spear he held in his hand, driving it into his shoulder-blade. Bjorn turned around, brandishing his staff, and drove it against Thord's ear so that he fell off his horse. There was no chance to do more, for now men jumped between them and separated them. Nothing is said other than that they allowed these deeds to cancel each other out, and then all was quiet for a while.

24 | Some years later, two brothers came from Hornstrandir to visit Thord at Hitarnes, and they spent a night there. The next day they asked Thord for protection and told him about the trouble they were in.

Thord said, 'I will make you an offer about this.'

This was early in spring. One of them was called Beinir, the other Hogni. They asked what the offer was.

'It won't seem very honourable,' said Thord. 'I will give you a hundred of silver to attack Bjorn and bring me his head. I will give you half the hundred now and half when you come back.'

That was the bargain between them. Thord promised them his protection on top of this. They said they would not shrink from attacking Bjorn if they got the opportunity.

They went up into the valley and came to Bjorn's house at Holm, where the cattle had been brought to the milking-shed for the evening. They met Bjorn's wife Thordis by the door and asked where Bjorn was, saying they had business with him. She pointed him out to them and said that he had gone to the pasture. And when she came in, she told Bjorn's mother Thordis about the talk of the men who had come. She said she thought they must be assassins. When Kolbein, Bjorn's servant, heard this, he took Bjorn's shield and sword and ran with them to where he knew Bjorn was. He got there before the attackers because he knew better where the shortest route lay. He told Bjorn that he believed killers were coming to find him.

Bjorn thanked him for this and made for the sheep-pen with his weapons, and went into the building. They saw him go and headed in that direction. When they reached the pen and were wondering how to attack him, Bjorn rushed out at them so suddenly that they were quite unprepared, and he laid hands on them both. There was a great disparity of strength between them; it did not turn out as they had intended. He bound them with their hands behind their backs, but left their legs free, and used no weapons on them. Then he stuck their axes under their bonds at the back and told them to go and show themselves to Thord. He took the silver from them and gave it to Kolbein. They went away, their venture seeming to have failed disgracefully, and came in this state to Hitarnes. Thord said that he had no men near him, though they were at hand, and drove them away.

25 | There was a woman called Thorbjorg who invited Bjorn for a visit for the sake of friendship. He accepted the invitation and stayed with her for three nights, hospitably entertained. The last night he was restless in his sleep, and when he woke up the mistress of the house asked him what he had dreamed, and why he had been so restless as he slept.

He said, 'It seemed to me that six men were attacking me, and I thought I almost lacked hands to oppose them. Perhaps that was when you heard me.'

'The meaning of that is plain to see,' said Thorbjorg. 'Those are the fetches of men who have evil intentions towards you. I don't want you to leave here until we have made sure that no one will hinder your going or lie in wait for you. Or go home by a different route from the way you came here even if it is rather longer, for those who want to meet you will watch the path that is shortest and most travelled.'

'Very well,' he said. 'I will go another way.'

Then he made ready for the trip home, and before they parted thanked her very much for her hospitality. But when he had left the yard he decided to go by the shorter way. He went on for a while, and then saw men ahead of him by some sheep-pens. He thought he could tell that it must be Thord with some others; he thought he could see six men. Bjorn prepared to defend himself if necessary. He was wearing a black cape, and he belted it firmly and then drew his sword. He had been carrying a spear in his hand, and as soon as he came within range of them he sent it flying forward along the track, and in its path was a man called Stein, son of Gudbrand. It pierced right through him, and he was killed at once. Then a man called Thorbjorn rushed at Bjorn, passing between him and Thord, but Bjorn was too quick for him and dealt him a blow on the forehead. It was only a small wound. Then Bjorn struck at Thord, who took the most prudent course: he let himself fall away from the blow, although he was just slightly wounded. When Thord stood up, Bjorn was not offered any further aggression, and at that they parted. Then both went home.

26 | Bjorn's sister lived at Knarrarness. He went there during the winter and stayed for three nights, and each night he had a dream that seemed significant to him. Before they parted, she asked him what had appeared to him in his dreams, and he spoke this verse:

30.
A dream I've dreamed, lady
with hair-land decked in river-fire: *hair-land*: head; *river-fire*: gold
Odin again to sword-play
will send the skilful poet.
Both hands were blood-covered,
blade of famed Maering reddened,
the cold hammer's comrade   *cold hammer's comrade*: sword
clasped in my hand, shattered.

Thord had learned of Bjorn's journey, and he travelled into his path with nine men, and lay in wait for him by the Hitara river. As he made his way home, Bjorn saw men ahead by the river. It seemed obvious now that it must be Thord. He made ready as he had done the time before, meaning to accept the challenge although the odds against him were great. When he reached them they attacked him from all sides; he could not keep up his defence, and they were able to wound him. He saw that he could not hold out in this situation. Then he rushed out into the river and swam across it with his weapons, holding his shield on his back. A Norwegian who was with Thord threw his spear after Bjorn, piercing his shield. When Bjorn got out of the river, Thord's son Kolbein threw a spear at him over the river, hitting him in the thigh. But Bjorn took the spear and threw it back across the river at them. There was a man in its path, and it passed through him and hit Kolbein Thordarson who was sitting behind him, and both were killed. There they parted, and Bjorn went home. It touched his wife deeply to see him come home covered in blood, and she thought that something terrible had happened. But Bjorn said it would not cause any trouble, and he recovered in a short time. Thord was very dissatisfied.

27 | There was a man called Thorstein, the son of Kuggi, who lived at Ljarskogar. He was a wealthy man and of good family, and was considered to be overbearing. He was related by marriage to prominent and worthy men. His wife was called Thorfinna, and she was second cousin to Bjorn's wife Thordis. Thord Kolbeinsson and Dalk asked Thorstein to support them against Bjorn, thinking that they would come off badly against him.

But Thorstein said that he was not ready to do so at that time: 'It would seem to me the best course to pursue against him would be for you two to pick some new quarrel with Bjorn. That will be easy, for I know the man is not shy of strife, and then I will give you support.'

Now Thord thought things were turning out well. And because of Thorstein's promise of help, Dalk invited him to the Yule feast, telling him to bring as much company as he liked. That was in spring before the Thing. And when people left the Thing in summer, they kept a watch about themselves. Meetings in the district were much in decline, and people tried to take care that Thord and Bjorn met rather less than more. But all was quiet.

The next winter, before Yule, Thorstein made ready for the journey to visit Dalk for the Yule feast. He rode out to Skogarstrond to his kinsman Thorgeir Steinsson at Breidabolstad, who urged Thorstein, if he wanted his advice, not to travel south. But Thorstein wanted nothing other than to go, and he set out with twelve people. His wife Thorfinna, who was the daughter of Vermund of Vatnsfjord, was there with him. They went to Dunkadarstadir to stay overnight with Kalf's father Ozur,[44] then went on the next day south to Knappafell heath and stayed at Hafursstadir in Knappadal. A man called Haf lived there. The next day, two paths lay before them over Hellisdal heath, which runs off from Klifsdal. They followed the path that goes up Hellisdal and down Klifsdal. The dale leads straight to Bjorn's farm at Holm. The weather became bad, with a heavy snowfall. They came down at last to a haystack yard belonging to Bjorn, which stood at Hjallar. There was a big snowdrift there. A man was there carrying out hay and giving it to Bjorn's horses; they exchanged greetings and asked for news.

Then Thorstein said, 'Will you tell us the way down over the lava field?'

The farmhand said, 'I don't suppose Bjorn's men owe you any friendship, so I won't.'

Thorstein said, 'What does it matter if you are forced to go, if you like that better?'

'You may be able to do that,' said the servant, 'if you try.'

The weather worsened, with both drifting snow and frost, and the farmhand had completely disappeared before they realized it. He went home and told Bjorn that he seemed to have got out of a tight corner, saying that Thorstein Kuggason and eleven others had met him and tried to force him to tell them the way.

Bjorn said, 'If Thorstein is as clever as he is bold and aggressive, he will come here tonight rather than risk his life where he is now. Whether he goes up into the valley against the storm or down over the lava field across the water and the difficult passages, it will not go well with him. Let's assume that he is coming here this evening.'

Thorfinna was riding, but the men were on foot, and they were all exhausted, having gone astray on the moor during the day. They saw that the farmhand had quite got away. They discussed what course they should take. The weather went on getting worse, and in any case the darkness of night was setting in.

Thorfinna said, 'If Bjorn slips through your fingers all the more easily than his farmhand, seeing that he is the greater man, your journey will not turn out particularly well. I know Thorstein thinks we have no choice but to be hostile to him, but I think it a better plan to honour our connection with my second cousin Thordis, and a bad plan to risk our lives out in the open by Bjorn's farm – and cowardly too, with much depending on how he deals with the matter. Let us rather go there, and if we seek him out at home, we will have a good welcome; he is a good man in that way.'

Thorstein was very reluctant to do this, but still he went.

Soon afterwards they saw a man by another haystack yard. Bjorn's farmhand Sigmund was there. Thorstein told him to show them the way down to Husafell.

He said, 'I can't show people the way through snowdrifts in the dark.'

But at last he mounted on Hviting's back and rode in front with Thorfinna. They came to the Hitara river, which had risen very high, and they got wet in the river. Then Thorstein grew rather suspicious about the path the man was taking. It turned out as he suspected: he was following the path that led up to Holm, and Bjorn was close by with thirty able-bodied men. It was difficult for Thorstein's men to find the farm, for it was no short distance. It stood under the Holmsfjall mountain. Bjorn's man rode in front of them all the way into the yard. And when they got there and knocked on the door, Bjorn spoke to the farmhand who had been by the haystack yard, and told him to go out and invite Thorstein to stay, if he had arrived.

'But I expect,' said Bjorn, 'that he will think you have no authority and little to offer, for people say "the man in charge invites". Say that he must accept your invitation or else go away.'

The man did as he was told, and as Bjorn had guessed, Thorstein said that he would accept no invitation from him, and told him to summon whoever was in charge. The farmhand told him to accept this invitation or go away. Thorstein accepted it, for he saw no way of reaching any farm if they left. And when they came in they were greeted, and then a table was set up. There were no fires made there and no change of clothes was offered, although they were wet and frozen. Bjorn asked for news in a leisurely way, without any enthusiasm, but the ladies entertained Thorfinna warmly. Thorstein debated with himself whether they should get away that night, for he thought he had been received with utter hostility. But Bjorn said he would not give him any man to go with them through the dark and the snowdrifts, and that the entertainment he would give them for the night would not be difficult to repay.

They were given cloaks to wrap themselves in, for their shoes and socks were frozen so that they could not get them off, as no fire had been kindled. Nor were they offered any dry clothes. There was cheese and curds for the evening meal, for fasts were not yet established by law.[45]

Bjorn asked Thorstein, 'What do people call this food in your district?'

He answered that they called it cheese and curds.

Bjorn said, 'We call this food "enemies' cheer".'

This was what their night's lodging was like: some of them got themselves out of their breeches, which hung, frozen, overnight on the partition, and then they lay down to sleep. Early in the morning Bjorn got up and looked at the weather, shutting the door when he came in. Thorstein asked what the weather was like. Bjorn said it was good weather for brave men. Thorstein called to his companions and told them to make ready, and so they did. Thorfinna had been taken to a seat in the main room. But when Thorstein went out the weather was abominable.

He said, 'Bjorn isn't choosy about the weather on our behalf; he doesn't know how short of heroism we are.'

Bjorn heard what he said: 'Yet it is fit weather for a begging journey to Husafell,' he said.

Thorstein grew angry at this response, went out to the main room and joined Thorfinna. There was one other woman there. They were quiet and said little; Bjorn had come in too. Frost followed the great storm, and at times there were bright patches in the sky.

Then Bjorn said, 'I will give you a choice: either you stay here till the fourth day of Yule and accept all the hospitality I can offer, or go away if you prefer; but Thorfinna, and the men who are frozen, will stay behind.'

Thorstein said that he did not want to harm his men, and that he supposed it was possible not to go at all; and that was what he would choose, he said.

'Good,' said Bjorn. 'You have made the wiser choice.'

Then Bjorn had great fires made, and told Thorstein to toast himself and dry his clothes. Thorfinna urged Thorstein to accept everything from Bjorn that would make him more comfortable: 'From now on we won't be stinted; his coldness to begin with was excusable. The temperaments of both of you are such that it will be more fitting for the two of you to be on good terms with each other.'

Thorstein now accepted the situation with a good grace and sat by the fire with his companions. Bjorn was very cheerful.

Then he said, 'Now, what has happened is that necessity more or less forced you to come here; and I was short with you the first night because I meant you to have other things to talk about over ale at Husafell than that I was making overtures of friendship to you. But from now on, I will entertain you as best I can.'

And now the entertainment was of the best. The mass for the second day of Yule[46] was sung, and they stayed there for four days of Yule, enjoying the hospitality as it deserved.

Then the storm abated. Thorstein said they must make ready, and so they did. Bjorn sent for his stud horses, which were close to the haystack yard since they had been fed there during the storm. The stallion, a son of Hviting, was pure white, but the mares were all red. There was another son of Hviting in Thorarinsdal, also white, but with black mares. Now Bjorn had one group of horses led to Thorstein,[47] saying that he wished to present them to him.

Thorstein replied that he did not want to accept them in these circumstances, 'for I don't yet deserve gifts from you; and if I did not repay you for the hospitality I have just received, it is unlikely that I would do so even if you added more to it. But if I do repay the hospitality suitably, I will accept the horses then, knowing that they in turn will have to be repaid in some way. I will offer myself as mediator between you and Thord in your dispute, for it cannot rest as it is. Although no compensation was due for the men you have killed, and you have not strayed far beyond the law, the two of you will come into collision unless the case is mediated; and I'll tell you what I will do. You must pay a certain sum for each of them, though it be less than will be wanted, and I will make up the difference; and then they will think they have put up a good fight.'

Bjorn said, 'I will agree to what you decide, and put the whole problem into your hands.'

'And I too,' said Thorstein, 'will now pledge myself to this.'

Bjorn went with them to the path. The horses he gave to Thorstein numbered four altogether.

28 | Now Thorstein and his party came to Husafell, where many other guests, including Thord Kolbeinsson, had already arrived; it was a fine feast. Thord greeted Thorstein politely, but was less pleased than he would have been if Thorstein had not been staying with Bjorn. And after the eighth day Thord went back to Hitarnes, together with Thorstein and his wife, and they stayed there for the rest of Yule. After Yule, Thorstein asked Thord whether he was willing to trust him to arbitrate in the case between him and Bjorn, saying that Bjorn had agreed to it. Thord said that it seemed promising.

'But it seemed extraordinary to me,' he said, 'that you stayed with Bjorn during that storm.'

Thorstein said that it would have been less promising to have ventured out in abominable weather and exposed himself and his men to injury.

Thorstein had broached with Dalk the subject of the settlement before he left Husafell, and he was not unwilling for Thorstein to arbitrate between them. Then Thorstein came very often to confer with Thord, who became altogether more reluctant than Dalk was. Thorstein said that people would say they had a good arbitration in the settlement if he carried it out, and that he had only recently made friends with Bjorn. The case progressed, through Thorstein's persuasions, so that Thord, and everyone else, agreed to his stipulations.

29 | It is said that the settlement meeting was to be held below Hraun. Then Bjorn was sent for with a great troop of men, and he stayed outside with his supporters while Thord and his men were inside. Then Thorstein proceeded with the settlement. And when they had conferred for some time, making reference to the settlement, the situation seemed rather good than bad, thanks to Thorstein's management.

Thord said, 'Something about the settlement is not yet clear.'

Thorstein asked what that was.

'You and I have not discussed my verses and Bjorn's. Now what I want is that we each recite everything we have composed about the other.'

Thorstein said that would be unnecessary.

'Not at all,' said Thord. 'I want to know which of us has composed more about the other, and in this respect I need not be at a disadvantage in relation to Bjorn.'

It went ahead as Thord asked, each of them reciting all that he had composed about the other, and of that entertainment only some was fit to hear. But it was established that Bjorn had composed one verse more than Thord. Thord said that he wanted to compose a verse in return, although Thorstein and many other people said that this was unnecessary. Bjorn said in reply that he did not want to be accused of giving Thord permission to compose the verse, 'but if you won't let the matter drop, then don't delay, and take care there is no open slander in it'.

But Thorstein said that Thord's faction had so little respect for him that they were not willing to keep to the settlement he had made, and that he was almost ready to wash his hands of their case. Thord said that he would take no notice, whether Bjorn gave permission or not, and spoke a verse:

31.
Boldly, Bjorn each morning
brews some scheme for evil,
the dolt, jaws dropping, always
dazed by every slander;

and the white-talking windbag,
wide of arse and loathsome,
stripped of sense and reason,
stays a useless loser.

'Now you can hear,' said Bjorn, 'that this scum doesn't want peace. He'll not throw away this verse unanswered any more than the others.'

And Bjorn spoke a verse:

32.
Don't claim, Thord, to down me;
debts I'll not leave unsettled.
You've a dearth of daring
and deeds, feeble trickster.
I've made no blacker metres
– I mix beer for Odin –
than for you, sword-inviter,
outlawed by your folly.

beer for Odin (Har): poetry
sword-inviter: warrior, man

The settlement was abandoned, and they left the meeting. Thorstein went to Hitarnes with Thord and stayed there for a short time. When he left, he got few gifts from Thord. Because Thorstein thought that it was Thord's fault that the settlement had come to nothing, their friendship was rather in decline, for he thought that Thord had little valued his contribution to this case. Thorstein went to visit Bjorn at Holm and stayed there for some time.

And when he left, Bjorn led him to the path up on to Hitardal heath, where they meant to part after speaking together in confidence, and Bjorn said that he thought he would have had the better part in the case against Thord, 'since I was willing to accept your judgement. But you and I have sworn friendship between us; I am determined to keep to that and be your friend, but we both have certain enemies. Now I would like to propose that whichever of us lives longer should avenge the other if he meets his death by weapons or man's contrivance.'

Thorstein said that he considered himself to have promised this much whenever he offered his friendship: 'But let us make some distinction, since you have spoken of vengeances, for people know better now than before what they must do. I want to stipulate that either of us should obtain the right to decide the terms of judgement, in a prosecution for the death of the other, to be either outlawry or compensation, rather than putting anyone to death, and that better befits Christian men.'

Then they made a firm agreement that either of them must avenge the other or pursue the prosecution of his killer as if they were brothers by birth.[48] Then the stud horses were led forward again, and this time Thorstein agreed and said that he would accept them by all means; the horses stayed there that winter and the following summer without being sent for, and Bjorn was to send them west the following autumn. Bjorn gave Thorfinna a gold ring, and the costly woven tunic that King Olaf had given to Thord Kolbeinsson, and that the king had given into Bjorn's possession after the robbery in the Branno islands. And then they parted good friends, and both went home.

Soon afterwards Bjorn had a pain in the eye which lasted for some time. It gave him some trouble, but improved as time went by. However, he was somewhat the worse for it: afterwards his sight was rather dim, not as keen as before.

It was very generally thought that all the dealings between Bjorn and Thord ended in the same way, and Thord and those who stood by him in the case were very dissatisfied. A great friendship now developed between Bjorn and Thorstein Kuggason.

30 | Now the winter and the summer passed, and their affairs seemed to be peaceful. That autumn, Thorfinn Thvarason went out to Ness[49] to visit his father in a party of fifteen; he took Bjorn's sword Maering, and Bjorn had Thorfinn's weapon. Bjorn was at home with few other men; some of the servants had gone to a common fold in Langavatnsdal, and some another way. Thord and Kalf were waiting with a large body of men at Hitarnes, unknown to Bjorn, and they meant, if they saw their chance, to burn Bjorn in his

house. Old Arngeir set out from home, meaning to pay a visit to his daughter in Knarrarness, and in the morning he took Bjorn's weapons, which were in the house, while Bjorn had gone out to his horses. Arngeir lost his way, and did not know where he was until he came to Thord's cow-byre at Hitarnes, and met a cattleman who at once sent him away. But there were some women in the byre who, when they went indoors, could not keep quiet about Arngeir's coming. And when Thord, Kalf and Dalk learned that there were few people at home with Bjorn, they discussed their tactics. And at this time Thord composed the following verse:

33.

Eagerly I ask all	
users of shield-clamour,	*users of shield-clamour*: gods
strong spear-gods, who fashioned	
the sky – I see clearly –	
that by the steel-chant stirrer may	*steel-chant stirrer*: warrior
stand – and I to cause it –	
bloody, red-bearded, over	
Bjorn's scalp, the eagle.	

And now Kalf was very insistent that they should kill Bjorn if they could, and said that he had been ready to fight against Bjorn long ago, when he had had more strength than he had now. Also, Dalk said that it was obvious that they should use this opportunity when Bjorn had few men about him. They had had an uneven struggle against Bjorn, he said, and it seemed about time to have his tyranny over their heads no longer, if matters could be put right.

He said that Thord was obliged to take charge and organize the attack, 'and the others to support you'.

Then they decided that Kalf should go to Eid's sons, Thorvald and Thord, at Hurdarbak, and give them a message from Thord Kolbeinsson telling them what they meant to do. They responded at once and set off to return with Kalf, and in the course of their journey they had to cross the Thorarinsdalsa river in Hitardal. There by the river they met Bjorn's servant-woman, who had to go out to Vellir. They asked her for news from Holm, what people were doing, and how many men were at home with Bjorn; and not being too slow of speech, she told them a good deal about it. She said that there were three men at home apart from Bjorn; she added, though, that they were in the forest cutting wood. Then they parted from her and hastened back to Thord and Dalk.

They made ready at once for the attack on Bjorn. Twenty-four men set out, one of them being Thord's son Kolli.[50] They stopped in the evening for their supper below Hraun, and then travelled overnight by the path that runs up into the valley from Vellir until they came on to the Holm land, and then took counsel.

Thord gave orders for how they were to go about taking Bjorn. They also made a firm agreement among themselves at this meeting that if they succeeded in bringing Bjorn down, they would all be obliged to pay if compensation were demanded for him: Thord in the first instance, and Dalk and Kalf, whichever of them was his killer. That day there were to be gatherings at the sheepfold in Thorarinsdal, and others in the upper part of Hitardal.[51]

31 | After that Thord made his arrangements. When morning came, he sent Kalf along the path that leads to Vellir, along which they had ridden during the night. He went in a troop of six men to lie in wait for Bjorn in case his movements took him that way. Meanwhile, Eid's sons Thord and Thorvald, and Kolli, the son of Thord Kolbeinsson, were to lie in wait on the path leading to Hvitingshjalli in case he approached that way, because the horses that Bjorn had given Thorstein were pastured there, and Bjorn often went to see them. Hvitingshjalli was named after the older Hviting. Dalk of Husafell was to lie in wait on the path leading to the mountains east of the lake and keep watch there, for they thought it not unlikely that Bjorn would go up the valley to the sheepfold, since few people were at home. But Thord was to wait on the path that leads out of Holm down to Husafell. Thord thought it likely that Bjorn would go to one or other of the sheepfold meetings, and more likely that he would go to the one at Thorarinsdal because more of Bjorn's livestock might be expected to be there, so Thord lay in wait

in case he came that way. There were six men in each ambush. And they guarded all the paths because they were sure that Bjorn would go out sometime, and they were unwilling to approach Holm until it was certain, if possible, that he was not at home. They thought it would be difficult for them to attack him there. Then they parted, and each made his way to the path to which he had been assigned, to lie in wait for Bjorn.

32 | It is said that Bjorn, for his part, was on his feet early that morning, and had breakfast; his farmhand Sigmund had gone up into the valley. Bjorn was not pleased when his people were away visiting other places, for he had many enemies, and thought there was never a moment when it was unlikely that he would need men by him. His brows were rather knit, and he told his wife Thordis that he would go to Hvitingshjalli and trim the manes of Thorstein's horses before he sent them west. And yet he said that he had had rather bad dreams that night, though he said he did not understand clearly what they might portend. He had very often dreamed in the same way, he said, but now it seemed more significant.

She said, 'I would rather that you didn't leave the house at all today. You are careless about your safety, while your enemies wait all around you. But what did you dream?'

'I will not let dreams direct my movements,' he said.

'I wish you would not leave the house, and would take special care of yourself, which never did anyone any harm. But I think your dreams were especially bad last night. Tell me what happened.'

So Bjorn spoke a verse:

34.
Strange if, far-seeing, no
sign the goddesses give me:
I often lie longer wakeful;
I've learned of men's hatred.

For now an arm-snake Ilm   *arm-snake*: ring; its *Ilm* (goddess): woman
of day-fire's lord, wearing   *day-fire*: sun; its *lord*: God
a helmet, each dream haunting,
homeward bids the poet.[52]

'This I have often dreamed,' he said, 'and now, last night, most forcefully.'

She urged him not to leave the house, but he would not be dissuaded. Those of their farmhands who were at home went into the forest to cut wood, and Bjorn was the only grown man left. Now he made ready to go to the horses, and had the large mane-shears at his belt, a hood on his head and a shield at his side. He had in his hand the sword belonging to Thorfinn Thvarason. Bjorn was a very tall man, handsome and freckled, red-bearded and curly-haired, weak-sighted, but an excellent fighting man. A fifteen-year-old boy went with him. And as they left the hayfield, Bjorn spoke a verse:

35.
I go out, few following,
fearing no man's vengeance,
my sword and splendid shield at
the ring-spoiler's side.   *ring-spoiler*: man, here the poet
Before I flee at Myrar
from any shrub of sea-beast,   *sea-beast*: ship; its *shrub*: man
in my hand the hilt-wand   *hilt-wand*: sword
has to be set swinging.

Then they went along the path leading to Hvitingshjalli; they had to cross the Hitara river close to where it flows out of the lake. And when they had been going for a while, the boy saw six men coming towards them from the haystack yard at Hvitingshjalli. Bjorn asked the boy whether he could see the horses at Hjalli,[53] saying they would be easy to see because of their colour. He said he could see the horses, and also six men coming towards them. Then Bjorn spoke a verse:

36.

We two, Eir-of-weapons'	*Eir* (goddess) *-of-weapons*: valkyrie; her
warden, once were many;	*warden*: warrior, man
often under shield this poet	
a wolves' feast attended.	*a wolves' feast*: battle
A band the man bold-minded	
brought east in the autumn;	
the tough treasure-giver's	*treasure-giver*: man
troop was not a small one.	

Bjorn had on a fine tunic and was wearing hose, and bound around his leg was the silk cross-garter he had got in the exchange with the blessed King Olaf.

He drew the sword that belonged to Thorfinn Thvarason, and said, 'Here a good man has a bad sword.'

Kalf saw them at once from where he had got to, and started in pursuit of them, saying, 'There is no small hope that our luck is changing. They thought they had [not] placed me in danger, but I think that now I am hunting the bear that we all want to hunt.'[54]

'They are not far from us now, Bjorn,' said the boy, 'for they are going hard.'

Bjorn answered, 'We will find it all the easier to catch the horses, the more people come to lend a hand.'

The boy said, 'These can't be men of peace; they are all carrying weapons. And I see still more men, for there are some coming behind us, also armed.'

'You mustn't make too much of it,' said Bjorn. 'It may be that they are people from the sheepfold meeting.'

The boy said, 'I can see still more men coming from Holm. The only thing for us to do is to turn towards Klifsdal, and then save ourselves by going through Hellisdal.'[55]

Bjorn said, 'I have never been chased away before, and that must not change now. I will not turn back. We will go along Klifsand to Klifsjorfi, and I would gladly go to the large Grastein rock if we could get there.'

'I can't tell,' said the boy, 'how that would help us, for they are attacking us from every side. I can see clearly that they are in groups of six, though some are further away from us than others, and now I see altogether no fewer than twenty-four men.'

Bjorn asked, 'How are the men closest to us dressed?'

The boy told him, and Bjorn thought he recognized Kalf from his description. Kalf was a tall dark man, and was only a short way off behind them, while Kolli and Eid's sons were coming from in front. Dalk was approaching from Holm, though he and those with him were still far away.

Bjorn said to the boy, 'Now you go up on to the ledge to the horses, but I will wait here. It would be of no use to go further.'

Then Bjorn sat down while the boy went to catch the horses. He tried to turn back, but could not, for their encounter had begun. First to come up to Bjorn were Kalf and his five men, and Kolli, and with him Eid's sons and the rest of their group of six. Thorvald Eidsson threw his spear at Bjorn as soon as he was within range. Bjorn caught the spear in the air and sent it back to its owner. It struck Thorvald in his middle, and he fell dead to the ground. They had come between Bjorn and the Grastein rock, so that he could not reach it. Thord Eidsson meant to avenge his brother, and struck a great blow at Bjorn, but Bjorn was holding his shield with his arm through the hand-grip, and the blow entered the shield with such force that Bjorn's arm was broken and the shield fell down. Then Bjorn grasped the narrow point of the shield[56] with his other hand, and drove it into Thord's head so that he was killed at once; but some people say that he stabbed him to death with the mane-shears.

Kolli attacked Bjorn fiercely, the most fiercely of all the men, though we are not able to record the extent of the injuries he dealt him. Kalf spoke, saying that it would all come to the same for Bjorn even if he did kill some men, and that he would not get away this time – 'Our numbers are not small now,' he said.

Some said that they should form a ring around Bjorn and guard him so that he would not get away, and wait for Thord Kolbeinsson to deal him the final blow. And while they were discussing this, Bjorn unfastened the mane-shears from his belt. They had just been sharpened before he came out, and were both large and keen. Then

Dalk arrived and wanted to attack Bjorn at once, for he was a bold man and felt himself to be hardly lacking a cause for duelling with Bjorn, since he had his son's death to avenge. But Bjorn drew Thorfinn's sword, which he had brought from home, and struck so hard at Dalk's leg that it broke, although the sword did not bite. Dalk was left disabled, and was taken away out of danger.

Next came Thord Kolbeinsson. And when Bjorn saw him, he said, 'You come late to such a meeting, little lad.'

'But that little lad will stand close to you today,' said Thord, 'and strike you a shameful blow.'

'Those are the only blows you will strike,' said Bjorn, 'as long as you live.'

For Thord had made a slip of the tongue; he meant to say that he would strike Bjorn a shaming blow[57] that day.

Then Bjorn gripped the shears, for he knew the sword was useless, and rushed at Thord, meaning to drive the shears into him. Thord dodged out of reach, but a farmhand of Thord's called Grim got in the way and was killed at once. And at that moment Kalf struck at Bjorn and gave him a great wound. Then Bjorn fell on to his knees, and defended himself with the shears with great courage (for he was a most gallant man, as had often been demonstrated), and dealt his attackers many wounds. They pressed him very hard now, and none more than Kolli.

Bjorn said, 'You are attacking me hard today, Kolli.'

'I don't know of any reason to show mercy,' he replied.

'But there is,' said Bjorn. 'Your mother must have told you that you must attack me very fiercely, but I think I see that you are more gifted at other things than at tracing family trees.'[58]

Kolli said, 'I don't think you have spoken too soon if I am related to you in any way.'

And at once Kolli stopped his onslaught and went away.

Bjorn defended himself for a long time with the shears, on his knees, and they all wondered how a man almost unarmed, under attack from so many, could put up such a defence; and yet all who came closest to him felt that they had a hard task. Now it is told that Thord struck at Bjorn and cut off his buttocks, and then Bjorn fell.

Then Thord did not pause between blows. His second blow cut off Bjorn's head, passing between trunk and head, and then Thord spoke a verse:

37.
Fate did not fail, warrior
fierce in war, to let me –
(blades bit him who doubted
my bravery, south of heathland;
I suffered robbery by the ruler   *death-rod*: sword; its *wood*: shield;
of death-rod's wood;   *ruler* of the shield: warrior, man
with good cause swords cut him)
– become his slayer.[59]

Thord picked up Bjorn's head and fastened it to his saddle-straps.[60] He let it hang there beside his saddle. Kalf said that they should go to Holm and announce the killing, and wanted to take them the ornament that Bjorn had been wearing round his neck. Dalk said that that was unnecessary and rash; that it would be more fitting to show themselves ready to redress Bjorn's kinsmen for what they had done than to increase the offence against them. Thord added nothing to either side of the dispute. Kalf rode away at once from the scene of action. As they rode off and were coming down over Klifsand, some ravens flew towards them, and then Thord composed this verse:

38.
Where are you racing, ravens,
in regiment black, so swiftly?
North-east of Klifsand, clearly,
carrion you are seeking.
There lies Bjorn, and bloody
birds his head are guarding.
Higher upon Hvitingshjalli
The helmet's staff fell.   *helmet's staff*: warrior, man

33 | Then they came to Holm, and Kalf went into the women's room where Bjorn's wife Thordis was, and told her of Bjorn's killing.

'And here for the taking,' he said, 'is the ornament that he was wearing round his neck.'

She took the ornament and asked whether Thord was there. Kalf said that he had arrived.

'Still, I want to meet him,' she said.

She went out of the room to where Thord was, threw the ornament at him, and told him to take it to his wife Oddny as a keepsake.

Then they rode down along the valley until they came to Husafell. Dalk stayed behind there while Thord rode to Vellir. Bjorn's father Arngeir had come home. Thord told the news to both him and his wife. She was outside, washing a child's hair. Thord loosed Bjorn's head from his saddle-straps and threw it to Bjorn's mother Thordis. He told her to see whether she recognized the head, and said that it needed washing just as much as the one she was washing at present.

Then she said, 'I know the head, and you should know it too, for you have often gone in fear before that head when it was attached to the body. Go now and take it to Oddny. She will like it better than that wretched little one dangling from your neck.'

Thord disliked her language. He left Bjorn's head there and rode home to Hitarnes, announced what had happened, and gave Oddny the ornament that Bjorn had been wearing around his neck. When she saw it she sank down and lost all consciousness of those around her; and when the swoon lifted from her she had fallen into weakened health and great restlessness. Thord tried many things to comfort her, and treated her well. But her state became so severe that she was overwhelmed with suffering, which was especially painful for the first year. She felt most relief if she sat on horseback while Thord led her to and fro. He did this because he thought it a most distressing situation, and wanted to comfort her. About this he composed:

39.

Weary, I walk leading
the woman on horseback; not
a speedy ride for the sickly
silk-Frid, day after day;   *silk-Frid* (goddess): woman
for the Hlokk of pool-fire   *pool-fire*: gold; its *Hlokk* (valkyrie): woman
finds nowhere rest from pain
in her mind's fort; to sword-Modi   *mind's fort*: breast
much sorrow that has brought.   *Modi*: a god; *sword*-god: man, here Thord

Thord thought he had suffered such a blow, because of the illness
that had come upon his wife, that people say that – if it had been
possible – Thord would rather have chosen that Bjorn should still be
alive, and that he himself should have the same love from his wife as
before. It seemed to him a great disaster that had come to them and
to Bjorn all together. She withered and shrank, and never afterwards
had any joy in life, yet lived for a long time in this discomfort.

Bjorn's family had his body sent for, and it was buried at Vellir in
the church that he had had built in honour of St Thomas the Apostle.
He was buried with his clothes and the cross-garter, as was said
before.

34 | Now the news of Bjorn's killing spread widely through the
     | land. His brother Asgrim[61] heard it at Rangarvellir in the east,
and came west to Ljarskogar to see Thorstein Kuggason, and he took
over the case from old Arngeir. Thorstein, Asgrim and Bjorn's friends
prepared the case for the Althing in spring. And when Asgrim left
Thorstein in the winter, he went to Holm and took care of the farm
that had belonged to Bjorn. In the spring he went from there to
prepare the case with Thorstein, and then to the Thing, with a great
following. Thord and those who were willing to support him did the
same.

It is said that when people arrived at the Thing, Thord sent men
to Asgrim in secret with the errand of making him a flattering offer,
and suggesting that they meet each other during the night. He said

that he wished him to win the greatest honour in the case, professing himself bound to that, since Asgrim had never opposed him during his quarrel with Bjorn. Asgrim was not used to taking part in lawsuits, and he met Thord at night. He greeted Asgrim warmly, and they spoke together at length. Thord was a skilful, smooth-tongued speaker, and related to him how he had been forced into this deed. He told him a great deal about his exchanges with Bjorn, what mean treatment he had long borne from him, and how Bjorn had now killed yet three more men in their last meeting, and maimed four.

'There are twelve men,' said Thord, 'for whom no compensation has been spoken of: Ottar and Eyvind, Thorstein Kalfsson, Thorkel Dalksson, two full outlaws, Stein Gudbrandsson, eighth a Norwegian, ninth my son Kolbein, Thorvald and Thord Eidsson, and twelfth my servant Grim. Dalk is maimed, and all of us hurt in some way. But I will pay you three hundreds of silver for your brother,[62] because I wish you well.'

Asgrim listened to Thord's recital and agreed to this. The silver was paid to him; he accepted it; and it was all rather hasty. It was obvious what had brought about their settlement: Thord's persuasions and Asgrim's rashness. Thorfinn Thvarason did not realize what was going on until Asgrim had taken the money. Then he went out of the booth to Thorstein Kuggason and told him that Asgrim had let himself be cheated in secret by Thord into accepting some settlement; he said he was busy counting silver.

Thorstein said this hastiness was more than enough, and that it was not easy to help men as self-willed as this, 'and yet it still isn't certain how much Thord will gain from it'.

No one had expected that Asgrim would consult nobody, not even Thorstein, who was associated with him in the case. Thorstein and Asgrim were in charge of the prosecution for the killing of Bjorn because the man who had begun it, old Arngeir, was now infirm with age. He had passed the case on to them since he thought he was too old to travel to the Thing, and he had not been used to conducting cases even when he was younger. But he knew that Thorstein had sworn to Bjorn that he would pursue the case after his death if necessary – whichever of them lived longer would do this for the other. Now Thorstein sent men to his kinsman Thorkel Eyjolfsson's booth, saying that he wanted to meet him. Thord Kolbeinsson was in Thorkel's booth. He had made the settlement with Asgrim without the advice of Thorkel, who knew nothing of it.

Now it is to be said of Thorstein that he gathered a large following, and at once rallied the men of Myrar, Bjorn's kinsmen. Then Thorstein and Thorkel met, and Bjorn's friends and relatives were with Thorstein.

Thorstein said that he was bound by oath to avenge Bjorn or to pursue the prosecution for his killing: 'Now we, his friends and kinsmen, are come together here, and it must be affirmed that we are all of one accord that we must invalidate this settlement that Asgrim has made with Thord.'

'It has often appeared,' said Thorkel, 'that Bjorn's kinsmen have not pursued his case correctly, and I expect it will seem a cause for concern if the chief plaintiff is not able to get the terms he hopes for.'

'That is out of the question,' said Thorstein. 'I alone will determine the outcome of the case, both the outlawing of men and the payment of compensation, as I am bound to do or else lose my life. You may oppose it by force, if you wish; we have enough support. It's not clear that we will win against those who oppose us, but we will risk it for the chance of taking the life of Thord or the others who killed Bjorn.'

Thorkel and Thorstein were first cousins, and Thorkel saw that it did not befit them to quarrel so keenly, but he knew Thorstein's pugnacity. Thord Kolbeinsson had not consulted him about the settlement beforehand; he was willing to direct the case on Thord's behalf, but not to go into battle against his own kinsmen for his sake. He said that he wished to stipulate that Thord be exempt from outlawry, and also from the payment of more money than he had already paid, but that Thorstein should proceed against the other men who were involved in the killing for as much money and outlawry as he wished.

Thorstein said that it was not acceptable that Thord should get off with no penalties at all, since all the evil in the case had sprung from him.

Thorkel said, 'I wish, then, that monetary atonement should suffice for the case, and let us discuss it and agree that Thord should escape outlawry by payment.'

Now the case proceeded so that terms were named and settled between them in this way. Thorstein and Thorkel were to confer, and Thord was to pay as much as Thorstein wished as a substitute for outlawry, but the other men involved in the killing were to suffer both outlawry and payment of compensation according to Thorstein's wish. They had to pay all the fines before leaving the Thing; and this was done. Thorstein had what amounted to sole control of the arbitration once Thorkel had reprieved his kinsman Thord from outlawry; he spared no money in the demand for compensation, for there was plenty of it. Now Thorstein's settlement was that Dalk was to receive no compensation for his own injury or his son's death, but would also pay nothing for his part in Bjorn's killing. Kalf, likewise, was to have no compensation for his son and was outlawed from the western district, leaving his land in Selardal to go south over the heath to his place of origin.

Thord was to pay Asgrim the three hundreds of silver that Asgrim had already accepted at his hands and taken possession of. A second three hundreds Thord was to give in exchange for his reprieve, and a third three hundreds for Kalf's reprieve. Thord's kinsmen who had been killed on the lava field were judged to have died having forfeited their immunity, therefore as full outlaws; likewise all the men who had died attacking Bjorn. Now there remained twelve men who had actually been present at the killing. All of these Thorstein outlawed, and they had to go abroad that same summer, and pay money for their passage, a mark for each of them. But if they did not go abroad as was laid down, they would be full outlaws, and could be killed wherever they were found.

Now they left the Thing, and Thorkel took the outlawed men with him, had their kinsmen contribute the money to help them to leave, and sent them abroad that summer. And now people said that there had hardly ever been such a suit for any man as for Bjorn, for the terms were all according to what Thorstein had determined, and Thord and his men were very dissatisfied, although they could do nothing about it. The men of Myrar, who were Bjorn's kinsmen, also received a lot of money from Thord Kolbeinsson in the settlement. Old Arngeir went to live with Thorstein Kuggason, taking with him the large sum of money that he had accepted, but Thordis took from it her bride-price and her dowry, and went west to her family at Bardastrond by Breidafjord. Asgrim went east to Rangarvellir with the money that fell to his share, and lived there after that.

Thord Kolbeinsson went back to Hitarnes, dissatisfied with the outcome of the case. From then on, interest in the affair began to die down. And here this narrative ends.

Translated by Alison Finlay

VIGLUND'S SAGA

VÖLUND'S SAGA

1 | Harald Fair-hair, the son of Halfdan the Black, was absolute
ruler of Norway at the time when this story took place. He was
young when he inherited the kingdom. Harald was the wisest of men
and well endowed with all those skills appropriate to his royal dignity.
The king maintained a large court and chose for it men of excellent
family who had proven themselves in prowess and many celebrated
deeds. Since the king desired to have the choicest men about him,
these were also better provided for than any other men in this realm,
for the king was sparing with neither money nor necessities, provided
his men knew how to manage them. But it was no less the case that
those who acted against his will did not thrive. Some were banished
from the country, others were killed. The king then seized everything
they left behind, and many men of high station fled from Norway,
for those who came from great families did not tolerate the king's
taxes. They preferred to leave their inherited lands as well as kin and
friends rather than be subjected to slavery and the king's yoke of
oppression, and so they emigrated to many lands.

It was in those days that Iceland became extensively settled, since
many who did not tolerate the power of the king found their way
there.

2 | Thorir was the name of an earl who ruled a portion of Norway.
He was an excellent man and was married. He had married an
excellent woman. The earl and his wife had a daughter whose name
was Olof. When she was still very young she was already very

gracious. Among the women who were then in Norway she was the most beautiful, and for this reason she acquired a nickname and was called Olof the Radiant.[1]

The earl loved his daughter very much and was so protective of her that no man was allowed to talk to her. The earl had a private dwelling built for her, constructed with every artistry. The dwelling was decorated all over with carvings inlaid with gold. It had a roof of lead and all the inside was painted.[2] A high fence surrounded it and the gate was made fast with strong iron locks. This dwelling was no less decorated on the outside than within. In this private dwelling the earl's daughter lived with her serving-women.

The earl also sent for those women whom he knew to be the most gracious, and he had them teach his daughter all those feminine skills suitable for noble women, for the earl wanted his daughter to surpass all other women in handicrafts just as she surpassed each of them in beauty, and indeed this is what happened.

And when she reached the appropriate age, many excellent men came to ask for her hand, but the earl was so exacting in his expectations for her that there was no one he wanted her to marry. He turned them all away with cordial words, while she showed no disdain in either her words or her deeds. Thus it happened that the earl's daughter was praised by everyone.

3 | Now other persons must be mentioned. There was a man called Ketil who ruled over Raumarike. He was a very honourable man, wise and popular, with great wealth.

Ketil was married and his wife's name was Ingibjorg; she came from a noble family. They had two sons, one named Gunnlaug and the other Sigurd. The two brothers had nicknames: Gunnlaug was called 'the Boisterous', but Sigurd 'the Wise'. Ketil had his sons taught all the skills common in those days, for Ketil was more adept in these skills than most other men. The brothers had companions to whom they gave gold and other valuables. The brothers used to go riding with their men to hunt animals and birds, and they were most accomplished.

Ketil was a great warrior. He had fought in duels twenty-four times and had been victorious each time. He and King Harald were good friends. Ketil was such a successful lawyer that, no matter with whom he dealt, he was never involved in a matter where he did not prevail, for when he began to speak, others came to think as he did. The king asked Ketil to assume a higher position and told him that this was appropriate both for the realm and for many other reasons, but Ketil did not want that; he said that he preferred to remain a simple farmer but nonetheless equal to those in a higher position. Ketil loved his wife so much that he could not bear to see any harm come to her.

Some time passed.

4 | It happened one time that King Harald was levying men and ships for war, intending to head south along the coast, and he carefully prepared both ships and men for the expedition. Ketil got his sons and a large, handsome following to accompany the king, but he himself stayed at home because by then he was quite old.

When the king was ready, he sailed south along the coast. And when he came south to Rogaland, an earl named Eirik was ruling there at that time.[3] He was a great leader and popular among his men. When he learned about the king's arrival, he ordered a fine feast to be prepared and invited the king to the feast with his entire entourage; the king accepted the invitation and proceeded on land with his entourage. The earl brought the king with all his men to his hall, to the accompaniment of all kinds of music, with songs and stringed instruments, and every kind of entertainment that was available. In this manner the earl welcomed the king into his hall, placing him on the high seat. There was a splendid feast, and the king was in very good spirits, as were his men, for the earl spared nothing in entertaining the king very warmly. The best of drinks were served and the men quickly became drunk.

The king always seated Ketil's sons close to him, and showed them great honour. The earl himself stood in front of the king and served at the king's table. Throughout the hall there was great merriment.

The king then assigned the brothers to serve as cupbearers, and he seated the earl on the high seat next to him. The brothers did as the king asked them and earned much honour for their noble bearing.

And when the tables were removed, the earl had precious objects brought out which he chose for the king and all his men. He gave away quite a few precious objects. And when the gifts had been distributed, the earl asked for a harp to be brought out. Its strings were alternately of gold and silver. It was a most remarkable piece of workmanship. The king reached for it and began to pluck the strings, and the harp emitted such a robust sound that everyone was astounded, for they did not think they had ever heard anything like it before.

Then the earl spoke: 'I would like you to amuse yourself by taking a walk with me, my lord. I want to show you all my possessions, both inside and outside, the fields and the orchards.'

The king did as the earl asked, and went along and was quite impressed. They then went to an apple orchard. A lovely grove stood there and under the trees three boys were playing. They were very good-looking, but one of them surpassed the others. They were playing a board game and two were playing against one. The two thought that the third was getting the advantage and upset the board. The one who was winning became annoyed and gave each of them a box on the ear. They then came to blows and the two went against the one, but he got the upper hand no less in wrestling than in the board game. The earl then asked them to stop and make peace, which is what they did, and then they went back to playing the board game as before.

The king and his entourage returned to the hall and sat down at their places. It was obvious that the king was quite taken by the youth, and he asked the earl who the boys were.

'They are my sons,' said the earl.

'Do they have the same mother?' asked the king.

'No, they don't,' said the earl.

Then the king asked, 'What are the names of the boys?'

The earl answered, 'Sigmund and Helgi, and Thorgrim is the name of the third. He was born out of wedlock.'

A little later the boys all came into the hall. Thorgrim came last because in other areas of repute he was the least respected.

The earl called the boys over and asked them to step before the king. They did so and greeted the king. When they stood before him, Thorgrim took each of his brothers by the hand, pushing them away from each other, and stepped between them and climbed up on to the king's footstool and greeted the king and hugged him. Laughing, the king took the boy and sat him down next to him and asked him about his mother's family. He said that he was the nephew of the hersir Thorir of Sognefjord. The king removed a gold ring from his arm and gave it to Thorgrim. Thorgrim then went back to his brothers.

The feasting went on with great magnificence until the king said that he wanted to depart, 'but on account of the munificence you have shown me, you may choose a reward for yourself'.

The earl was pleased by this and asked the king to take his son Thorgrim with him, and said that he thought this better than money, 'for what you will do for him seems to me much better than all the things you do for me. Moreover, I would also like him to go with you because I love him most of all my sons.'

The king agreed to this.

Then the king left, and Thorgrim went with him. He quickly became most skilled at serving the king, and soon many of the king's men envied him.

5 | One time, it is told, the king went to a feast arranged by a man named Sigurd. This feast was quite elaborate with regard to provisions. The king told Thorgrim to serve as cupbearer to him and his friends that day. Many of the king's men thought it excessive that the king promoted Thorgrim so obviously by showing him every honour.

Sigurd had a relative named Grim. He was a powerful man because of his wealth. He was such an arrogant man that he thought everyone else quite beneath him. He was present at the feast and had his place on the high seat on the higher bench.

Thorgrim served that day, and when he carried a large goblet to Grim, because Thorgrim stumbled some of the contents spilled out of the goblet and spattered on to Grim's clothing. Grim got angry at this and jumped up, exclaiming loudly, and said that it was obvious that the whore's son was more accustomed to herding swine and giving them slop to drink than to serving respectable men. Thorgrim was furious at these words, drew his sword, and ran Grim through. Men pulled him out dead from under the table. Sigurd called upon his men and told them to get up and seize Thorgrim.

The king said, 'Don't do this, Sigurd. Grim brought this on himself with his words, but if you are willing to let me do as I please, I intend to pay full compensation for him, for that is how we can best preserve our friendship.'

The king had his way, and he paid all the money, so Sigurd was very pleased. The feasting now came to an end, and nothing else of note happened. The king headed home.

The king invited many great men to his court. He first invited Earl Thorir, and Ketil from Raumarike. He had lost his wife when she died in childbirth, but she had given birth to a daughter who was named Ingibjorg after her mother. Thereafter, the king invited all and sundry, because there was no shortage of necessary provisions. People came to the feast as soon as they were invited. Olof the Radiant attended the feast with her father. People were now assigned their places and excellent drink was brought out. Thorgrim went around serving, and people were impressed by what a worthy and honourable man he was. He was fittingly attired, since the king bestowed much honour on him, but many of the king's men thought this excessive, and for this reason they disliked Thorgrim intensely. He received a nickname and was called Thorgrim the Elegant.

When Thorgrim saw Olof, he immediately fell in love with her and she in turn fell in love with him, but other people were not aware of this. As soon as they had the chance, they met, and each was attracted to the other. Thorgrim asked how she would answer if he were to ask for her hand. She replied that she would not object if her father gave his approval. And when the feasting came to an end,

Thorgrim proposed marriage, and asked for the hand of Olof the Radiant. Earl Thorir was not quick to respond, and they parted without settling the matter.

6 | Some time later Thorgrim came to talk with the king and asked him for leave to seek out Earl Thorir, and the king granted him that. And when Thorgrim arrived at Earl Thorir's he was well received. Thorgrim once again proposed marriage and wanted to know the earl's response on the spot. However, the earl said that he would not give him his daughter in marriage. Thorgrim stayed there for three nights and he and Olof were on good terms, and some people said that they had promised to marry each other. Thorgrim then returned to the king's court for the time being.

Thorgrim now went harrying; by this time he had come of age. He harried all summer long and was considered braver than anyone else no matter how great the danger. On this expedition he built up both wealth and prestige.

The next thing that happened was that Ketil of Raumarike rode over to Earl Thorir's with thirty men. King Harald was also present at the feasting. Ketil then proposed marriage and asked for the hand of Olof the Radiant, and, given the support of the king, Earl Thorir betrothed his daughter Olof to Ketil. Olof gave neither her approval nor her consent to this.

And when the marriage contract was to be ratified, Olof spoke this verse:

1.

I know the glad gold-warden   *gold-warden*: man
wields better words than others.
The sound of those words
will wound me in this world.[4]
Here dwells no handsome man
who'll draw my love to him.
But one received my oath,
and ever that bright man I'll love.

Most people were convinced that Olof would rather have had Thorgrim, but things were the way they were. The date was now set for when the wedding would take place. It was going to be held during the Winter Nights at the home of Earl Thorir. The summer now drew to a close.

In the autumn Thorgrim returned from harrying. He learned that Olof had been promised to another. He immediately sought out the king to ask for his support in obtaining the woman, whether Earl Thorir – and Ketil – liked this or not. The king refused all support to Thorgrim, however, saying that Ketil was his best friend.

'I'll give you some advice,' said the king. 'Don't quarrel with Ketil. I intend to ask for the hand of his daughter Ingibjorg on your behalf, and thus the two of you will be fully reconciled.'

Thorgrim said that he did not want that. 'I want to keep my word and the vows with which Olof and I have pledged ourselves to each other. I intend to marry her and no one else. And if you do not want to support me, then I will no longer serve you.'

The king said that Thorgrim could decide as he pleased, 'but most likely your reputation will not be greater anywhere else than with me'.

Thorgrim then took leave of the king. At their parting the king gave Thorgrim a gold arm-ring weighing a mark. Thorgrim then returned to his men. Three nights remained before the wedding was to take place.

Thorgrim then went ashore, alone and without his men, and headed for Earl Thorir's dwelling. By that time the bride was sitting on the bench and the drinking-hall was full of men; the king was in the high seat and the feasting was in full swing. Thorgrim went into the drinking-hall, into the middle of the floor, and stood there. There were so many lights in the room that not a single shadow was cast. Everyone recognized Thorgrim, but many did not consider him a welcome guest.

Thorgrim said, 'Has Olof been betrothed to you, Ketil?'

Ketil said that was the case.

'Was this done with her consent?' asked Thorgrim.

'I thought that Earl Thorir himself had the right to make decisions for his daughter,' said Ketil, 'and that the contract he made was legal.'

Thorgrim said, 'I declare that Olof and I have sworn to each other that she would marry no one but me. Let her say whether this is so.'

Olof said that it was the truth.

'In that case I consider the woman mine,' said Thorgrim.

'You will never get her,' said Ketil. 'I have contended with men who are superior to you, and yet have held my own against them.'

Thorgrim said, 'Then I suspect that you are doing this with the king's approval, and for that reason I challenge you to a duel. Let us fight and let him who defeats the other in the duel win the woman.'

'I intend to benefit from having more men than you,' said Ketil.

And as they were talking, it happened that all the lights were extinguished in the room. There was much pushing and shoving. When the lights came back on, the bride had disappeared, as had Thorgrim. Everyone now realized that he must have been responsible. As a matter of fact, Thorgrim had made off with the bride and taken her to his ship. His men had made the preparations he had ordered, so that they were ready to cast off to sea. They now raised their sails as soon as Thorgrim was ready to sail, since the wind was blowing off shore.

At that time the period of the settlement of Iceland was at its height. Thorgrim realized that he could not stay in Norway after what he had done, and he wanted to go to Iceland. They headed out to sea and got a good wind, so that they were only a short time at sea. They arrived at the Snaefellsnes peninsula and made land in the harbour of Hraunhofn.

The king and the earl learned that Thorgrim had sailed off, and Ketil thought that he had suffered an enormous dishonour: he had lost the woman, and it was uncertain whether he would be able to gain redress from Thorgrim. The king, under pressure from Ketil, outlawed Thorgrim for this deed.

For the time being we leave Norway.

7 | There was a man called Holmkel who lived at Foss by the river Holmkelsa on the Snaefellsnes peninsula. He was married to a woman called Thorbjorg. He had two sons by her, one of whom was called Jokul and the other Einar. Holmkel was the son of Alfarinn, who was the son of Vali. His brothers were Ingjald at Ingjaldshvol, Hoskuld at Hoskuldsstadir, and Goti at Gotalaek.[5]

Thorgrim the Elegant bought land at Ingjaldshvol, but Ingjald bought a place to live elsewhere, and he does not play any role in this saga. Thorgrim quickly became a great leader and a most munificent man. He and Holmkel of Foss became great friends.

It is told that Thorgrim held his wedding with Olof. The following winter, when they were living at Ingjaldshvol, Olof gave birth to a child and it was a boy; he was named Trausti. A winter later Olof gave birth to another boy, and he was named Viglund. Early on he was already big and good-looking. During this same year Thorbjorg at Foss gave birth to a baby girl who received the name Ketilrid.[6] She and Viglund were the same age, but Trausti was a year older. They grew up in the district and everyone said that there was no man or woman from those parts who was in any way fairer or more gracious than Viglund and Ketilrid. Holmkel loved his daughter so much that he was incapable of opposing her in anything, but Thorbjorg loved her somewhat less.

When Viglund was ten years old and Trausti eleven, there was no one in the district as strong as they, but Viglund was the stronger of the two. They started to learn all kinds of skills and Thorgrim spared no efforts to teach his sons.

Thorbjorg did not want to teach her daughter any handicrafts. Her husband Holmkel considered that a great shame, and therefore he decided to ride over to Ingjaldshvol with his daughter. Thorgrim received him warmly, since there was great friendship between them. Holmkel wanted his daughter to be fostered by Olof so that she would instruct her in handicrafts, for Olof was considered the most cultivated of women in Iceland. She was delighted to do this and she loved her foster-child greatly. Olof herself had a young daughter named Helga, who was a year younger than Ketilrid. These young people passed the time together in fun and merriment, and in every game where they ended up partners, it always turned out that Viglund and Ketilrid ended up together, and then Trausti and his sister Helga. Viglund and Ketilrid came to love each other deeply. Many said that they were well matched in every way. Whenever they were together, Viglund and Ketilrid had eyes only for each other.

One time Viglund said that he wanted them to pledge their love, but Ketilrid was not much interested.

'There are many things speaking against this,' she said. 'First of all, you may not be so inclined when you have grown up. You men are always fickle in such matters. Furthermore, it is not appropriate for me to go against my father's wishes – nor do I desire it. The third reason, which settles the matter, is that I cannot do as I choose, and I know that most things go as my mother dictates. She has little love for me. Nonetheless, I know of no one whom I would rather marry than you if I myself could decide, but my heart tells me that we'll encounter great obstacles no matter how things turn out.'

Viglund kept bringing up the matter with Ketilrid, but she kept answering in the same way. Nevertheless, people said that they must have vowed to marry each other.

8 | Turning now to the brothers Jokul and Einar, who had become very unruly in the district: they very much followed in their mother's footsteps in this respect, and Holmkel was displeased, but there was nothing he could do. The brothers became very unpopular because of their behaviour.

The brothers had a stallion, black in colour, and it was very savage. It put to flight every horse against which it was pitted. It had such large incisors that they were unlike those of any other horse.

Viglund too had a stallion, a yellow dun, the best and most beautiful of horses. He prized the horse greatly.

Thorgrim, his father, had two oxen, brindled-brown in colour and with cross-markings on their foreheads. Their horns were the colour of bone. He set great store by them.

One time it happened that Einar got into a conversation with his mother. 'I'm not pleased that Thorgrim is so highly respected here in the district. I think that if I could seduce his wife Olof, he would have to try to avenge the deed, otherwise his reputation would suffer; and if he were to avenge himself, it is not certain that he would come out ahead.'

She said that this was a good idea and in tune with her own thoughts.

One day, when Thorgrim had left home on his errands, Einar rode over to Ingjaldshvol, and his brother Jokul went along. Olof, the mistress of the house, had told one of her maids that she should lock the door each morning when the men went off to work, and this is what she did. On this morning, when Einar and Jokul came to the farm, the servant-woman noticed them and went to Olof's bedroom to tell her that the men from Foss had come.

She stood up quickly, got dressed, and went to her sewing-room, where she sat her servant-woman down and laid her own cloak over her and said, 'Don't be startled if Einar thinks you are me. I'll see to it that he does not disgrace you.'

She sent another servant-woman to the door, because none of the men was at home. Einar asked where Olof was, and the servant-woman said that she was in her sewing-room. Einar and his brother headed there. When they entered the room, they saw Olof sitting on the cross-bench. Einar sat down beside her and talked to her. At this moment a man dressed in black walked into the room; he was holding a drawn sword. The man was not particularly tall, but he was extremely angry. They asked him who he was and he said his name was Ottar. They did not know the man, yet they were somewhat afraid of him.

He began to speak: 'It's time to go out and welcome Thorgrim, for he's riding towards his farm.'

Both of them jumped up and went out, and they saw that the farmer was approaching with a large group of men. They jumped on their horses and rode off home. What really happened is that the cattle were being driven in, and the man in black was Olof herself.

When the people from Foss found this out, they realized that their errand had ended most disgracefully. Once more great animosity arose towards the people at Ingjaldshvol. When her husband Thorgrim came home, Olof told him everything that had happened.

Thorgrim said, 'We should not bring charges against my friend Holmkel for this, since Einar was not able to have his way.'

9 | It happened one day that the brothers Jokul and Einar rode over to Ingjaldshvol. They were all at home, the father and his sons, and were standing outside. Jokul asked whether Viglund wanted to give him his yellow dun horse. Viglund said that he did not intend to do so. Jokul said he had pursued the matter as men of old would have done, but Viglund again said he was not inclined to give in.

'Would you then be willing to have our horses pitted against each other?'

'It seems to me that we could do that,' said Viglund.

'I think that is even better than the gift of your horse,' said Jokul.

'Why shouldn't the matter run its course?' said Viglund.

They agreed on the date when the horse-fight should take place.

When the time came for the horses to fight against each other, the Foss brothers' horse Blackie was led out, and it carried on frightfully. The brothers got ready to accompany it. Viglund's stallion Yellow Dun then came out and as soon as it came into the paddock, it kept circling, finally raising both front legs and ramming them into Blackie's muzzle with such force that all its incisors were knocked out. Yellow Dun then made for Blackie's haunches with its teeth and ripped a gaping hole in the body. Blackie fell down dead and when Jokul and Einar saw that, they ran for their weapons, as did the others, and they fought until Thorgrim and Holmkel were able to separate them. One of Viglund's men had then been slain, and two of the Foss brothers' men. And this is how they parted.

Still, the friendship between Thorgrim and Holmkel was kept as before. Holmkel now discovered that Viglund and Ketilrid loved each other, but he did not forbid it. Thorbjorg and her sons, however, were most displeased.

With the passing of time, everyone said that in Iceland at that time there was no one as good-looking as Viglund or Ketilrid, or as talented and gracious.

10 | Once, it is told, the brothers Jokul and Einar left Foss by night. It was a bright night and they headed for the common pasture where Viglund's stallion Yellow Dun was with the stud mares. They approached the horses and wanted to drive them home with them but they were unable to do so. The stallion guarded them so well that they could not drive off the horses in single file together with the stallion, as they had intended. When they were unable to do this, they got very angry and attacked the stallion with weapons, intending to kill it, but the stallion defended itself so fiercely with both teeth and hooves that the night wore on and they achieved nothing. At last they struck the horse down with their spears and thus killed it. After they had done this, they no longer cared to drive the horses away with them, because they thought it would then be obvious that they had killed the stallion. They wanted to hide the fact that they had killed the horse and dragged the body to a cliff and pushed it off so that people would think that the stallion had fallen off by itself.[7] Then they went home and pretended that nothing had happened.

Some time later the brothers Jokul and Einar went to the common pasture belonging to Thorgrim the Elegant in which his oxen were kept. In all there were fifty oxen in the herd belonging to Thorgrim. They recognized the two prized cross-marked oxen, seized and haltered them, and took them home to Foss. There they killed the two beasts and hung them up in a storage shed. This happened one night, and they had finished their work before the farmhands got up. Their mother knew all about this, and in fact enthusiastically supported what her sons had done.

11 | Now to turn to the other brothers, Viglund and Trausti: one day when they went to their horses in the pasture, the stallion was missing. They looked far and wide and finally found the horse dead at the foot of a high crag. They discovered many deep wounds

on the body; the stallion had suffered internal wounds. Viglund and Trausti suspected that the people from Foss had done this. They went home and reported that their stallion was dead, and that Jokul and Einar must have done it.

Thorgrim asked them not to do anything: 'Remember, they lost their own stallion earlier, and you'll be able to take some other action, even if you ignore this, if things turn out as I think they will.'

They let the matter rest for the time being.

Not long afterwards Thorgrim was told that his prize oxen, the cross-marked ones, which he valued above the others, had disappeared and that people thought some men were responsible for this. Thorgrim commented little about the matter except to say it was likely that thieves hiding out in the mountains would have done this kind of thing. He did not have his men search for the oxen.

This became widely known and people thought that the family at Ingjaldshvol had suffered great damage. Thorbjorg over at Foss made great sport of this and had the slaughtered oxen served at meals. When Holmkel found out where the oxen belonging to Thorgrim had ended up, he got on his horse one day and rode to Ingjaldshvol. When he found Thorgrim, Holmkel told him that he thought the prize oxen had found their way over to his own place and that his sons must have been responsible for this.

'I want to settle on a sum for the oxen as high as you want, provided you do not bring charges against my sons.'

Thorgrim agreed to this and took as much money as he wanted. Holmkel and Thorgrim parted in great friendship.

12 | Kjolvor was the name of a woman who lived at Hraunskard. She was very skilled in magic and was completely given to evil, so that she was quite unpopular with people everywhere. She and Thorbjorg at Foss were great friends.

Thorbjorg and her two sons Jokul and Einar negotiated with Kjolvor and gave her a hundred of silver to destroy the brothers Viglund and Trausti by any magic she chose. They did this because they were extremely envious of Viglund and Trausti and, moreover, had found out that Viglund and Ketilrid loved each other. They begrudged them their love, as they demonstrated later. Viglund and Ketilrid loved each other even more ardently now than they had while growing up. They had such a secret love concealed in their hearts that their deeply entrenched love and the fruit of their affection could never be uprooted from their hearts, since this is the nature of true love. For the fire of affection and the flames of love burn all the more intensely, and weld together the hearts and minds of lovers all the more tightly, the greater the number of those who wish to injure them and the greater the obstacles that families place in the path of those whom love and affection have brought together, as was the case with these two, Viglund and Ketilrid. They loved each other so ardently all their lives that, if they could do as their hearts told them, neither ever wanted to be without the other from the time they first laid eyes on each other.[8]

There was a man named Bjorn who was one of the farmhands of Thorgrim the Elegant. He was such a bold sailor that no matter how terrible the weather, he was not afraid to sail. He always said that he did not worry about the size of the swells. He had emigrated to Iceland with Thorgrim and had been put in charge of his boats, since there was good fishing in the bay. He never rowed out with more than two men, even though he had a seaworthy ten-oared boat.

It happened in the autumn that both of Bjorn's fishing companions got sick because of Kjolvor's magic. All the men were employed at haymaking when Bjorn wanted to row out for fish, and he asked the brothers Viglund and Trausti to row out with him for the day. They did so, since the weather was fine and they were good friends of his. Kjolvor knew all about this and climbed up on the house and waved her hood in an easterly direction, and all at once the weather turned bad. When the three had reached the fishing bank, there were quite a few fish, but then they saw a cloud rising in the east-north-east.

Viglund said, 'I think it advisable to head for land. I don't like the look of the weather.'

Bjorn said, 'We're not going to do that until the boat is full.'

'You're the one who's in charge,' said Viglund.

The cloud approached quickly, accompanied by wind and frost, and such heavy seas that the water was very rough and pelted them as though with grains of salt. Bjorn now said that they should head for land.

Viglund said that they should have done so earlier – 'but I'm not going to object now'.

Bjorn and Trausti rowed but could make no headway; instead they were driven out to sea towards the south-west. The boat now began filling with water. Viglund asked Bjorn to bail and Trausti to steer, while he himself took to the oars and rowed so vigorously that they reached land at Dagverdarnes, the home of Thorkel Skin-swathed, who had immigrated with Bard Snaefell's As,[9] and was now quite old.

When Ketilrid learned that they had been driven out to sea by the storm and that they were dead, she fainted. When she came to, while looking out to sea she spoke this stanza:

2.
I cannot gaze to sea
without grief-filled weeping,
since dear friends drowned
deep below the bay.
I loathe the swarthy sea,
the soughing of the waves.
Dire distress befell me
from the billows' burden.   *billows' burden*: drowned men

Thorkel welcomed the brothers, and they went home the next day. There was a joyful reunion between Viglund and Ketilrid.

13 | Now we must return to Norway where we left off earlier. Ketil from Raumarike was displeased with the way things had turned out between him and Thorgrim the Elegant. He was rapidly ageing and did not think it would be easy to pursue any action in the matter. His sons Sigurd and Gunnlaug had become valiant and good-looking men, while his daughter Ingibjorg had turned out to be a most beautiful woman.

There was a man called Hakon whose family came from Vik; he was wealthy and headstrong. He set out to see Ketil in Raumarike in order to ask for the hand of his daughter.

Ketil answered the suit as follows: 'I will give you my daughter in marriage provided you first go to Iceland to kill Thorgrim the Elegant and bring me back his head.'

Hakon said that he did not consider this a great matter and they agreed on it. Hakon went to Iceland that summer, and his ship sailed into the mouth of the river Froda. The people from Foss, Jokul and Einar, arrived at the ship first. The skipper welcomed them and inquired about all kinds of things. They were generous with information. He asked what prospects there were for lodging.

They told him that there was no place better than their father's at Foss: 'We have a sister who is so beautiful and gracious that no one can compare with her. We'll see to it that you either win her in marriage or enjoy her as your mistress. We would like to invite you to take lodging with us.'

The skipper thought this was an attractive offer, and told them that he would go with them. He told them about his mission in Iceland, and they thought this was a great plan; they all agreed to carry out the plot together.

Some time later the skipper went to Foss. This was not at all to Holmkel's liking, but that is the way things turned out. In time the skipper became friendly with Thorbjorg and he gave her many a precious object.

On one occasion Hakon struck up a conversation with Thorbjorg and her two sons. He inquired where the young woman the brothers had told him about lived: 'I want to see her.'

They said that she was being fostered by Olof at Ingjaldshvol.

Hakon asked that she be brought home – 'and I trust that you, Thorbjorg, and your sons will assist me for the sake of our friendship, so that I can have my way with her'.

Shortly afterwards Thorbjorg got into a conversation with her husband Holmkel.

'I want my daughter Ketilrid to come home to me,' she said.

'I think it advisable for her to stay where she is,' said her husband.

'That won't do,' she said, 'for I would sooner fetch her myself than for her to stay there any longer, subject to likely gossip because of Viglund. I would rather marry her to Hakon, since that seems to me an honourable match.'

With this their conversation ended.

Holmkel now realized that Thorbjorg would have Ketilrid fetched, and he preferred to get her himself. Subsequently he rode to Ingjaldshvol, where he was warmly welcomed.

After he had arrived, Viglund went to Ketilrid and said, 'Your father has come here. I realize that he intends to fetch you and take you home with him. He has the power to decide in this matter, but I want you, Ketilrid, to remember all we have said to each other. I know that I will never stop loving you.'

Ketilrid wept copiously and said, 'I've known for a long time that we would never be able to enjoy our love in peace. I now think that it would have been better if we had talked less about it, for I am not at all sure that you love me more than I love you, even though I talk less about it than you. Now I realize that my mother's plotting is at the bottom of this. For a long time now I have received little love from her, and if she is in charge, it is most likely that our joyous time together has come to an end. In spite of everything, I would be satisfied if I knew that things were going well for you. Either we will never be able to enjoy our love, or my father will have to find a way to help us; but he has his hands full if my brothers and mother are involved, since they will do anything to oppose me. But don't let on how you are taking this.'

Viglund then approached her and kissed her. It was obvious that she, and in fact both of them, took the parting at this time much to heart.

Viglund spoke this verse:

3.
I'll never love on earth
a young valkyrie of silk   *valkyrie* (Gunn) *of silk*: woman
– men will not observe this –
other than you, woman.

Fair maiden, mind the oaths
and vows made long ago;
though an arrogant woman
is eager to destroy us.

Ketilrid then went inside to look for her father. He informed her that she was to go home with him.

Ketilrid said that it was for him to decide – 'but I think it's good to be here'.

'I know that,' he said, 'but that's the way it will have to be.'

Everyone was unhappy at having to part with Ketilrid, because they were all fond of her. Father and daughter now rode home to Foss, and when Ketilrid arrived, the skipper was pleased and happy. Her mother Thorbjorg ordered her to serve Hakon, but she did not want to do this at all. In tears, she told her father about it, but he said, 'You don't have to wait on Hakon unless you want to, and you only have to do what you yourself want. Just stay close to me night and day.'

She said that she would gladly do so. This went on for a time, and Hakon never got a chance to talk to her.

14 | The games now started up on Esjutjorn[10] and the people from Foss headed there to have some fun. When the men came home from the games on the first day, Ketilrid asked whether people had not come from Ingjaldshvol. She was told that all of them had come, the father and his sons, as well as Olof and her daughter Helga.

The next day Ketilrid asked her father for permission to go to the games. He granted it, and that day they all went together. Everyone was very happy because the sons of Thorgrim, Viglund and Trausti, had come, but nobody else from Ingjaldshvol. The two brothers went over to the slope where the women were sitting. Ketilrid stood up and greeted them warmly. Then they sat down, with Viglund and Trausti on either side of her.

Ketilrid then said, 'Now I'm going to make a show of acting equally affectionately towards each of you.'

All this time Ketilrid was looking at Viglund, and she said, 'I am now going to lengthen your name and call you Viglund the Handsome. Here is a ring I want to give you. My father gave it to me when I cut my first tooth, and I want to give it to you as a token of your new name.'

Viglund accepted the ring and put it on his hand. In exchange he gave her the ring his father had received from King Harald, called Harald's Gift,[11] which his father had given him. They talked together for a long time, and when the men from Foss saw this, they were most displeased. Each group then went home.

That evening Hakon went to talk to Thorbjorg. He asked her not to let her daughter go along to any social gatherings, 'considering the frame of mind she is in'.

Thorbjorg agreed. She told her husband Holmkel not to let Ketilrid go along to any more games, but rather to have her stay at home. He did as she said, but as a result Ketilrid became very downcast. Her father told her that he would stay at home with her if that would make her feel better, and she said that she wanted him to do so.

The men now continued going to the games and the groups, those from Foss and the sons of Thorgrim, were on opposing teams.

On one occasion it happened that Viglund knocked the ball past Jokul. He got angry, and when he got hold of the ball, he struck Viglund's face so hard with it that his eyebrow split open. Trausti tore a piece off his shirt and wound it around Viglund's brow. When that occurred, the brothers from Foss had already gone home.

Viglund and Trausti went home and when they walked into the main room Thorgrim was sitting on the cross-bench, and he said, 'Welcome back, my son and daughter.'

'Which one of us are you calling a woman, father?' asked Trausti.

'It seems to me,' said Thorgrim, 'that the one with the headgear must be the woman.'

'I'm not a woman,' said Viglund, 'even though it may seem that I'm not far from being one.'

'Why didn't you avenge yourself on Jokul when he struck you?'

'They were gone,' said Trausti, 'by the time I had bandaged Viglund's forehead.'

At this point their conversation petered out.

The next day the two brothers went to the game, and when it was least expected, Viglund struck Jokul's brow with the ball so that it split open. Jokul sought to strike Viglund with the bat, but he ducked, and instead he knocked Jokul down on to the ice so that he lost consciousness. The men separated them and each side went home. Jokul was not able to get on a horse by himself and he was carried home on a makeshift litter. He recovered quickly.

The games began again at Foss, and Thorgrim's sons prepared to go. Thorgrim tried to dissuade them from going by saying that nothing but trouble would result, but they went nonetheless.

When they walked into the main room at Foss, the game had already begun. Everyone was seated, and Viglund went to the cross-bench where Holmkel and his daughter were sitting. Ketilrid greeted Viglund joyfully. He pulled her out of her seat, sat down himself, and then put her on his lap. When Holmkel saw this, he moved aside, making room, and Ketilrid sat down between them. They then started talking. Holmkel had a game board fetched for them and they played the entire day. Hakon hated the brothers, and he had often approached Holmkel that winter about giving him his daughter Ketilrid in marriage. But Holmkel always answered the same way – that he would not do so. The day passed until it was time for the brothers to go home.

When they had come out into the yard, Ketilrid was also there, and she asked the brothers not to go home that evening – 'because I know,' she said, 'that my brothers will be waiting to ambush you'.

Viglund said that they would nonetheless leave as he had planned, and that is what they did. Each brother was carrying his axe in his hand. When they came to one of the haystacks, they saw that twelve men from Foss had assembled there.

Jokul then said, 'It's a good thing we have met, Viglund. You'll now be repaid for having struck me with a ball and making me fall down.'

'I can't blame you for that,' said Viglund.

The people from Foss then attacked the two brothers, but they defended themselves well. Viglund had not fought long before he killed one man, and then another. In the meantime Trausti had killed a third.

Jokul then said, 'Let's hold off now, but then blame the whole incident on the brothers.'

That is what they did. Both sides then went home.

Jokul told his father that Viglund and Trausti had killed three of his men – 'but we did not want to take action against them until we had talked to you'.

Holmkel was very angry when he heard the story.

15 │ Jokul then egged his father on to marry Ketilrid to Hakon, and at the brothers' insistence Holmkel gave Ketilrid in marriage to Hakon, but she did not give her consent to this. Hakon intended to settle down here in Iceland, since he realized that he had not managed to kill Thorgrim the Elegant.

News of this now reached Ingjaldshvol, and Viglund was much taken aback at it. When Holmkel learned the truth about the brothers' ambush, he realized that he had gone too far in marrying Ketilrid to Hakon.

The sons of Thorgrim now frequented the games at Foss again, just as before, and Viglund got into conversation with Ketilrid and reproached her greatly for having married. When the brothers prepared to go home in the evening, Hakon and Holmkel's sons had vanished and many men with them. Holmkel approached Viglund.

'I don't want the two of you to go home this evening,' he said, 'because I don't think Jokul's and Einar's doings are to be trusted.'

Viglund said, however, that he would leave as he had intended. When Viglund and his brother came out of the door, Ketilrid was standing there, and she asked Viglund to go home by another way, one he had not taken before, rather than the usual one that he planned to take.

'I'm not going to be disquieted at your words,' he said, and he spoke this verse:

4.

The spoiler of battle   *spoiler of battle*: man
trusted you, bearer of gold.   *bearer of gold*: woman
I balked at believing
you betrothed to another.
No use to us now are
our oaths and many kisses.
Baffling is a woman's mind.
The woman broke her pledge.

'I don't think that I have done that,' said Ketilrid, 'and I don't want you to leave now.'

'That can't be,' said Viglund, 'for I am more inclined to meet up with Hakon so that the two of us can settle this between us, than for him to embrace you while I stand by watching', and he spoke a verse:

5.

Like other men I must
endure the valkyrie's fire   *valkyrie's* (Thrud's) *fire*: sword
– fate weighs heavy on me –
wielded by warriors.
It is better than to know
another man, not I,
can hold you, woman,
clasped in his embrace.

16 | Viglund and Trausti then went on their way, until they came to the haystacks where they had previously fought. Twelve men from Foss were there. Thorgrim's sons climbed up on to the hay in the enclosure so that the others did not become aware of them until they had loosened a large, heavy piece of frozen turf. When the group from Foss saw Viglund and Trausti, they jumped up and attacked them, and a very fierce battle broke out. The people from Foss realized that as long as the two brothers were on top of the hay they could not attack them.

Then Jokul said, 'Now it's advisable not to yield, Viglund, and we know as a matter of fact that you are not a real man unless you come down off the hay and fight till the end.'

Egged on by Jokul, Viglund jumped down off the hay, as did his brother Trausti. A hard fight ensued and all of Hakon's men were slain, so that only three men from Foss – Jokul, Einar and Hakon – remained standing, and two other men, but they could no longer fight.

Jokul said, 'Now it's time to fight manfully and win. Trausti will fight against Einar, and Viglund against Hakon, but I'll sit and watch.'

Trausti was both wounded and tired. They fought until each of them fell.

Then Viglund and Hakon began to fight. Viglund was extremely tired but not wounded. Their struggle was hard and long because Hakon was both strong and courageous, while Viglund was strong and skilled with weapons and fierce. Their encounter ended when Hakon fell down dead, while Viglund was seriously wounded.

Jokul then sprang to his feet. He was neither tired nor wounded, and he turned towards Viglund. They began to fight and their struggle was fierce and went on for a good part of the day, and it was impossible to guess who would win. Viglund realized that he could not continue to fight against Jokul on account of his wounds and his exhaustion. Therefore he threw up the shield and the axe, and since he could fight equally well with either hand he caught the shield with his right hand and the axe with the left. Jokul could not follow this manoeuvre and Viglund cut off his right arm all the way to the elbow. Jokul then got away. Viglund was not able to pursue him, and he reached for one of the many spears lying near him and hurled it after Jokul. The spear struck him between his shoulders and came out in front through the chest. Then Jokul fell down dead, but Viglund was by then so weakened by loss of blood that he fell down unconscious and lay there as though dead.

The two who were left of the men of Foss saw this. They mounted and rode back home to Foss and walked into the main room. Holmkel was sitting on the cross-bench with his daughter and wife on either side of him. They reported that Hakon, Jokul and Einar, as well as seven others, were dead and that Viglund and Trausti had fallen as well. When Ketilrid heard this, she fell into a faint.

When she came to, her mother Thorbjorg said, 'Now you show what a loose woman you are and how much you loved Viglund. It's a good thing that you had to part.'

Holmkel said, 'Why do you interpret Ketilrid's fainting in this manner? She loved her brothers so much that she was no less affected when she heard that they had been slain.'

'That may well be the case,' said Thorbjorg, 'but that's not what I think, and it's time to round up the men and kill Thorgrim the Elegant and to avenge the deed as fiercely as possible.'

'Is that really the best course of action?' said her husband. 'It seems to me that he is innocent of the killing of our sons, while Viglund and Trausti could not do any more than lose their lives. What else could they do but defend themselves?'

17 | While Viglund and Trausti were now lying among the slain, Viglund regained consciousness and looked for his brother, and realized that he was still alive. He tried to help him right there because he did not trust his strength to carry him to shelter. Then he heard the sound of cracking ice; it was their father who had come by sled. He put Trausti on the sled and took him back to Ingjaldshvol, while Viglund rode on alone. He put them into a cellar under the beds, and Olof was there to bind up their wounds. They stayed there in secret and recovered their health, but this took twelve months.

Holmkel had a mound placed over his sons and the men who had been slain alongside them. That place has since been called Kumlahaugar (Grave mounds). News of this travelled far, and everyone thought the news remarkable. Everyone believed it quite true that Viglund and Trausti had been killed.

Holmkel and Thorgrim met, for this did not destroy their friendship. They agreed not to bring the case before the law courts. When Thorbjorg learned of this, she sent word to her father Einar from Lon to prosecute the case regarding the slaying of her sons and to seek full outlawry for Viglund and Trausti should they be alive. Even though Einar was old, he took on the case and prosecuted Thorgrim's sons at the Thorsnes Assembly and had them sentenced to full outlawry. News of this now got back to the district.

Hakon's shipmates sailed away in the summer as soon as they were ready, and arrived in Norway. They sought out Ketil and told him everything that had happened. He thought that it would be a while before there was a chance to take vengeance against Thorgrim and his sons. Ketil's sons, Gunnlaug and Sigurd, had recently returned from Viking voyages. They were most renowned men. Gunnlaug the Boisterous had made a vow never to refuse a man passage if his life was at stake, while Sigurd the Wise had vowed never to repay good with evil.

Ketil now told his sons of the slaying of Hakon and asked them to go to Iceland to avenge his dishonour and to kill Thorgrim the Elegant. They were reluctant to do so, but finally went because of their father's pleading. When they got out to sea, they encountered gales and tempestuous weather and were tossed about at sea until the Winter Nights. They reached Snaefellsnes in a terrible fog and got shipwrecked off Ondvertnes. All the men made it to land, but they saved very few of their possessions.

Thorgrim found out about the shipwreck and about the men involved. He rode out to meet them and invited Gunnlaug and Sigurd and all their men to go home with him. They accepted the invitation and stayed there for the winter. Sigurd was quite taken by Helga, even though he said little to her. They never realized that Viglund and Trausti were in hiding.

One time Gunnlaug got into a conversation with his brother Sigurd, and this is what he said: 'Should we not attempt to take vengeance on Thorgrim? I know that we have a very good chance to do so.'

Sigurd said, 'That would have been better left unsaid. I think it would be repaying good with evil if I were to kill the man who has taken me in after the shipwreck and has treated me better with each passing day. I should rather defend him than do him evil if I had to choose.'

They broke off their conversation and Gunnlaug never broached the matter again.

The winter now passed and the brothers had their ship prepared, and when summer came they got ready to sail off. Some said that things must have gone well between Helga and Sigurd, but the rumour did not really spread to the general populace.

18 | The story now returns to Earl Eirik. He grew elderly and died of old age. His son Sigmund inherited all his possessions, but King Harald did not bestow a title on him because the king nurtured ill-will against all of Thorgrim's kinsmen on account of his friendship with Ketil. Helgi[12] had married in Norway and his wife had died at this point in the story. He had only one daughter, whose name was Ragnhild, a most beautiful woman. Helgi was not happy in Norway and went to Iceland. He reached the East Fjords late in the period of the settlement of Iceland. He bought land in Gautavik from Gauti, who had settled on that land, and lived there until old age.

Several persons will now be introduced. There was a man called Steinolf who lived in Hraunsdal. He had a son named Thorleif, a big and promising man. He asked for Ketilrid in marriage, but she did not want him. Thorleif talked a lot about this, saying that he was going to marry her even though she did not give her consent. Thorbjorg was all in agreement with him.

When the time came that Viglund and Trausti had quite recovered from their wounds, they asked their father Thorgrim what advice he might have for them.

He answered: 'I think it advisable for you to be taken on board by the two brothers, Gunnlaug and Sigurd. Ask Gunnlaug for passage to Norway and tell him that your lives are at stake, which is true, and keep your identity concealed. Gunnlaug will keep his oath and give you passage. Sigurd is quite a decent person and you will receive nothing but good from him. And you'll need it, because over there you're going to have to answer for me.'

The matter was now settled.

People say that Ketilrid was very depressed during the winter. Often she slept little and spent the nights awake in her sewing-room. The very night before Viglund intended to board the ship – Ketil's sons were now ready to sail – the two brothers went over to Foss and walked into the room where Ketilrid was sitting up awake, while her servant-women were sleeping.

She welcomed the two brothers warmly: 'It's been a long time since we've met,' she said, 'and everything is all right again since you are well and in good shape.'

The two brothers sat down beside her and talked with her for a long time. Viglund now told her all his plans.

She was pleased by this: 'I think everything is fine,' she said, 'if things are going well for you, no matter how things are going for me.'

'Don't get married while I am away,' Viglund said.

'My father will decide,' said Ketilrid, 'because I am not allowed to, and I do not want to go against his will. It may happen that I will be no happier than you if things turn out other than we want, but what will be, will be.'

Viglund asked her to cut his hair and to wash it, and she did so. And when this had been done, Viglund spoke: 'I swear that no one but you will cut my hair or wash it as long as you are alive.'[13]

Then all of them went out together, and they parted in the hayfield. Viglund kissed Ketilrid, and she wept painfully; it was obvious that they took their parting much to heart, but that was the way it had to be. She then went back into her chamber, and the brothers went their way. However, Viglund spoke a verse before he and Ketilrid parted:

6.
Pretty maiden, take
my poem if it please you;
delivered to delight you,
brooch-bearer, now and then.   *brooch-bearer*: woman
When your eyes, Freyja,   *Freyja*: a half-kenning for 'woman'
espy the islet garth,   *islet garth*: sea
your mind will seek me,
slender maid, each time.

And when they had come a short distance from the farm, Viglund spoke this verse:

7.
We stood in the meadow.
Then the noble maiden,
blessed with beauteous hair,
embraced me broken-hearted.
Weeping tears, the woman
expressed her grief and wishes;
with a snow-white kerchief
her fair white brow she wiped.

A little afterwards, when Ketilrid walked into her room, Holmkel came in and saw his daughter weeping copiously.

He asked why she could not sleep, and she said, 'Because I am remembering the slaying of my brothers.'

'Do you want to have them avenged?' asked Holmkel.

'Clearly, if I were a man with the power to act, but I am in fact a woman.'

Her father said, 'You may be sure, my daughter, that for your sake I have not moved against Viglund and Trausti even though I know that they are alive. Don't conceal from me what you want done, since I intend to kill them when I can, if that is your will.'

Then she responded: 'They would no more be killed – if I had my way – than they would have been outlawed – if I had my way – and they would be given money for their journey – if I had it – and I would marry no man but Viglund – if I could choose.'

At this Holmkel stood up and went out. He took his horse and rode after the brothers.

When they saw him, Trausti said, 'Here comes Holmkel, and he is alone. There's one way for you to get Ketilrid, but it is not advisable to kill Holmkel and carry off Ketilrid.'

Viglund said, 'Even if it were to happen that I should never see Ketilrid again, I would prefer that to doing Holmkel any harm, for I would be remembering but little the loyalty he has shown me, considering the suffering for which he ought to repay me; further-more, Ketilrid is already suffering enough without having her father killed – someone who wants nothing but what is good for her.'

'That's the better thing,' said Trausti.

'Now we are going to ride into the hayfield to make way for Holmkel,' said Viglund. 'That's more respectful to him.'

They did so. Holmkel now passed them but then turned around to go home. The brothers now returned to the path and saw a money-pouch lying on the path and a golden ring along with a rune stick,[14] on which was inscribed the entire conversation between Ketilrid and Holmkel and, furthermore, that she was giving Viglund this money.

19 | The brothers then rode to the ship. Gunnlaug and his brother were ready to sail, and the wind was blowing off shore. Viglund called up to the ship and asked whether Gunnlaug was willing to give him passage to Norway. Gunnlaug asked who they were. One of them said that his name was Trouble-prone and the other one Problem-prone. Gunnlaug asked them the reason for their trip, and they said that their lives were at stake. He then told them to board the ship, and they did so. They then hoisted the sails, and headed out to sea. When they had been sailing for a time, Gunnlaug asked the tall man why he was called Trouble-prone.

'I call myself Trouble-prone,' he said, 'because I have more than enough troubles, but my real name is Viglund, and this is my brother Trausti; we are the sons of Thorgrim the Elegant.'

At this Gunnlaug was silent, but then he said, 'What should we do now, Sigurd, my brother? I think we now have to get ourselves out of a tight spot, since I know that our father Ketil will have them killed when they arrive in Norway.'

Sigurd said, 'You did not ask me about this when you let them come on board, but I recognized Viglund when I saw him, because of his sister. It seems to me that you are decisive enough not to let father have more power over them than you want. That way you can also best repay them for everything Thorgrim has done for us.'

'Now that's good advice,' said Gunnlaug. 'We'll do that.'

They now got a good wind and reached Norway and went home to Romsdal. Ketil was not there. When he came home, his sons were in the main room, and the sons of Thorgrim sat between them. Altogether there were twenty-four people present. They did not greet their father, and he sat down in his seat. He recognized his sons but not Thorgrim's. He asked them why they had not greeted him, and who the strangers were.

Sigurd said, 'One of them is called Viglund, and the other Trausti; they are the sons of Thorgrim the Elegant.'

Ketil spoke: 'Stand up, men, and seize them. I only wish that Thorgrim the Elegant were now here, and they could all share the same fate.'

Sigurd the Wise answered: 'There's a great difference between Thorgrim the Elegant and us, since he rescued us two brothers from a shipwreck, and he dealt with us all the better when we were completely at his mercy, but you now want to kill his sons without cause. We two and our companions would sooner wound you than have Thorgrim's sons killed, because we are all going to meet the same fate.'

Ketil said that it was unthinkable to attack one's own sons. His anger then left him.

Sigurd then spoke: 'I suggest that my brother Gunnlaug arbitrate the whole affair, since he has shown himself to be a just man.'

Ketil said, 'That is to be preferred rather than that we, father and sons, start quarrelling.'

They agreed on this.

Gunnlaug spoke: 'I arbitrate that Thorgrim be given a legal right to Olof, but she will have to forgo her entire inheritance upon the death of her father Earl Thorir. My father will receive her inheritance instead, but my father will have to give his daughter Ingibjorg in marriage to Trausti Thorgrimsson, while Sigurd the Wise is to marry Helga, Thorgrim's daughter. This is my arbitration in the matter.'

Everyone thought that this was well done and wise. Ketil was quite pleased with matters as they stood. They stayed there for the winter enjoying good hospitality. Trausti married Ingibjorg. In the summer the four sworn brothers[15] went on warring expeditions. They were most renowned men, but Viglund was foremost by far. The next three winters they engaged in these warring expeditions. Viglund never looked as happy as formerly, however, because he could not get Ketilrid out of his thoughts.

20 | Now it is time to return to Holmkel, who was at home at Foss. One day it happened that he rode over to Ingjaldshvol, and he and Thorgrim sat together all day in conversation, but no one knew what they were talking about. After that Holmkel went back home. Thorleif Steinolfsson went on wooing Ketilrid, but she was not quick to respond. A little while later Thorgrim sent three of his men on an errand, and they were gone for three weeks before they came home again. No one knew what mission they had undertaken.

One day it happened that thirty men came to Foss. Holmkel asked their leader his name, and he responded that he was called Thord and had his home in the East Fjords. He said that he had come to ask for the hand of Ketilrid in marriage. The farmer went to discuss the matter with his daughter. She was asked what she thought and she reacted negatively to this. She thought the man was old and said that she did not in any case have a mind to marry. Thorbjorg was very anxious for the marriage contract to be made, and the matter ended with Holmkel marrying his daughter to Thord, whether she liked it or not, and she left at once with Thord. The wedding was to take place in the East Fjords. Thord and Ketilrid did not stop until they arrived at his home there. Ketilrid took charge of everything, but people never saw her in a happy mood. Thord did not celebrate his wedding with her. The two lay together in one bed; one blanket covered them. This went on for a long time.

Thorleif was displeased when Ketilrid was given away in marriage, but he did not think it possible to do anything about it, since she was so far away.

Thord did everything he could for Ketilrid, but she did not appreciate it because of her love for Viglund, for in her breast she nourished the flames of a burning love for him.

21 | Viglund and the sworn brothers returned that summer from their warring expeditions. Ketil welcomed them.

One day when they were called together to get their hair washed, Viglund said, 'I'm not going to have my hair washed nor have I had it washed since Ketilrid and I parted.'

Then he spoke a verse:

8.

The faithful linen-tree   *linen-tree*: woman
gently stroked my locks.
Hence, I'm in no hurry
to have another wash.
Never shall another
– though near to her in grace –
goddess of the bowl   *goddess* (Aud) *of the bowl*: woman
bathe me in my lifetime.

Viglund refused to have his hair washed.

They stayed there without stirring that winter, but in the summer they got ready to go to Iceland in their ships, and they set out to sea. Ketil's sons arrived at the Hvita river and got lodging at Ingjaldshvol. They told Thorgrim about the settlement of the case between him and Ketil, and also that Thorgrim's sons were expected to arrive. Thorgrim was happy at the news.

Viglund and Trausti sailed on until they saw the Snaefellsjokul glacier.

Viglund then spoke a verse:

9.

Whenever with loving eyes
I look upon the slope
beneath which she dwells,
my thoughts dart to her.
Great is the mountain's fame,
the lace-goddess standing there   *lace-goddess* (Thrud): woman
endears to me the mount
more than all the others.

258

And then he spoke another verse:

10.

It's light enough to look,
bearer of herbs, on the heath.   *bearer of herbs*: woman
The sun sinks late o'er the slopes,
there where I seek to be.
For her I love the slopes.
Thus I am silent, woman.
I must praise the fairest woman,
who dwells beneath the hawk's land.   *hawk's land*: mountain

All at once such a strong wind blew from the headland that they were driven out to sea, where they got into a west wind. There was such a fierce storm that they had to keep bailing water.

One day Viglund was sitting on some cargo, and the weather was terribly stormy. He then spoke a verse:

11.

Ketilrid bade the young man
not to cower in the deep,
wildly though the waves crash,
wash upon the ship's prow.
Take to heart the words
– let's be doughty, Trausti,
though I am lashed by grief –
uttered by Ketilrid.

'That's quite remarkable,' said Trausti, 'the way you name Ketilrid at both the beginning and the end of your verse.'

'You really think so, kinsman?' said Viglund.

They were out at sea for fifty days and with difficulty made land at Gautavik in the East Fjords.

Then Viglund said, 'It seems best to me, brother, since we are in trouble with a number of people, that you call yourself Hrafn and I'll say I'm Orn.'[16]

The farmer of Gautavik came to the ship. The two brothers welcomed him and asked him to take from the cargo whatever he wanted.

The farmer said that he had a young wife – 'She can come to the ship and choose from your wares whatever she wants.'

The farmer then rode home, and the lady of the house came in the morning. She recognized Viglund as soon as she saw him, but reacted little. Viglund, however, was quite upset when he recognized her. She chose whatever she wanted from the wares; everything was at her disposal.

The farmer had invited the two skippers to stay with him, and when they arrived, the farmer together with the lady of the house went to meet them. Then the farmer lost his footing because he was stiff with old age.

The lady of the house said, but quite softly, 'It's a nuisance to be married to an old man.'

'It was quite slippery,' said her husband.

They were then taken into the house with great respect. Viglund did not think that Ketilrid would recognize him.

Ketilrid then spoke a verse:

12.

I see noble Viglund,	
decked in flood's fire at evening,	*flood's fire*: gold
– strange that the seafarer	
should seek me – and Trausti.	
The slim perch of gold-lace	*perch of gold-lace*: woman
is given to another.	
Older than her husband	
no man is here on earth.	

They now stayed there for the winter, and Viglund was most unhappy, but Trausti was as cheerful as could be; the farmer, too, was most cheerful and treated his guests warmly. They say that Ketilrid wore a veil in front of her face, since she did not want Viglund to recognize her, for it would not have been a good thing if he had done so.

22 | It happened one day that Ketilrid was outside. She was very
warm. She had just taken the veil off her face when Viglund
walked out and saw her face clearly. He was very upset and turned
as red as blood.[17] Thereupon he went back into the main room, where
Trausti was, and his brother asked him what was the matter with
him, or what it was he had seen that had so upset him.

In response Viglund spoke this verse:

13.

Never have I looked into
fairer eyes of dragon's lair   *dragon's lair*: gold;[18] its *eyes*: beautiful eyes
– I would not tell a lie –
since we two went our way.
I'll cut off the craven's head
who caresses the maid;
– from him I earned harshness,
but from the gold spangle, grief.   *gold spangle*: woman

From that time on Ketilrid never again wore the veil before her
face, now that she knew that Viglund had recognized her.

Trausti answered his brother: 'It would be most inadvisable to
harm her husband, considering how well he has treated us. It will be
our misfortune if you kill her husband without cause. You should
forget it.' And he spoke a verse:

14.

You'll never, breaker of rings,   *breaker of rings*: man
win the maid in wedlock,
if you harm the good ruler
of Fafnir's great realm.   *Fafnir's* (a dragon's) *realm*: gold; its *ruler*:
Dealing blows with weapons   generous man
does not solve dilemmas.
We two brothers must behave
beyond blame and reproach.

The evening now passed and people went to bed. During the night
Viglund got up and went to the bed where the farmer and his wife

slept. There was a light high up in the hall so that one could see everything above, but below it was dark. Viglund raised the bed-curtains and saw that Ketilrid was turned towards the wall but her husband towards the bed-board, and he had laid his head as best he could on the board. Viglund was going to draw his sword, but at this moment Trausti came up and said: 'Take care not to carry out so heinous a deed as to kill a sleeping man. Don't let anyone catch on that you yearn for this woman. Behave like a man.'

Trausti then spoke a verse:

15.
Recall, my friend, the maid
who robs you of good cheer;
mark here the man of honour,
I say with happy mien.
Don't have it prattled
– though a perch of splendid silk   *perch of splendid silk*: woman
deprives you of your joy –
around to everyone.

Viglund then calmed down. He nonetheless wondered why there was such a big space between the two in bed. The brothers then went to bed, but Viglund slept little that night.

The next morning Viglund was most dejected, but the farmer was very cheerful and asked Viglund why he was so unhappy. Viglund, whose name everyone thought was Orn, then spoke a verse:

16.
Bright with hand's icy silver
she has bereft me of my bliss,
I'm cast into the currents
of a cursed sea of woe.
Never will the young maid,
– no matter my resolve –
your wife, wounding me sore,
depart from my thoughts.

'That may very well be,' said her husband. 'I think it would be a good idea if we amused ourselves by playing a board game.'

And that was what they did. Orn paid little attention to the board game, because his mind was only on the lady of the house, so that he was checkmated. At this the lady of the house came into the main room and looked at the board; she spoke this half-stanza:

17.
You, generous man, should
merrily move your piece
– a woman's word to the wise –
to another square.

Her husband looked at her and said:

18.
Still contrary to me
is the necklace-goddess.   *necklace-goddess* (Hlin): woman
Wealth-Balder needs suffer nothing   *Wealth-Balder* (god): man
from you save old age alone.

Orn then played as he was told to do, and the game was a draw. The lady of the house and Orn spoke little to each other.

One time the two of them found themselves outside alone. They exchanged a few words but did not speak long. Orn then went to see the farmer. He was glad to see the skipper.

Orn then spoke a verse:

19.
Won't you keep a watch, friend,
on your fair young wife;
do not let the goddess   *goddess* (Gna) *of the fire*: woman
of the fire cause me grief.
If often we meet outside,
who knows to which of us
the valkyrie of gold   *valkyrie* (Hlokk) *of gold*: woman
will prove to be disposed?

And then he spoke another:

20.

Never, warlike Viglund,[19]
do I want to bear the blame
of yearning so for a woman
as to steal another's wife.
Though should the maiden
meet me by cover of dark,
I will not swear to you
I'll not seek that sweet embrace.

The farmer said that things would turn out well, even though she was in charge. They broke off their conversation.

The farmer outdid himself in doing kind things for the skipper, but it was of no avail. He was such an unhappy man that he never spoke a cheerful word. His brother Trausti thought that was a great shame, and he often spoke to him about it, and said that he should stop thinking about it and get himself a wife.

But Orn said that it would not happen – 'I will never love another one like her. I can't keep on like this.'

He then spoke a verse:

21.

I love another's lady,
though on a fair oaken keel
I seek the distant seas;
some won't think me manly.
I can not imagine
another woman ever
would be to me so dear.
The winds bear me from peril.

'That may well be,' said Hrafn.

They then went into the main room. The farmer was sitting there with his wife on his lap. He had his arms around her. Orn saw that she was not very happy about this. She then slid off his lap and sat down on the bench and cried. Orn went over and sat down beside her, and they talked for a while in a rather low tone of voice.

264

Then he spoke a verse:

22.

I wouldn't ever want,
radiant bride, to see you,
linen-decked, a dotard's
doddering paws around you.
It's I should stretch my arms,
woman, as I would wish,
bright stand of arm's fire,   *arm's fire*: gold; its *bright stand*: bejewelled woman
on shore around you.

'We have no certainty that this will ever be,' said the lady of the house.

She got up then and went away.

The farmer was again most cheerful and spoke: 'Skipper Orn, I would now like you to take care of my farm and whatever else concerns me, because I have decided to take a trip. At the shortest, I'll be gone for a month. I trust you more than anyone else with everything that is of greatest concern to me.'

Orn did not react to this.

23 | The farmer then departed together with fourteen men.

Orn spoke to his brother: 'I think that we should leave, so that we are not here while the farmer is away, because otherwise people will think that I am seducing his wife, Ketilrid. Besides, there's quite a difference in character between the farmer and me.'

They then rode off and stayed with some of their customers until the farmer returned at the appointed time. Now he had an even larger company of men. Thorgrim the Elegant and his wife Olof had come with him, as had their daughter Helga and Sigurd the Wise, and the latter's brother Gunnlaug as well as Holmkel from Foss. There were fifty of them altogether, and now the skippers Viglund and Trausti also returned. Ketilrid had prepared everything as her husband had asked her to. He now intended to celebrate his wedding.

When they were all sitting in the main room, the farmer stood up and said, 'It has now turned out that you, Skipper Orn, as well as your brother, have been here all winter. I know that your real name is Viglund and your brother is Trausti, and you are the sons of Thorgrim the Elegant. I also know how much you love Ketilrid. I have given you many tests of character and you have passed them all; at the same time your brother has made sure that you did not do anything dishonourable, but the whole time I was the one really controlling things. I will not conceal from you any longer that I am Helgi; I am the son of Earl Eirik and I am your father's brother. I asked for Ketilrid in marriage in order to be able to save her for you, and I have not taken advantage of her. Ketilrid has borne all this well and in womanly fashion, for I and your father kept her completely in the dark. Furthermore, we have never slept together between the sheets because a bed-board separated us, even though we shared one coverlet. I hardly think that she considered it an ordeal or a punishment not to have relations with anyone as long as she knew you were alive. All of this was Holmkel's plan and now I think it advisable for you to make peace with him and to ask for the hand of his daughter in marriage. He will reach a settlement with you, since he has dealt with you even better and more nobly in the past.'

Viglund then walked over to Holmkel; he knelt down and placed his head on Holmkel's knees, and asked him to do with him as he wished.

Holmkel answered as follows: 'Better that your head stay on your neck, for that would please my daughter Ketilrid more. You and I will certainly make peace.'

Then Holmkel bestowed his daughter Ketilrid on Viglund, and Thorgrim gave his daughter Helga to Sigurd the Wise, while Helgi gave his daughter Ragnhild to Gunnlaug the Boisterous. The weddings were celebrated together, and then everyone went to his own home.

Viglund and Ketilrid were very content with their lot, and they lived at Foss after the death of Ketilrid's father Holmkel, while Trausti stayed on at Ingjaldshvol after the death of his father Thorgrim; but Gunnlaug and Sigurd went abroad and settled in Norway. Here ends this saga.

If the story has been a pleasure,
it's God who has sent us this treasure.
The tale has now come to an end,
into the world God will us send.
And if others with these stories you wish to regale,
you must not too long hold back with the tale.

Thanks be to the one who composed the stories and wrote them down. Amen.

Translated by Marianne Kalinke

Notes

For the sagas and other literary works mentioned in the notes, see Further Reading (pp. xlvi–l) and 'Early Icelandic Literature' (pp. 317–21).

KORMAK'S SAGA

1. *King Harald Fair-hair*: On Harald and other rulers, see 'Rulers'.

2. *Helga, the daughter of Earl Frodi*: These characters are not recorded elsewhere, and the whole Norwegian prelude of the saga is somewhat unlikely.

3. *Helga's foster-mother ... battle*: The motif of a foster-mother with special powers of palpating men's flesh to determine whether they will be wounded in combat appears in several sagas.

4. *high-seat pillars*: Various accounts depict immigrants using these as a means of obtaining guidance from the gods as to a fortunate place to settle, by throwing them overboard, then searching for them and settling in the spot where they landed. They are normally assumed to have been carved with figures of gods and to have been of religious significance.

5. *Kormak had dark curly hair ... like his mother*: Kormak's name is clearly Irish (Cormac), and his dark hair points in the same direction, despite the saga's claim that his grandfather in Norway was also Kormak (ch. 1). The name Dalla has also been interpreted by some as Celtic. People of Celtic origin formed a significant proportion of the population of Iceland from its settlement from *c.* 870 onwards.

6. *Dolluson brothers*: i.e. 'the brothers who were the sons of Dalla'. Icelandic names in -son or -dottir are usually patronymics, incorporating the father's name, but here because Ogmund is deceased the brothers are known by the matronymic Dolluson, in which Dollu- is the possessive form of Dalla.

7. *wood stacked by the door*: This, and 'fire-hall's felled wood' in v. 2, are somewhat obscure. An alternative interpretation of the prose is that Steingerd

is peeping over a wooden partition or an internal half-door set into vertical posts with runners.

8. *troll-woman's breeze: mind* (line 2): A kenning pattern that has been thought to spring from folk-beliefs in winds produced by sorcery which carry with them the sorcerer's spirit, or possibly a blast of disease.

Gerd: The specific 'goddess' named in the original text is Gerd, a giantess who became wife of the fertility god Frey. In a piece of wordplay typical of the skalds, her name matches the second part of Steingerd's, and it appears again in Kormak's last verse (v. 85). On the use of names of gods and goddesses in kennings, see 'The Techniques of Skaldic Poetry' (pp. 322–6).

9. *dark, narrow passage*: This ran along the perimeter of a hall, separated by partitions from the main living-space.

the carved beard of Hagbard: While the original simply has 'Hagbard's beard', this appears to be an image carved on a post or partition. Hagbard is a shadowy figure – a legendary sea-king in Norse tradition, but also a tragically ill-fated warrior and lover in Book VII of Saxo Grammaticus's *History of the Danes* (early thirteenth century).

10. *The moon . . . ring-goddess herself*: Verse 3 is also attributed to Gunnlaug (as v. 20 of his saga), but most scholars have assumed that it properly belongs in *Kormak's Saga*.

will later bring trouble (line 7): An alternative reading is 'has brought trouble'.

11. *Kormak made a habit . . . Steingerd*: Despite – or perhaps because of – prohibitions on approaches to unmarried women, the 'illicit love visit' becomes a topos in the sagas.

difference between the parties involved: Dalla is presumably thinking of the lower social status of Steingerd and her family. One interpretation sees this as a factor in Kormak's failure to marry Steingerd.

12. *There was a man named Narfi living with Thorkel*: The loafing Narfi is unknown from other sources and possibly a pure fiction. Steingerd addresses Narfi as 'kinsman' when asking him a favour in ch. 7, and one manuscript specifies that he was being fostered at Thorkel's home.

13. *snakes of the cauldron* (v. 11), *suet* (v. 12): Icelanders were often mocked abroad for their suet-eating habits, but Narfi's taunts about sausages are clearly sexual.

14. *They adopted this course of action . . . Saurbaer*: As becomes clear, it is Thorkel the younger (Tooth-gnasher) and Narfi who travel.

15. *against Steingerd's wishes*: Women in the sagas are frequently not consulted or even informed about their betrothal until after the event, but for the bride to be left in the dark until the wedding day itself is exceptional.

16. *saw then that Bersi had boarded Thorveig's boat*: The awkward handling of

complex narrative strands here and elsewhere in the saga is often attributed to its (presumed) early date.

iron-bordered targe: A circular shield.

17. *Muli*: The farm of Bersi's ally Thord Arndisarson, introduced in ch. 7.

18. *the sword Skofnung*: Swords were prestigious weapons in the Viking Age, and swords with names, individual 'personalities' and magic attributes often feature in saga fights. Skofnung and its healing-stone (which heals wounds made by the sword) appear in other sagas.

19. *pommel of the sword hilt*: Sword hilts comprised three parts: the pommel or knob at the top; the middle section, i.e. the main part by which the weapon was held; and the guard between the hilt and the blade.

a little snake will crawl out from under the hilt: That this and other legendary swords harbour snakes has been explained as a fanciful extension of the fact that some early sword-blades had serpentine designs which may have shown more clearly when breathed upon.

20. *duel . . . single combat*: See Glossary (pp. 327–38). The distinction is not made in other sources.

21. *four strings, named hazel poles*: Hazel poles and cordons marking out ground are standard in duels, but the equivalence of the two here is puzzling. *Strengir* 'strings' could possibly be an error for *stengr* 'posts'.

22. *hit the targe*: Bersi seems to have kept the magic shield given him in ch. 8 as a last resort, but there is inconsistency with the previous statement that both combatants had used up the three shields allowed them.

23. *Steinar, the son of Onund Sjoni*: See *The Saga of Gunnlaug*, n. 10.

24. *dwellings of the sea-king (Ati)*: Although this is not a standard 'shield' kenning pattern, shields are often associated with ships (being set along the gunwale), or are referred to as the buildings of heroes.

25. *Glum or Skuma*: Like many temporary aliases in the sagas, these names suggest concealment and menace. Glum (*Glúmr*) is also recorded as a name for a bear, while Skuma (*Skúma*) is from a root meaning 'dark'.

26. *The duel-challenge . . . spear-river*: This verse is partially echoed in v. 45.

27. *the pouch it was in*: It seems from this and the following verse that Bersi's sword Hviting was accompanied not only by a healing-stone but also a pouch of herbs and moss with healing properties.

28. *A long time . . . my life still*: The short lines here and in v. 48 are characteristic of the 'metre of ancient utterance' (*fornyrðislag*), which is also used in Old English, Old High German and Old Saxon poetry.

29. *Skrymir*: Also the name of Steinar's sword in *Egil's Saga*, ch. 81, but more famous as the name of a giant in *Lokasenna*, v. 62, in the *Poetic Edda* and in a story in the *Gylfaginning* section of Snorri Sturluson's *Edda*, chs. 45–7.

30. *wished to divorce him*: Divorce, on a variety of grounds, is quite frequent in the sagas, and is most often initiated by women on grounds including male violence and incompatibility of various kinds. The issue for Thordis seems to be that her honour is diminished by Thord's humiliating injury (see further Jenny Jochens, *Women in Old Norse Society* (Ithaca: Cornell University Press, 1995), pp. 57–60).

31. *discussing who were the greatest in the district*: The comparison of men is something of a set piece in early Norse poetry and saga. It often sparks off violence.

32. *Both of us . . . none at all*: This verse also occurs in *The Saga of the People of Laxardal*, ch. 28, where Halldor, more appropriately, is still an infant.

33. *go to Vali and pour out your woes*: The plan for Steinvor to contrive a quarrel with Thordis, then to run to Vali complaining about Bersi siding with Thordis, is rather curious, given that Vali is Thordis's brother.

34. *rode around five farms*: The thirteenth-century Icelandic law code *Grágás* (literally, 'Grey Goose') does not mention five farms, but it does stipulate that a killing should be announced the same day at the nearest farm where it is safe to do so. This was among the conditions for a killing to qualify as manslaughter rather than murder.

Valafall (Vali's fall): An example of a place-name that pins a saga incident into the local landscape. Like many stories attaching to Icelandic place-names, this one is incapable of proof.

35. *Thorvald Tintein . . . Thorvard . . . Skidi clan*: Thorvald is recorded in *The Book of Settlements*, but his brothers are named there as Thorstein and Orn (ch. 187). In 'Tintein' the first element means 'tin', the second probably 'twig' or 'bar', and Kormak jibes at Thorvald as a tinsmith in v. 51. The family are named from a distant ancestor, Skidi the Old.

36. *asking her to make him a shirt*: A sign of intimacy found elsewhere in the sagas, e.g. *Gisli Sursson's Saga*, ch. 9.

37. The last six lines of this verse are repeated in v. 65.

38. *Thorveig's eyes when they saw it*: Clearly the fetch of Thorveig, presumably come to damage the ship. There is some doubt as to the exact sea-mammal indicated.

39. *Harald Grey-cloak*: Kormak is named in the *List of Poets* (*Skáldatal*) as skald to Harald.

40. *so dear. . . to the sword of the love-hair's island*: Only a slight emendation to this problematic text would give a more predictable and less sexually explicit reading: 'sea-goddess [woman], dear to the tree of the island of sword-din', where 'sword-din' is battle, its 'island' a shield, and the 'tree of the shield' a warrior, Kormak.

41. *Stones will stand . . . will be born*: This stanza is noted for its use of the

rhetorical topos of adynaton – claiming that impossible or cataclysmic events are more likely to happen than that anyone will surpass the subject of the praise (cf. also v. 19). The apocalyptic image of the earth sinking into the sea is associated with the final 'doom of the gods' (*ragnarök*).

42. *That human spawn ... set in train*: This verse is a reprise, with a different opening couplet, of v. 52.

43. *slander and other insults*: It is not certain what is meant here, unless Thorvald is pretending to believe that Kormak composed v. 64. The 'other insults' may be Kormak's intimacies with Steingerd and perhaps the killing of Narfi.

44. *heart, albeit of clay*: This seems to refer to Mokkurkalfi, a cowardly giant made of clay who, according to Snorri Sturluson's *Edda*, stands beside Hrungnir in his fight against Thor (see v. 15).

45. *a daughter's gift*: Some editors emend this puzzling phrase to 'Odin's [gift]', referring to poetry.

46. *see her eyes in the sunlight*: This may be connected with fears of the evil eye, though the normal way of dealing with that is to put a bag over the evil one's head.

47. *saw a bull standing nearby and killed it*: Cf. ch. 23, where the sacrificial nature of the act is clearer. Such sacrifices were customary after duels.

48. *make the elves a feast of the meat*: A rare reference to sacrificing to elves, which was possibly for fertility.

49. *went to the duel*: There are striking parallels between this and the duel in ch. 22; this is one of several doublets in the saga.

50. *Those two rings that I lost earlier*: Strictly, it was Thorvard who surrendered the rings in chs. 22 and 23, but he was acting for Thorvald. The fine for two kisses seems heavy, but the *Grágás* law code stipulates lesser outlawry as the penalty for illicit kisses.

51. *Steingerd asked Thorvald Tintein to travel abroad with her*: A rare venture for an Icelandic woman in the Viking Age, though less so later.

52. *The king said, 'Let one kiss ... Steingerd'*: The king's version of the attack is more precise than the original description, as he specifies that it happened as Steingerd and Thorvald came to land and implies that Steingerd was actually seized. The episode is duplicated in ch. 26.

53. *Permia*: The area around the White Sea, prized for products including furs and walrus ivory. Harald's expedition is also recounted in *Heimskringla* and *Fagrskinna*.

54. *drinking with Steingerd out of the same vessel*: Men and women drinking in mixed pairs was one of the accepted patterns of communal drinking, although it is often, as here, suggestive of intimacy.

Vig: *Vigr* in the original is itself a poetic word for 'spear', as in v. 79, line 5. The prose-writer may or may not be correct in taking it as a proper name.

55. *Ash-sides*: The nickname is not mentioned when Asmund is first introduced (ch. 1), but it is said there that Ogmund's weapons will not pierce his side.

56. *demanded a report of events from the cooks*: Kormak's order of priorities at a moment when his beloved is in the embrace of a Viking marauder is only one of the bizarre features of this narrative; another being the fact that he and Thorgils board by the stern gangway, but then swim ashore, Thorgils with Steingerd.

57. *Scarborough [Skarðaborg]*: Thorgils had the nickname Skardi (Skarði), to judge from vv. 53–5, and adding to that the claim here that Thorgils and Kormak founded the stronghold, it is widely held that the place-name derives from the nickname.

58. *a giant whom the Scots worshipped as an idol*: i.e. with sacrifices, which is a unique concept, since giants are not usually recipients of sacrifices in Norse sources. Celtic influence has been suggested.

59. *steerer of rigging-steeds*: i.e., a seafarer – a very unlikely way of referring to a Scottish giant, and only one of the problems of mismatch between the final verses of the saga and the prose narrative in which they are set.

drinking ale in the high seat in Odin's hall: This seems to allude to the belief that men slain in battle earned a place in Valhalla, in which case a negative has been lost in lines 6–7: logically, Kormak would have been slain if he had not had the help of the sword Skrymir. Either way, the verse is difficult to reconcile with the surrounding prose, since Skrymir does help, but Kormak is fatally injured. Verses 83 and 85, meanwhile, indicate that Kormak, to his chagrin, dies in bed.

60. *Ireland*: A clue that this verse may belong more properly within the campaign described in ch. 19.

THE SAGA OF HALLFRED TROUBLESOME-POET

1. *Thorgerd Hallfredardottir*: i.e., daughter of Hallfred, who is the great-grandfather of the poet.

2. *sons of Gunnhild, who ruled Norway at that time*: Notably King Harald Grey-cloak, who ruled from *c.* 960, after defeating Hakon, Athelstan's foster-son, at the battle of Fitjar. Since the battle is mentioned later in the chapter as taking place seven or eight years later, the rule of Gunnhild's sons is placed too early.

attack the farm with fire: To burn enemies inside a building was a desperate act, undertaken either by villains, as here, or by men of general goodwill who are driven to it by circumstances, as in the burning of Njal, mentioned in *The Saga of Gunnlaug*, ch. 11, and narrated in *Njal's Saga*, chs. 129–30.

3. *Ottar fought at Fitjar . . . fell*: The other *Hallfred* manuscripts (see Note on the Translations), probably correctly, say not that Ottar was at Fitjar but that a battle (*orrusta*) took place there. On the battle of Fitjar, see n. 2 above.

4. *All the girls . . . in my upper gum*: The first half-stanza is also in *The Saga of the People of Vatnsdal* (ch. 8), where it is the sole verse, cited within a telling of the story of Ingolf and Valgerd.

go with (lines 2 and 6): Could imply either courtship or marriage.

5. *autumn feast*: Autumn was a traditional time of feasting, when travel was still relatively easy and meat was plentiful after the annual slaughter of beasts not to be kept over the winter.

6. *Ingolf took to visiting . . . Valgerd*: The placing of this romance here provides a foreshadowing of Hallfred's courting of Kolfinna, but forces events out of chronological sequence. The other main version of the saga ('O', see Note on the Translations) has the episodes in reverse order.

the way things were in the valley: i.e., given that his father is chieftain.

7. *love poem about Valgerd*: The laws encoded in *Grágás* made it illegal to compose love poems about women over the age of twenty.

8. *Constantinople and won great honour there*: Presumably Gris served in the famous Varangian Guard, an elite, mainly Nordic, corps within the Imperial Guard of the Byzantine emperor (cf. ch. 10).

9. *all-heathen* (line 3): Since Hallfred himself is still heathen at this point, this has been taken as a sign that the verse is either displaced or not authentic.

I swell the poetry: Both the insertion of one sentence within another, and boasting references to their own art, are characteristic of the skalds.

10. *a hundred of silver to Hallfred*: A substantial sum – equivalent to the standard compensation for a killing.

11. *a drapa*: Nine surviving half-stanzas are assumed to belong to this poem. They are remarkable for the recurring mythological image of Hakon as lover of the earth goddess, the personified land of Norway. Hallfred is not, however, listed among the poets of Earl Hakon in the *List of Poets* (*Skáldatal*).

12. *Frey . . . Iceland*: The association of the fertility god Frey especially with Sweden and of Thor and Odin with Iceland is authentic. The thunder god Thor may also have had a role as a wind god.

13. *Anchor-fluke*: The anchor-fluke (*akkerisfrakki*) mentioned here and in vv. 5 and 6 is the metal barb that pins the anchor into the sea-bed. Rightly or wrongly, the prose writer has taken it as a name, but it could, instead or

additionally, simply be the common noun; another possible meaning is 'anchor-bold'.

14. *the man in the cloak*: i.e. 'Anchor-fluke'. In his zeal for brevity, the writer of this version of the saga has omitted to mention that he was wearing a green cloak.

15. *Jostein*: Maternal uncle to Olaf Tryggvason.

16. *Nordri's kin*: Nordri, Austri, Sudri and Vestri are in mythology the four dwarfs who hold up the north, east, south and west corners of the sky. The 'burden of Nordri's kin' is hence the sky.

17. *a flokk*: Despite the later statement that the poem was a drapa. Five stanzas and four half-stanzas are believed to belong to this poem.

he did not wish to hear it: The king's reluctance presumably reflects the association of poetry with pagan inspiration and pagan imagery. This exchange is reminiscent of one between the poet Sighvat and King Olaf Haraldsson.

18. *Troublesome-poet*: While *The Saga of Hallfred* links the nickname 'Trouble-some-poet' to the conflict that Hallfred sees between his poetic art and the new religion, it is associated in sagas of King Olaf Tryggvason with his driving of a hard bargain. In the saga by Odd Snorrason Hallfred agrees to baptism only on condition that the king personally stands sponsor to him (ch. 40), while in Snorri Sturluson's saga in *Heimskringla*, Hallfred swears allegiance to the king in return for a pledge that he will never reject him, whatever happens (ch. 83).

19. *his skiff of Austri's son* (line 4): Austri's son is a dwarf, since Austri, one of the sky-bearing dwarfs (see n. 16 above) can stand for dwarfs in general. The 'skiff' or rowing-boat of dwarfs is figuratively 'poetry', since at one stage of the intricate account of the mythical origins of poetry in Snorri Sturluson's *Prose Edda*, chs. 57–8, some treacherous dwarfs marooned on a tidal rock by the giant Suttung buy their release by giving up the precious mead of poetry. *the king's gift*: Or *King's Gift*. Expressions like this, which are used virtually like names, refer to weapons and other treasures that have been obtained, normally by gift, from the person identified in the first element (here King Olaf).

20. *Grimnir*: Odin, literally 'masked one'; the thought behind line 3 is obscure.

21. *It was different in former days ... and pray to Christ*: Verses 9–13 underpin one of the main themes of the saga, and are a rare and precious expression of the anguish experienced by a pagan convert to Christianity at the end of the first millennium. Their authenticity has been questioned, but the evidence against them is far from conclusive.

22. *Hakon's Gift*: Hallfred's reward for the poem in ch. 5.

it was the law ... should be executed: An anachronism, since the death sentence for such a crime under old Norwegian law postdates the time of the action.

23. *sward-strip*: A whimsical comparison seems to be made here between the sheath and the raised arch of turf under which men passed in certain ancient rites and ordeals.

24. *Thor amulet*: Figurines of the god, and miniature replicas of his famous hammer, are quite common finds in Nordic archaeology.

25. *Let my money-bag be searched now*: The slight lack of fit between charge and response is another example of over-zealous shortening (cf. n. 14 above). In the 'O' version the king asks specifically about the amulet.

26. *I will grant this my luck*: The personal luck of the two missionary King Olafs is frequently mentioned in the sagas. It comes to Hallfred's aid as he grapples with Onund in ch. 7.

27. *mound on which he was sitting*: Rulers are often said to do this; cf. n. 11 to *The Saga of Gunnlaug*.

28. *Hallfred told the whole story*: As the following conversation shows, this is not strictly true. The 'O' version's 'Hallfred said that he had blinded Thorleif' is more apt.

29. *perilous*: Literally 'unclean'. The same word describes the 'bad place' from which King Olaf rescues Hallfred and crew in ch. 5, and in both cases physical perils seem also to symbolize the dangers of paganism. In heading east into present-day Sweden, Hallfred ventures into territories that converted to Christianity later than the rest of Scandinavia, as a gradual process in the eleventh century.

30. *White Christ*: The expression is often found in narratives of conversions, and is used by Sighvat Thordarson, an early Christian poet of the eleventh century. White clothes were worn at baptism.

31. *a man was there chopping wood ... a red beard*: The folk-tale atmosphere hereabouts matches the fact that this scene, like the threefold division of labour in the previous chapter, has parallels in sagas of an obviously fictional sort. Men with red beards frequently prove treacherous in other sagas, e.g. the killer Thorir Red-beard in *The Saga of Grettir the Strong*, ch. 56.

32. *valuables ... which Audgisl had sent her*: Audgisl met his death entirely unexpectedly (ch. 7), so could not have sent treasures to Ingibjorg.

33. *in his tributary land*: Vastergotland was under Swedish sovereignty.

King Olaf: Tryggvason, king of Norway.

34. *Uppreistardrapa*: An atonement poem – literally a poem about advancement/restoration or about the Creation. The 'O' version asserts 'and it is a very fine poem', but no trace of the poem survives, and its existence has been doubted.

35. *coloured clothing*: Contrasting with the neutral colours of local homespun wool, coloured clothing spoke of foreign travel and the kudos it conferred.

36. *like a swan swimming*: An alternative translation is 'like a swan in a bay'. Explicit similes, as distinct from the comparisons implied by kennings, are rare in skaldic verse, but v. 19 caps the image of Kolfinna as swan-like with one of Gris as a fulmar, a bird of the petrel family whose name means 'foul gull', while v. 28 contains a spectacular image of Kolfinna gliding like a ship.

37. *white fellow* (line 1): 'White' probably has implications of cowardice here and in *The Saga of Gunnlaug*, v. 13, and *The Saga of Bjorn*, vv. 3 and 11.

enjoys his livestock: Probably innuendo about bestiality; and *wide milking-shed* and *long sheep-pen* may have sexual reference.

38. *giant-stories: gold*: Snorri Sturluson, in his *Prose Edda*, chs. 56–7, explains how the giant Olvaldi divided up his treasure-hoard among his three sons by having them take mouthfuls in turn. Since speech is another kind of mouth contents, any phrase meaning 'utterance of giant(s)' comes to mean 'gold'.

goatskin: May have associations with (homo-)sexuality, cowardice and sorcery, and *hog* plays on the name Gris (young pig).

39. *the cloak King's Gift*: Hallfred's impulse breaches King Olaf's injunction earlier in this chapter.

40. *Einar, son of Thorir Thrandarson*: Gris's cousin, according to the 'O' version of the saga.

41. *the arm-rings, Earl's Gift and King's Gift*: The rings given by Earl Sigvaldi in ch. 7 and King Olaf in ch. 9. The fate of Earl's Gift is noted at the end of ch. 10.

42. *parried with a sacrificial trough and was not wounded*: Mar's curious choice of weapon seems to derive from v. 26. Indeed, the ambush episode is a narrative dead-end, probably created as a context for the verse.

43. *scared of the hog*: A play on Gris's name, which means 'young pig'; cf. the play on Bjorn's name at the climax of his saga (ch. 32 and n. 54).

44. *the fall of King Olaf*: Olaf Tryggvason fell *c.* 1000 at the sea-battle of Svold (of uncertain location) against a confederation of Swedes, Danes, and Norwegians led by Earl Eirik Hakonarson. A contemporary rumour that he might have escaped by swimming is mentioned in v. 24 of Hallfred's memorial poem for Olaf.

45. *Olafsdrapa*: Some twenty-nine surviving verses are believed to come from this poem.

46. *compose a drapa about the earl*: Olaf Tryggvason's command may be an

authorial attempt to justify Hallfred's composing for the enemy and displacer of his beloved lord.

47. *Thorleif the Wise*: Last seen in ch. 6.

48. *compose ... within three nights*: In other cases where a poet composes a 'head-ransom' poem his life depends on it more urgently than is the case here. The most famous example is Egil composing to mollify his foe Eirik Blood-axe (*Egil's Saga*, chs. 60–2).

49. *Onund*: Father of Hrafn, chief antagonist of *The Saga of Gunnlaug*.

50. *between him and Hrafn*: A fuller account of Hallfred's journey with Gunnlaug and a shorter one of his contretemps with Hrafn are given in *The Saga of Gunnlaug*, ch. 10.

51. *Thorvald*: The 'M' version (see Note on the Translations) omits to mention that Thorvald sailed with Hallfred.

52. *if I die*: In the 'O' version of the saga, Hallfred speaks a verse declaring that he would be content to die, but for his anxiety for his soul and fear of Hell.

Holy Isle (Iona): Site of a monastery founded by St Columba in the sixth century, which became the centre of a network of religious foundations in the Hebrides and western Scotland.

53. *Hallfred ... Troublesome-poet*: The younger Hallfred and his descendants are not mentioned in other sources.

THE SAGA OF GUNNLAUG SERPENT-TONGUE

1. *This is the saga ... in Iceland*: This preamble, like the remainder of the translation, follows the early fourteenth-century Stockholm manuscript Holm. perg. 18 4to. Ari Thorgilsson (1067–1148) wrote the first known vernacular history of Iceland, *The Book of the Icelanders*, and probably contributed to an early version of *The Book of Settlements*. Some material, especially genealogical, in *The Saga of Gunnlaug* may go back to Ari, but the attribution is otherwise far-fetched. The other principal manuscript is simply headed 'The Saga of Gunnlaug Serpent-tongue'.

2. *and many others*: Einar Skulason was a distinguished twelfth-century poet. Snorri Sturluson was a thirteenth-century magnate who probably wrote *Egil's Saga* as well as *Heimskringla* and the *Prose Edda*. The earlier generations of Myrar folk are central to *Egil's Saga* and prominent in several other sagas including *The Saga of the People of Laxardal*.

3. *Dreams don't mean anything*: A proverb.

4. *They were both dead*: Two main literary influences on Thorstein's dream

have been suggested: a dream of two eagles killing a falcon which portends the death of Siegfried/Sigurd within the love-triangle plot of the German *Niebelungenlied* and the Norse *Saga of the Volsungs*; and Hecuba's dream in *Trójumanna saga*. The queen is warned in a dream that her unborn child will be the destruction of Troy, whereupon her husband orders it to be exposed, but, seeing the beauty of the newborn child, Alexander, she secretly has him fostered.

5. *have their children exposed*: According to the *Saga of St Olaf* in *Heimskringla* (chs. 58–60), it was early in the eleventh century, and at the insistence of King Olaf Haraldsson, that this practice was discontinued. In the sagas, exposure has become almost a romantic motif, since the victims, often girls, are always saved, which cannot have been the norm.

6. *Hermund and another Gunnlaug*: Most of the genealogical information about Illugi the Black matches that in *The Book of Settlements*, chs. 15, 43, 99, 174, and in other sagas. Hermund Illugason is the central character of *The Saga of the Confederates*.

7. *Lawspeaker*: Skafti in fact held office somewhat later, for the exceptionally long period between 1004 and 1030.

8 *Their names were*: The copyist has presumably skipped a section in his exemplar, where the names of Thorfinn's remaining four sons were recorded.

9. *the farmer thought that was too little*: Gunnlaug could have been subject to full outlawry if the shepherd was a free man rather than a slave. On the other hand, the scale of penalties for riding another man's horse without consent went right up to full outlawry.

10. *Neither Onund . . . father*: Possibly a reference to Onund in Thorstein's speech has dropped out of the text.

Thorgrim Kjallaksson . . . there was to be had: Illugi disputed with him over his wife's dowry; cf. *The Saga of the People of Eyri*, ch. 17.

Steinar, the son of Onund Sjoni: Maternal uncle of Kormak (*Kormak's Saga*, chs. 11–12). He got into a dispute with Thorstein through encroaching on his grazing land (cf. *Egil's Saga*, chs. 83–7). Steinar is also mentioned in *The Book of Settlements*, ch. 60.

11. *Borg*: A fortress, either man-made or natural, in this case the steep, rocky hill from which the farmstead of Borg took its name. Private conversations are often held out in the open in sagas, and there may be a trace of an ancient belief in hills and burial mounds as a supernatural source of wisdom.

12. *Trondheim to Nidaros*: Nidaros is part of the city now called Trondheim, while Trondheim (*Þrándheimur*) referred to the district now called Trøndelag.

13. *white breeches*: Integrated trousers and socks, made of undyed cloth – a

contrast with the finery Gunnlaug later acquires (ch. 11), and presumably with the courtly splendour around him.

14. *foster-brother*: Since Gunnlaug had spent part of his teens at Borg in the household of Skuli's father Thorstein.

15. *We should test him a bit*: Cf. the widespread motif of the challenge to the hero on arrival in the hall of strangers. A famous example is Unferth's dispute with Beowulf in the Old English epic *Beowulf*.

16. *Earl Hakon did*: According to the Sagas of Kings, Hakon the Powerful was murdered *c.* 995 by his slave Kark while hiding in a pigsty. He was under threat both from the gathering forces of Olaf Tryggvason and from farmers infuriated by his exercise of *droit de seigneur* over their wives and daughters.

17. *the language in England ... Denmark*: The Scandinavian languages and English are 'genetically' related within the Germanic family, and because of ninth- and tenth-century emigrations to parts of eastern and northern England, Scandinavian or Scandinavianized speech would have been current there at this time. The saga's claim is therefore exaggerated but not wholly false.

William the Bastard: William is so called in Icelandic and other sources because he was the illegitimate son of Duke Robert of Normandy.

French language ... from then on: Norman French became the language of the court and to some extent of officialdom, but Latin was the main documentary and ecclesiastical language, and English continued as the spoken language for the great majority.

18. *scarlet*: A fine cloth from the Low Countries and Germany, frequently but not necessarily red in colour.

19. *Northerner*: Norðmaður, i.e., someone from the Nordic lands, often specifically 'Norwegian'.

20. *the berserk said ... sword*: Thororm does not exhibit the extremes of behaviour of the stereotypical berserk, such as howling in an animal frenzy of aggression or biting shields, but his ability to blunt weapons by looking at them is a berserk characteristic.

21. *a short while*: Sigtrygg appears to have ruled in Dublin from *c.* 996 to 1042. The chronology of the saga suggests that Gunnlaug visited him in 1003.

22. *To the troll-wife's stallion ... in drapa metre*: The short, end-rhyming lines of the original vv. 6–8 are composed in the *runhent* metre which seems to be particularly associated with the British Isles.

23. *An earl named Sigurd ... was ruling there*: Not recorded in other sources, and there is no room for him in the contemporary political world.

24. *Yule*: A thirteen-day pagan winter festival, fairly easily accommodated, after the Conversion, to Christmas. The eighth day was New Year's Day.

25. *only a flokk ... merited a drapa*: Gunnlaug composes in the form of the flokk for earls, reserving the more grandiose drapa for kings. According to *Heimskringla* (*Saga of St Olaf*, ch. 172) King Canute threatened Thorarin Praise-tongue with hanging after he had offered him a flokk. Thorarin saved his head by hastily composing refrains and extra verses.

26. *Canute the Great, the son of Svein*: According to the saga's chronology, the date at this point would be *c.* 1004, but as in other Icelandic sources Svein's death is placed over a decade earlier than its actual date in 1014.

27. *Hallfred Troublesome-poet ... yesterday*: Cf. accounts of the episodes involving him in *The Saga of Hallfred*, ch. 11.

28. *living on ... gold-breaker*: Gunnlaug clearly means that he fears dishonour more than death, which has led some editors to emend to 'not living'.

29. *paid him a mark*: Hallfred escaped lightly, in fact. Under a normal legal settlement, he would have had to pay double the original debt, and a fine of at least three marks.

30. *looking after their property there*: According to *The Saga of Hallfred*, ch. 10, Galti was killed some three or four years previously.

31. *Oxararholm*: A sandy island in the river flowing into Thingvellir lake, and a customary duelling-ground.

32. *the burning of Njal ... the Slayings on the Heath*: Both climactic events in famous sagas. They are set in 1010 and 1014 respectively by the *Icelandic Annals*.

33. *The moon of her eyelash ... ring-goddess herself*: Probably the most lyrical verse attributed to Gunnlaug, this also appears – more plausibly – as v. 3 of *Kormak's Saga*.

34. *Thorkel*: Not hitherto mentioned on this journey, but he was on Gunnlaug's previous one.

35. *gone across into Sweden*: The saga-writer's location of Dingenes in Sweden may reflect a tradition that Earl Eirik banned duelling in his realm, but Dingenes is the name of a place on the west coast of Norway.

36. *Thord Kolbeinsson*: Poet to Earl Eirik and King Olaf Haraldsson, father to Arnor Earls'-poet (see n. 43 to *The Saga of Bjorn*), and one of the two main antagonists in *The Saga of Bjorn*.

37. *a dream*: The atmospheric use of dreams after an event rather than as a portent is somewhat unusual.

38. *Bjorn killed and Thorgrim's foot cut off*: Revenge was quite often taken against family members uninvolved in the original dispute. Maiming, however, is unusual in sagas set in this period; it is more characteristic of the thirteenth century, as documented in *Sturlunga Saga*.

39. *My Helga ... be yet living*: Two lines, probably 5–6, appear to be missing

from this verse in the manuscript text, but only 'river' has been supplied in order to make sense of the kenning here.

THE SAGA OF BJORN, CHAMPION OF
THE HITARDAL PEOPLE

1. *Now some account . . . friends*: The unusual start to the saga is due to the fact that the first five chapters are imported from *The Great Saga of St Olaf*, since the original opening is missing from the manuscripts.

Gudrun Osvifsdottir: Central character of *The Saga of the People of Laxardal.*

2. *Skuli Thorsteinsson at Borg*: Bjorn is hence connected both by birth and fosterage to the mighty dynasty of the Myrar folk. In fact, Skuli's father Thorstein was still alive and patriarch at Borg, rather than Skuli, at this date (cf. *The Saga of Gunnlaug*, ch. 1 onwards).

3. *she consented*: The consultation with Oddny, and her very positive response, are both rather unusual, as is the fact that Bjorn's visits to Oddny in the previous chapter do not cause offence.

4. *Hroi*: The name is probably extrapolated from the Danish place-name Roskilde (*Hrói's-kelda*), and the material about Hroi seems fanciful.

5. *Bag-Shaking*: Fifteen stanzas and two half-stanzas attributed to Thord and in praise of Eirik survive, some of which are believed to be from this poem.

6. *Kaldimar*: Vladimir I ruled the partially Norse kingdom of Gardariki from 980 to 1015. The name of the challenger, Kaldimar, seems to be a fictitious imitation of the king's name.

7. *Maering*: According to *The Great Saga of St Olaf*, Bjorn was given this sword by Olaf Haraldsson. *Mæring* means 'noble, excellent one'.

8. From this point the text followed is that of the surviving portion of the saga itself.

9. *dragon . . . fell down dead*: Dragons are rare in the Sagas of Icelanders and fabulous events of any sort mostly confined to distant and exotic lands, or to less 'realistic' types of saga.

Audun Back-flap: The second part of Audun's nickname, *bakskiki*, refers to a patch of land or a trailing piece of fabric; homosexual implications may be intended.

10. *change of rulers in Norway*: The following account tallies quite well with the Sagas of Kings.

St Olaf: King Olaf Haraldsson came to be venerated as a saint throughout the Nordic lands (though never formally canonized). He was credited with a martyr's death, an uncorrupt body and miracle-working in the years immediately after his fall at Stiklestad in 1030.

11. *a letter*: Possibly an anachronism.

the sons of Eid, Thord and Thorvald: There is some inconsistency in the manuscript over these brothers, who are Thorkel and Thorgrim here, but Einar and Thorvald in ch. 19 (where they are introduced as if for the first time), then Thord and Thorvald several times in chs. 30–2. These last two names have therefore been adopted throughout the translation.

12. *Branno islands*: 'Where Vikings used to lie in wait in those days for the many trading ships that sailed through them' (*Egil's Saga*, ch. 48).

13. *father and foster-father are still alive*: Although Bjorn spent his teens in Skuli's household (ch. 1), the foster-father must be the otherwise unknown Ingjald who appears unannounced alongside Bjorn's father Arngeir in ch. 10. He was presumably introduced in the original, lost opening of the saga.

14. *with the king at several feasts*: A glimpse of a largely itinerant monarchy in which the king and his company were entertained for a few days at a time by a succession of prosperous magnates. 'Feast' refers both to great social meals and to this whole form of hospitality.

no other kind of bath in Norway: Unlike Iceland, where geothermally heated springs and pools are quite widespread.

15. *cross-garter remained uncorrupted*: This motif resembles narratives about the uncorrupt bodies or possessions of saints. The point that the uncorrupt cross-garter revealed the sanctity of Olaf Haraldsson is made more explicitly in *The Great Saga of St Olaf*.

16. *Ingjald*: This may be the name of Bjorn's foster-father, previously mentioned (see n. 13 above).

17. *the dog V—*: The manuscripts have only *V*, but the dog may have shared the name of King Olaf Tryggvason's famous hound Vigi. Since Bjorn must have been abroad for some twelve years, this would be an elderly dog by now.

18. *spreading out the linen*: Bjorn's assisting with the laundry – women's work – is exceptional, and his peaceful occupation contrasts vividly with the menacing approach of the black-cloaked Thord (whose mission, however, confounds expectations).

19. *One oath broken . . . others*: A proverb known as early as the eleventh century, in a verse of Sighvat Thordarson.

20. *Out you must go . . . Out you must go*: In v. 4 (also vv. 5, 14 and 15) the metre is the short-lined 'metre of ancient utterance' (*fornyrðislag*).

more of the same metre as before: Possibly referring to an insult in the lost opening of the saga.

21. *Our meeting ... Thraelaeyri once*: This was narrated in ch. 7.

22. *The tree ... in my image*: This stanza and another versified paternity claim, v. 29, closely resemble vv. 28 and 27, respectively, of *The Saga of the People of Eyri*. The poet there is named as another notable Bjorn who also gained his nickname ('Champion of the Breidavik People') abroad.

23. *to pasture in Hitarnes*: The headland on which the farm of the same name stands.

24. *Out you must go ... Quiet I'll stay*: Verses 14–15 are a partial reprise of vv. 4–5.

25. *the serving-woman who helped them off with their clothes*: The loose sleeves of garments had to be sewn to tighten them at the wrist, so that putting on and taking off clothes daily was laborious.

26. *the cloak that had been Thord's*: Not mentioned elsewhere, but possibly among the goods that Bjorn seized from Thord in ch. 7 and was granted by King Olaf in ch. 8.

27. *he said ...*: There follows a lacuna of about a page and a half in the surviving saga manuscripts. The missing text presumably told of Bjorn's return from Hitarnes to Holm, of his building a farm at Vellir, and of his marriage to Thordis, whose family background must also have been described.

28. *a summons ... as he claimed the law allowed*: The law code *Grágás* stipulated outlawry as the penalty for composing or reciting so much as half a verse of mockery.

29. *pay a hundred of silver for the verse*: A heavy penalty, being the standard compensation for the killing of a man.

30. *an indecent encounter*: A similarly offensive carving is described in *Gisli Sursson's Saga*, ch. 2. Accusations of passive homosexuality or behaviour perceived as womanish are usually associated with taunts of cowardice in the sagas.

31. Two lines are missing from v. 20 in the manuscripts, perhaps omitted because of indecency.

spear-pointer: man: In the context, this and the preceding *weapon-wielder* appear as blatant sexual innuendo, cf. *Kormak's Saga*, v. 64.

32. *Beruhraun*: A variant of 'Beruvikurhraun' on p. 184.

33. *to have*: Probably in the sense of 'lay hold of', though it is unclear which party is which in this sentence.

34. *Hraundal, as was said before*: Presumably in the original, lost, opening or in the section missing after ch. 14.

Grettir ... Vellir: Grettir Asmundarson, the famous outlaw who combined prodigious strength with unusually bad luck, is said to have spent three years under Bjorn's protection (*The Saga of Grettir the Strong*, chs. 58–61).

Runolf Dagsson: This is assumed to be Runolf Dalksson, a learned priest of the mid-twelfth century. It has been suggested that Runolf wrote an account of Bjorn's association with King Olaf and his acts of devotion, and that this was the original kernel of Bjorn's saga.

35. *strangled him until he was dead*: This is presumably based on v. 25 ('without ... weapons'), but it is also tempting to note that Bjorn's name means 'bear', and that bare-handed killings appear in versions of the international story-pattern known as the 'Bear's Son Tale', whose heroes have names and/or natures associated with bears.

36. *the wood*: Although Iceland today is virtually treeless, it appears that woodland, or at least low scrub, covered the habitable parts of the land at the time of the settlement. Many place-names such as Fagriskog in ch. 23 or Ljarskogar in ch. 27 contain the word *skógr* 'wood'.

37. *grey-belly*: Presumably a lumpfish.

38. *A fish came to land ... brave as a she-goat*: The end-rhyme in the translation of vv. 26–8 reproduces that of the original.

39. *Kolla-verses*: Cow-verses – these may have been something like v. 19. It is impossible to know whether particular verse libels truly existed, but if they did their illicit status would have reduced their chances of survival. There is also some doubt as to whether one verse or more is meant here, since the original contains both singular and plural forms.

40. *forfeit his immunity*: The Law Council placed an injunction on reciting verses in ch. 16, and the law provided the general sanction of outlawry for libellous verses; but neither covers this particular case.

41. *Thord prosecuted Bjorn ... last case against him*: The penalty for harbouring outlaws was lesser outlawry.

42. *Thord was asked ... did not refuse*: A rare glimpse of a social context in which poetry is recited as a form of entertainment.

Beam of Day ... Light of Lands: Thord's names for both poem and woman are poetic terms for the sun, and both seem to echo Oddny's nickname 'Isle-candle' and the verses about her. No trace of either set of verses survives, and their existence has been doubted. Bjorn's marriage to Thordis, and her genealogy, were doubtless covered in the section of the saga now lost after ch. 14.

43. *Arnor*: Arnor Thordarson became a distinguished poet of the earls of Orkney and of Magnus and Harald, Kings of Norway.

44. *Kalf's father Ozur*: It is not clear whether this is Kalf the Ill-willed who appears in ch. 7, or a different man.

45. *not yet established by law*: Thorstein and company arrive on the eve of Yule or Christmas. Christian laws on fasting introduced to Iceland in the early twelfth century forbade the eating of meat and often of dairy produce at this and other designated times.

46. *mass for the second day of Yule*: 26 December. This seems to imply the existence of a priest and a chapel at the farmstead Holm, though there is no other evidence of this.

47. *one group of horses led to Thorstein*: Presumably the stallion, Hviting's son, and his mares, as distinct from the horses at Thorarinsdal.

48. *as if they were brothers by birth*: Bjorn and Thorstein thus effectively became sworn brothers.

49. *Thorfinn Thvarason*: i.e. son of Arnor Thvari (Cross-stick). Patronymics were sometimes formed from the father's nickname rather than his forename. *Ness*: i.e. Snaefellsnes, where Thorfinn's parents lived (cf. ch. 18).

50. *Thord's son Kolli*: Note, however, Bjorn's paternity claim in ch. 21.

51. *gatherings at the sheepfold . . . Hitardal*: The autumn round-up and sorting of sheep was also a social occasion for the district.

52. *Strange if . . . homeward bids the poet*: Verse 34 is remarkable for its combination of pagan and Christian (or at least monotheistic) motifs. The 'goddesses' of line 2 are *dísir*, or female guardian-spirits, and the helmeted woman is surely a valkyrie, despite the association with God, lord of the sun, while her summoning gesture is reminiscent of a fetch.

53. *Hjalli*: i.e. Hvitingshjalli, the shelf or ledge on a hillside named from the horse Hviting (ch. 31).

54. *hunting the bear that we all want to hunt*: Kalf, who had been posted on one of the routes Bjorn was thought unlikely to take, puns on the meaning of Bjorn's name, 'bear' (cf. n. 35).

55. *Klifsdal . . . Hellisdal*: These names are in the reverse order in the manuscript, but this makes better geographical sense.

56. *narrow point of the shield*: Viking Age shields were either circular, reinforced with a metal rim, or, as in this case, an elongated triangle tapering towards the bottom.

57. *shaming blow*: A blow, often to the back of a retreating opponent, which brings dishonour to the recipient. Thord spoke instead of a 'shameful blow', which brings dishonour to the one who delivers it.

58. *tracing family trees*: cf. Bjorn's paternity claim about Kolli, ch. 21.

59. *Fate did not fail . . . to let me . . . become his slayer*: This extreme suspension of the syntax, stretching over the whole verse, is unusual and splendidly expressive.

60. *Bjorn's head . . . saddle-straps*: The barbaric practice of parading the enemy's head is found in other sagas, e.g. *Orkneyinga Saga*, ch. 5, but the motif has been considered to be of foreign origin.

61. *as was said before*: i.e. at the end of ch. 9. Bjorn's building of the church of St Thomas at Vellir is mentioned in ch. 19.

his brother Asgrim: Probably introduced in the lost original opening of the saga.

62. *three hundreds of silver for your brother*: Since the normal compensation for the killing of a man according to the sagas is one or two hundreds, this is certainly among the highest sums paid.

VIGLUND'S SAGA

1. *Olof the Radiant*: Olof's nickname *Geisli* literally means 'Sunbeam'; cf. the nicknames of the central women in *The Saga of Bjorn* (ch. 23 and n. 42).

2. *roof of lead . . . painted*: There is some evidence of the use of lead on Icelandic church roofs in the later Middle Ages, but they would have been extremely rare. This detail is therefore almost as exotic as the others in the passage.

3. *an earl named Eirik was ruling there at that time*: Typifying the non-historical nature of this saga, this character is otherwise unknown and presumably fictional, despite his high status.

4. *world*: This translates what appears to be an unusual kenning for 'world' in the original text. Several kennings and half-kennings have been simplified or replaced in the translation of the *Viglund's Saga* verses.

5. *Holmkel . . . Gotalaek*: Holmkel and his three brothers are recorded in *The Book of Settlements*, ch. 77.

6. *received the name Ketilrid*: Ketilrid, and Viglund's verses about her, are mentioned in *Bard's Saga*, ch. 3, and they are named in one late manuscript of *The Book of Settlements*, but the entry there may derive from the sagas.

7. *stallion had fallen off by itself*: A Bleikshamar (Bleikr's/Blackie's crag) rises east of the Holmkelsa river, and may well have been the inspiration for this story. A similar incident and place-name occur in *The Saga of Hrafnkel*, ch. 6.

8. *Viglund and Ketilrid loved each other . . . each other*: This stylistically remarkable passage is not in all manuscripts, and has been suggested to be an interpolation. That it is strongly influenced by foreign writings is obvious from the concentration on abstract emotion, the complex sentence structures (slightly adapted in this translation) and the vocabulary, which includes the words *náttúra* 'nature' and *amor* 'love' adopted from Latin.

9. *Thorkel Skin-swathed*: This nickname is explained in *Bard's Saga*, ch. 3, as

deriving from the fact that Thorkel when a child was wrapped in sealskins because of a local shortage of woollen cloth.

Bard Snaefell's As: The eponymous protagonist of *Bard's Saga*, whose name derives from the fact that he settled at the foot of the mountain Snaefell (ch. 3) where he eventually comes to be called Bard the As (guardian spirit) because men attribute supernatural powers to him and call upon him in times of need (ch. 6).

10. *Esjutjorn*: A small upland lake or tarn – these games are evidently played on ice.

11. *Harald's Gift*: The gold ring given to Thorgrim in ch. 6.

12. *Helgi*: The other son of Earl Eirik, last mentioned in ch. 4. Helgi and Sigmund are hence half-brothers of Thorgrim and uncles of Viglund.

13. *I swear that no one but you . . . alive*: Viglund's vow, though purely romantic, is reminiscent of King Harald Fair-hair's refusal to cut or wash his hair before he had subdued the whole realm of Norway (see, e.g., ch. 4 of his saga in *Heimskringla*).

14. *rune stick*: A stick inscribed with runes, the main form of writing in pre-Christian times, is occasionally mentioned in sagas including *Egil's Saga*.

15. *sworn brothers*: The two pairs of brothers, Viglund and Trausti and Gunnlaug and Sigurd, are now brothers-in-law, in fact or in prospect. That they also regard themselves as sworn brothers is suggested by Sigurd's declaration that one fate should befall them all, although they have not made formal vows of mutual allegiance.

16. *Hrafn . . . Orn*: Quite common names in early Iceland, meaning 'Raven' and 'Eagle' respectively.

17. *He was very upset and turned as red as blood*: Viglund has, of course, already recognized Ketilrid in the previous chapter. His reaction here could be ascribed to the emotion of their eyes meeting, or more prosaically to a minor continuity lapse on the part of the writer.

18. *dragon's lair: gold*: Gold is, in legend, the lair of dragons. 'Gold-eyed' seems to mean 'beautiful-eyed'.

19. *warlike Viglund*: Though addressed to Thord, this plays on the hero's name, which can be taken either as an adjective meaning 'battle-minded' or as a kenning for warrior, 'battle-grove' or 'battle-tree'.

Plot summaries

Events abroad are shown in italics.
(1), (2), (3) etc. refer to chapter numbers.

Kormak's Saga	Saga of Hallfred	Saga of Gunnlaug	Saga of Bjorn	Viglund's Saga
Prelude: Norway and emigration, love and rivalry	*Prelude: Norway and emigration*	*Prelude: Helga's childhood*	(No prelude, possibly because first chapters are missing.)	*Prelude: Norway, love and rivalry, emigration*
(1) *Ogmund defeats the Viking Asmund in battle, marries Earl Frodi's daughter Helga and vanquishes the jealous Asmund in a duel.*	(1–2) *The foster-brothers Ottar and Avaldi escape from a Viking arson attack which kills their fathers. They take revenge, then emigrate to Iceland.*	(1–2) Thorstein Egilsson's prophetic dream: his wife will give birth to a daughter who will occasion the death of two men, after which she will marry a third.		(1–4) *The reign of King Harald Fair-hair in Norway, when many great men emigrate to Iceland.*
(2) *Ogmund emigrates to Iceland.* Helga having died, he marries Dalla and	Their children include Hallfred (H),	(3) Thorstein orders his wife Jofrid to		(2–3) *Introduction of Olof, beautiful daughter of Earl Thorir, and Ketil and his sons Gunnlaug and Sigurd.*

290

fathers Thorgils and Kormak (K).	son of Ottar, and Kolfinna, daughter of Avaldi.	expose the newborn child, if a girl, but she disobeys, sending her in secret to Thorstein's sister Thorgerd. Six years later, Thorgerd reveals Helga's identity to Thorstein, who takes her home.			
Love and emmity	*Love and emmity*	*Love*	*Love and emmity*	*Love and emmity*	*Love and emmity*
(3) K meets Steingerd (S), daughter of Thorkel, and begins courting her. (4) Thorkel disapproves, and K's hostilities with Narfi, a member of his household, begin.	(2–3) Ingolf woos Valgerd, Ottar's daughter. In resolving the resulting discord, Ottar is forced to move south. (3–4) Hallfred woos Kolfinna, but when he refuses to commit	(4) Gunnlaug Illugason (G), aged twelve, goes to stay with Thorstein after his father has refused to let him go abroad. He falls in love with Helga, now a fully grown beauty,	(1) Introduction of Thord Kolbeinsson, Bjorn Arngeirsson (B) and Oddny Thorkelsdottir. The young B lodges with his cousin Skuli Thorsteinsson to avoid Thord's	(7) Thorgrim's and Olof's sons are Trausti and Viglund (V); their daughter is Helga. Holmkel's daughter Ketilrid (K) is fostered by Olof. She and V fall in love.	*(4) Thorgrim, illegitimate son of Earl Eirik, taken into the king's service.* *(5–6) Thorgrim falls in love with Olof and asks for her hand, but Thorir betrothes her to Ketil.* *Ketil refuses a duel and Thorgrim abducts Olof from her wedding feast. They sail to Iceland.*

Kormak's Saga	Saga of Hallfred	Saga of Gunnlaug	Saga of Bjorn	Viglund's Saga
Love and enmity	*Love and enmity*	*Love*	*Love and enmity*	*Love and enmity*
(5) With Thorkel's encouragement, Odd and Gudmund, sons of the sorceress Thorveig, mount two ambushes against K; the second ends in their deaths. K demands that Thorveig leaves the district; she curses his relationship with S. (6) K continues to visit S and mollifies Thorkel, who agrees to their betrothal, but K fails to come to the wedding.	himself, she is betrothed to Gris. After defying Gris and his friend Mar, H is pursued, attacked and captured. His father rescues him and presses him into going abroad.	and play-acts a betrothal with her. (5) Hrafn Onundarson introduced. G's quarrelsome nature revealed in a minor dispute. G's father provides for him to go abroad. Thorstein agrees to G's informal betrothal to Helga, conditional on his return within three years.	aggression. B courts Oddny. (2) B seals a betrothal with Oddny, conditional on his return within three years.	(8) Einar, Holmkel's son, jealous of Thorgrim's standing, intends to seduce Olof but is outwitted by her. (9–11) Einar and his brother Jokul start a vendetta against V. Their fathers remain friends and settle matters. (12) With their mother Thorbjorg, Einar and Jokul pay the sorceress Kjolvor to destroy V and Trausti. She raises a tempest in which they almost drown. (13) *In Norway, Ketil*

Marriage and rivalry	Events abroad	Events abroad and rivalry	Events abroad and rivalry	Marriage and rivalry
				Bersi
promises Hakon his daughter Ingibjorg in marriage if he avenges him against Thorgrim. Hakon goes to Iceland and lodges with Holmkel and Thorbjorg, who insists that K is brought home. (14) At a games meeting, K and V exchange rings.	(5–6) H spends several years travelling. Honoured by Earl Hakon in Norway. King Olaf Tryggvason rescues him from a storm and preaches Christianity to him,	(6) G is ejected from Earl Eirik's court for insolence. (7) G composes for King Ethelred in England, and kills the thug Thororm in a duel. (8) Visits King Sigtrygg	(2) B visits Earl Eirik in Norway. (3) Thord arrives and the two Icelanders stay there on reasonable terms. B entrusts Thord with a message of reassurance for Oddny.	(7) S is married to Bersi to spite K. She sends word to K. (8) K rides after Bersi and S. Thorveig sabotages

Marriage and rivalry

(14) Thorbjorg, at Hakon's urging, has K kept at home. In another game, Jokul wounds V. Taunted by his father, V avenges himself by knocking

Kormak's Saga	Saga of Hallfred	Saga of Gunnlaug	Saga of Bjorn	Viglund's Saga
Marriage and rivalry	*Events abroad*	*Events abroad and rivalry*	*Events abroad and rivalry*	*Marriage and rivalry*

the boat she lends to K. Catching up with Bersi, K demands S but is offered Bersi's sister instead.

(9–11) First duel: K refuses the offer and challenges Bersi to a duel. K borrows the magic sword Skofnung but mistreats it. K loses the duel.

(12) Thord Arndisarson falls out with his neighbour Bersi. Second duel: K's uncle Steinar challenges Bersi. After taking away Bersi's magic

which H reluctantly accepts.

H kills Ottar, a rival follower of King Olaf. Narrowly escapes execution.

H partially fulfils the king's order to blind the pagan Thorleif the Wise, but also maims Ottar's brother Kalf.

(7) H visits Earl Sigvaldi in Eyrar. He kills the robber Onund, who has murdered Audgisl.

(8) H narrowly escapes death by killing his treacherous host Bjorn. Ingibjorg Audgisl's

in Dublin and Earl Sigurd in Orkney, with poems of praise. G arbitrates wisely between factions at the court of another Earl Sigurd, in Vastergotland.

(9) At the court of King Olaf of Sweden, G's fellow poet Hrafn develops a bitter grievance against him.

Hrafn, returning to Iceland, presses a suit for Helga and is promised her if G fails to return at the agreed time.

(10) G visits King Ethelred and stays, pending

Thord returns to Iceland and fulfils the commission, adding that B has made over the betrothal to him if he does not return.

(4) B overcomes the champion Kaldimar in Russia. After recovering from his wounds, be reaches Norway too late to sail to Iceland that summer.

(5) Thord reports B dead and marries Oddny.

Learning of this, B stays abroad, slaying a dragon in the service of Canute.

Jokul unconscious. Enraged by V's affection for K, Jokul ambushes V and Trausti, but loses three men in the fight.

(15) Holmkel, angry at this and swayed by Jokul, marries K to Hakon.

Later, he warns V of a possible attack by Jokul and Einar.

(16) In an attack amidst the haystacks, Jokul, Einar, Hakon and seven of their men are killed by V and Trausti, who are

badly wounded and thought dead.

(17) Ketil in Norway sends Gunnlaug and Sigurd to avenge Hakon and kill Thorgrim. They are shipwrecked and taken in by Thorgrim, who is unaware of their identity.

Thorbjorg's father, at her urging, has V and Trausti outlawed, if alive.

(18) Helgi, son of Earl Eirik, settles in Iceland.

One Thorleif presses his suit on K.

On Thorgrim's advice, V and Trausti decide to go to Norway.

They bid farewell to

---

(6) Thord and Oddny have eight children.

(7) Thord, abroad to claim an inheritance in Denmark, delivers a poem to King Olaf. B corners Thord off the Brunno islands but spares his life in deference to King Olaf, whose guest Thord has been.

(8) Both Icelanders visit King Olaf, who arbitrates between them.

(9) Thord returns to Iceland.

---

a possible attack from King Camute.

---

widow, saves him from pagan retribution, and he marries her.

(9) H delivers a poem to King Olaf of Sweden. First dream of King Olaf Tryggvason, whom H visits with Ingibjorg and their sons.

Ingibjorg dies, H leaves King Olaf for Iceland.

---

healing-stone during a swimming contest, Steinar wounds him in the duel.

(13) Thord and Bersi reconciled.

S leaves Bersi because of his injuries.

(14) Third duel: S's brother Thorkel fights Bersi over her dowry and is killed.

(15–16) Bersi rescues the abducted Steinvor, then uses her as a decoy to facilitate the killing of Vali.

Thorvald

(17) S is married to Thorvald Tintein. K, preparing to sail abroad, has a brief

Kormak's Saga	Saga of Hallfred	Saga of Gunnlaug	Saga of Bjorn	Viglund's Saga
Marriage and rivalry				*Marriage and rivalry*
exchange with S, including verses against Thorvald.				K, who is overjoyed to see them alive. V vows that no one but K will cut or wash his hair as long as she lives. Holmkel, realizing K's feelings, assists V and Trausti rather than taking revenge on them.
Events abroad				*Events abroad*
(18) *K and Thorgils go raiding.* (19) *They fight for King Harald Grey-cloak in Ireland.* *Unable to forget S, K returns to Iceland.*				(19) *Once out to sea, V and Trausti reveal their identity to Gunnlaug and Sigurd, who decide to protect them against their*

Marriage and rivalry	Marriage and rivalry	Marriage and rivalry	Marriage and rivalry	Marriage and rivalry
(19) K spends a night with S, separated by a screen. (20) Thorvald, his brother Thorvard, and Narfi commission an obscene verse about S which they attribute to K. She shuns K, who	(9) H spends a night with Kolfinna, reciting slander against Gris. (10) Pursued by Gris, H kills Einar Thorisson. H ambushed by Mar. H composes verses against Gris.	(10) G returns home via Norway, but does not arrive until the day of Helga's marriage to Hrafn. (11) Hrafn and Helga are married. She feels cheated of G. At another wedding attended by all three,	(10) B returns to Iceland. Oddny, learning he is still alive, bitterly reproaches Thord. (11) Thord invites B to stay with himself and Oddny. (12) Frictions and scurrilous verses	(20) In Iceland, Holmkel and Thorgrim have discussions. Holmkel promises K to Thord, a wealthy farmer from the East Fjords, who takes her home with him.

father Ketil's anger. Gunnlaug arbitrates, stipulating compensation for Ketil and marriages of Trausti to Ingibjorg and Sigurd to Helga.

The four young men distinguish themselves raiding though V cannot forget K.

Kormak's Saga	Saga of Hallfred	Saga of Gunnlaug	Saga of Bjorn	Viglund's Saga
Marriage and rivalry	*Marriage and rivalry*	*Marriage and rivalry*	*Marriage and rivalry*	*Events abroad*
kills Narfi.	Gris summonses H for killing Einar. Brand, Kolfinna's brother, kills Galti, H's brother, then escapes.	Helga's and G's feelings for one another are confirmed. G almost rides Hrafn down but they are restrained from a fight.	create a strained ménage à trois.	(21) *After a winter in Norway, the two pairs of brothers sail to Iceland.*
(21) Fourth duel: Thorvard fails to turn up to fight K.			(13–14) Tensions continue. Oddny offers B one of her and Thord's daughters in marriage.	*Love prevails*
(22) Thordis's attempt to reverse Thorveig's curse on K is thwarted by K himself.	H challenges Gris to a duel. Second dream of King Olaf, who tells him to withdraw from it. Thorkel arbitrates a settlement for the killings of Einar and Galti and the verses against Gris.	At the Althing, G challenges Hrafn to a duel; the outcome is disputed. Duelling is then permanently banned. Helga's and G's love is renewed. Hrafn challenges G to a duel in Norway.	(15–16) Scornful verses; eventually B and Thord are forbidden to recite verses against each other.	(21) V and Trausti are blown to the East Fjords, where, concealing their identity, they winter with Thord.
Fifth duel: K defeats Thorvard and, though S refuses to go with him, K continues to see her. K helps Thorvard in his healing ritual, but demands a ring belonging to S.	*Events abroad*	*Events abroad and rivalry*	(17) B has to pay compensation for an obscene verse following hints of homosexuality against Thord.	(22) V, upset by recognizing K, makes to kill Thord, but is calmed by Trausti.
(23) Sixth duel: K wins another ring from Thorvard	(11) *H travels to Orkney and Scandinavia. Third dream of King*	(12) *Hrafn winters in*	(18–24) Escalating feud with repeated	He reveals his feelings for K in a verse.

(24) K kisses S twice and has to pay the two rings to Thorvald Tintein in compensation.

Events abroad and rivalry

Thorvald and S sail abroad; K rescues them from Vikings.
More kisses; King Harald arbitrates between the Icelanders.

(26) Off the Branno islands, K rescues S from Vikings again. Thorvald offers S and K the chance to unite, but both decline. K and Thorgils resume

---

attacks on B prompted by Thord, and exchanges of slanderous verses. They come to blows at a horse-fight.

(25–6) B repels two attacks by Thord and his men.

(27–8) Thorstein Kuggason mediates between B and Thord.

(29) Thorstein's peace agreement is overturned; Thord and B resume verse-making.

(30–1) Thord and Dalk organize a massive ambush of B.

(32) Despite bad dreams and his wife's entreaties, B sets out to trim the manes of

---

Norway. G fights in the Hebrides and Scotland for Earl Sigurd of Orkney, then follows Hrafn to Norway and to Dingenes.
Hrafn and G fatally wound one another; Hrafn through an underhand trick.

Olaf, who dissuades him from killing Earl Eirik.
H arrested at Earl Eirik's court for his mutilation of Thorleif the Wise; he is rescued from execution by Thorleif's mediation.
H goes to Iceland but without seeing Kolfinna or Gris, then to Sweden to visit his son Audgils.

Sails for Iceland, intending to collect his property then settle in Sweden.
Fatally injured off the Hebrides. Speaks a verse remembering Kolfinna and parts from his fetch.
His body is washed ashore. After a dream

Thord entrusts the farm to the brothers during a short absence.

(23) At V's urging, he and Trausti withdraw from the farm to avoid impropriety. Thord soon returns with a huge company including Thorgrim and Holmkel, as though to celebrate his marriage. Instead, he reveals that he is Helgi, uncle to V and Trausti, who has been keeping K for V.

The marriages of V to K, Thorgrim's daughter Helga to Sigurd, and Helgi's daughter Ragnhild

Kormak's Saga	Saga of Hallfred	Saga of Gunnlaug	Saga of Bjorn	Viglund's Saga
Marriage and rivalry	*Marriage and rivalry*	*Marriage and rivalry*	*Marriage and rivalry*	*Love prevails*
their raiding voyages. In Scotland, K kills a giant, but is fatally injured in the fight.	*appearance of King Olaf; he is buried on the Holy Island of Iona.*		some horses, and after a valiant defence against his attackers, B falls. (33) The killing is announced. Oddny, inconsolable, lapses into lifelong illness.	to Gunnlaug are celebrated.
Epilogue	*Epilogue*	*Epilogue*	*Epilogue*	*Epilogue*
K bequeaths his property and followers to Thorgils, who continues in Viking warfare.	H's son H takes over his farm in Iceland and prospers greatly.	(13) The two fathers, Illugi and Onund, dream that their sons appear to them, covered in blood. After failing to gain compensation at the Althing, Illugi and G's brother	(34) B's brother Asgrim takes over his farm. He is talked by Thord into accepting three hundred of silver in compensation for B, but Thorstein secures	The Icelanders and Norwegians return to their respective homes and settle there.

massive payments
from Thord, as well
as outlawry for the
others present at B's
killing.
Normal life resumes
for the survivors.

Hermund take
revenge against
kinsmen of Hrafn.
Helga is married
to Thorkel Hallkels-
son, and has children
by him, but con-
tinues to think of G
until she dies.

REFERENCE SECTION

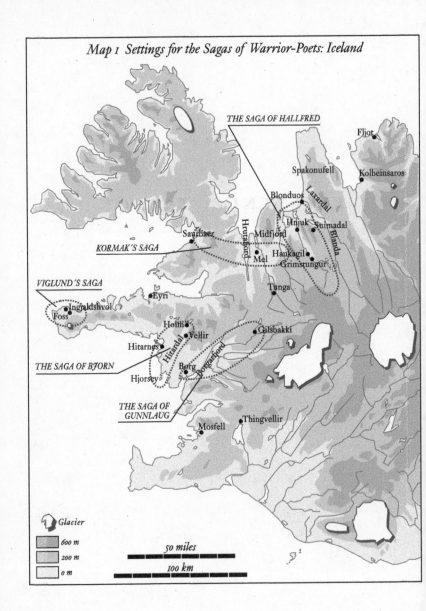

Map 1 Settings for the Sagas of Warrior-Poets: Iceland

THE SAGA OF HALLFRED

Fljot

Spakonufell

Kolbeinsaros

Blonduos

Laxardal

Hnjuk   Suimadal

Midfjord

Blanda

Saurbaer

KORMAK'S SAGA

Hrutafjord

Haukagil

Mel   Grimstungur

VIGLUND'S SAGA

Tunga

Eyri

Ingialdshvol

Foss

Holm

Vellir   Gilsbakki

Hitarnes

Hitardal

THE SAGA OF BJORN

Borg

Borgarfjord

Hjorsey

THE SAGA OF
GUNNLAUG

Mosfell   Thingvellir

Glacier

600 m

200 m   50 miles

0 m   100 km

304

Map 2 Settings for the Sagas of Warrior-Poets: Abroad

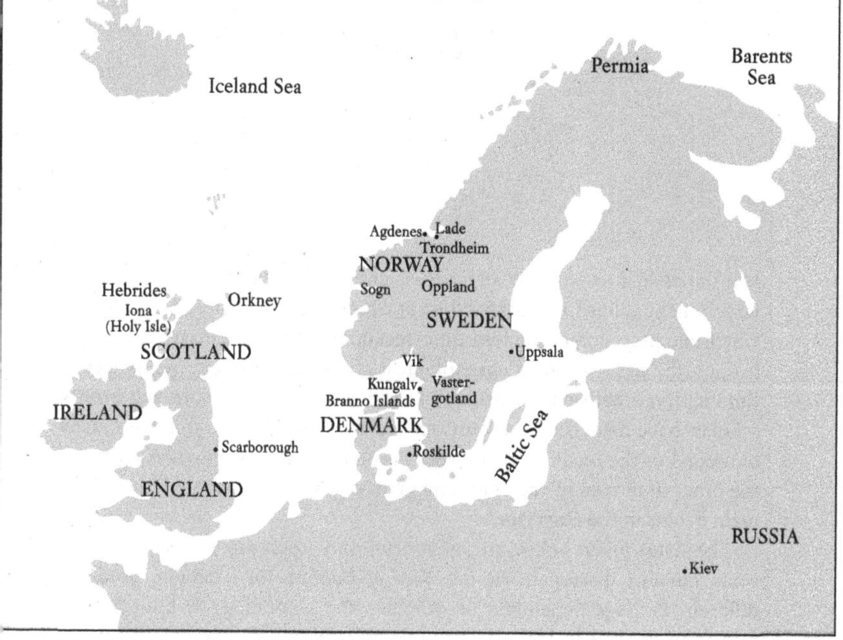

Iceland Sea

Barents Sea

Permia

Agdenes. Lade
Trondheim
NORWAY
Sogn Oppland

Hebrides
Iona
(Holy Isle)
Orkney

SCOTLAND

SWEDEN

•Uppsala

Vik

IRELAND

Kungalv. Vaster-
Branno Islands gotland

DENMARK

Baltic Sea

• Scarborough

•Roskilde

ENGLAND

RUSSIA

•Kiev

Chronology

It is impossible to establish any precise chronology for the sagas, which are largely fictionalized reconstructions of events written down in a society in which the precision of modern time-reckoning was unnecessary. Nonetheless, on the basis of broad chronological consistency, precise references to time intervals between events, and known and datable persons and events, scholars have managed to reconstruct a fairly plausible time-frame for many of them. For the reader, a framework chronology at least provides a view of the inner time span of each saga and gives it a rough position relative to the main events in the Saga Age.

The dates given below are, of course, only approximations. There are some obvious discrepancies: the *Saga of Hallfred*, for example, produces different findings depending on whether the chronology is built around Ottar's settlement in Iceland or the death of King Olaf, and the events of *Kormak's Saga* have proved extremely difficult to date. Although its reference to historical persons places it in the period 900–950, *Viglund's Saga* is considered almost purely fictional, and therefore no attempt is made at a detailed chronology for it here.

Key historical events (see also the next section, 'Rulers')

Settlement of Iceland	870–930
Battle of Havsfjord (Harald Fair-hair takes control of Norway)	*c.* 885–900
Establishment of the Althing	*c.* 930
The division of Iceland into quarters	*c.* 965
Iceland converted to Christianity	*c.* 1000
Battle of Svold (death of King Olaf Tryggvason of Norway)	*c.* 1000

Key events in the sagas (approximate dates)

KORMAK'S SAGA

Birth of Steinar	910–20
Birth of Bersi the Dueller	920
Birth of Kormak	940
Main action of the saga	955–70

THE SAGA OF HALLFRED TROUBLESOME-POET

Ottar and Avaldi go to Iceland	950
Trouble with Valgerd, Ottar moves south	970
Gris marries Kolfinna, Hallfred starts his travels	970
Hallfred visits King Olaf Tryggvason and is baptized	996
Hallfred in Vastergotland	997–9
Hallfred returns to Iceland	1000
Death of Hallfred	several years later

THE SAGA OF GUNNLAUG SERPENT-TONGUE

Birth of Gunnlaug and Helga	984
Gunnlaug goes to Borg	996
Gunnlaug goes abroad	1002
Gunnlaug stays with King Ethelred	(winter) 1002–3
Gunnlaug in Skarar	(winter) 1003–4
Gunnlaug and Hrafn meet, staying at the court of King Olaf of Sweden	1004
Gunnlaug with King Ethelred	1004–6
Hrafn asks for Helga's hand	1005
Helga betrothed and married to Hrafn, Gunnlaug arrives	1006
Gunnlaug at Gilsbakki	1006–7
Gunnlaug and Hrafn duel at the Althing, then go abroad	1007
Gunnlaug in the Orkneys, Hrafn in Trondheim	1007–8
Gunnlaug goes to Norway	(summer) 1008

THE SAGA OF BJORN, CHAMPION OF THE HITARDAL PEOPLE

Rulers

Rulers of Norway

King Harald Fair-hair Reigned in Norway for some sixty years, until *c.* 932. His nickname, according to tradition, commemorates his vow to his betrothed Gytha that he would not have his hair cut or combed until he had subdued all Norway. The main emigration to Iceland took place during his reign, and is often attributed to his tyranny (e.g. *Viglund's Saga*, ch. 1; though cf. *Kormak's Saga*, ch. 2). Several of the Sagas of Icelanders begin at this point in history.

King Eirik Blood-axe Favourite son of Harald Fair-hair, so nicknamed for his ruthless elimination of some of his many (half-)brothers. Together with his queen Gunnhild (a witch, according to some accounts) he was ejected from Norway and ruled in York until his death in battle in 954.

King Hakon, Athelstan's foster-son Also known as 'the Good', reigned in Norway *c.* 934–60. One of the numerous sons of Harald Fair-hair, he was fostered as a boy by King Athelstan in England.

King Harald Grey-cloak Pre-eminent among the sons of Eirik Blood-axe and Gunnhild, he ruled *c.* 960–*c.* 970, after defeating Hakon, Athelstan's foster-son, at the battle of Fitjar.

Earl Hakon the Powerful Ruled *c.* 970–*c.* 995, gaining a reputation for political brilliance, a victory against the mighty Jomsvikings, paganism and lechery.

King Olaf Tryggvason Despite his short reign, *c.* 995–1000, famed for presiding over the Christianization of Norway and Iceland, and for a dramatic last battle, at sea off Svold.

Earl Eirik, son of Earl Hakon Ruled *c.* 1000–13, partly in conjunction with his brother Svein.

King Olaf Haraldsson Reigned, with some interruption through exile, *c.* 1015–30. His death in battle at Stiklestad quickly turned him into a Christian martyr.

Other Rulers

King Sigtrygg Silk-beard Ruled the Viking kingdom of Dublin for some fifty years to *c.* 942, though as under-king to the king of Meath.

Earl Sigurd Hlodvesson 'The Stout', ruled Orkney and beyond from *c.* 980 until his death at the battle of Clontarf in 1014.

Valdimar Vladimir I, who ruled a partially Norse kingdom in north-west Russia, 980–1015.

King Olaf the Swede Reigned *c.* 995–1021/2; so named in the sagas to distinguish him from the two contemporary King Olafs of Norway.

King Ethelred, son of Edgar Ethelred II of England, who reigned 978–1016.

Canute the Great, son of Svein King of England 1016–35, and of Denmark from 1018.

Social, Political and Legal Structures

Human conflict, acted out in particular types of feud pattern, is a constant feature of the world portrayed in the sagas, whether it stems from competition for land or goods, for women or for honour. The social and political structure that evolved in Iceland from the Settlement in the late ninth century and beyond the adoption of Christianity in A D 1000 reflected the need to establish order by resolving such frictions. However slight the grounds on which they developed, the chief motive force behind feuds was the concept of honour. Society at this time saw honour in wide perspective, as an almost tangible property of the family or kin, not merely of the individual at the centre of the conflict. To some extent the social aspect of honour is played down in the sagas of poets, because of their strongly biographical tendency, but the sense of family still looms.

Kinship essentially involves a sense of belonging not unlike that underlying the Celtic clan systems. The Icelandic word for kin or clan (*ætt*) is related to other words meaning 'to own' and 'direction' – the notion could be described as a 'social compass'. Establishing kinship is one of the justifications for the long genealogies that are found in the sagas and which tend to strike non-Icelandic readers as idiosyncratic detours, and also for the preludes set in Norway before the main saga action begins. Close relatives or members of the 'nuclear' family are only part of the picture, since kinsmen are all those who are linked through a common ancestor – preferably one of high birth and high repute – as far back as five or six generations or even more.

Marriage ties, sworn brotherhood and other bonds could create conflicting loyalties with respect to the duty of revenge, as we see in so many sagas, but by the same token they could serve as instruments for resolving such vendettas. A strict order stipulated who was to take revenge within the more or less immediate family, with a 'multiplier effect' if those seeking vengeance were killed in the process. The obligation to take revenge was inherited, just like wealth, property and other claims.

Patriarchy was the order of the day, although notable exceptions are found. Likewise, the physical duty of revenge devolved only upon males, but women were often responsible for instigating it, either by urging a husband or brother to action with slurs of cowardice, or by bringing up their sons with a vengeful sense of purpose and even supplying them with family heirlooms in the form of old weapons.

Iceland was particularly prone to feuding in the tenth to thirteenth centuries because of its unique social and political structure, with no king and no executive power to follow through the pronouncements of the highly sophisticated legislative and judicial institutions by which order was supposed to be maintained. Since there was no 'state', resolution of conflict depended greatly on individual consent, local political dynamics and the fighting strength of those involved, and there was no means of preventing men from taking the law into their own hands. While this was a productive process from a strictly literary point of view for the wealth of heroics that it engendered, it also led to the gradual disintegration of the Commonwealth in the thirteenth century.

In a kingless country, legislative and judicial functions were exercised by assemblies, or Things (Icelandic *þing*): a national assembly or Althing, and local assemblies such as the Hunavatn or Thorsnes Assemblies. The local assemblies, after *c.* 965, numbered thirteen, three in three of Iceland's quarters, but four in the northern quarter. They met twice yearly: the Spring Assembly (*vorþing*) attempted to resolve local disputes before the Althing convened, while the brief Autumn Meeting (*leið* or *leiðarþing*) reported back from it. If local procedures failed, matters were referred to the appropriate Quarter Court at the Althing, which was held for two weeks each June at Thingvellir ('Assembly Plains'). Laws were made or revised there in the Law Council (*lögrétta*). The Althing was presided over by a Lawspeaker, who was required to recite the law code over a three-year term. Decision-making was mainly in the hands of thirty-nine chieftains, or godis (*goðar*, singular *goði*), whose followers were known as their 'thingmen'. All assemblies were also an opportunity for socializing, for exchanging news, and for negotiating marriages, business deals and so on. The assembly sites were wide areas, where – at least at the Althing – the Law Rock was the focal point where public announcements and speeches were made. Those attending stayed in booths – huts with permanent walls of turf and stone which were temporarily roofed for the duration of the assembly.

Deadlock sometimes arose because the decisions of the Quarter Courts had to be unanimous, so around 1005 a Fifth Court was established as a kind of court of appeal to hear cases that they could not resolve. The godis appointed forty-eight members to the Fifth Court, of which the two sides in the case were allowed to reject six each. A simple majority among the remaining thirty-six then decided the outcome, and lots were drawn in the event of a tie. With the creation of the Fifth Court, the number of godis was increased correspondingly, and with their two thingmen each and the Lawspeaker, the Law Council then comprised 145 people in all.

Legal disputes feature prominently in the Sagas of Icelanders (though less so in the sagas of poets than in most others), and the prosecution and defence of a case followed clearly defined procedures. Cases were prepared locally some time before the Thing, and could be dismissed at that stage if they were technically flawed. Preparation generally took one of two forms. A panel of 'neighbours' could be called, comprising five or nine people who lived near the scene of the incident or the home of the accused, to testify to what had happened. Alternatively, a party could go to the home of the accused to summons him during the Summons Days, two weeks before the Spring Assembly but three or four weeks before the Althing. The accused generally did not attend the Thing, but was defended by someone else, who called witnesses and was entitled to disqualify members of the panel of neighbours. Panels did not testify to the details and facts of the case in the modern sense, but merely determined whether the incident had taken place. The case was then summed up and a ruling passed on it by the Quarter Court.

Penalties depended on the seriousness of the case and took the form of either the payment of monetary compensation or the imposition of 'outlawry'. Lesser outlawry meant a term of three years' exile, while full outlawry meant that a man must not be fed or helped and was tantamount to a death sentence. A confiscation court would seize the belongings of a person outlawed, whether for three years or for life. Cases were often settled without going through the complex court procedure: either by arbitration, in which a ruling by a third party was accepted by both sides; or by self-judgement by either of the parties involved in the case.

Duelling was another method of settling disputes. Duels originally took place on an islet in a river and proceeded according to strict rules (described in detail in *Kormak's Saga*). The duel features in a number of sagas but was formally banned in Iceland in 1006, after the thwarted clash related in the *Saga of Gunnlaug Serpent-tongue*. To sidestep the ban, the eponymous hero and his adversary Hrafn go all the way to mainland Scandinavia to settle accounts.

The Farm

The farm was a basic social and economic unit in Iceland. Although farms varied in size, there was presumably only one building on a farm at the time of the settlement, an all-purpose building known as a hall (*skáli*) or longhouse (*langhús*), constructed on the model of the farmhouses the settlers had inhabited in Norway. Over time, additional rooms and/or wings were often added to the original construction.

The Icelandic farmhouse shown in the illustrations opposite is based on information provided by the excavations at Stong (Stöng) in the Thjorsardal valley in the south of Iceland. Stong is regarded as having been an average-sized farm by Icelandic standards. The settlement at Stong was abandoned as a result of the devastating ash-fall from the great eruption of Hekla in 1104.

Figure 1, the plan of the farmstead, shows the overall layout of a typical farm. It is fictional, but based on the measurements carried out by the archaeologist Daniel Bruun. It should be stressed that the layout of farms was far from fixed. Nonetheless, the plan indicates the common positioning of the haystack wall and yard (*stakkgarður*) in the often-mentioned hayfield (*tún*). The hayfield wall (*túngarður*) surrounded the farm and its hayfield. Also placed outside the main farm are the animal sheds. With the exception of one cowshed, no barns or other animal sheds came to light in the excavation at Stong, but these must have existed as they did on most farms. In some cases, they were attached to the farmhouse, but more often they took the shape of independent constructions some distance away from the building. Sheep sheds, in particular, tended to be built some distance away from the hall, closer to the meadows used for grazing.

The smithy was also separate (for safety reasons), and the same appears to have applied on occasion to the fire room/fire hall (*eldhús*/*eldaskáli*). The latter was essentially a form of specialized kitchen, but was not used only for cooking. It was also the site of other daily household activities carried

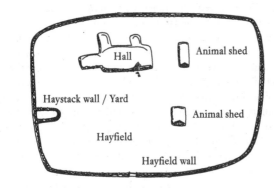

Figure 1. Plan of an Icelandic farmstead

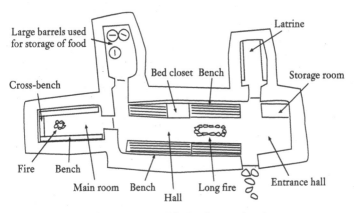

Figure 2. Cross-section of the hall at Stong

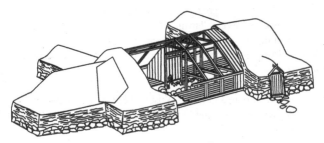

Figure 3. Layout of the farmhouse at Stong

out around the fire. Indeed, sometimes the term *eldhús* seems to refer not to a separate building, but to the farmhouse, instead of the word 'hall' (*skáli*), stressing the presence of the fire and warmth in the living-quarters.

Figure 2 shows a cross-section of the hall at Stong, giving some idea of the way the buildings were constructed. The framework was of timber; the main weight of the roof rested on beams which, in turn, were supported by pillars running down either side of the hall. The frequently mentioned high-seat pillars (*öndvegissúlur*) that some settlers brought with them from Norway may have been related to the pillars placed either side of the high seat (*hásæti*). The outer walls of most farms in Iceland were constructed of a thick layer of turf and stone which served to insulate the building. The smoke from the main fire was usually let out through a vent in the roof, but this would not have prevented the living-quarters from being rather smoke-ridden.

Figure 3 depicts the layout of the farmhouse excavated at Stong. The purpose of the area marked 'latrine' is uncertain, but this role makes sense on the basis of the layout of the room, and the description given in *The Tale of Thorstein Shiver*, for example. For information about the bed closet, see the Glossary.

See further: P. G. Foote and D. M. Wilson, *The Viking Achievement* (London, Sidgwick & Jackson, 1979); and James Graham-Campbell, *The Viking World* (London, Frances Lincoln, 3rd edn, 2001).

Early Icelandic Literature

Works mentioned in the Introduction, Further Reading and Notes

Following the advent of Christian learning *c.* 1000, writing on vellum flourished in Iceland from the twelfth century onwards. Native traditions combined with narrative materials and influences drawn from foreign literature, especially medieval Latin and, later on, French, though the 'native' strand predominates in the most famous branch of the literature, the Sagas of Icelanders. The word *saga* in Icelandic derives from the verb *segja*, 'to say, tell', and denotes an extended prose narrative which may (to modern perceptions) be located anywhere on the spectrum between seriously historical and wholly fictional, and various groupings of sagas are customarily identified especially on the basis of content and degree of apparent historicity. Some but by no means all of these saga genres were recognized in medieval Iceland. Literacy also enabled poetry to be recorded, some of it oral composition dating from the Viking Age (approximately ninth to mid eleventh centuries). Some poetry, especially the earlier compositions, and certain prose genres had their genesis in Norway, and for a few texts Norwegian or Icelandic origins are equally possible.

POETRY

Skaldic poetry

Usually attached to named poets and specific occasions, skaldic poetry includes praise of princes, travelogue, slander verses, love poetry and, especially as regards the earliest surviving poetry (late ninth and tenth centuries), pagan mythology. Metre, diction and word order tend to be elaborate (see the next section, 'Techniques of Skaldic Poetry'), though the style of later religious poetry (twelfth to fourteenth centuries) is simpler. Skaldic poetry tends to be preserved as fragmentary citations within prose works, including the sagas of poets. The names of 146 poets, and the rulers they composed for, are preserved in the *List of Poets* (*Skáldatal*), *c.* 1260.

The Poetic Edda/Eddic poetry

The poems of this genre are mainly composed in older, simpler metres, and span the ninth century to the twelfth or thirteenth. Topics are drawn largely from pagan mythology or legend. The works were composed in Norway, Iceland or the wider Nordic-speaking world, but preserved mainly (as complete or near-complete poems) in the Icelandic *Codex Regius*, *c.* 1270.

THE SAGAS

Sagas of Icelanders/Family Sagas (*Íslendingasögur*)

Composed from the early thirteenth century to *c.* 1400 and beyond, the group to which the sagas of poets belong is based on characters and events from the Icelandic past, especially from the settlement period (*c.* 870–*c.* 930) to the early eleventh century. Most are concerned with feuding in a pastoral setting, and feature in varying proportions both exceptional individuals and neighbourhoods: hence titles such as *Egil's Saga*, *Njal's Saga* and *The Saga of the Sworn Brothers* on the one hand, and *The Saga of the People of Eyri* and *The Saga of the People of Vatnsdal* on the other. *The Saga of the People of Laxardal* is unusual in featuring a woman, Gudrun Osvifsdottir, as its central figure. Many sagas, including *The Saga of Hrafnkel* and *The Saga of the Confederates*, are concerned with chieftainly power. In *The Saga of Grettir the Strong* and *Gisli Sursson's Saga* the titular heroes spend long periods of outlawry in the Icelandic 'wilderness', and many depict episodes abroad, including *Bard's Saga*, a late work of *c.* 1400 which differs from the 'classic', feud-based sagas in narrating adventures of an often fantastical kind. On the style of the Sagas of Icelanders, see the Introduction, pp. x–xi.

Contemporary Sagas (*Samtíðarsögur*)

Sturlunga Saga, 'The Saga of the Sturlungs': a compilation, from *c.* 1300, of sagas by various authors based on Icelandic events from the twelfth century to the end of the Icelandic Commonwealth in the 1260s. Sturla Thordarson's

Saga of the Icelanders (*Íslendinga saga*) is the most substantial; shorter items include *The Saga of Thorgils and Haflidi*, which relates the dispute between these two early-twelfth-century characters.

Sagas of Kings (*Konungasögur*)

These sagas feature mostly Norwegian kings and earls, but also Danish kings and earls of Orkney (*Orkneyinga saga*). They began to be be written, in Latin and in the vernacular, in Norway and Iceland, in the later twelfth century. Some sagas concern individual kings, especially the two missionary Olafs: for instance, the sagas of Olaf Tryggvason by Odd Snorrason and Gunnlaug Leifsson, both written originally in Latin, and Snorri Sturluson's *Great Saga of St Olaf.* Others cover a broad sweep of reigns, including the anonymous *Morkinskinna, Fagrskinna* and Snorri Sturluson's massive *Heimskringla*, all from the first decades of the thirteenth century. *Flateyjarbók*, a huge manuscript compilation mainly from the late fourteenth century, contains many kings' sagas.

Short tales (*Þættir*)

Brief narratives, often of encounters between Norwegian kings and low-born but canny Icelanders; these are more or less independent stories, but are incorporated especially in major compilations of the Sagas of Kings such as *Morkinskinna, Fagrskinna* and *Hulda-Hrokkinskinna*. Other tales, including some contained in *Flateyjarbók*, are in effect miniature Sagas of Icelanders, or Legendary Sagas.

Sagas/Lives of Saints (*Heilagra manna sögur*)

Mainly translations from Latin; some fragments are preserved from the mid twelfth century, putting these sagas among the earliest type of literature produced in Iceland.

Legendary Sagas/Sagas of Ancient Times (Fornaldarsögur)

Usually set in remote times and locations, showing stereotypical heroes in racy though sometimes tragic adventures involving the supernatural – hence giving a generally unrealistic impression. They include *The Saga of the Volsungs (Völsunga saga, c.* 1260–70) and *Fridthjof's Saga (c.* 1400).

Chivalric Sagas (Riddarasögur)

Romances, some of them adaptations of French originals such as the *Saga of Tristram and Isond (Tristan and Isolde,* Norwegian, *c.* 1226); others are original Icelandic compositions in a similar mode. The latter have sometimes been termed 'lying sagas' (*lygisögur*).

Translated quasi-historical works

These include *The Saga of the Trojans (Trójumanna saga,* first half of the thirteenth century), a retelling of the story of the Trojan Wars, mostly based on classical sources, especially the late Latin *De excidio Troiae historia* attributed to 'Dares Phrygius'.

OTHER PROSE WORKS

Works on Icelandic history

The Book of the Icelanders (Íslendingabók), by Ari Thorgilsson: *c.* 1122–33, on the Settlement and the establishment of Christianity.

Kristni Saga: a narrative of the Christianization of Iceland, probably late-thirteenth-century.

The Book of Settlements (Landnámabók): gives names, often accompanied by genealogies and anecdotes, of over four hundred settlers, region by region. There are five main versions, the earliest thirteenth-century, but including still older materials.

Icelandic Annals: lists of dates and events (Icelandic and foreign), existing in numerous versions, the oldest compiled in the late thirteenth century from older sources.

Legal writings

Grágás, 'Grey Goose': the laws of the Icelandic Commonwealth, as preserved in a range of mainly thirteenth-century manuscripts. These are Christian laws, but to some extent founded on the pre-Christian Norwegian laws brought by the early settlers of Iceland.

Works on poetry, language and grammar

The *Prose Edda* of Snorri Sturluson (*Snorra Edda*, probably composed in the 1220s) comprises a prologue and three parts: on Nordic mythology (*Gylfaginning*, 'The Deceiving of Gylfi' – the most comprehensive medieval account we have); on the diction of skaldic poetry (*Skáldskaparmál*, 'The Language of Poetry'); and on metre (*Háttatal*, 'List of Metres', 102 illustrative verses, with commentary).

The Third Grammatical Treatise, by Olaf Thordarson: mid-thirteenth century, and the fullest of four prose treatises applying classical grammar and rhetoric to Icelandic language and poetry; it is rich in poetic quotations.

The Techniques of Skaldic Poetry

METRE

The poetry of the skalds is usually composed in the eight-line stanzas of the 'court metre' (*dróttkvætt*), an ambitiously elaborated version of its ancient counterparts in Old English, Old Saxon and Old High German, though some verses are cast in the shorter lines of the 'metre of ancient utterance' (*fornyrðislag*) or other metres. In 'court metre', the number, length and stressing of syllables in the line are tightly regulated, as is the placing of alliteration and internal rhyme, while word order often departs quite radically (though not lawlessly) from that of everyday speech. To illustrate these features, here is v. 18 from *The Saga of Hallfred*, with a more or less word-for-word translation. (Words necessary in English but not in Icelandic are in square brackets, and some hyphens are inserted in order to make the English word boundaries match those of the original, e.g., 'bright-slope' (line 1) is all one word in Icelandic):

Leggr at lýsibrekku	[There] streams on to bright-slope
leggjar íss af Grísi	of-arm's ice from Gris
– kvöl þolir Hlín hjá hánum –	– anguish suffers Hlin beside him –
heitr ofremmðar sveiti;	hot, most-rank, sweat;
en dreypilig drúpir	while gloomy droops
dýnu Rán hjá hánum	eiderdown's Ran beside him
– leyfi'k ljóssa vífa	– praise I [the] bright lady's
lund – sem ölpt á sundi.	nature – like [a] swan swimming.

arm's ice: silver; its *bright slope*: lady (envisaged as a wearer of jewellery), Kolfinna.

Hlin: the goddess Frigg, here Kolfinna (a half-kenning); an alternative reading would be *hún/hon* 'she'.

Ran: sea-goddess; *eiderdown's Ran*: woman, Kolfinna.

The main metrical features are:

- six syllables per line (seven in line 3, since the two short syllables of *þolir* resolve into one)
- alliteration linking each couplet, placed on the initial sounds of two syllables in the odd line (lines 1, 3 etc.) and the first stressed syllable of the even line (lines 2, 4 etc.; shown in **bold**)
- full internal rhyme of vowel and consonant(s) between the penultimate syllable of each even line and a preceding syllable (<u>double underlined</u>) and
- half internal rhyme of consonant(s) only between the penultimate syllable of each odd line and a preceding one (defective in line 1; <u>single underlined</u>).

The device of suspending a sentence while interposing another one is also characteristic (see, for example, lines 1–4 of the translation above).

DICTION

Skaldic diction is richly varied and, as the verse above shows, often compressed and riddling.

Heiti

Much of the skalds' virtuosity goes into expressing recurrent key concepts such as man, woman, battle, sword, ship or gold, by means of poetic appellations known as *heiti*, many of which are not just synonyms, but descriptive terms with specific connotations. Among the many words for 'sea', for instance, are 'roaring' (*gjallr*), 'salty one' (*salt*), and other terms meaning 'broad', 'swelling', 'dark' and so on.

Kennings

The *heiti*, together with mythological and legendary names, are frequently combined to form kennings, which are the most distinctive feature of skaldic poetry. These at their simplest are two-part expressions which refer to a single concept, as when a sword is called 'shield's snake' or 'snake of the shield'. They can also take the form of compounds, hence 'shield-snake'. Kennings can be embedded within each other, making structures of three or more parts. The 'storm of the snake-shield' would mean 'battle', for example.

Some kennings, though stylized, have an approximately literal meaning. Men can, for instance, be referred to as feeders or cheerers of ravens or wolves, implying that they turn their enemies into carrion. Many others are metaphors based on shared attributes. A man stands tall, with branch-like arms, and hence can be 'tree of treasure' or 'rowan of weapons'. A sword is long, slender and venomous, hence 'snake of the shield', an image possibly also encouraged by the serpentine patterns that ornamented some swords. A further range of kennings draws its being from legend and folklore. Gold is the 'lair of dragons', both because of widespread notions of dragons guarding gold, and because of the particular story of the dragon Fafnir in the legend of the Volsungs. Gold is also 'flame of the sea/river', which may have roots both metaphorical and legendary: it is a shining substance often found under water, and the famous hoard of the Niebelungs was hidden in the depths of the Rhine. Myths, too, are a rich source of kennings, none more so than the story of Odin winning the 'mead of poetry' from giants and dwarfs, which gives rise to the 'poetry' kenning 'Odin's mead', and many more.

A great many kennings make rather casual use of mythological names by referring to men and women as gods or goddesses, always with some attribute, as in 'Odin of swords' or 'Freyja of the necklace'. Commonly used gods' names in the sagas of poets include Balder, Njord, Ull, Tyr, and (from among the numerous names of Odin) Gaut, Ygg and Fjolnir, and there is a splendid variety of goddess names, including Eir, Sif, Syr, Gefn (an alternative name of the fertility goddess Freyja) and Hlin (probably identical with Odin's wife Frigg). In some cases, reference to a specific deity may be significant, but on the whole these mythological names seem to be used interchangeably, chosen more for metrical reasons than because of the particular nature of the deities in question. In the verse translations in this volume, the specific names may be retained, or they may be translated as 'god' or 'goddess', in which case the original name is mentioned in the note to the verse. Names of valkyries (e.g. Hlokk, Hrist) and sea-kings (e.g., Ati,

Haki) are also used generically by the skalds, in fact still more so than those of deities, since next to nothing is known about individuals.

As discussed opposite, some of the images and implied comparisons contained in kennings are apt, vivid and richly suggestive, but kennings also tend to be highly stereotyped, one term being readily substituted for another. Because a prince or distinguished man can be designated as 'giver of treasure/rings', for example, he can also be 'flinger' or 'destroyer' of treasure. The conventional equation of 'god of weapons' with 'man' sometimes leads the skalds into designating enemies and cowards, as well as heroes, in this complimentary way, though not without pungent irony, and the 'weapon-wielder' pattern can be reshaped into splendid insults such as 'scythe-shover'. The heroines in the sagas of poets, meanwhile, are repeatedly idealized as 'goddesses of treasure' or of fine clothes, but either of the terms can be substituted, sometimes with less flattering results, as in 'valkyrie of lace', or 'goddess of furniture'.

Kennings are explained individually as they occur in the verses in this volume, but it may be useful here to lay out the patterns most commonly represented in the sagas of poets.

Man (*warrior, seafarer*) is usually referred to in relation to fighting, seafaring or treasure-giving:

a (named) god tree/post	} *of*	battle, sometimes personified as a valkyrie weapon/armour ships treasure

or, with an agent noun as the basic word:

wager of battle, wearer of armour, wielder/reddener of weapons, feeder/cheerer of carrion-beasts; steerer/launcher of ships; distributor/destroyer of treasure

Woman is usually referred to in relation to fine goods:

a (named) goddess valkyrie ground/stave/tree	} *of*	treasure/jewellery/gold/silver fine clothing/fabric/decorative lace etc. drink/drinking vessels herbs/dulse bed/furniture/household items arm

Battle is:

$$\left.\begin{matrix} \text{storm/weather/noise} \\ \text{assembly} \end{matrix}\right\} \ of \ \left\{\begin{matrix} \text{weapons} \\ \text{Odin} \\ \text{valkyrie} \end{matrix}\right.$$

Sword is:

$$\left.\begin{matrix} \text{fire/light} \\ \text{snake} \\ \text{thorn} \end{matrix}\right\} \ of \ \left\{\begin{matrix} \text{battle} \\ \text{shields} \\ \text{wounds} \end{matrix}\right.$$

Shield is the door/cloud of Odin/valkyrie; plain of the sword; wall of battle; foot-stand of the giant Hrungnir

Ship is the horse of the sea/river/wind/launcher

Sea is the sea-king's realm; land or path of sea-creatures/waves

Gold is the fire/gleam of the sea/river; fire of the hand/arm; rock of the hand/arm; lair of dragons/snakes; dew of Draupnir; story of giants

Poetry is the drink of Odin; ship of dwarfs

Half-kennings

Some kenning-like expressions appear to be truncated, one-part, kennings, the most common being references to women by the name of a goddess or valkyrie, without a qualifying element meaning 'of treasure' or similar. An example is the use of Hlin, one of the names of Odin's wife Frigg, in the stanza above. Half-kennings are especially common in later skaldic verse, for instance in the poetry of *Viglund's Saga*.

Glossary

*The Icelandic terms are printed in italics,
with modern spelling.*

Althing   *alþingi*: General assembly. See 'Social, Political and Legal Structures'.

Autumn Meeting   *leið, leiðarþing*: Held after the *Althing* and generally lasting one or two days at the end of July or beginning of August. Proceedings and decisions from the Althing were announced at the Autumn Meeting, which had no judicial role.

ball game   *knattleikur*: Played with a hard ball and a *bat*, possibly similar to the Gaelic game known as hurling which is still played in Scotland and Ireland. The exact rules, however, are uncertain.

bat   *knattdrepa, knatttré*: See *ball game*.

bed closet   *hvílugólf, lokrekkja, lokhvíla, lokrekkjugólf*: A private sleeping area used for the heads of better-off households. The closet was usually partitioned off from the rest of the house, and had a door that was secured from the inside.

black   Often used here to translate *blár*, which in modern Icelandic means only 'blue'. The colour was a dark blue-black, often worn by saga characters setting out with murderous intentions.

board game   *tafl*: Probably often refers to chess which had plainly reached Scandinavia before the twelfth century. However, in certain cases it might also refer to another board game known as *hnefatafl*. The rules of the latter game are uncertain, even though we know what the boards looked like.

booth   *búð*: A temporary dwelling used by those who attended the various assemblies. Structurally, it seems to have involved permanent walls which were covered by a tent-like roof, probably made of cloth.

bride-price *mundur*: In formal terms, the amount that the groom's family gave to the bride's. According to Icelandic law it was the personal property of the wife. See also *dowry*.

compensation *manngjöld, bætur*: Penalties imposed by the courts were of three main kinds: awards of compensation in cash; sentences of *lesser outlawry*, which could be lessened or dropped by the payment of compensation; and sentences of *full outlawry* with no chance of being moderated. In certain cases, a man's right to immediate vengeance was recognized, but for many offences compensation was the fixed legal penalty and the injured party had little choice but to accept the settlement offered by the court, an arbitrator or a man who had been given the right to *self-judgement* (*sjálfdæmi*). It was certainly legal to put pressure on the guilty party to pay. Neither court verdicts nor legislation, nor even the constitutional arrangements, had any coercive power behind them other than the free initiative of individual chieftains with their armed following.

cross-bench *pallur, þverpallur*: A raised platform, or bench at the inner end of the *main room* (see 'The Farm'). Women were usually seated there, but in *Viglund's Saga* male heads of households are pictured there, at least on informal occasions (chs. 14 and 16).

directions *austur/vestur/norður/suður* (east/west/north/south): These directional terms are used in a very wide sense in the sagas; they are largely dependent on context, and they cannot always be trusted to reflect compass directions. Internationally, 'the east' generally refers to the countries to the east and south-east of Iceland, and although 'easterner' usually refers to a Norwegian, it can also apply to a Swede (especially since the concept of nationality was still not entirely clear when the sagas were being written), and might even be used for a person who has picked up 'Russian' habits (see *Russia*). 'The west', or to 'go west', tends to refer to Ireland and what are now the British Isles, but might even refer to lands still further afield; the point of orientation is west of Norway. When confined to Iceland, directional terms sometimes refer to the *quarter* to which a person is travelling: e.g., a man going to the *Althing* from the east of the country might be said to be going 'south' rather than 'west', and a person going home to the West Fjords from the Althing is said to be going 'west' rather than 'north'.

dowry *heimanfylgja*: Literally, 'that which accompanies (the bride) from her home'. This was the amount of money (or land) that a bride's father contributed at her wedding. Like the *bride-price*, it remained legally her property. However, the husband controlled their financial affairs and was responsible for the use to which both these assets were put.

drapa *drápa*: A heroic, laudatory poem, usually in the complicated metre preferred by the Icelandic poets. Such poems were in fashion between the tenth and thirteenth centuries. They were usually composed in honour of kings, earls and other prominent men, living or dead. Occasionally they were addressed to a loved one or made in praise of pagan or Christian religious figures. A drapa usually consisted of three parts: an introduction, a middle section including one or more refrains, and a conclusion. It was usually clearly distinguished from the *flokk*, which tended to be shorter, less laudatory and without refrains (see *The Saga of Gunnlaug Serpent-tongue*, ch. 9).

duel *hólmganga*: A formally organized duel, literally meaning 'going to the island'. This is probably because the area prescribed for the fight formed a small 'island' with clearly defined boundaries which separated the action from the outside world; it might also refer to the fact that small islands were originally favoured sites for duels. The rules included that the two duellists slashed at each other alternately, the seconds protecting the principal fighters with shields. Shields hacked to pieces could be replaced by up to three shields on each side. If blood was shed, the fight could be ended and the wounded man could buy himself off with a ransom of three *marks* of silver, either on the spot or later. The rules are stated in detail in *Kormak's Saga*, ch. 10. The duel was formally banned by law in Iceland in 1006, six years after the Icelanders had accepted Christianity: see *The Saga of Gunnlaug Serpent-tongue*, ch. 11.

earl   *jarl*: A title generally restricted to men of high rank in northern countries (though not in Iceland), who could be independent rulers or subordinate to a king. The title could be inherited, or it could be conferred by a king on a prominent supporter or leader of military forces. The earls of Lade, who appear in a number of sagas and tales, ruled large sections of northern Norway (and often many southerly areas as well) for several centuries. Another prominent, almost independent, earldom was that of Orkney and Shetland.

east   *austur*: See *directions*.

fetch   *fylgja*: Literally 'someone who accompanies', a fetch was a personal spirit that was closely attached to families and individuals, and often symbolized the fate that people were born with. If it appeared to an individual or to others close to him or her, it would often signal the impending doom of that person (e.g., *The Saga of Hallfred Troublesome-poet* , ch. 11). Fetches could take various forms, sometimes appearing in the shape of an animal. As with most ghosts mentioned in the sagas, Icelandic fetches tended to be corporeal.

flokk   *flokkur*: An extended praise-poem, but less prestigious than the *drapa* and lacking refrains.

follower   *hirðmaður*: A member of the inner circle that surrounded the Scandinavian kings, a sworn king's man.

foster-   *fóstur-, fóstri, fóstra*: Children during the saga period were often brought up by foster-parents, who in return received either payment or support from the real parents. Being fostered was therefore somewhat different from being adopted: it was essentially a legal agreement and, more importantly, a form of alliance. Nonetheless, emotionally, and in some cases legally, fostered children were seen as being part of the family circle. Relationships and loyalties between foster-kindred could become very strong. It should be noted that the expressions *fóstri/fóstra* were also used for people who had the function of looking after, bringing up and teaching the children on the farm. See also *sworn brotherhood*.

full outlawry   *skóggangur*: Outlawry for life. One of the terms applied to a man sentenced to full outlawry was *skógarmaður*, which literally means 'forest man', even though in Iceland there was scant possibility of his taking refuge in a forest. Full outlawry simply meant banishment from civilized society, whether the local district, the province or the whole country. It also meant the confiscation of the outlaw's property to pay the prosecutor, cover debts and sometimes provide an allowance for the dependants he had left behind. A full outlaw was to be neither fed nor offered shelter. According to one legal codex from Norway, it was 'as if he were dead'. He had lost all goods, and all rights. Wherever he went he could be killed without any legal redress. His children became illegitimate and his body was to be buried in unconsecrated ground. See also *lesser outlawry*.

games   *leikar*. *Leikur* (sing.) in Icelandic contained the same breadth of meaning as 'game' in English. The games meetings described in the sagas would probably have included a whole range of 'play' activities. Essentially, they involved men's sports, such as wrestling, *ball games*, 'skin-throwing games', 'scraper games' and *horse-fights*. Games of this kind took place whenever people came together, and seem to have formed a regular feature of assemblies and other gatherings (including the *Althing*) and religious festivals such as the *Winter Nights*. Sometimes prominent men invited people together specifically to take part in games. In some cases it is clear that the games were played on ice, or else indoors (see *Viglund's Saga*, ch. 11).

godi   *goði*: This word was little known outside Iceland in early Christian times, and seems to refer to a particularly Icelandic concept. A godi was a local chieftain who had legal and administrative responsibilities in Iceland. The name seems to have originally meant 'priest', or at least a person having a special relationship with gods or supernatural powers, and thus shows an early connection between religious and secular power. As time went on, however, the chief function of a godi came to be secular. The first godis were chosen from the leading families who settled Iceland in *c.* 870–930. See 'Social, Political and Legal Structures' (pp. 311–13).

godord *goðorð*: The authority and rank of a *godi*, including his social and legal responsibilities towards his *thingmen*.

hall *skáli*: Refers both to large halls such as those used by kings, and to the main farmhouse on the typical Icelandic farm. See 'The Farm' (pp. 314–16).

hayfield *tún*: An enclosed field for hay cultivation close to or surrounding a farmhouse. This was the only cultivated part of a farm and produced the best hay. Other hay, generally of lesser quality, came from the meadows, which could be a good distance from the farm itself. See 'The Farm' (pp. 314–16).

hayfield wall *túngarður*: A wall of stones surrounding the hayfield in order to protect it from grazing livestock. See 'The Farm' (pp. 314–16).

haystack yard *stakkgarður*: A small enclosed yard to protect the haystacks from the livestock. See 'The Farm' (pp. 314–16).

hersir *hersir*: A local leader in western and northern Norway; his rank was hereditary. Originally the hersirs were probably those who took command when the men of the district were called to arms.

high seat *öndvegi*: The central section of one bench in the *hall* (at the inner end, or in the middle of the 'senior' side, to the right as one entered) was the rightful high seat of the owner of the farm. Even though it is usually referred to in English as the 'high seat', this position was not necessarily higher in elevation, only in honour. Opposite the owner sat the guest of honour.

homespun   (cloth) *vaðmál*: For centuries wool and woollen products were Iceland's chief exports, especially in the form of strong and durable homespun cloth. It could be bought and sold in bolts or made up into items such as homespun cloaks. There were strict regulations on homespun, as it was used as a standard exchange product and often referred to in *ounces*, meaning its equivalent value expressed as a weight in silver. One ounce could equal three to six ells of homespun, one ell being roughly 50cm. A homespun cloak was woven from wool with a shaggy exterior like sheepskin.

horse-fight   *hestaat/hestavíg*: A popular sport among the Icelanders, which seems to have taken place especially in the autumn, particularly at *Autumn Meetings*. Two horses were goaded to fight against each other, until one was killed or ran away. Understandably, emotions ran high, and horse-fights commonly led to feuds.

hundred   *hundrað*: A 'long hundred', or one hundred and twenty. A 'hundred of silver', the standard compensation for the killing of a man, was probably, though not certainly, the value of a hundred ells of *homespun* cloth, paid in silver. In some contexts, 'hundred' is used rather loosely to refer to a large number.

knorr   *knörr*: An ocean-going cargo vessel.

Law Council   *lögrétta*: The legislative assembly at the *Althing*. See also 'Social, Political and Legal Structures' (pp. 311–13).

Law Rock   *lögberg*: The raised spot at the *Althing* at Thingvellir, where the *Lawspeaker* may have recited the law code, and where public announcements and speeches were made. See also 'Social, Political and Legal Structures' (pp. 311–13).

Lawspeaker   *lögsögumaður*, *lögmaður*: Literally, 'the man who recites the law', referring to the time before the advent of writing when the Lawspeaker had to learn the law by heart and recite one-third of it every year, perhaps at the *Law Rock*. If he was unsure about the text, he had to consult a team of five or more 'lawmen' (*lögmenn*) who knew the law well. The Lawspeaker presided over the assembly at the *Althing* and was responsible for the preservation and clarification of legal tradition. He could exert influence, as in the case about whether the Icelanders should accept Christianity, but should not be regarded as having ruled the country. See also 'Social, Political and Legal Structures' (pp. 311–13).

lesser outlawry   *fjörbaugsgarður*: Differed from *full* (or greater) *outlawry* in that the lesser outlaw was banished from society for only three years. Furthermore, his land was not confiscated, and money was put aside to support his family. This made it possible for him to return later and continue a normal life. *Fjörbaugsgarður* means literally 'life-ring enclosure'. 'Life-ring' refers to the silver ring that the outlaw originally had to pay the *godi* in order to spare his life. (This was later fixed at a value of one *mark*.) 'Enclosure' refers to three sacrosanct homes no more than one day's journey from each other where the outlaw was permitted to stay while he arranged passage out of Iceland. He was allowed limited movement along the tracks directly joining these farms, and en route to the ship that would take him abroad. Anywhere else the outlaw was fair game and could be killed without redress. He had to leave the country and begin his sentence within the space of three summers after the verdict, but once abroad regained normal rights.

longship   *langskip*: The largest warship.

main room   *stofa*: A room off the *hall* of a farmhouse. See 'The Farm' (pp. 314–16).

mark   *mörk*: A measurement of weight, eight *ounces*, approximately 214g.

neighbour   *búi*: In a legal context, 'neighbour' often has a formal meaning: people who were called on to 'witness' the testimony of principal figures in a case, and form a panel.

north   *norður*: See *directions*.

ounce   *eyrir*, pl. *aurar*: A unit of weight, varying slightly through time, but roughly 27g. Eight ounces were equal to one *mark*.

334

outlawry   *útlegð, skóggangur, fjörbaugsgarður*: *Útlegð*, literally meaning 'lying, or sleeping, outside', and *skóggangur*, 'forest-walking', stress the idea of the outlaw having been ejected from the safe boundaries of civilized society and being forced to live in the wild, alongside the animals and nature spirits (elves and guardian spirits, for instance), little better than an animal himself. The word *útlagi* ('outlaw') is closely related to *útlegð*, but has also taken on the additional meaning of 'outside the law', which for early Scandinavians was synonymous with 'lying outside society'. Law was what made society. See also *full outlawry* and *lesser outlawry*.

quarter   *fjórðungur*: Administratively, Iceland was divided into four quarters based on the four cardinal directions. See 'Social, Political and Legal Structures' (pp. 311–13).

Quarter Court   *fjórðungsdómur*: Four Quarter Courts were established at the *Althing* in *c.* 965. See 'Social, Political and Legal Structures' (pp. 311–13).

Russia   *Garðaríki*: Literally means 'the realm of towns', and refers very generally to the area running between the Baltic Sea and the White Sea in the north and the Black Sea and the Caspian Sea in the south.

sacrifice   *blót*: There is great uncertainty about the nature of pagan worship and cult activities in Scandinavia, and just as the theology and mythology of the Nordic peoples seem to have varied according to area, it is highly questionable whether any standardized rules of ritual practice ever existed there. It should also be remembered that the population of Iceland came from all over Scandinavia, as well as from Ireland and the islands off Scotland. Religion was very much an individual matter, and practices varied. The few references to sacrifices in the sagas are somewhat vague, but these sometimes seem to have involved the ritual slaughter of animals (see *Kormak's Saga*, chs. 22 and 23).

scorn-pole   *níð*: In the sagas *níð* refers to two forms of slander that need to be distinguished. The physical form, scorn-pole, generally refers to figures made of wood that were understood by all to represent one or more persons in local society. These figures were sometimes depicted in some compromising sexual position. Such a public insult attracted attention and seriously damaged the honour of the person or persons in question. The figures were strictly illegal, and a common reason for killings and/or local feuds. See, for example, *Gisli Sursson's Saga*, ch. 2. In *Egil's Saga*, a scorn-pole with a horse's head on it is used to place a curse on the king. For the verbal form of *níð*, see *slander*.

self-judgement   *sjálfdæmi*: A means of settling disputes whereby one party hands over exclusive power of judgement to the other.

shape-shifter (-changer)   *hamrammur*, adj.: Closely associated with the berserks, those who were *hamrammir* (pl.) were believed to change their shape at night or in times of stress, or leave their bodies (which appeared asleep) and take the physical form of animals such as bears or wolves. There are faint associations with shamanistic activities and figures known in folklore throughout the world, such as the werewolf. The transformation was not necessarily intentional.

shieling   *sel*: A roughly constructed hut in the highland grazing pastures away from the farm, where shepherds and cowherds lived during the summer. Milking and the preparation of various dairy products took place here, as did other important farm activities like the collection of peat and charcoal-burning (depending on the surroundings). This arrangement was well known throughout the Scandinavian countries from the earliest times.

single combat   *einvígi*: The less formal fight between two men, differentiated from the formally organized *duel* which was fought according to defined rules and rituals.

slander   *níð*: In the sagas *níð* refers to two forms of slander that need to be distinguished. The verbal form commonly consisted of slanderous verse containing hints of lack of masculinity or deviant sexual practices. Such verses obviously spread like wildfire, and were capable of doing great damage to a person's honour and respect. Insults of this kind were not only illegal, they also tended to start or escalate serious feuds because of the element of dishonour. As the Eddic poem *Hávamál* ('The Words of the High One') states, 'the tongue is the slayer of the head' (*tunga er höfuðs bani*, v. 73). For the other form of *níð*, see *scorn-pole*.

slave   *þræll*: Slavery was quite an important aspect of Viking Age trade. Judging from their names and appearance, a large number of the slaves mentioned in the sagas seem to have come from Ireland and Scotland. Stereotypically they are presented in the sagas as being stupid and lazy. By law, slaves had hardly any rights at all, and they and their families could only be freed if their owners chose to free them, or if somebody else bought their freedom. In the Icelandic Commonwealth, a slave who was wounded was entitled to one-third of the compensation money; the rest went to his owner.

south   *suður*: See *directions*.

Spring Assembly   *vorþing*: The local assembly, held each spring. These were the first regular assemblies to be held in Iceland. Held at thirteen sites and lasting four to seven days between 7 and 27 May, they were jointly supervised by three *godis*. The Spring Assembly had a dual legal and economic function. It consisted of a court of thirty-six men, twelve appointed by each of the godis, where local legal actions were heard, while major cases and those which could not be resolved locally were sent on to the *Althing*. In its other function it was a forum for settling debts, deciding prices and the like. Godis probably used the Spring Assembly to urge their followers to ride to the Althing; those who remained behind paid the costs of those who went. See 'Social, Political and Legal Structures' (pp. 311–13).

sworn brotherhood   *fóstbræðralag*: Seen as another form of foster-brotherhood, but instead of being arranged by the parents (see *foster-*), it was a relationship decided by the individuals themselves. Sworn brothers literally were 'blood-brothers': they swore unending loyalty to each other, sealing this pact by going though a religious ceremony involving a form of symbolic rebirth, in which they joined blood and passed beneath an arch of raised turf.

tale *þáttur*: A short narrative, often included as an episode in a larger whole, in many cases in a saga based on the life of a king.

Thing *þing*: An assembly. See 'Social, Political and Legal Structures' (pp. 311–13).

thingman/men *þingmaður/þingmenn*: Every free man and landowner was required to serve as a thingman ('assembly man') by aligning himself with a *godi*. He would either accompany the godi to assemblies and other functions or pay a tax supposed to cover the godi's costs of attending them. See 'Social, Political and Legal Structures', (pp. 311–13).

Viking *víkingur*: Normally has an unfavourable sense in the Sagas of Icelanders, referring to violent seafaring raiders, especially of the pagan period (as in *The Saga of Hallfred*, ch. 1). It can also denote, in a more general sense, bullies and villains. The reference to Kormak's company as 'Vikings' in *Kormak's Saga*, ch. 18, seems less pejorative.

west *vestur*: see *directions*.

Winter Nights *veturnætur*: The period of two days when the winter began, around the middle of October. In the pagan era, this was a particularly holy time of the year, when *sacrifices* were made to the *disir* (female guardian spirits who watched over farms, families and, occasionally, individuals), and other social activities such as *games* meetings and weddings often took place. It was also the time when animals were slaughtered so that their meat could be stored over the winter.

Index of Characters